She glanced back, the dim red glow of their survival tents receding into the darkened underbrush. What could Orna be doing, ranging this far from safety?

Nilah hoped it wasn't some amorous scheme—she wasn't in the mood. Orna had to be just over the next little hill, in a clearing, and Nilah was about to give her a piece of her mind.

The clearing fell dead still as Nilah took a few silent steps into it, slinger at the ready. Tumbled boulders and soft moss carpeted the western side, and she thought she could see the opening of a cave beneath an overhang. Nilah's anger flared as another sharp rock cut her foot.

"Orna!" she hissed, trying to keep her voice low. "Orna, damn it, don't do this to—"

Another sharp cut on her foot interrupted her, and Nilah fell, trying to keep her weight off the dangerous rocks. At her wits' end, she let her dermaluxes flow free, and what she saw turned them green.

They weren't rocks. They were bones.

Praise for the Salvagers series

A BIG SHIP AT THE EDGE OF THE UNIVERSE

"A clever fusion of magic and sci-fi makes this book a total blast. I was hooked from page one."

—V. E. Schwab, author of the Shades of Magic series

"*A Big Ship at the Edge of the Universe* is perfectly paced, full of intense, inventive action, and refreshingly honest characters. It's the seamless hybrid of fantasy and sci-fi that you didn't know you always needed. Do you miss *Firefly*? Do you want it back? Well, sorry, not gonna happen. But this book is damn close."

—Nicholas Eames, author of *Kings of the Wyld*

"*A Big Ship at the Edge of the Universe* is a raucous genre-buster that careens through a series of heart-stopping curves and roars to a podium finish. Bratty, brilliant racer Nilah and hard-boiled cynic Boots are as winning a pair of strong female characters as I've met in years. A pacy plot, a diverse supporting cast, and a vivid set of worlds round out this highly entertaining series opener. Alex White is going to be leading the pack for years to come."

—Claire Humphrey, author of *Spells of Blood and Kin*

"*A Big Ship at the Edge of the Universe* starts in high gear and never lets up. Boasting action, intrigue, and deadly fusions of technology and magic, you have to remember to put the book down now and then to take a breath!"   —Mike Brooks, author of *Dark Run*

"An exciting, fast-paced, magic-fueled treasure hunt across the galaxy."   —Corey J. White, author of the Voidwitch series

"A crazy blend of SF and fantasy concepts, with exciting characters and a brilliant universe—highly recommend!"
                    —Jamie Sawyer, author of the Lazarus War series

"Racing! Treasure and smuggling! *A Big Ship at the Edge of the Universe* is a gripping quest for justice among salvage and magic—I really loved it."   —Mur Lafferty, author of *Six Wakes*

"This universe's thrilling combination of technology and magic traps two tough women in a fight for their lives, and although Nilah has a better life to fight for, Boots is marvelously stubborn. Guaranteed to make you wonder what kind of sigil you'd draw in their world."   —R. E. Stearns, author of *Barbary Station*

"To call this book fast-paced or action-packed is underselling it. Buckle up, readers: this is a ride you won't want to get off until the end."   —*B&N Sci-Fi & Fantasy Blog*

"White's assured debut is an entertaining throwback with some fun worldbuilding and two great lead characters."
                    —*Publishers Weekly*

"*A Big Ship at the Edge of the Universe* is a rollicking fun ride. I enjoyed it a lot, and I'm looking forward to the sequel."   —*Locus*

"This ambitious start...combines magic and space opera to create a fast-paced adventure with charismatic characters and formidable enemies in a realized universe of greed and power."
                    —*Booklist*

By Alex White

A BAD DEAL FOR THE WHOLE GALAXY

The Salvagers: Book Two

ALEX WHITE

www.orbitbooks.net

Copyright © 2018 by Alex White
Excerpt from *The Worst of All Possible Worlds* copyright © 2018 by Alex White
Excerpt from *One Way* copyright © 2018 by S. J. Morden

Author photograph by Rebecca Winks
Cover design by Lisa Marie Pompilio
Cover images by Shutterstock
Cover copyright © 2018 by Hachette Book Group, Inc.

Orbit
Hachette Book Group
1290 Avenue of the Americas
New York, NY 10104
orbitbooks.net

First Edition: December 2018

Orbit is an imprint of Hachette Book Group.
The Orbit name and logo are trademarks of Little, Brown Book Group Limited.

The publisher is not responsible for websites (or their content) that are not owned by the publisher.

The Hachette Speakers Bureau provides a wide range of authors for speaking events. To find out more, go to www.hachettespeakersbureau.com or call (866) 376-6591.

Library of Congress Cataloging-in-Publication Data:
Names: White, Alex (Novelist), author.
Title: A bad deal for the whole galaxy / Alex White.
Description: First edition. | New York, NY : Orbit, December 2018. | Series: The Salvagers ; Book two
Identifiers: LCCN 2018044714| ISBN 9780316412100 (trade pbk.) | ISBN 9780316412094 (ebook)
Subjects: | GSAFD: Science fiction.
Classification: LCC PS3623.H5687 B33 218 | DDC 813/.6—dc23
LC record available at https://lccn.loc.gov/2018044714

ISBNs: 978-0-316-41210-0 (trade paperback), 978-0-316-41209-4 (ebook)

Printed in the United States of America

LSC-C

10 9 8 7 6 5 4 3 2 1

For my spouse,
Renée, because no one writes alone.

Chapter One

Polyphony

The crowd writhed and swayed, bodies in motion to a blistering-hot beat. Wisps of arcane fireworks drifted overhead—glimmering wireframe dragons and murmurations of cormorants spraying cool flakes of magic as they passed.

At the premier concert event in the galaxy, every stare that wasn't trained on the light show overhead should have rested on the singer Indira Panjala, whose silvered hair flowed in time with the kick drum. No one should've been looking at Nilah Brio.

But Aaron Forscythe was, recognition in his expression.

She'd taken every precaution. She'd stuffed her now-famous mohawk under a purple wig. She'd done up her face, accenting different contours, flowing lines of neon makeup covering most of her features. She'd worn the sort of short party dress she hated. The glowing, tattooed dermaluxes that covered her arms were covered in translucent sleeves, obscuring the patterns.

Confirming her fears, Aaron spun and began shouldering through the crowd away from her.

"I've been made!" Nilah shouted into her comm, taking off after him.

"Hunter Two, hit him with a sleeper, say he's drunk, and bring him back to the ship." Cordell Lamarr's deep voice entered her ear, overpowering Indira's crescendo.

Aaron shoved a woman so hard she went sprawling to the floor. He plowed through the bystanders with an unnatural strength, creating a rising chorus of protestations.

"I'm bloody trying," snapped Nilah, vaulting over a stumbling drunk before juking past another. Her dermalux tattoos filtered through her translucent sleeves with strobing white light, temporarily blinding anyone unfortunate enough to look directly at them. The crowd parted before her as people covered their eyes and looked away.

If Aaron hadn't been smacking everyone around, he might've disappeared into the crowd with little difficulty. The shifting light show of the Panjala concert made him tough to track across a sea of bobbing heads. A few meters away, hands flailed as Aaron shoved another concertgoer, drawing Nilah's attention. He'd almost reached the exit to the arena.

"Planetwise exit! Hunter One, block him off," she called out into her comm.

"Damn." The gruff voice of Orna Sokol, quartermaster of the *Capricious*, joined the radio chatter. "I'm too far away. There are a lot of tunnels down there. Don't lose him. ETA two minutes."

"I'm not going to lose him," said Nilah, dodging a spilling drink. "I'm the one that found him."

"You're also the one that got spotted," said Orna, chuckling.

"We'll talk about this on the ship," hissed Nilah.

"Focus up," said Cordell. "We're hearing a lot of chatter from concert security. You might want to shut those tattoos off."

"Blast it," Nilah grumbled, suppressing her dermaluxes as her target made it to the arena's emergency exit.

Aaron kicked the door open and stormed out into the balconies above Goldsmith Park, leaving Nilah to wrestle through the remainder of the crowd. By the time she pushed outside, the only sign of him was the clang of his feet on the stairwell below. Cool, night-cycle air tickled her bare skin, and this high up, wind whipped at her dress. She leaned over the railing to see if she could spot him—and was rewarded by the sizzle of a flame bolt passing by her head.

"He shot at me!" she said, ducking away from the edge.

"That slinger fire triggered the detectors," said Cordell. "Cops are on the way."

"Hang back, babe," said Orna. "Wait for backup."

Nilah quickly leaned out once more to catch a view of her quarry near the base of the stairs, headed for the lush greenery of Goldsmith Park. If she didn't stop him now, he'd get into the Morrison Station superstructure and vanish. All the hunting they'd done would be worthless if he went to ground. She took hold of the handle on the stadium's emergency descender box and swallowed. It was only sixteen floors or so to the sidewalk.

"Not the stupidest thing I've done," she muttered.

"Wait. ETA eighty seconds," said Orna.

Nilah pulled open the emergency box, finding ten shiny descenders inside. She took one of the clear discs and pressed the tester just to make sure the binary spells inside were still good.

A former race car driver, she would've been an Ultra GP galactic champion if Mother and her crew hadn't ruined her last shot at the crown. At least her experience made her an expert at judging speed over distance. Forty-eight meters to the ground would make for a pretty quick fall. She spied Forscythe's shadow as he rounded the final corner and burst out into the open.

Now or never.

Nilah swung her legs over the railing and leapt into the neon haze of Morrison Station's downtown, the descender clutched tightly in her hand. Wind roared in her ears. The shadowy figure of her target grew exponentially in size.

She snapped the descender mere feet away from Aaron's head, gelatinous phantoplasm instantly enveloping the both of them, blunting the kinetic energy of her fall. Their limbs interlocked as they bounced across the park grounds, the world free-spinning.

Eventually, the bubble of goo burst, spitting them out onto the summery grass beneath the statue of Carrie Morrison. The pair arose, dripping with smoky gelatin, and regarded each other. Nilah brought her fists to a fighting posture, and her dermaluxes began to pulse in time with the distant music.

Aaron was doughy and soft, not exactly the image of a dangerous criminal and cultist—and a lot younger than expected. He couldn't have been much older than eighteen.

"Nilah Brio," said Aaron, smirking. "The little racer who never did."

" 'Never did' what?"

"Win the Driver's Crown," he said, a tremor entering his voice. "He'll be pleased when I bring him your body."

She narrowed her eyes and smiled. "You can't be serious. I saved the universe from your lot and literally punched out a horde of springflies. It was all over the Link."

"The news always lies," he said, whipping his slinger level with her face and blasting off a few spells.

She tumbled away from his wavering aim with little difficulty, rolling to her feet and bolting forward. Two more shots erupted in her direction, but Aaron didn't have the military precision required to make them land. His grip on the slinger was too tight, too amateurish.

Nilah whipped her arms toward him, momentarily blinding Aaron with the spray of light, then sent a kick straight into his jaw, lifting him up off the ground. He came down hard on his back, going slack.

"ETA thirty seconds," said Orna, her voice almost panicked. "What's going on over there, babe?"

"I just took him down. Glass jaw, as they say—"

Two figures emerged from the shadows around the Morrison monument, daggers in their eyes. One male, one female, clad in fine suits, their postures spoke of expertise. Perhaps they were bodyguards for Aaron. Perhaps they were assassins come to cut her throat. Either way, she'd have to deal with them alone—thirty seconds would be an eternity once the spells started flying.

"Forscythe has friends," said Nilah. She squared herself to the newcomers, her dermaluxes gently pulsing, like lightning in a storm cloud. "Hello, chums."

They spread out to flank her, silent as ghosts. Aaron began to stir. His beady eyes flew open, and he scrambled to his feet, dashing away between the two goons. In two seconds, he'd be into the access corridors.

"Why don't we skip all of this?" Nilah asked of the closest one. "You can just walk aw—"

They slashed glyphs from the air with their fingers—one elemental sigil of ice, the other of wind. Together, the spells could form a flash-freeze that would kill her instantly. Her eyes darted from spell to spell, searching for the more powerful of the two casters.

Nilah dashed for the wind caster, peppering her with a hail of flashing blows. The caster flipped out a baton and took a swing, but she kicked it away; the woman's wind spell fizzled in the jolt. With the killer's guard softened, Nilah leapt for her like a great cat, latching on and attacking. The woman shouted in pain as Nilah wrapped her legs around her chest, boxing her ears and eyes with punishing fists. Uncoiling like a spring, Nilah kicked off of her, knocking her backward against a rock, where she lay still.

Nilah rose to her feet to find the frost caster's glyph engorged with power. The fellow moved with surprising alacrity, ripping arcane ligatures from the night. She'd misjudged their skill, taking out the wrong target first. The ice caster's fingers brushed closed the last throbbing line of the glyph, and the air crackled with frost.

He released the spell, and it was like being thrust into the raw vacuum of space. Every inch of her overexposed skin seared with pain as frigid air wicked moisture away from the surface. Her eyes stung, and she shut them on reflex. Nilah wanted to shout, but when she opened her mouth, freezing air bit her throat. Orna had been right; she shouldn't have engaged them alone. The spell howled, wrapping around the distant sounds of Panjala.

Then came another noise: a familiar, mechanical galloping.

A metallic screech erupted from above them, and a suit of bloodred robotic battle armor landed on the ice caster, crushing him into the dewy grass. As soon as Nilah could move a muscle, she looked away, shivering. She was glad to see Charger but would've preferred a less lethal resolution.

Charger's cockpit hissed, popping open to reveal Orna strapped inside, a smile on her face. "Told you to wait, babe."

"And how were you supposed to come to my rescue if I did?"

"Hunters, enough banter," interrupted Cordell. "Have we got eyes on Forscythe?"

Nilah bounded up to Charger and mounted his back plate, sinking her feet into his vents like stirrups. "In pursuit, Boss."

Orna shut herself back inside the cockpit, and the battle armor rocketed in the direction of the Morrison Station access corridor.

Nilah held on for dear life, her arms around Charger's metal neck as the creature beneath her loped along. "We really should put some handholds on the big guy for this! Some up top, and footholds on the side."

"I'm not putting love handles on my killbot."

They reached the superstructure access hatch, which poked out from between a pair of bushes. Charger's claws left long ruts in the grass as the pair skidded to a halt. Caution flashers blinked around the thick door frame, indicating the lack of gravity beyond—the grav drive range didn't extend to the outer hull. Charger stepped inside, and Nilah's stomach flipped as she adjusted to weightlessness.

The superstructure was a mesh of translucent tunnels with running lights, punctuated every now and again by a viewport. Between racing seasons, Nilah had enjoyed using the tunnels for fitness training, working her legs by leaping between the various observation decks dotting Morrison's expansive hull. She could do a hundred kilometers of low-grav kicks easily.

The bright corridor extended before them, splitting into three branches. They launched to the end of the corridor, and Charger sampled the air as they flew. His neck snapped to the right, polychroic lenses flashing green with excitement.

"Good boy," Orna murmured through his speakers, and they sailed down the right side of the split.

They raced through the superstructure, Charger scenting out their prey with little trouble. Each of the bot's powerful pushes left an unfortunate red stain on the pristine walls, and Nilah wondered what they'd tell the police. When they reached the first observation deck, they found Aaron Forscythe trembling and red-faced, his slinger placed against his temple. He hovered before a wide cupola window, Taitu glinting in planetrise behind him.

Charger's high-cal slingers swung out from their hip holsters before Nilah could even blink, but Orna stayed her hand.

"This isn't how it was supposed to happen," said Aaron, his voice cracking. "I had a destiny."

Nilah pushed off of Charger's back, grabbing onto one of the floor's many handrails. If he decided to fire at her, it'd be tricky to get out of the way. She couldn't maneuver as unpredictably in zero gravity—it'd just be a straight line. "We traced your message. We know you work for Henrick Witts. Tell us who you're here to meet, and we can protect you."

"No one can protect me," he said, gritting his teeth. "Now that I've failed, I'm dead."

"If you don't drop your weapon," said Orna, locking back the hammers on Charger's massive slingers, "I don't think they'll get the chance."

"That's open space behind that window," Nilah warned, placing a hand atop one of Charger's weapons.

"Yeah, well I'm sick of going after these middle-management dorks," said Orna. "Bunch of rich idiots with almost no intel."

Aaron sneered. "The Children of the Singularity will end you, too!"

Nilah drew up short. "The what now, mate?"

"We're going to expose all of your lies," said Aaron.

Orna's laugh came out tinny through Charger's speakers. "The only thing you're doing is boring me to death."

"Stop, darling." Nilah tensed her legs, preparing to leap away in case he took a shot at her. "I'm sure he thinks he's very important."

"You ruined this for me!" screamed Aaron. "I was chosen by the gods!"

Nilah and Charger exchanged glances.

"I mean," Nilah began, "not really. I've met the chosen ones. They're stonking powerful, and you can't even shoot straight. Just give up."

A shaft of sunlight warmed the window as their star crested

Taitu's horizon. Nilah prayed no civilians would come around for a morning constitutional.

"Look, let's work something out," said Nilah. "I want to get back to my comfy clothes."

"'Work something out'?" he laughed, a tear rolling down his cheek. "You've robbed me of my place among the gods."

"We already killed two of them," said Orna. "Mother and Dwight Mandell. A place among the gods is six feet under, as far as I'm concerned."

"You got lucky once," said Aaron. "Surprised them. It won't happen again."

"Can I shoot him yet?" growled Orna through Charger's speakers. "He's getting annoying."

"Let us save your life," said Nilah, motioning for Orna to lower her weapons. "We might be able to arrange protection. Who were you here to meet?"

She raised a hand and tentatively floated closer. Maybe she could talk him down and compel him to help her.

"No. I...I'd be killing everyone I ever loved if I came with you," said Aaron, shaking his head. His face twisted with something like shame. "I was a Child of the Singularity. Now I'm a liability...so I have to die."

His face darkened and he pointed his slinger at Nilah. "Just like you."

"Down!" Orna shouted, and Charger knocked her flat against the floor, pinning her underfoot with its prehensile toes. The bot placed a single devastating shot through Aaron's chest—and melted the window behind him.

The world went red. Charger held Nilah in place despite the sudden decompression. Klaxons screeched in her ears. Her wig was sucked away, tearing to purple strands as it caught a jagged outcropping. Through the crack into the stars beyond, Aaron

Forscythe clutched his chest and struggled against the inevitable. Then, glowing nanotubes healed over the station's wound, and the crying wind grew higher in pitch before winking out. The air pressure returned to normal.

Emergency responders would be inbound. They had to leave.

"*Capricious*, this is Hunter Two," huffed Nilah. "Mission failed. He's dead, blown out into space."

"We're headed for your coordinates. Get to the rendezvous," said Cordell in her earpiece. "We'll grab Forscythe's body before the cops get here."

Charger hoisted Nilah to her feet and looked her over. "Thought we were finally going to take one of them alive."

"Yeah, well"—Nilah coughed, staring out the window at the body—"better we get the scraps than nothing."

"Okay, let me see if I've got this straight."

Elizabeth "Boots" Elsworth looked over her old companions, nursing her glass of clear, unaged whiskey. The crew of the *Capricious* had landed in her backyard on Hopper's Hope, uninvited. Now, Cordell, Armin, Nilah, Orna, Aisha, Malik, and the strange pair of gingers were gathered in the uncomfortably large kitchen of Boots's obnoxiously huge house; for the first time since Boots had moved into her mansion by the distillery, the place felt full.

She raised her tumbler to the crew, pointing at them with her metal index finger. She'd worked with doctors to upgrade it in the months since they'd seen her, converting it to full regraded steel. It looked a little more human—but not enough. It was nothing like a magical prosthesis. "Two weeks ago, your big plan was to extract this Forscythe character and...force him to talk? From Morrison Station, no less." She took a long pull of her white dog whiskey and coughed. It was well and truly awful stuff.

Cordell looked just like Boots remembered him—dense black hair in spongy curls, dark skin, and a perpetual sly smile. The old Arca Defense Force captain hadn't aged a day since the *Harrow*. "We've been catching bagmen for bad guys all across the galaxy, and you know what we find? Million-argent bank accounts. Sometimes two million. Whatever they're doing, it's some serious scratch."

"You keep any of it?" Boots asked into her glass.

"They keep draining the bank accounts as fast as we can kill their foot soldiers," said Cordell. "Three missions have ended in suicides."

First mate Armin Vandevere hadn't changed much either—his dour expression could still wilt a flower. "We have reason to believe Henrick Witts has a massive financial engine at his disposal—some sort of self-replicating system."

Boots gulped her whiskey a little too hard at the mention of Henrick Witts and coughed. The madman behind the Winnower Fleet and its flagship, the *Harrow*, had drained all life away from her homeworld, casting it into perpetual civil war.

"And the Children of the...uh?" asked Boots.

"Singularity. We're looking into Forscythe's comment with all available intelligence sources," said Armin. "It looks like a cult, but we're not sure."

She cleared her throat and shrugged. "If these Children of the Whatever are cultists, you were never going to get this guy to talk."

"We absolutely were," said Cordell, leaning forward with his unlit cigarette dangling from his lip, "because we had something you didn't figure into your calculations." He wore the same gold captain's jacket as usual, and he adjusted the cuffs with a flourish. He might've dressed like the veteran of a dead world, but he still swaggered like a cadet.

"That's where we come in," said the male ginger, subdued confidence on his face. "We're here to change the game."

The pale, freckled pair had to be in their twenties, and Cordell had scarcely introduced them when he'd arrived, just calling them "the Ferrier twins." They cut their hair in the same short fashion, and Boots had to do double takes to remember which one was the woman and which one was the man.

Boots gave them a bemused glance. "I don't mean to be rude, but 'change the game'? Unless you can conjure an armada and unlimited resources from thin air, you're not changing much."

The young man froze, silenced by her rebuke. His sister pursed her lips.

Cordell raised an eyebrow. "Really, Bootsie? Be nice. These two still have a twinkle in their eyes. No need to undo all the kind things we been saying about you."

"She can be a bit spiky," said Nilah to the twins. She sported the sort of formfitting athletic clothing she always wore, but her muscles filled it out more than they once had. "Don't worry about it, loves."

Boots narrowed her eyes and surveyed the crowd. "Never known you to be gentle with tenderfoots, Cordell. What's the angle?"

"Another time," said the captain.

"What my brother was trying to say," said the female twin—Boots was pretty sure that one was "Jeannie"—"is that we both have the reader's mark."

"So you're not siblings?" asked Boots. "Because you can't be if you have the same spell, right?" She wasn't an expert in arcane physiology, but she knew that siblings never shared a mark.

The twins exchanged glances.

"We are," said Jeannie.

Boots narrowed her eyes. "Then...how?"

"That's not your concern right now," said the male twin, clearly annoyed with her for shooting holes in his "change the game" bravado.

"Listen, Alan—" said Boots.

"Alister," he corrected. "And what's important right now is that we're both mind readers."

Boots eyed them warily—these legendary telepaths. A reader never had to resort to torture or bribery. All they had to do was ask simple questions, and the target's answers would come to the top of their mind—or so the rumors went. The closest Boots had ever come to one was the hack mnemonimancer who'd helped her make Kinnard, her old AI. A true reader was supposed to operate at another level. "You've got to be kidding me."

Cordell raised his eyebrows, his signature grin widening. "That's right, Bootsie. We've got the tools now."

She leaned back in her chair. "Okay, but how did you straight-up murder someone and then get off Morrison Station? That's Nilah's old stomping ground, and I know how security must be."

Armin steepled his fingers, leaning back in one of Boots's overpriced chairs. "That's where it gets interesting. The Taitutian Special Branch has become...amenable to our extrajudicial operations. After we took down Dwight Mandell, Prime Minister Bianchi cleaned house. Current leadership loves asking us for favors, and they're willing to turn a blind eye to our activities."

"Yeah, but they might still be compromised, sir—" Boots said, halting as she accidentally addressed Armin as an officer. She wasn't a crew member anymore. Judging from Cordell's chuckle, he was thinking the same thing.

"Look," said Boots. "We don't know how deep Henrick Witts's network goes, or who's a part of it. You're trusting intel agencies with your plans."

She hadn't said Witts's name in months, and it was like ash in her mouth.

"We...may have told them after the fact this time. We didn't want interference," said Armin. "But the Taitutians came and covered for us in the two weeks since then. The public thinks it's a suicide, and Forscythe's body was never found."

"And the splattered goons in the park?" asked Boots.

"Taken care of," said Cordell. "That's all you've got to worry about."

"That's some dubious reckoning, at best," said Boots. "They might just squirrel away these murders and have a case against you when they need it. I don't get much news out here, but I know they could spin a fall from grace story about heroes like us."

The rest of the crew quieted down, but Cordell pressed on. "I know that, but honestly, we need all the friends we can get."

"Yeah, you do," said Boots.

"And we need air support," added Orna. She was clad in a casual yet fashionable suit, all soft fabrics free of grease stains. Boots almost didn't recognize her, but her face was still hard as ever, covered in scars. And she still wore a silver circlet for her new battle armor, which she'd dubbed "Charger." "No one's taken the Midnight Runner for a walk since you left."

"Come with us," said Cordell, just laying it out there. "There's more cash in it, if that's your thing. Those bastards are rolling in dough, and we can keep what we find."

Boots had to admit that she missed the feel of a flight stick in her hand and the thrusters at her back. "I've got money, and I barely know what to do with it. You know this is a fool's errand, right? We nearly wound up dead last time."

"The job ain't done, Bootsie," said Cordell. "Witts and his pals destroyed our planet, and a man who'd do that doesn't just walk away because we screwed him up once. No one is safe until he's dead. We're already prepped to go after the next bagman."

He pulled out his lighter and gave her an expectant look. "If we can catch one of these bastards alive, we can take apart Witts's funding."

Boots wanted to tell Cordell to go smoke outside, but the truth was that she didn't want him to leave. She missed all of them so badly, but she'd be damned if she said so. "They're going to kill every last one of us," she said, watching him with disgust as he lit up his smoke.

He exhaled a huge cloud, looking away. "You know...I didn't even ask how you've been doing. Everything okay out here in paradise?"

"Of course you didn't ask!" said Boots. "You just busted up in my place and destroyed my staging area."

The captain made with his innocent eyes. "Well, I'm asking now."

Boots gave him a scowl. "You can't just change the subject from planet-killing to distilling!"

"The hell I can't." He drained his glass and put it in front of her. "Damn, that's good," he sighed, obviously lying. "Any chance I can get another?"

She filled his tumbler and, in her quest to calm her nerves, poured herself another, too. She added some sugar and a crushed basil leaf in an effort to wipe away the mouth-incinerating taste, but it did little.

"Come on, Boots," he said. "We can talk business soon enough."

He always did that when she got too gloomy—tried to distract her with chitchat. It didn't help that she wanted to share the details of her new life with them. Before long, the rest of the crew asked for seconds, even Nilah. Boots had never seen her tipsy and hoped it'd be funny.

Boots told them of her new hires, the bums who manned the

distillery, and of the easy life on Hopper's Hope. She told them how she didn't know how to spend her money, and how she'd given a bunch away to the various veterans' memorial funds. Her house was too large and too luxurious for her tastes. She asked Cordell about Silas and some of the other Fallen refugees from Gantry Station, and learned that Silas had beaten a man for insulting Boots in the Widow's Watch. They'd put her portrait up on the wall, and some folks had taken to saluting it.

They'd even put up a portrait of Kinnard, to commemorate the human voice of Boots's lost AI. It'd been just as much a part of that mission as anyone.

Boots tried to muster some saltiness at Silas, the idea of him touting her glory after years of antagonism, but it touched her. The Fallen had found a measure of closure in her actions.

Her speech became slurred as the night wore on. She belted out a rendition of Arca's national anthem with Cordell, Doctor Malik Jan, and Armin. Nilah and Orna started making out in the corner, suffused by the pink light of dermaluxes. Armin tried to explain his datamancy to Boots, saying it was "no big deal, anyone with the mark can do it." Aisha Jan, the ship's pilot, said little until Alister bet her twenty argents that her marksman's magic wouldn't work while intoxicated. Jeannie begged Boots to stop them, but Boots wanted to know as badly as Alister. The rest of the night turned into Aisha casting spells and throwing knives while piss drunk. Malik fell asleep on a couch, his glass still in his hand. The ship's doctor may have possessed powerful sleep magic, but he had no trouble napping without it.

Seeing the crew of the *Capricious* lose all sense of decorum or orientation got Boots thinking about all the Arcan crews that had come before. She had her favorites. There was Pete Masters, who could whistle so loud the cargo bay would ring; he'd been transferred, and she never saw him again. There was Anna Fenton, who'd convinced Cordell to let her keep a dog on the ship; she'd kicked the bucket on a resupply mission, and the dog got lost shortly after. Some of those crew members had been happy. Plenty were dead. The ghosts of people she'd tried to forget came riding in on the memories of ship life, and old fears mixed inside her stomach with the whiskey. No one had mentioned Didier yet. Kinnard was just a portrait now, hung on the wall of a dried-up bar in Gantry Station.

Why did she always end up hanging around a bunch of fools?

"Don't know why you want to team up with the Taitutian Special Branch, Cordell," Boots said, rising to her feet, attempting to keep her level of intoxication a secret. "Bastards never gave me back my computer. Bunch of lying double-crossers, I bet. I want Kin back."

The party stopped.

"I miss Kin," she added before sipping from her glass.

Nilah put a hand on her shoulder, concern in her eyes. "Boots…"

Of course Boots had ruined the vibe. She'd always been the exact opposite of fun.

"I'm…" she mumbled. "I'm going to bed. Y'all are free to sleep where you can find a spot. It's a mansion. Beds and crap everywhere."

Then she hobbled off into the darkness of her house, cursing every wall she fell against.

A distant snore roused Boots from her slumber, and she pulled the sheets tight around her shoulders. Her head swam from the white dog, so she was still a ways away from a hangover. Most nights, she found it difficult to sleep on such soft bedclothes—the ones made from rare fibers. Those were for rich people, and Boots sucked at being rich.

She shouldn't have gotten wasted on her own supply. She needed to bottle it one day, and Kinnard's Way was far from mature enough for copious consumption. Most nights, she'd taken to downing a quarter of Flemmlian Ten just to get some sleep.

Hadn't this been the dream: get money and cash out? Her room was too big, sprawling overhead with intricate designs of stars and nebulae. The furniture was too nice, lacking the dents and dings that had always marked her things. The architect had called her house "Cozy, for its size" and encouraged her to spend more money decorating the place, but Boots had gotten accustomed to living in a garbage studio apartment, a crew bunk, a cockpit... and this mansion made her skin crawl.

At least she had some nice paper archives at the house—not that she had to sell legends anymore. There had been a time when every scrap of paper, every old auction note, every invoice, every report had represented a piece of her livelihood. Those papers had been the seeds of lies and the keys to selling salvage maps. Even after accumulating her wealth, Boots hadn't broken the habit of snapping up any old records she could find. She'd built herself an archive and taken to searching for the clues to lost treasures. She hadn't stumbled upon any great finds, but there was bound to be more out there for her.

She'd told herself not to let Cordell and his clowns inside her home. He hadn't come there to visit, and both of them knew it. He just wanted to recruit her so he could fill out his roster. But then, he could've gotten any jackass fighter jockey; why choose her?

Boots swung her legs over the side of the bed and stood up, maybe a little too quickly. The room spun, and she felt the familiar cold sweat of sickness bead up on her forehead and upper lip.

"Ai, open the windows," she grunted.

"Yes, ma'am," came the voice of "Ai," the AI, its vocalization lacking any personality or identifying characteristics.

Boots couldn't envision what Ai would look like as a person—not male or female, not old or young. She hadn't even given it a real name. She couldn't bear to, after what'd happened to Kin.

The floor-to-ceiling windows slid open. A gentle breeze wafted into the room, and her gauzy curtains danced in the moonlight like ghosts.

"Ai, water."

It dinged an acknowledgment, and a recess on her dressing table slid open, a glass of cold water ready and waiting. Boots took it, drained the contents, and replaced it, where it disappeared into the cycler. Then she stepped out onto her back porch into the fresh night of Hopper's Hope.

The twin moons of her planet shone brightly overhead, washing everything in their thin light. Grasshoppers sang their chirping love songs to the stars. Green waves of rye undulated before her in all directions like an ocean, and she sighed. This, and the hard work of running a still, were the only parts of her new life that gave her peace. A shack, a tractor, a still, and a warehouse would've done the trick—no need for a fancy mansion. The fields were enough: all that green food, healthy and perfect. It was as far as she could get from the dusty world that almost killed her.

She leaned against the faux stone railing, letting it pull the intoxicated heat from her body. She almost jumped out of her skin when the double doors in the room next to hers opened and Nilah stepped out, wearing one of the guest sets of pajamas—some striped linen threads that'd come with the house.

Boots smirked. "I don't think I've ever seen you look so frumpy."

"These are Beton Chic, Boots," said Nilah, obviously impressed. "That's a nice label."

"Keep them. I don't get many guests out here anyway."

Nilah came and stood beside her, both of them barefoot, leaning against the railing. They listened to the whispering crops, the soft snoring of a farming colony. Nilah's dermaluxes went snowy white, then dimmed as the racer suppressed them.

"How'd you get the ginger weirdies to help you?" asked Boots.

"They have their reasons for hating Witts, but they're not mine to share."

"That's good. Everyone ought to hate him, after how close humanity came to extinction."

"You know, I don't think..." Nilah began, but trailed off.

"What is it?"

She shook her head. "No, I'm being selfish."

Boots looked her up and down. "Say what you've got to say."

Nilah turned and looked her in the eyes. "I don't think I've ever missed anyone as much as I've missed you."

"Aw, now. I'm cranky and awful."

"I know."

Nilah wrapped her arm around Boots and pulled her in for a tight hug. Boots jolted with the sudden contact, then rested her head against her companion's shoulder. She let out a long breath.

"What the hell is wrong with me? Why can't I be happy?" asked Boots.

"The same thing that's wrong with me," said Nilah. "We need to struggle."

"No, I'm sure that's not it," said Boots, laughing softly and pulling away. "I was struggling on Gantry Station, and I wasn't happy then, either."

"Maybe you just like to fight."

"Yeah." Boots chucked Nilah on the shoulder. "Maybe so, kid."

Nilah turned to face the breeze, the black curls of her mohawk dancing over her dark skin. "I don't feel much like a kid anymore. I'm twenty-one."

Boots guffawed, and her head ached in retaliation. She'd have Ai mix her up some medicine to stave off the alcohol's effects. "Okay, kid. You're twenty-one now."

"Twenty-one can be pretty old. What were you doing at twenty-one?"

Boots nodded, conceding the point. "Watching my friends die...I guess you're right."

"I usually am," she replied with a wink. The trio of scars across Nilah's cheek crinkled up.

"When I remembered you this past year," Boots said, searching for the words, "I always thought of the pampered racing champion who became a badass, right there in front of me. I always forgot the scars."

"I always forgot the arm," said Nilah.

"It's got some tricks," said Boots, snapping out a hidden blade. She locked back a chamber in the forearm to reveal a space for a large slinger shell—the kind used in ship-to-ship combat.

"Boots, that's an arm cannon."

"And so it is. If I had to replace my arm, I figured it's best to put in an upgrade. Orna's new bot carries around that kind of firepower."

"One: no, it doesn't." She circled Boots like she was inspecting a dangerous breach in engine containment. "Two: not in a prosthetic stump. Bloody hell, Boots, do you have any kind of recoil compensation?"

"No."

"Safeties?"

"Only mechanical. Low tech keeps it reliable. You never know when a bunch of dangerous yahoos might drop out of the sky and kidnap me."

"Hey, now. I'm more of a hooligan than a yahoo."

Boots snapped the hidden chamber shut. "Maybe Witts's folks want some revenge on us. Best to plan for trouble."

Nilah placed a hand against her chest with a theatrical flourish. "Well, darling, trouble is here. Are you going to follow it out into space, or sit at home?"

Boots leaned back against the railing. "If I lose my other arm, do you people promise to leave me alone?"

"That depends. How do you feel about those legs?"

In the early hours of the morning, Boots packed her things to go. It'd been easier than she expected. She maintained a top-quality emergency bag with cash, slinger, ammunition, clothing, and false identification, on the chance she needed to get the hell off-world in a hurry. She'd long ago given Ai instructions on how to run the distillery and schedule employees, just in case she needed to disappear for a while. There was a large sum in escrow to pay folks while she was gone, and Ai could call her lawyer about any estate troubles.

Maybe that's what she hated about this life—she could leave, and no one would even notice.

As pink predawn washed over her fields, she shouldered her duffel and hiked up the gentle slope, past her warehouse, to where the *Capricious* lay dormant. The ship was the same bucket he'd always been, his bulbous body scarred and scorched by so many years of turmoil. In this, he was Boots's brother.

She glanced back to her mansion: the sprawling, stark house in the valley, all flat lines and luxury trim. It was supposed to be her future, her escape. "Ai can handle it," she muttered to herself.

Cordell shambled out of Boots's front door and onto the porch to smoke. Even at this distance, he looked like death. She saw the short flare of a lighter, and his eyes rose to meet hers. He straightened and cocked his head.

It was as though they'd switched places for a moment: him at the homestead, her on the path to the ship.

"Well?" she shouted at him from the hill, even though it felt like a hammer on her skull. "You going to open the big guy up or what?"

Chapter Two

Flanking Maneuvers

Despite her better judgment, Boots found herself in the soaring cargo hold of her old warship—the one in which she'd ridden out the Famine War twenty years prior. The level of magical talent among the crew was far beyond that of the average slouching scribbler. Sure, everyone had a cardioid to give them magic, but the members of the *Capricious* were like endurance athletes, able to cast bigger, better spells, more often. It was enough to give her a complex, since she was one of the ultra-rare people born without the spellcasting organ. "Arcana dystocia," the doctors called it. Boots simply called it a goddamned curse.

Now she was supposed to tag along with these heroes into the stars. She'd barely finished the thought when she spotted the greatest piece of aeronautical hardware ever crafted by human hands.

"There he is," she said, dropping her duffel onto the deck of the cargo bay and staring up at the MRX-20 Midnight Runner strike fighter. It still laid in mag lock, suspended from the rafters, though Orna's rigged scaffolding had been replaced with an actual docking system. With her *Harrow* salvage rights, Boots had considered buying a fighter of her own, but keeping a weapon of war at her house seemed a little foolish—especially when she didn't have Orna doing all the tough maintenance. Most MRX-20s were scrap on Clarkesfall's surface or carbon in its atmosphere, and finding a local mechanist would be a real pain.

Gone were all the scratches and dents of her last three sorties. They'd given him a fresh coat of paint, Clarkesfall purple with the orange half-moon of Arca slicing across the tail fins. Beams of moonlight radiated from the Arcan sigil, winding over the hull, tracing the lines of the keel. It was a bit wild for a military craft, more like an exotic flier, but Boots liked the look. If they got revenge on Grand Admiral Henrick Witts and the rest of the *Harrow* conspirators, by god, everyone would know who flew that Midnight Runner. Witts had destroyed her country of Arca, sucked the life from her homeworld of Clarkesfall, but looking at that strike fighter reminded Boots that she could always fight back.

"I bet you missed him," said Orna, clomping up behind her in combat kicks. The quartermaster rubbed her eyes and yawned. "Had to repair the main cannons after the *Harrow*. Your overcharging them scored the spell boreshafts." Orna pointed to the keel. "The landing skids are no longer held together by patch tape and good feelings."

"Did you make any upgrades?"

"Nah," she replied, and Boots relaxed. "Still all standard issue. Being honest, it would've been easier to replace the main cannon with something newer. Arcan parts are getting harder to come by."

"I don't doubt it," said Boots, remembering how Orna and the crew had descended to abandoned military outposts to salvage parts for the first Runner. "How'd you get the stuff?"

Orna arched an eyebrow and smirked. "We've got some serious fans now. A lot of Fallen are grateful for what we did. Speaking of which, there's something for you in the cockpit. It's a..." There came a rummaging sound from the tool chest. "Charger!"

Boots turned to see Orna's new battle armor comparing wrenches to the bolts on its chest, its head cocked to one side as it considered them.

"Charger, no!" shouted Orna, and it looked up at her. "You leave that plate on! I know it causes you to run hot, that's what I'm counting on. No, I'm trying out a new engine spec." Her circlet flashed around the edge, almost like the light spoke to her. "Well, you'll get used to it!"

It tested the fit of the wrench and gave one of the bolts a half turn.

"Damn it, Charger!" Orna clenched her fists. "Never should've upgraded his intelligence," she mumbled, stomping after him.

Boots watched Orna chew out her own battle armor before snatching the wrench out of his hand and chucking it back in the tool box. She then locked it with a palm print.

"I've got to show him his design spec again," Orna called over to Boots. "You've got a present in the cockpit." The quartermaster and her battle armor disappeared into the bowels of the ship.

At least Orna had learned to put her tools away.

Boots walked to where the scaffolding ladder was before and found that Orna had replaced it with a more traditional "rocket rung" ascender. Boots grasped the metal and put her foot on the kickplate, then hit the go button. The ascender rose with such violence that it nearly tore her off, and when it stopped at the ship, Boots held on for dear life, quivering.

Had she really used it one-handed back in her military days? Even in full grav or plus halfs, she could remember leaping onto the rocket rung with one arm and leg hanging off. She huddled close to the rung, not daring to look down at the deck fifteen feet below.

When she felt steady enough, she slowly stepped onto the catwalk, then made her way to the open cockpit. She looked inside, spotting exactly what Orna had meant.

Boots lifted the yellow polybuff jacket from the seat, holding it up in disbelief. Emblazoned across the front pocket were the swooping red letters of Rook Velocity Corporation's logo. She turned it this way and that, admiring the way the light caught inside the raised type. She inspected the black trim and piping, still unable to wrap her head around what she was holding.

She'd seen those jackets on the flight lines as a child, when she went to air shows in Arca's capital. RVC mechanics used to run around the bays in Brandenburg Base wearing them while they serviced the MRX-20s, much to the envy of all the fighter jocks. Only five-year employees of RVC ever got a jacket, and they'd never part with them. She turned it to look at the shoulder patch, where a name should've been stitched.

It said, Boots.

"What the hell?" she mumbled. It didn't look new. She opened it up to check the country of origin, just to see if it was Arcan, and found a note made of real paper pinned to the inside:

We had a few of these lying around after we evacuated Clarkesfall. I thought you might like one. Thanks for keeping the stars over Arca. Forever your fan.

—Jack Rook

Boots admired the note for a long while, enjoying the feel of it in her hands. She'd held a lot of paper in her day, but a handwritten note from the legend himself was something else. Jealousy needled her heart; someone on the crew had to have met the guy. She tried the jacket on, and it fit like a dream. She wished she had a mirror.

"He threw us a big party at his place on Taligola. You could've come if you hadn't run off," Cordell called up to her, and she peered down to find him standing on the deck, hands on his hips. "It was a veterans' benefits thing. That jacket is the real deal."

"I can't believe you did this," she said, trying to hold her elation inside. She couldn't stop beaming.

"Well, now...you actually look happy for once in your life."

"It's only the greatest article of clothing ever made."

"Girlie, there is nothing better than an Arcan captain's jacket—giving orders and breaking hearts. Don't even come with that weak sauce."

"Yeah, all right, Captain. Sure," she said, gingerly straightening out her cuffs and savoring the weight on her skin. "I'm never taking this thing off, you hear me? I want to be buried in this."

"And just think," said Cordell, "all you had to do to get one was save the damned galaxy. Now stow your crap. I want to brief the crew in thirty."

"Gather round, boys and girls!" Cordell called, stunning Nilah's hungover ears. "We've got work to do."

They'd all assembled in the *Capricious*'s ready room, otherwise known as the mess. Cordell hadn't wasted a second once Boots came on board, rousting everyone from their hangovers and cajoling them onto the ship. He'd ordered them into orbit and summoned everyone to the mess without a second's reprieve. Armin, Orna, and the twins—Alister and Jeannie—stood beside Nilah, all blinking the boozy sleep out of their eyes. Aisha and Malik appeared stone sober, much to Nilah's jealousy. Boots was surprisingly alert, sporting a flight jacket twenty years out of style and preening like a princess.

Cordell nodded at the party. "Mister Vandevere has worked his magic on the data cube we found on Forscythe's body, and he's got news."

"It's just as we suspected," said Armin. "Aaron Forscythe was a bagman for Witts's financial engine, which I have dubbed the 'Money Mill.'"

Boots smirked. "Money Mill, sir? Are you sure a silly name fits the situation?"

Armin scowled, and Nilah didn't envy Boots in that moment. "Are you sure you want to get off on the wrong foot with the first mate right after boarding his ship?"

Boots reddened. "No, sir."

"As I was saying," Armin continued, "Aaron Forscythe was a bagman for the Money Mill. Once again, we weren't able to liberate his funds before someone drained them—someone knew he was dead and took immediate action . . . but we got two key pieces of intelligence. First, Forscythe was there to pay off someone in the Taitutian Special Branch. He carried this missive, and the crypto was pathetic. Took me a half hour to crack."

Armin waved his hand, and the projectors spun out a set of light spells. Text formed, garbled at first, then sorting into the words:

Children infiltrated. Pinnacle. Buy identity. Liaison to follow.

"Told you we couldn't trust the Special Branch," muttered Boots.

"Who's the liaison, sir?" asked Nilah, and Armin shook his head.

"No idea," he replied. "That's the only message I could get out of the crystal. Most of the rest of its contents had been zeroized several thousand times."

Cordell patted down the sides of his hair and glanced at Boots's ugly jacket. Nilah could swear the two were competing over something—maybe the world's worst fashion show.

The captain stroked his chin. "But that ain't the whole story. Mister Vandevere, you found something else?"

"Yes, sir," said Armin. "All of Forscythe's bank accounts were unsigned IGFs, *but*...one of them lined up with an account used by an arms dealer, active during the Famine War."

"This ugly cuss," Cordell began as the lights in the mess came down, "is Maslin Durand, and he's our next target in the Money Mill chain."

The light of the text dispersed and formed anew, crafting something that looked like a human head for all the crew to see. Nilah didn't have the words to describe the horrible visage that appeared; he looked as though half of his head had been blown off and chewed on by rats.

"God, he looks like a marpo threw up on another, uglier marpo," said Orna.

"Not everyone wears their scars as well as you, Miss Sokol," said Cordell.

Nilah thought of how she'd chosen her own scars, and a pang of sympathy came over her. Without thinking, she touched her cheek, then put her hand down when she caught the captain's eye.

Cordell cleared his throat and gestured to Armin. "Thanks to Mister Vandevere, and a bit of extra access from the Taitutian Special Branch, we found a ton of anomalous bank activity around the same time Miss Brio was framed for Cyril Clowe's murder. We believe there's a good chance that Durand was selling weapons and laundering money for the Gods of the *Harrow*. His transactions line up precisely with the locations and dates that Mother popped up and...." He paused a moment to chew on the sentence. "It's highly likely that he contributed materiel for her battlegroup and arranged transport for her."

"That means he helped kill Didier," said Boots. "And almost killed us."

"Do we have to call them the 'Gods of the *Harrow*'?" asked Nilah. "It sounds so dreadfully complimentary."

"They have godlike power, and there's not a word awful enough to describe them," said Cordell. "Besides, it's going to make it that much sweeter when we kill their sorry asses."

"Right," said Nilah. "Of course."

"There was another lucky break," Cordell continued. "We checked out the Special Branch dossier on Maslin Durand and found out he recently got religion. Guess which denomination he chose?" He paused. "No one's going to guess?"

Nilah raised her hand half-heartedly. "The... Children of the Singularity?"

"Exactly!"

"Do we know what their deal is yet?" asked Boots.

"You know how everyone was happy that we took down Witts's plan to kill all humans?" said Cordell.

"Oh hell, I see where this is going," said Boots.

"Yeah, there's a group on the Link—a massive one—that believes the entire thing was a setup by the current Taitutian prime minister, Angela Bianchi, to execute her predecessor, Dwight Mandell," replied the captain.

Dwight's last moments alive flashed through Nilah's mind—his choking, blood-soaked face. "Well, that's bloody stupid."

"We shot him on a live broadcast!" Boots said. "Mandell manifested a massive glyph right in front of everyone in the goddamned galaxy! We parked the *Harrow* in the Taitutian stratosphere! What else were we supposed to do?"

Cordell held up his index finger. "No one is disputing that the *Harrow* returned, nor are they saying we didn't shoot Mandell. But the conspiracy theorists say the *Harrow*'s location was fed to us by the Taitutian government to justify a coup, and we were hired to assassinate him."

"And his godlike glyph that spontaneously manifested in the middle of a live broadcast?" asked Boots.

"They also believe that part," said Cordell. "The Children of the Singularity have code-named him 'Big Daddy' and say he was the pinnacle of magical prowess. They worship him. That's the cult part; got a bunch of weird allegorical myths, too. It's like, half self-help, half religious nonsense."

"I've been aggregating their posts on the Link," said Armin. "There's a strong nationalist component to the Children's rhetoric. They love Witts, love Mandell, hate anything that challenges Taitutian hegemony, like GATO."

"Gate-oh?" asked Boots. "I must not be hearing you right."

Armin smirked. "The Galactic Alliance Treaty Organization. Yes."

Boots smacked her lips. "Because it totally makes sense to hate a galaxy-stabilizing humanitarian organization."

"They're just a bunch of doddering diplomats," said Nilah. "My father always said they could barely negotiate getting out of bed."

Armin shook his head. "It doesn't matter. The Children of the Singularity have created their own version of reality on the Link, complete with incriminating imagery, alternative timelines, and dossiers on each one of us. The fakery is actually quite compelling. In your case, Boots, they're saying your treasure show was a front for you to conduct a wide-ranging espionage operation."

"Oh!" Nilah said, brightening at the prospect. "And what do they say about me, sir? Anything exciting? Am I a spy, too?"

Armin sniffed. "The politest thing they say is that you cheated your way to the top of the PGRF to get close to Claire Asby, and that you framed her. There are less-savory items in their repertoire, which you can peruse later if you're so inclined. I wouldn't."

Nilah was ambivalent over the thought of a bunch of cultists fuming over her picture. On the one hand, it was disturbing that anyone could hate her for helping save every human alive. On the other, it warmed the cockles of her spiteful heart that a bunch of nationalist fascists lost sleep over her.

"We know Durand is a bagman for Witts," said Armin.

"And if he's giving to the Children of the Singularity," said Boots, "we need to look into that angle, too."

"Bingo," said Cordell, pointing at her with a finger-slinger. "Wouldn't it be nice if these cultist assholes gave us a reason to have them all arrested?"

Armin nodded. "We have it on good authority that Durand's accounts are in overdrive again, but no one knows where he's funneling the cash. It's going into an unsigned IGF account, then disappearing from there."

"That cash could be anywhere," said Nilah.

"That's where we come in," said Jeannie, nudging Alister. "Can't hide the money trail from a pair of readers. We can probe Durand's mind and get the truth out of him, regardless of whether or not he uses unsigned accounts."

"Can you really get that specific?" asked Boots. "I'd always heard there were limitations."

"There are," said Alister, crossing his arms. "But there's no one who can keep me out of their head forever."

Boots crooked an eyebrow. "Aren't you the eager one?"

Alister shook his head. "You wouldn't say that if you'd ever been inside someone's mind. I just want a chance to do some damage."

"We're at your service," Jeannie added with a smile. "We want to help."

"So it's a repeat of the previous mission," said Nilah. "The one I screwed up."

"That was a team effort," said Orna, crossing her arms.

"This might be the last bone Taitutian intelligence throws us," said Cordell. "They're happy we cleaned out their ranks, but their goodwill only goes so far. They gave us Durand because they believe he murdered one of their operatives."

"So, if we accidentally kill him . . ." said Boots.

"It's a win-win," replied Cordell. "With Durand dead, they

take one wanted man off their list and get plausible deniability. If we're captured or killed, they get to call us vigilantes and disavow all knowledge."

"Seems like Taitutians do a lot of disavowing," grunted Boots, and Nilah gave her a sour look. "Present company excluded, of course."

Cordell jammed his hands in his pockets. "Our intel states that Durand is on safari in the forests of Corva, on Blix, for the next six days. A lot of endangered game in that biome, and there are more than a few lucrative contracts for some of the magical species there."

"Cutting it close, aren't we?" said Boots. "I thought Blix was at least a five-day jump from Hopper's Hope."

"We'll make it." Cordell quirked his lips. "Our boy *Capricious* has all sorts of new surprises. Miss Sokol overhauled our Flow systems to speed them up a touch. Mister Vandevere?"

Armin gestured, and the face mercifully disappeared, replaced by a map of the region. "Not a lot of settlements here," said the first mate. "The locals consider these woods to be a death trap. That's in large part because of these creatures here." He gestured again, and the rendering of a colorful bat appeared, its fur startling shades of crimson and blue. "They call them 'sirathica,' or 'sirens' in Standard. The creatures live in eidolon crystal caves and possess a crude form of the inveigler's mark."

"The inveigler's mark...They charm people?" asked Nilah, her stomach sinking. "Why?"

Armin gave her a wan smile. "To lure them away from the group, so they can bite their heads off. The creatures have a particular taste for gray matter."

Nilah waited for the joke, even though she knew Armin was never one for humor.

"And how big are they?" asked Nilah.

The first mate frowned, considering the question. "A fully grown adult is roughly the size of the Midnight Runner in the hangar. In flight, they can reach speeds of up to a hundred and sixty kilometers per hour. They give off little noise profile but, mercifully, light up like bonfires on infrared."

Nilah grimaced and looked to Boots, Orna, and the twins, whose white skin went a few shades lighter. They'd be on the ground team, and she'd be right there with them.

Armin gave her a thin smile and folded his hands behind his back. "Sirens will only attack if certain they can lure a member of the pack away. The favored tactic among poachers is to hunt alone to appear more attractive. They haul around expensive portable disperser towers to stop the charms."

"Aren't those heavy?" asked Boots.

"Probably fifty kilos," said Orna. "It's no picnic."

"Then Durand is strong," said Boots, "if he's carrying that along with his hunting gear."

Armin waved his hand, and a topographical map appeared. He pointed to the peak of a mountain. "We believe Durand will pop up an encampment here. We'll wait until he's alone, then kidnap him before we're attacked by sirens."

Cordell took a deep breath, surveying his crew with a smile. "Any questions?"

Every hand slowly rose.

Within two cycles, they were standing in the woods of Corva, drenched and miserable under the orange light of a single full moon.

When Nilah thought of big game and hunting, hot climates always came to mind, with enormous fern fronds and colossal insects... though what did she know, since most Taitutians were vegetarians and rarely engaged in such savagery. The fog-glazed mountain forests of Corva were anything but temperate, full of evergreens and ivy, frigid and devoid of human settlements as far as the eye could see. The only group of humans that made enclaves in these woods were closed off and provincial, and the crew of the *Capricious* wasn't welcomed into the village where they landed.

In other parts of Blix, they had vineyards and olive orchards with beautiful country châteaus. Not Corva.

After they departed the village, Orna had led them into the woods alongside Malik and the Ferrier twins. Boots remained in the skies on patrol, and Aisha, Armin, and the captain stayed in orbit, awaiting exfiltration requests.

Alister traced his reader's mark and closed his eyes, inhaling with arms outstretched. "I bet I can sense the sirathica's minds. I bet I can read them."

"I bet you can shut up," said Orna. "I'm the mission lead, and I say save your magic, greenhorn. Don't you cast again without telling me."

Alister deflated and Jeannie scowled.

"No call to be rude," said the female Ferrier.

Nilah patted Jeannie's back as she passed, giving her a sympathetic look.

They pushed through along game trails in the ruddy afternoon, quieter than a funeral procession. The speed at which Charger could move over the ivy truly impressed Nilah. She'd been a party to Orna's battle armor testing, but Charger was next-level weapons design. Most times, Nilah couldn't even see the bot. It darted about the undergrowth, silent as a cat. Occasionally, it'd come into view, only to leap away. The same onboard AI that gave it improved speed, agility, and target triage also gave it an attitude like a whiny child.

In the temperate forests of Corva, Charger was at home, dashing among the boulders, leaping from tree to tree like a bloodred cat. Nilah imagined what it would be like to be hunted by it, the primal fear its claws could inspire, and shook the thought from her head. With Charger as their pathfinder, they made speedy headway through the woods in search of data sources—the satellite uplinks that could give Maslin Durand away. Within an hour, they found their first signal, and Orna guided them toward it.

Six hours into their hike, the sun ran out. Charger dropped down in front of them and signaled for absolute quiet. Nilah, Malik, and the Ferriers waited, slingers in hand, while Charger scouted ahead. When Orna called the all-clear, they approached to find the ruins of a camp.

Shelters lay empty, their flaps open and the woods creeping inside one leaf at a time. The satellite radio was still in operation, requesting periodic updates from geolocation, despite being buried by months of mossy growth. Its eidolon crystal likely still had another year in it. The remains of the campers were considerably less intact.

Nilah swore aloud when Charger gestured to the bodies. Flesh had rotted to a mottled gray. Clothing had moldered to ribbons. Neither of the corpses possessed a head, but a tattered stump at the end of their necks. At the party's approach, a single carrion bird rose into the night.

Nilah had seen murder victims a few times before—the crew of the *Harrow* had been gassed and stuffed into a vacuum-sealed cargo bay, left ageless by Henrick Witts's mutineers. The people entombed in the ice of Alpha, the conspirators' planning base on Wartenberg, were distant and frozen—their presence impersonal. Nothing prepared Nilah for the stench of these camp corpses.

The Ferriers hunkered down together, Jeannie's hand upon Alister's, looking anywhere except at the bodies. Alister always acted tough, but Nilah had seen Jeannie comfort him more times than she could count.

"It doesn't take a ship's doctor to know what made these wounds," said Malik, crouching over the deceased. "The torn flesh around the neck indicates that these heads were pulled off, likely in a single bite. I would've expected the sirens to carry their prey away and eat them in the comfort of a den or nest. Looks like they just bite the heads off and leave. I'm surprised the other animals haven't cleaned this up."

"Why do you think that is?" asked Nilah.

Malik stood, pulled out a handkerchief, and blew his nose. In spite of his cool demeanor, the smell had to be getting to him, too. "I'm guessing that any animal large enough to eat the lion's share also gets hunted by the sirens."

Charger turned one of the corpses up by the arm, its bloated flesh making a gruesome slurp.

"It's not our guy," said Orna, her voice a hoarse whisper through Charger's speakers.

"Oh?" asked Nilah.

Charger nodded. "Durand is supposed to have a tattoo on his inner forearm. No such markings. Got another data source three klicks east of here. Let's go."

After another hour, they had to take a break, making camp for the evening. Charger was a godsend, hammering the deep tent spikes and unloading the heavy packs as though they were feathers in its claws. They popped up a heater and tucked into their rations, Orna stretching her arms after being inside the bot for so long. Nilah had taken to the Fallen military bars with zeal, pleased to wolf down loads of carbs, fat, and sugar. She thought back to the night that she first smelled one of those heavenly, enchanted ration bars, sitting in a bunk next to Boots.

She'd been running for her life, framed by Mother, kidnapped by the crew of the *Capricious*, but she'd had no idea how much stranger things would get.

"This is Hunter One," said Orna, yawning. "We're done for the night. Going to catch a few hours of sleep."

"Boots, acknowledged," said Boots over the comm. "Returning home."

"Boss, acknowledged," said Cordell. "See you in the morning."

As they finished making camp, Orna set Charger to patrol a square kilometer. "Everyone," she said, "get some rest. If you have to leave your tent, take a buddy."

Orna came over to Nilah and kissed her. She looked her in the eyes and said, "I love you. Going to be okay out here?"

She rolled her eyes. "Of course, darling."

"Good," said Orna, pulling back and gesturing to her tent. "I won't be far if you need me."

"Oh, I need you," Nilah shot back with a wink, and Orna hesitated. "Not really, babes. Pretty knackered. Get some sleep."

Nilah settled in to her survival tent, a duraplast-plated shelter rooted to the ground by mechanical pegs. Sloped as it was, the structure could weather gale-force winds or even avalanches. She felt certain that the sirens would have trouble getting to her in there, but she still couldn't sleep.

The captain didn't object to Nilah's relationship with Orna because it'd formed before Nilah was a part of the crew. When they were on a mission, however, they were required to sleep apart, as were Malik and Aisha; Cordell wouldn't tolerate "distractions."

She supposed he was right, that it wouldn't do to get into a fire-fight with her pants down. Still, it felt cruel to deny her the chance to push in close with Orna, to feel the skin of the quartermaster's bicep and soft breath in her ear as they both drifted off to sleep. Over the past year, Orna had been more than a wild fling: she'd been an anchor. With the quartermaster around, Nilah could get comfortable anywhere.

Instead, Nilah fell back on her old sleep routine: she closed her eyes and mentally rehearsed the curves of Wilson Fields, her home racetrack on Taitu. She imagined the starting line from pole position, the mad dash for the inside of turn one, the right braking sequence for the Chicane Olivier complex. When she got to the long back straight, she considered the markers along the sides of the track. Did she downshift at 450 meters? That couldn't be right. There was only a 300-meter marker.

A footstep sounded outside, startling Nilah from her near sleep. She snatched her slinger from its holster in the ceiling and checked the clip as her dermaluxes went purple with anxiety. Another two footsteps came, and Nilah sat back in exasperation, tattoos fading to white. Orna was out there creeping around, probably too cool to take a partner to the bathroom. Nilah checked her watch; she must've drifted off, because three hours had passed. What was Orna doing, wandering around like that?

Nilah climbed out of her tent wearing only skivvies, ready to chew her girlfriend out, but in the darkness, she could only see Orna's silhouette receding into the woods. Nilah's skin pebbled with gooseflesh, but the longer she took to get properly dressed, the longer her fool girlfriend was out in the woods alone. The terrain didn't look too treacherous; if she went back inside for her shoes, she might lose sight of Orna. Nilah suppressed her dermaluxes, hoping not to draw any more attention to herself as she went after her girlfriend.

Getting through the undergrowth without shoes was tough, and every stray rock and stick scratched the soles of Nilah's feet. She hoped none of it was poisonous, but they could sort that out back on the ship. Each cut was something she could use to guilt Orna into taking on some of her watch duties later.

She glanced back, the dim red glow of their survival tents receding into the darkened underbrush. What could Orna be doing, ranging this far from safety? Nilah hoped it wasn't some amorous scheme—she wasn't in the mood. Orna had to be just over the next little hill, in a clearing, and Nilah was about to give her a piece of her mind.

The clearing fell dead still as Nilah took a few silent steps into it, slinger at the ready. Tumbled boulders and soft moss carpeted the western side, and she thought she could see the opening of a cave beneath an overhang. Nilah's anger flared as another sharp rock cut her foot.

"Orna!" she hissed, trying to keep her voice low. "Orna, damn it, don't do this to—"

Another sharp cut on her foot interrupted her, and Nilah fell, trying to keep her weight off the dangerous rocks. At her wits' end, she let her dermaluxes flow free, and what she saw turned them green.

They weren't rocks. They were bones.

A sudden wind ruffled her short hair, and clawed red feet scratched the ground before her. Moist, rotting breath warmed the top of her head. She didn't want to look up. She knew what she'd see.

Her hand holding the slinger wouldn't move. She couldn't raise her eyes to the attacker.

Before the beast could take Nilah's head off with its massive jaws, Charger slammed into its side, sending both of them flailing across the pile of bones. The creature batted Charger away as though the battle armor was a simple nuisance. When the siren beat its wings, the wind bowled Nilah over. She scrambled to her feet to get back to the camp.

The siren landed opposite them, blocking Nilah's path with a bloodcurdling screech. Charger regained its footing and scooped Nilah up, shoving her into the small cave, where it would have an easier time defending her. She went sprawling across the mossy rocks, bruised and scratched, but still alive. Nilah clambered back to the opening to see what became of Charger and found him wrestling with the siren in the moonlit clearing. The bot clawed at the leathery wings of the creature but appeared to be losing.

"On my way!" said Orna, Charger's eyes flickering green as her words came out of his speaker.

"Hurry!" was all Nilah could say. She took careful aim at the beast but stayed her shot for fear of hitting Charger. If the bot was disabled, she'd be all alone with the creature.

The tiny cave began heating up, stinking of the same rotten breath as the siren. When she turned to look behind her, Nilah found a dozen of the creatures scratching up through the caverns, maneuvering through the tight space with their barbed foreclaws.

She screamed, strobed her dermaluxes at full blast, and bolted from the cavern.

Nilah didn't know which way her friends were, but as sirens poured out of the earth in a writhing cloud, she found it safer to flee into the darkness of the foggy woods.

They'd parked the *Capricious* in a nearby valley, and Boots was glad of it—since they were apparently going to rumble with a flock of magic bats.

She ran for the cargo bay as fast as her legs would take her. Good thing she'd observed scramble protocol—when the call came in, she'd been asleep in her flight suit.

"Remember, Boots," said Cordell, his voice tinny in her comm. "This is an atmos deployment. You've got to keep it tight. Hunter One, Sleepy, Spyglass, and Pensive are hunkered down in the survival tents. For now, the sirathica haven't cracked them, but that won't last forever."

This time, Boots took the rocket rung much better, cleanly stepping off onto the catwalk in a practiced motion. She climbed into the cockpit and tapped her paragon crystal to the pad.

"Boots here, requesting departure," she said, closing the canopy and strapping herself in. She flipped the ready switches in sequence, powering up all the subsystems.

"Departure acknowledges," said Armin. "Opening the cargo bay. Get ready to drop."

The cargo bay growled as the door opened, wind whipping through its cavernous space. Dark clouds rolled past outside, and in the distance, a rising sun began to tint the sky pink.

"Hunter One here!" shouted Orna, and Boots could hear unnatural hissing and screeching in the background. "Hurry the hell up!"

Boots mashed the full-start, and her engine roared to life. "The bay is open enough, Departure. Let me out!"

"Cleared for launch," said Armin.

The mag-lock system ejected the Midnight Runner out of the rear of the *Capricious*, where the ship fell for a hundred meters before executing a hard burn and picking up enough speed to fly. Boots's head grew light and her vision dimmed as she pulled out of the stall.

"We don't expect the bats to be able to harm the *Capricious*," Cordell began, "but we can't take chances. Stay close. You're my only wing."

"So I'd better stay on this bird," said Boots.

"I can hear her screaming out there, Boss!" said Orna, terror in her voice. "I know it's not really her, but it sounds so real!"

"Hold tight," said Boots. "Boss, I'm requesting permission to engage."

"Prince here," said Armin. "Those animals are endangered. If you shoot them, we're in violation of intergalactic treaties."

"I already shot three of them!" shouted Orna. "We're the endangered ones here!"

"Boss here," said Cordell. "Boots, you're cleared hot."

"Solid copy," said Boots, throttling up to speed across the upper atmosphere. "Hunter One, give me a beacon on Hunter Two."

"We can't just step outside, Boots!" said Orna. "Please, just find my—just find Hunter Two."

"Can you send out Charger?" asked Boots.

"Charger is down," Orna replied. "One of them ripped his head off. Not irreparable, but he's done for now."

"Copy. Sit tight."

Dark mountains swam out of the mist. Boots's passive scanners picked up three dozen data signals and relayed them to the heads-up display. The survival tents, which held a transponder each, showed up as a set of green triangles, and Boots dialed them in as no-fire. As she closed the distance, her sensors illuminated the swarm of sirathica attempting to tear the tents from the ground. Boots came in low and fast, dropping flares every hundred meters over the tents.

Her proximity alarms went wild as the swarm of sirathica peeled off and gave chase. The Midnight Runner's dispersers fired with each second, blowing apart the creatures' crude inveigler's marks.

"These things are fast," said Boots, banking hard, "but they can't keep up. This ought to be a shooting gallery, Boss."

"Heard that," said Cordell. "You see Hunter Two?"

"No, sir, I—" Boots paused as a strobing light illuminated a furious swarm of black shapes from the ground. "I've got her! Just up the ridge. Can't see her, but she's alive. I'm beaconing her location. Can we get some ground support in there? Did I pull off enough heat with those flares?"

"Hunter One here." Orna's voice was interrupted by the loud snap of slinger fire. "We've got breathing room. Just get me the coordinates."

Boots lined up on Nilah's position: a craggy outcropping with a thin crevasse. If her slinger spells struck the bluff face, she might cause a collapse and squish her friend like a bug. Boots flipped her fire selector and hit the target with a beacon spell, sending a flashing infrared flare high into the sky.

"Prince here. We see your beacon," said Armin. "We can't set up an LZ in that area."

"It's okay. I've got this," breathed Boots, and she pulled the trigger, shredding the top of the sirathica swarm with bolts of fire. She pulled up at the last second, loosing another round of flares in a wild spiral as she banked away. She swiveled the keel cameras to focus on Nilah's position, and the flashing got brighter. A few of the creatures tried to follow the Runner, but broke off as Boots sped away.

"Boots, if you slow down, more of them might follow you," said Armin.

"I know," Boots replied, dialing in her next run. "That's why I'm going fast."

"You're safer in your ship than Nilah is out in the open," said Cordell. "You need to run a diversion and get them to chase you."

Boots grimaced. "What am I supposed to do, Boss? Ask nicely?"

"This is Pensive," said Alister. "We've got a dying sirathica here, and I swear I can read its mind. Just give me a chance!"

Oh, okay. I'll just twiddle my thumbs until you figure it out. Boots lined up another strafing run, but she couldn't aim much closer to Nilah without hitting the cliff.

"Pensive says not to shoot them and to fly directly at the moon," said Orna. "He says they'll all follow you if you—"

"I'm not sure my dispersers can handle all of them," interrupted Boots.

"Just do it, Boots! My girlfriend is down there!"

She did as she was told and throttled down, popping her impulse thruster to keep her nose up. She passed over the swarm without incinerating any of them, and this time, her dispersers kicked into overdrive. The horde of sirathica gave chase, and as much as Boots wanted to throttle up, she kept her hand steady, allowing the creatures to close ranks.

Any second, they'd attach to the Runner's hull and start chewing. Surely, they would crash her. As she turned toward the full, tan moon, she couldn't believe she was trusting her fate to Alister, the cocky rookie. Yet the blows never came.

When Boots switched her heads-up display to the rear imager, she found a gaggle of crimson-and-blue bats flying peacefully in vanguard behind her. They lazily flapped their leathery wings, riding the currents with no indication of the violence they'd shown before.

They were following her in formation.

"It's working!" said Orna. "Keep them busy while we find Hunter Two."

"*Capricious*," said Boots, keeping an even tone. "What the hell is going on?"

"You're at the head of a pack of ravenous freaks who can't decide if they love you or want to bite your head off," said Cordell. "I'd say you're learning what it's like to be a captain."

The screaming died down, and the creatures vanished as quickly as they had come.

Nilah lay panting in the tiny crevasse, her eyes bulging from all of the fading charms cast on her. It'd taken every ounce of will to resist the spells, though it was a bit easier when she could see their dripping maws.

In her desperation, she'd tried punching one in the eye, but the creature had scarcely flinched. If she wanted to use her Flicker on targets larger than humans, she was going to need some kinetic amplification. Maybe she ought to build her own battle armor...

But those were thoughts for another time. As she scrambled free of the crack in the cliff face, she was scratched, half-naked, and sore. She wouldn't be venturing far, lest she get lost again. She could only wait.

She carefully made her way down the pile of fractured shale that led up to the crack and sat down on the flattest rock she could find, which was still a bit jagged.

A rustle in the trees startled her, and she sat upright, ready to bolt. Her slinger had been lost in the cave, and she prayed the rustling wasn't a wounded siren come to finish its horrid work. Her dermaluxes mirrored her fear with a dim purple glow.

Instead of an animal, a cloaked figure emerged, encumbered by a bulky backpack. His polybuff poncho shimmered with optical deflection, but he made no effort to hide his goggles, his pack, or his long-range slinger. He was either a poacher or a ranger, but he was too far away to identify.

He surveyed the remains of a sirathica that Boots's ship had annihilated and laughed out loud. "Well, that's one way to do it," he croaked, setting down his pack. Now that she got a better look, Nilah could see the scanning head of a portable disperser peeking out of the top. "I don't think I've ever seen a swarm of them, but I'm no expert. Second hunt, you know."

She crossed her arms to shield herself from the cold, raising a hand to wave with fingers only. "Hello."

"In a lot of cultures..." His voice sounded like a frog caught in a fan belt. He lumbered closer. "They have a tale where they sacrifice the most beautiful to the awful monsters that live on the edge of the village."

She squinted, just able to make out the jagged scars across his face. This had to be her target. She feigned nonchalance. "Usually, we start with 'Hello,' then say what our names are."

He pulled off his goggles, revealing scars that confirmed Nilah's suspicions; she wouldn't forget Maslin Durand's face. Rummaging around his pack, he drew out a knife and clicked it on, filling the clearing with the dull glow of a cauterizer.

"No need to introduce ourselves," he grumbled. "I'll have done my deed and been long gone by the time your friends get here."

Her dermaluxes went bright white, her fingers curling into fists.

"Whoa there, my little beauty. I'm just here for this," he said, plunging the hot knife into the skull of the sirathica, splitting it in half like an overripe melon. He dug around in its brainpan with the steaming implement before drawing out a jagged piece of bone, suffused with a slimy pink light. "From where I stand, you've got more than a few kills to harvest. Surely your friends won't miss just one."

Nilah scowled. She'd never deliberately kill a wild animal, but if she had, she'd expect claim on the carcass. "You by yourself?"

"Yeah. Wanted to face the great beast alone." He gestured to her body with the knife and gave her a lascivious smile. "They'll still eat you with clothes on. You don't have to pull the whole virgin sacrifice act to lure them out."

She rolled her eyes. "They attacked our survival tents...but I found their nest. If you want to help us get home, I'm sure the captain will cut you in on a share."

He grunted and stood up, wiping his hands on the slick poly-buff poncho. "No thanks. I wanted the souvenir and I got it." He winked and turned to leave. "I'm just here for the adventure."

If he turned and vanished into the woods, they could chase after him, but they might never catch up before he made it offworld.

"Wait!"

"No dice, gorgeous," he croaked, taking a few more steps toward the woods. "They might come back, and there's no way in hell I'm going to be here—"

He'd almost disappeared into the tree line when she finally figured out how to stop him in his tracks.

"Enjoy it while you can," she shouted. "We're going to kill every last sirathica on Blix. Our trophies will be worth a fortune on the black market. You saw how many we could lure out."

"What are you talking about?"

"In a lot of cultures," she said, parroting his phrase, "rich patrons would destroy the works of great artists, or even the artists themselves, to raise the value of what remained. Think of how much that bone will be worth when all of them are extinct."

Maslin eyed her.

"Now imagine owning two or three of them. Ten of them. Twenty of them. It'd be enough to buy anything your heart desired."

"I don't think you know how rich I am," he replied. "I'm only here for the sport."

She put her hands on her hips and craned her neck to look down at him. "And you got rich by passing on brilliant opportunities? This will be a tale for the ages. After all, isn't that why you hunt? For the stories you can tell the other hunters?"

He chewed the remains of his lip and held the severed bone to his eye, peering into the depths of its arcane energies. After a long moment, he pulled aside his poncho and tucked the trophy into a bag at his waistband. "I don't think so, dearie. Good luck getting home."

Orna crashed through the tree line, leveling her slinger on the unprepared Maslin. The twins followed, both keeping their weapons trained on the poacher.

Orna smiled. "Looks like luck was on our side today. Tell us everything you know about the Children of the Singularity, and I don't melt what remains of your face."

"I don't think you understand who you're—" Maslin began,

but a purple ball of light splashed against his back, and his eyes rolled back in his head. He fell forward onto his face, erupting in loud snores.

Malik emerged from the shadows at the edge of the trees, dusting the violet smoke of the sleep spell from his hands. "If he's going to threaten us, he can do it back on the ship. Let's go home."

Chapter Three

Melody

Boots here," came the radio call in Nilah's ear. "Ditched my flock with the afterburners before any of them could mate with the ship. Returning to home."

"Nice work," Nilah replied, already grateful to have the pilot back on the crew. Without the Midnight Runner, she'd have lost her mind—and her head.

Halfway back to the ship, Maslin Durand awoke to threaten Nilah, and she made sure to tighten his restraints. In response, Durand delivered every clichéd line in the criminal handbook. *They had no idea who they were messing with. They would be sorry. He'd kill all their loved ones. His men would come for him.* On and on he went until Nilah and the others loaded him into the cargo bay of the *Capricious*.

Extraction had been a bit of a trick, since the marauder-class vessel wasn't designed to land in mountainous terrain. It was made to touch down in battlefield conditions, but with cleared, mostly level landing zones. Getting Maslin up to the *Capricious* without repeatedly knocking him unconscious at the end of a wench line meant a forced march through the mountains during the hottest part of the day.

The Ferrier twins hated him and wanted to put him back to sleep. Nilah was solidly in favor, but Malik wanted to rest his cardioid for any coming interrogations. There was only so hard he could work the organ before he'd be exhausted.

With so many sirathica dead and the large party of humans clumped together, the creatures didn't mount another attack. That didn't stop Nilah from flinching every time the trees rustled. It didn't unglue her eyes from every cave they walked past. She'd have nightmares about those snapping jaws for days to come.

When they were finally back on board the *Capricious* with the cargo ramp closed, she breathed a sigh of relief. Cordell and the others escorted Maslin to the reconverted brig, and Nilah fell into Orna's arms for a deep kiss.

"Oh, I don't think so," said Orna, dodging away. "You stink of the woods."

Nilah's jaw dropped. "I snog you all the time when you've been bathing in engine grease!"

The quartermaster waved her away. "That's perfume, babe. You smell like ticks and desperation. Go get a bath. Besides, Cap forbids making out on a mission."

Nilah raised her hands, flexing her fingers and grinning madly. Her dermaluxes went a solid pink, and her nostrils flared. "The mission is over. If you don't kiss me, there'll be consequences."

Orna popped her neck and flexed her back, limbering up with a grin. "I can handle anything you've got, Brio." She cracked her knuckles and spread her stance ever so slightly. "Tell you what: I'll fight you for it. If I win, you have to do anything I say for twenty-four hours."

Nilah tongued the inside of her cheek and began bouncing

on the balls of her feet, dermaluxes pulsing in time. "I already would've done anything you asked me to. You know that, darling."

Orna took a few steps back. "I'm going to make you clean the brig after Durand does something awful to it. Prisoners always mess up the place."

"Wicked," said Nilah, keeping her beat steady. She recalled one of Indira Panjala's songs and began keeping time. "But I'm so much stronger than I once was. You know I'm the fastest."

Orna rolled her eyes. "You should trademark that, babe. You say it enough."

Nilah put down her hands and shut off the dermaluxes. "Are you really going to deny me?"

The quartermaster sighed, exasperated. "Look, if you're not going to play the game—"

Nilah ducked in and slung her girlfriend to the deck with a hip check, shielding Orna's head so she didn't hit too hard. Orna lay beneath her, flushed and panting, her scars white against her apple-red cheeks. A drop of sweat descended the quartermaster's forehead, racing down her temple to hide behind her neck. Orna stunk; Nilah didn't care.

"Looks like you've won," said Orna. "Should've made your own wager."

"I just wanted the kiss," said Nilah, leaning in with lips parted.

A freezing-cold spray splashed the side of Nilah's face, and she gurgled in surprise. She sat upright, blinded by the constant rush of water over her. Nilah raised her hand to shield herself, and Orna caught her forearm, rolling and twisting it behind Nilah's back. Within a half second, Orna had pinned her facedown to the deck with no hope of escape.

Nilah craned her neck to find Charger holding the cargo bay hose, which still dripped from the end. She started to feel indignant when Orna's warm breath brushed her ear.

"I told you to take a bath," whispered the quartermaster.

"So you did," grunted Nilah. "And now I'm yours for the next twenty-four hours."

Orna's rough hand seized Nilah by the scalp, sending a tingle down her spine. "Don't kid yourself. You're mine forever."

Nilah bit her lip. "So am I supposed to go peel out of these clothes, or..."

Orna stood up, leaving a shock of cold air on Nilah's back. "No, we attend the questioning of the prisoner, and then you clean up his jail cell when we're done."

Nilah rolled over, shielding her eyes from the deck lights. "Must we? Couldn't we simply slip away and find some time to... reconnect?"

Orna grinned. Charger turned the hose back on.

Boots had never seen a reader at work before. She'd expected some kind of torture, perhaps a villainous monologue about "extracting secrets from an unwilling mind."

Instead, the Ferrier twins escorted Maslin Durand from the brig to the mess, where they began to cook a nice meal for him of fried liver and onions. The scent saturated the galley, driving Nilah from the room, dermaluxes green with disgust. The pair of gingers worked as a single machine, one raiding the larders while the other pillaged the spice racks. Their cuisine carried a uniquely Tormish flair, heavy on the cumin and thyme. Boots remembered reading Maslin's dossier; Torm was his homeworld.

Maslin's stomach growled, and he placed an arm across his gut to silence it.

Boots sat down across from him, sizing him up. For a legendary arms dealer, the man had little presence. She'd expected to feel him like a high-pressure storm front, but his diminished stature and looks did little to accent that.

Malik remained behind Durand, just a few paces away. Boots guessed the doctor was there for medical support, just in case Maslin tried anything too dangerous.

The entire prep time, Maslin stared daggers at Boots, his dark eyes glinting underneath mottled brows. If he was trying to intimidate her, it wasn't working.

"Dinner service is slow around here," Maslin grumbled, straining at the calcifoam shackles on his arms.

Boots arched an eyebrow and glanced at Cordell in the corner, who shrugged.

The arms dealer scratched his cheek with a grimy hand. "What happened to your arm?"

Boots was only there as a guard, not supposed to engage, but she said, "Those people you ran the money-laundering operation for, they had this witch working for them who called herself Mother. She ripped up my shoulder pretty good. Returned the favor by crushing her throat."

Realization dawned on Maslin's face. "I know you lot! You're the ones that killed Mandell. That bird that took off, that was Nilah Brio. You're... You're, uh..."

Boots smirked, not answering him.

"You're Shoes," he said.

" 'Boots,' " she corrected.

"Don't look so tough to me," said Maslin, raking his eyes over the mess as though looking for escape routes. "A couple of my boys could work this place over lickety-split."

Boots leaned onto her elbows, grinning from ear to ear. "Your 'boys' ain't here. So what are you going to do in their place?"

"Why don't you take off these handcuffs, baby doll, and we can find out?"

"Baby doll" had to be a first for Boots, but she let him enjoy goading her. She secretly hoped that when Cordell had extracted all of the secrets from his mind, the captain would hand Maslin to the crew to do with as they wished. After all, he'd helped Mother get around, which meant he'd helped kill Didier.

She glanced up at Cordell to find him gesturing for her to stop, then pointing to the Ferriers in the kitchen. Malik echoed the captain's concern with an urgent expression. Boots frowned but did as she was told, ignoring the prisoner's further attempts at repartee.

Maslin wasn't looking when Jeannie and Alister each cast the reader's mark from the confines of the kitchen. The spells were dark magenta glyphs, innards radiating with anti-light that sucked from the world around them. Boots was happy that Maslin remained focused on her, because the effect was wholly unsettling.

Hands charged with their spells, the twins set the food before Maslin, and he took a deep breath of steaming fried livers.

"What was the cruelest memory of your childhood on Torm?" asked Alister, his voice cold and clinical. He laid his hand upon Maslin's shoulder, even as the prisoner flinched and protested.

"Get off me, you little wanker!" Maslin cried, writhing away from Alister, who held fast.

"You were tortured," said Alister, "by your classmates in primary school. It's how you got the burns on your head."

Maslin's face dropped, and Alister craned his neck, a frisson of excitement sparkling in his eyes. The ginger inched closer to get a better look at the scars, peering at them as though they were some venomous snake.

"They held you down outside of your house," said Alister. "They used a wilting spell. You'd never felt uglier in your life."

Maslin leered. "Cute trick, but don't try to shame me. I can buy all the birds I want with a couple of argents, and I got plenty."

Alister straightened. "Women? They don't help you forget what your father did." He turned to all present. "Patrice Durand, upon seeing his son's injuries, refused to pay for a usurer's mark to heal him. Patrice said you were weak for being so easily beaten."

Alister got right in Maslin's face. "But you didn't take revenge on those who wronged you, did you, Maslin? You slit your father's throat in his sleep and set the house on fire. The boys who scarred you were later the bankers who gave you your first loan." He squinted. "You've had a lot of work done, too. This hideous face is so much better than it once was. You've never found a sculptor who could fix it to your satisfaction. The last one told you it was like trying to paint a broken wall."

Boots sat up straighter. Alister Ferrier didn't say much of merit, but when he did, it disturbed her. Guilt needled her heart at the fact that he had attacked Durand over his disfigurement, but he had it coming. She hazarded a glance back at Cordell, but the captain simply stood cross-armed and steely-eyed in the back corner of the room.

Alister continued. "You wanted to prove that you were better than everyone else, and you thought money was the way to do it, right? That's why, when you came upon a wounded military unit on Torm, your gangsters ambushed them and took their materiel, selling the guns offworld. You killed those men and women who were defending *your* homeworld, all so you could prove that you were better than the children who tortured you."

Maslin rolled his eyes. "If you think I'm going to apologize for taking candy from babies, you've got another—"

"But you went and did business with those bankers again and again, bowing and scraping all the while," interrupted Alister. "Every time you improved your station, so did they, and many times, they did so with your help. It caused you horrendous pain every time you came to them for money, but you did it anyway. You came to believe they liked you. You came to love them."

Maslin squirmed. "Shut up."

"But you never beat them. If we blew you out of the airlock, those children would never notice you were gone. You'd be the ghost of minor troubles faded into obscurity. You'd be regrets unfelt: less than nothing."

Maslin choked on his replies, red-faced and furious.

Jeannie caught Maslin by the jowls and twisted his face toward hers, their eye contact intense. "What are you most afraid to tell us about your mission?"

Boots thought she'd see more resistance from Maslin, or wicked cackling or something. She readied her arm to sink its hidden knife into his shoulder. Instead, Maslin's stunned eyes flickered over Jeannie's features, helpless and fearful. After a moment, she stepped back.

"I have the information he possesses, Captain," she said. "You're free to space him whenever you like."

Maslin shook the stunned look from his face and he began to understand how hard he'd been played. They'd forced him to drop his guard, so they could get the information that really mattered. He shouted aimlessly in fear, filling the small mess hall with cries for his safety. He begged and pleaded, snot running down his ruined features.

"Okay," said Cordell, stepping out of the shadows. "Okay, Mister Durand! That's enough! You know good and well we're not going to blow you out of the airlock."

"Thank you," grunted Maslin, panting after the show of fear. "Thank you. I knew you could be reasonable."

"Maslin Durand," said Cordell, grinning, "you're wanted on Taitu for three counts of murder, as well as obstruction of justice. We're turning you in for the bounty."

Boots and Orna escorted Maslin to the brig, where he willingly took his place, rocked from the interrogation. He gave little resistance, his face ashen and hands shaking. Seeing the raw panic in his eyes, Boots couldn't help but feel a tiny shred of sympathy.

"They're going to kill me for this," he whispered, as he sat down on the bed. "They're going to kill everyone I love."

Orna laughed bitterly. "So just you, then?"

"I have a family," said Maslin.

"You said you were going to kill my family when we were loading you in," said Orna. "Why should I care?"

"Because I would've been kinder about it than the Children of the Singularity."

Boots jammed her hands into her pockets. "Then I'd suggest you cooperate with the Taitutian authorities as much as possible, if you want to get your loved ones to a safe house."

"You wouldn't be so cavalier if you knew what was about to happen to me!" He bucked in his restraints, almost getting free.

Orna fell upon him like a hawk, seizing him by his collar and slamming him against the bulkhead. "They going to starve you? Going to leave you on a desperate planet, huh? You know, I had to fight for my food every day!"

Boots grabbed her, pulling her back before she could do something damaging and permanent. Orna brushed her off with little effort, sending Boots stumbling back onto the far bunk.

"You move money for Witts, you get what you deserve," said Orna.

"Witts? That guy from the Link?" He shook his head. "I don't know him...please. I'm a nobody. I just sell the stuff, push a bit of money around. I don't ask questions! It's not my problem where it ends up!"

Boots tensed. She didn't know what Orna was planning, but she'd have to stop the quartermaster if she assaulted the prisoner. It could get messy, and Maslin might try to make an escape or hurt someone in the chaos.

Orna let him go, and he deflated. "You're right. You're a nobody." She wiped her nose on the back of her hand. "But today, you're collateral damage. Don't ask us to care if they kill you."

She walked to the edge of the shield barrier and gestured for Boots to follow.

Maslin looked to Boots, who recoiled at the fear in his gaze.

"You're going to die horribly going after the Children, and for nothing," he said. "There's nowhere safe for me now. Nowhere safe for you, either."

She stepped out of the barrier threshold, and Orna switched it on, filling the cell with the spell's orange light.

"You read about us on the Link, right?" asked Boots. "You know most of us are from Clarkesfall."

"I didn't do that. I didn't kill all those people," he said.

"No," said Boots. "But you're a collaborator."

Maslin regarded his hands for a long time, as if timing the shake of his fingers. Finally, he looked up and asked, "Can I have a knife? I don't want to see what's coming."

"You're worth money alive," said Orna, baring her teeth in a dark smile. "Not that we need it. I can't wait to see what happens to you."

He ignored Orna's sneering and pleaded with Boots. "I'm asking you as a human being."

Boots stood over him, the thin shield spell separating them. "You'll be accorded all the rights of a prisoner of war, but...no aid, no comfort."

They left him to weep in his cell. Boots knew that brig better than anyone, since she'd lived in it during the *Harrow* conspiracy. There were no sheets to turn to rope, no purchases upon which to hang. The spells powering the barrier were well encapsulated. There were no sharp edges. They'd never lost a prisoner, save for one escape that ended in a firefight, but Maslin wasn't equipped for that. According to the Taitutian Special Branch, he possessed the lamplighter's mark, and making random things glow wasn't going to kill him.

Unable to shake what they'd done from her mind, Boots found herself wandering toward Alister's quarters—a screened-off bunk on the lower deck. She hadn't visited him since rejoining the crew; in fact, she'd barely spoken two words to the boy. She'd believed him arrogant, but seeing the terrible gleam in his eye as he stood over Maslin, she'd ejected everything she thought about him from her mind.

Boots had done awful things to survive, too: lied, cheated her old friends, lost her way countless times. What the Ferriers did to Maslin, emotionally, wasn't much different from torture. She wasn't excited about being a party to it.

What if, in his desperation to destroy Witts, Cordell had jumped into bed with a pair of monsters?

She arrived at the converted storage bay and knocked. The twins hadn't installed any of the niceties of Boots's quarters, like a doorbell or camera. Whether this was because Orna had lacked the time or the Ferriers weren't familiar with social nuance, Boots couldn't say. When no answer came, she knocked again.

"Come in," said Alister, his voice muffled by the thick metal.

Boots slid it open to find a makeshift corridor made from medical screens, evenly dividing the space into two rooms: one for Alister and one for Jeannie. "It's me," she said, moving toward the entrance to his room.

She'd been prepared for the sparse furnishings: a cot, a washbasin, a personal cycler, a military-issue crew trunk for the four outfits she'd seen him wear. Those sorts of accoutrements made it clear to her that he didn't understand or care for modern design.

She hadn't, however, expected to find him cross-legged on his bed, eyes red and puffy from crying.

Boots glanced back into Jeannie's partition, but the other twin was nowhere to be found. She considered leaving, concocting some excuse to escape, but this was out of the way for normal foot traffic. He'd know she came on purpose, even without reading her mind.

He looked up at her, eyes twinkling. "I'm not really in the mood to talk, ma'am—"

"Boots."

"What?"

She quirked her lips. "Please, just call me Boots. Ain't ready to be called 'ma'am' for at least another fifteen years."

He smiled weakly. "Sorry. That's just what my tutor always told me to call people."

"You were tutored? Private school?"

"You could call it that."

She tongued the inside of her mouth, unsure of where to take the conversation. Whatever was happening with Alister, she still wanted to understand his treatment of the prisoner—the things he'd done under Cordell's watchful eye.

"Why…" she began. "What were you, uh— Why bring up Durand's childhood torture like that?"

"I'm not sure you'd understand. Most people never do."

"Try me," she said.

He looked away, his freckles fading into his reddening face. "I don't want to uncover scars, but I have to. I didn't want to feel what he felt. He kept thinking about the pain of that withering spell. You could hear those kids laughing. Maslin was so wrapped up in his wealth and status, in his criminal empire, so I had to make him feel small, had to strip away his power so Jeannie could break him."

"Do you feel bad for him?"

"Of course I do," he whispered. "Orna can pretend they're soulless, but I know the truth."

"Which is?"

"Everyone can be sick in their soul and still think they're the good guys."

Maslin's father had called him a coward for getting scarred up. He spent his whole life trying to make up for that.

"Can't you ignore that stuff?" asked Boots. "Not dive so deep into their minds or whatever?"

Alister shook his head. "That's not how it works. You know how Miss Brio got combat training so she wouldn't be kidnapped?"

"Yeah. And then Orna kidnapped her anyway."

He smiled wanly. "There are a lot of types out there who don't want their minds read—criminals, spies, powerful folk. They can learn mnemonics to clear out their brains and make them hard to see into. Even I can't force my way past someone's guard."

"That's why you started cooking Tormish food," said Boots. "The smell. Scent is the most nostalgic thing you can conjure."

He nodded.

"And when he's the most distracted, most devastated, you can ask him anything."

It was clever, yet cruel. Alister had felt everything going through Maslin's mind, but kept a straight face during the interrogation. Any display of weakness might've inspired Maslin to rebel, ruining the result. That's why they had Jeannie standing by to ask the follow-up.

"I was surprised...when the captain said he'd found two readers," said Boots.

"I know you think we're freaks, Boots," he said. "You don't have to hide it."

Boots chuckled, and he stared at her, wide-eyed and wounded. She waved at him with her metal appendage. "Missing arm," she said. "Did Cordell tell you about my arcana dystocia?"

Alister shook his head.

"I don't have a spell like you, so...I'm the last person who'll call you a freak. I want to know: how is it that both you and your sister have the reader's mark?"

He pulled his knees to his chest, shrinking back. He looked so young. The twins had to be Nilah's age, but they made the ex-racer look downright old by comparison.

"I'm not talking about that right now. I don't want to think about it."

She shrugged, feigning nonchalance. "Then don't, but as your crewmate, I want to tell you something."

He frowned and closed his eyes as though bracing for a blow.

"Come to me if you ever want to talk," she said.

The door slid open, and Jeannie appeared at the end of the screen corridor, her face etched with surprise. For a moment, Boots thought she spied a flash of anger, but it dissipated like mist on the wind. Jeannie donned a polite smile and approached.

"Boots," she said. "Nice of you to come by. Any particular reason?"

"Just wondering how you two were doing down here," Boots replied. "We used to store some pretty strange chems in this bulkhead. If memory serves, there's a loose panel over there where one of the boys kept his strongest stash during the war." Boots pointed.

"Very colorful," said Jeannie. "You know all the secrets on the *Capricious*?"

Boots lightly pounded her heel against the deck. "Rode out the war in this rust bucket. Then rode out that whole *Harrow* business in here. He's been my ship off and on for too many years. Still can't get away from him. Anyway, I need to be hitting the sack so I'm ready for the night cycle. Just wanted to have a quick chat."

"Good night, then," said Jeannie.

Boots looked to Alister, who pressed his cheeks to his knees.

His eyes remained fixed upon some point on the far wall. He wouldn't look at her, so she nodded to Jeannie and took her leave.

Boots had almost made it to the door when he called her name. "Yeah?" she asked.

He peered at her around the screen, like a child ready to bolt for a hiding place. "They're human, people like Maslin. You know that."

"Everyone is," said Boots.

"But they still have to die. They can't keep doing what they're doing."

Boots scratched her temple and gave him a thin smile. "Too right, kid. Try to take it easy."

She turned and left. She'd only made it about ten paces down the hall when Jeannie stopped her.

"Boots," she called. "What did you say to him?"

Boots shrugged. "The same thing I'm going to say to you: feel free to talk to me."

The two women looked each other over, and Boots spotted annoyance in Jeannie's gaze, seeping out between the cracks of her polite veneer.

"Don't...don't just show up like that," said Jeannie.

"Just wanted to have a friendly chat."

"I know how to take care of my brother."

Raising her hands, defeated, Boots said, "No one was suggesting—"

"He's been through a lot. You can't simply talk him out of the things he's seen."

"We've all seen things, sister. The sooner we learn to get along—"

"Not like Alister," Jeannie said, interrupting again. "You're not qualified to care for him, psychologically. Not after he's been inside the minds of these bastards."

"Oh? Well, if you're taking new patients, where do I sign up?"

"I keep up Alister's well-being. That's my job—something only another reader can do. Please don't get in the way with your heartfelt speeches. He can truly share his burden with me in a way you won't understand."

Boots sized up Jeannie, suppressing the urge to explain how ship life is supposed to work. Jeannie never blinked, never looked away, defiant, yet professional.

"Okay," sighed Boots, resting her hands on her hips. "You take care of him. Who takes care of you?"

Jeannie's eyes widened in momentary surprise, like Boots had spoken another language. Had anyone ever asked after her happiness?

"No one," said Jeannie. "I'm fine on my own."

"I'm just trying to make this easier on you."

"Please start by staying out of my way," she said, but her matter-of-factness melted a touch as she added, "You seem nice...but you're out of your depth."

Then Jeannie disappeared back into her room. Boots stared at the door as it sealed the pair of enigmatic twins inside. She wasn't the comfort-giving type; she wasn't sure why she'd even tried. Feelings had never been her strong suit.

She jammed her hands into her pockets and sauntered away.

"Don't have to tell me twice."

The night cycle darkened the bridge, dimming all but the faint running lights lining each console. Nilah lay on the second dais, her back on the deck, hands folded behind her head. Above her, long star streaks wheeled across the canopy as the ship gently spun along its axis. The extravagant yachts of her youth tended to downplay the jumps between worlds, disguising the space outside with projections of idyllic beaches or distant nebulae.

When Nilah was on the Lang yacht, she spent every night

practicing for the next race, having the track beamed into her mind by expert trancers. She'd never allowed herself to experience the engineering wonder of a ship slipping through the Flow.

Once she'd gotten used to it, Nilah preferred the *Capricious* to the frilly ships of yesteryear. As a mechanist, her magic gave her a psychic interface with any tech, and she had a natural affinity for the presence of powerful machines like the *Capricious*. Without a layer of cloying luxury, she felt an intense connection to the inner workings of the vessel. It was elemental and unprocessed, like the rough sport shocks of her Hyper 8 race car. Within the hardened hull of the *Capricious*, Nilah felt the whole of the stars upon her skin.

"You're in my spot, kid," said Boots, and the older woman clomped across the deck to stand over her.

Nilah grimaced. "I don't believe I saw you here before."

Boots sat down next to her and laid back, arm clanking against the deck. "Used to do this all the time when I was on night watch. Just lay back and stare at the Flow. When it's just you and the stars, there's no war."

"Do you mind if I ask you something about your time on this ship?" said Nilah.

Boots gave her a look of trepidation but nodded.

"How did you spend much time in the Flow if the Famine War was on Clarkesfall?"

Boots snorted. "There's a lot more to a war than the battles on home ground. As things got worse, Arca's national coffers were exhausted. We flew a lot of supply missions to Harvest and Hopper's Hope. That's when I first laid eyes on the plot where my distillery is. Thought I could buy it with my hazard pay when everything was over. But...the longer the war went on, the less you got in pay and the more you got in food and fresh water."

"Did the *Capricious* have his own jump drive?"

"No. Almost none of our ships did. Poor planet. Not much of an armada. The Gate Cartel, however, propped up a provisional jump gate. Both the Arcans and the Kandamili were allowed through, and there could be no fighting within ten thousand klicks of it. Always a race to get from our defense grid to that safe zone..."

Nilah listened in silence as Boots spoke. The older woman hadn't shared much of her military history. Neither had Cordell, for that matter, even if he liked to wear the regalia.

"We used to call it the 'trash bubble,'" said Boots. "The jump gate had this thin layer of debris almost exactly ten thousand klicks out, and the Kandis would hide in it and ambush you. Our scanners couldn't penetrate it by the end of the war. The orbital dynamics kind of massaged it into a shell. Ships and corpses, ours and theirs."

Boots sat up, resting her elbows on her knees. "So you'd have to pop the bubble on the way in, interdictors blasting your back the whole time, then you'd slip into the Flow for some nice peace and quiet. You'd have your shore leave on Hopper's or wherever, then it was back into the Flow. And when you came home, it was a full-on slugfest just trying to get to the surface again."

Nilah tried to imagine the difference between the peaceful magical field surrounding them and the few ship-to-ship actions she'd witnessed.

"I can understand... why you get along so well with the other Fallen," said Nilah. "I never had to experience anything like that when I was growing up. Orna talks about it sometimes, and I'm scared to say anything, because I know it'll be wrong. We've, uh... We've had a few fights from time to time."

Boots ejected the small knife blade from her finger and picked at her teeth before flicking away a sliver of food. "Trouble in paradise, eh?"

"I'm the only one who hasn't lost anything, not really," she said, but raised her hands as Boots made a face. "No, I'm not saying that's regrettable. No one should want to suffer as you all have. I'm only saying that it makes you a family, and I feel a little outside sometimes."

Boots chucked Nilah on the shoulder and smiled. "Kid, you're crew on this ship. You helped kill one of the guys that took out my homeworld. You don't need to be worrying about crap like that. Every Fallen on every world probably toasted you last year when the news broke."

"It's hard to believe the rough-and-tumble refugees identify with someone like me. I sometimes worry that I'm insufferably posh."

The older woman shook with quiet laughter. "You? No. Who would ever say such a thing? But seriously, I wouldn't talk about this crap with any offworlder, and here you've got me rambling on like one of those clowns from the refugee bars. Of course you're cool with us. Just…with Orna…she doesn't want you to act like you know what she went through. She just wants to tell you."

"Okay. Yeah. I get that," said Nilah, and she hoped she did.

Boots laid back again, her eyes dimly illuminated by the changing stars. "So, Taitu, huh?"

"Captain says we're going to drop off the prisoner and prep for the next mission. The sooner the better, if you ask me."

"Ready to get to work, then?" asked Boots.

Nilah shuddered. She'd gone to check on Maslin to make sure that nothing was amiss and had found him wailing in his cell, eyelids aglow. Malik, upon examining the arms dealer, said he was trying to kill himself with sleep deprivation—the only weapon he had left. It was nothing the doctor couldn't fix.

"I just want Durand off the ship," said Nilah. "Have you talked to the captain about our next mission?"

"Not yet," said Boots. "You?"

"Yeah. Jeannie pried a name from Durand's mind when she

asked about the mission: Izak Vraba—the head of the Children of the Singularity. We don't know much else about the bloke, but Durand is scared to death of him. Considers him a godlike being. And then there's something about a contract, but we couldn't quite understand. I think it's probably the Money Mill."

"That's a good sign."

"How is that good?" asked Nilah.

"Means we're on the right track and not just chasing down some cult for no reason."

Nilah nodded and closed her eyes. She took long, slow breaths, feeling the hum of the ship through the back of her skull. It had become as familiar to her as the gentle sighs Orna made when she slept.

Boots sucked her teeth. "What are we doing, kid?"

"Lying on the floor?" said Nilah.

"No, like where's the sanity? We're not soldiers, we're salvagers. The police ought to be handling this."

"As my beloved likes to say, 'We can steal all their crap.' "

"I'm rich enough," said Boots, "and I still haven't figured out how to spend it. I want to take out Witts, like, more than anything. Never wanted someone dead so badly in my life..." She held up her hands as though gesturing to everything out there. "But those people have unbeatable magic. They have an empire of spies. One tiny marauder ain't going to cut it, kid. This is a problem for the GATO authorities."

"Yeah," said Nilah. "But in the year since we found the *Harrow*, they haven't caught any more of the gods. You trust them to do it?"

She watched Boots's lips work over an answer, opening and closing without any sound. Boots squinted and let out a hissing breath through her nose. "No."

"I guess it's up to us, then. Maybe we'll find some more treasure along the way, so we don't have to operate at a loss."

Boots watched the stars roll by, contemplating them. "All right, Nilah. It's my watch, and your girlfriend is all alone, so get out of here. Check on Maslin on your way to bed."

Nilah did as she was asked and left Boots lying on the bridge. She was right—it'd been a few hours since anyone had seen Maslin, and he'd probably woken up. Low, orange light suffused the night cycle corridors as Nilah wound her way through the ship down to the brig. When she'd gone to the bridge, she'd been alert, unable to sleep after seeing Maslin. Now her heart had calmed, and she hoped he wouldn't rile her up again.

The door to the brig slid open, and blinding light filled her vision. Nilah narrowed her eyes and shielded her face, trying to adjust. Blurry details swam into focus: the walls of the cell, the active shield barrier. Maslin was still in there, but he'd painted the walls with his magic, covering every inch in white light.

From her vantage point, she could only make out the shadow of a boot. They'd taken his laces from him, afraid he'd wedge them into the bunk and hang himself. The polybuff of his shoe was ragged from where a buckle had been ripped free; it looked as though it'd been chewed off. Nilah's dermaluxes went purple as she crept closer.

The spreading pool of red on the cell floor told her what she'd find before she saw the body. She gritted her teeth and moved to get a better look.

Maslin lay facedown, eyes wide and shining under the light of his spell. His throat held angry red streaks along one side, leading to an open gash where sticky blood spilled forth. His limp hand clutched the chewed-off boot buckle, its steel having been crudely filed to a sharpened edge against the nearby deck.

They should've taken all his clothes and left him in there naked. Nilah remembered being so desperate to die, once, when Prime Minister Dwight Mandell used his power to bend her mind. Whoever this Izak Vraba was, the mere idea of his wrath had caused Maslin to kill himself.

Nilah turned to the console and tapped the intercom. "Bridge, this is Nilah."

"Durand okay?" asked Boots.

"No," she said. "Wake the captain. Durand is dead."

Chapter Four

Fans

Taitutian Special Branch Agent Cedric Weathers obviously
disliked Boots.

From the moment she'd entered his office and they'd
locked hands she knew. It was the look in his eyes, the grip of his
handshake, and the way he said, "Everyone likes you, Miss Elsworth, but I don't."

He was a short, athletic fellow in his thirties, with carefully
coiffed hair and clean, manicured fingernails. He kept the lines of
his suit as straight as the lines of his office, which were all either
parallel or perpendicular, but never anything in-between. His
face fit that mold, too, with its monolithic nose and flat, plucked
brow, which mirrored his scowl.

Boots gave him a thin smile with a wink and said, "I'm sure the
genocidal maniacs agree with you, at least."

And that had been the inauspicious start of their meeting.

He grilled her for two hours about the fate of Maslin Durand,
seething with prepackaged fury over the death. She shouldn't
have been answering questions at all, but Cordell had sent her and
Nilah to act as government liaisons for the transfer of Maslin's

corpse. The Special Branch had immediately separated the two of them and boxed her in with their most obnoxious agent.

"Listen, *Cedric*," she said, adding mocking emphasis on his first name. "You folks made a deal with the devil. You sent an extra-judicial, paramilitary group—us—to take care of a threat *you* should've handled. Since we're the ones doing your jobs, I don't think you have a right to complain."

He finally opted to settle into his chair across from her. He'd been looming over her for the past fifteen minutes, doing his version of what passed for intimidation. "Taitutian citizens should abide by the laws of—"

"We're not citizens of any world."

"Miss Brio is a Taitutian, subject to our laws, Miss Elsworth. I would hate to have her arrested," he said with the sort of relish that indicated otherwise.

"Cedric—"

"Agent Weathers."

"*Cedric*," Boots continued. "We cured the galaxy of your prime minister Dwight Mandell, who was a planetary embarrassment... in addition to being a war criminal. The people of Taitu erected a huge statue of Nilah on Capitol Square."

"I don't see how that makes her anything but a citizen," he said, leaning forward and folding his arms at a ninety-degree angle to his torso.

Boots rocked back in the office chair. "I'm saying she's more than a Taitutian. Go ahead and charge her. Have her arrested for the death of your cop-killing arms dealer. I would love to see Prime Minister Bianchi's reaction to that."

Cedric cocked his head to one side, falling out of sync with the vertical angles of the room for the first time. He regarded her and pursed his lips, clearly weighing his options.

Boots picked up one of his styluses and fiddled with it before putting it back at an off angle. "You're right, little guy. Durand died in our custody, under suspicious circumstances. We need to be punished or whatever, so do your thing and arrest her," said Boots, maintaining unwavering eye contact. "But I'm going to leak every word of this conversation to the press. I'll give the first exclusive interview I've ever given. They've been asking for my side of the *Harrow* story for a while, and I'll tie it in to the Special Branch blowhard who had my friend arrested."

"I'm a police officer, not a politician, Miss Elsworth."

"But you're wrong, Cedric, and you serve at the pleasure of fickle masters," she replied, rising. "If you don't mind, I'm going to walk out that door. If you want to commit career suicide, now is the time."

She took a step, grinning. "Eh? We going to have a problem?"

"Just get out."

"Aw, Cedric. Don't get all warm and inviting on me! Should I stay? Maybe I should stay."

"Miss Elsworth, I would like nothing less," he replied through gritted teeth.

She arched an eyebrow. "Too much of a good thing. I hear you."

When Boots emerged into the lobby, she found Nilah standing amid a gaggle of cops, signing autographs with her tattoos flowing gold. Nilah glanced up at her and smiled brightly before placing a rare Lang Autosport hat back into the hands of its owner.

"Can we please get out of here?" asked Boots.

Instead of hopping up and heading out, Nilah gestured to Boots, and three of the cops descended with pictures of the *Capricious* crew, their styluses at the ready. She recognized the picture immediately, the whole of them in hero poses before the open cargo hold—everyone except Didier and Ranger, who hadn't survived to be part of any press tour.

Boots's heart throbbed at the absence of the *Capricious*'s former cook. She and Didier had spent a wild night on Carré before he was cut down by Mother. Boots tried to imagine what he would've looked like in the picture—no doubt striking a goofy pose, no matter what he'd been directed to do. He'd have been popular—deserved to be.

It was only sex, but he was a good man. Maybe they could've been something.

She was about to demure from the autographs when she saw another cop holding a replica of the Chalice of Hana. Boots's network had made cheap imitations when *Finding Hana* was popular—for the children to enjoy. Despite the poor detail of the toy, the sight of it still sucked her breath away.

During the Famine War, Arca had loaded the Chalice of Hana onto their culture arc, the *Saint of Flowers*. But the ship never reached its destination, and the artifact was considered lost to history. After the war, Boots had teamed up with a fellow veteran, Stetson Giles, and a producer from Gantry Station, Gemma Katz, to find it. According to legends, the chalice was supposed to grant its owner an ultra-powerful barrister's mark, and Boots thought she'd finally be able to cast magic with it. Their show, *Finding Hana*, took the Link by storm before its tragic end.

The only time Boots had seen the chalice in person was when Stetson Giles used it to curse her and kill her producer.

The police officer held out the toy and a paint pen for Boots. Stunned, she took it and signed her name across the inside of its golden rim, then handed it back to its beaming owner. In a fugue, she signed the other pictures thrust in her direction. She frowned when the cops returned to their desks to register her autographs with the various digital authenticators.

"Remember to smile, darling," whispered Nilah.

They'd reached the lifts when Boots finally asked, "How can you stand all that?"

"The love and adoration?" chortled Nilah as the doors swooshed open. "Yes, it's all so very terrible."

They stepped inside, the building's AI directing them to the first floor.

"That's not love," said Boots. "Those people don't know you at all."

"Do you think the people who want us dead hate us?" asked Nilah.

"Some of them, yeah."

Nilah smoothed back her hair. "And they don't know us, either. Honestly, sweetie, you must get better at having fans."

Boots filled her in on the conversation with Special Agent Weathers as they walked. When they reached the lower floor and emerged into the Capitol Gardens, Aisha was waiting for them. On the ship, Aisha always wore her pilot's jumper. On Taitu, she was far more fashionable, sporting a silvery top and clip-on sun lenses.

"How did it go?" asked Aisha.

"The cops hate us," said Boots.

"Just the one cop," said Nilah. "And he'd probably like me."

Boots shrugged. "Anyway, thanks for agreeing to help out today. I can use all the hands I can get with the archives."

As they walked toward the tall, windowless building that housed the thousands of Taitutian Special Branch Archives, Boots took in the mild coastal air. She loved her farm on Hopper's Hope, but it lacked the bay breeze. The next dozen blocks would be filled with a pleasant, salty breeze, sunshine, and the glorious architecture of Taitu's capital, Aior.

"What are we looking for in the archives?" asked Aisha.

Boots glanced around to make sure no one was too close— being an old veteran had taught her to be cautious about classified conversations.

"First: anything about Izak Vraba. Second: active case files. If we've got an insider, we need to know who it is before the Children do. Third: bank routing records," said Boots, keeping her voice low. "Those are the most reliable sources of tracking. That's how I found the Chalice of Hana."

"I know," said Aisha. "I watched the show back when it was coming out."

Boots stopped and grimaced. "You serious? Why haven't you ever said anything?"

Aisha tapped her sun lenses, lightening them a shade. "It seemed like a bad memory. I was...well..." She shuffled slightly, embarrassed.

Boots glanced at Nilah, who was similarly thunderstruck by Aisha's sudden shyness.

"I was one of the crew who voted in favor of buying that salvage map from you," said Aisha. "Because of your reputation, you understand."

Boots hadn't thought about the crock of crap she'd sold Cordell for a long time. She'd screwed them over, and in return, they'd saved her life.

Hell, they'd saved everyone's lives.

Boots bit her lip. "I don't think I've ever formally apologized for that."

"There she is!" came a distant voice, and Boots looked up to see a group of ten people walking purposefully toward them.

Boots shook her head. "Oh, great. More 'fans.'"

But the newcomers seemed anything but pleased to see them. There was something off about them: the way they walked, the certainty in their faces, the uniformity of their outfits. They weren't actual uniforms, but this group must've all shopped at the same place.

Boots crossed her arms as nonchalantly as possible—considering that she'd taken hold of the slinger in her Rook Velocity jacket. She glanced back at Aisha and Nilah to find them similarly on guard.

"Keep walking," muttered Nilah, pulling back her sleeves. "I've dealt with my share of dangerous obsessives. Let's cross around here."

"These losers better not scuff my jacket," mumbled Boots.

The trio made their way over a bridge to put a reflecting pool between them and the rapidly approaching gang. The strange folk didn't speed up to catch them. The leader, a scruffy fellow in his early twenties, shouted: "You stopped it once, but you can't stop transcendence forever!"

"Oh god. I think those might be Children of the Singularity," said Nilah.

A crackle of fury went up Boots's spine, and her thumb came to rest against the knurled surface of her safety. "So when do we start shooting?"

"Not yet," said Aisha. "We don't know anything about them, and they're not breaking any laws."

Nilah's pace quickened. "Aside from those fashion crimes. At the very worst, this is harassment. Aisha is right. Even if they're Children, we can't know if they're working for Witts."

"Your day will come! Aisha Jan! Elizabeth Elsworth!" cried another cultist. "We're watching you!"

"I ought to sock you just for showing your fascist faces," Boots called back to the cultists. "You want to go? Get over here, you callow—"

"Don't look at them," said Nilah. "We're almost to the rail station, and we can lose them in there."

"We were going to be beautiful!" screeched the leader, agony in his voice, hatred twisting his features. "You stole our choice!"

Elba Pool Station, Aior's busiest terminal, loomed large before them. Aisha quietly traced her marksman's spell, clutching the glyph in her hand. Boots tightened her grip around her slinger, ready for the first spell to come her way. She'd been practicing her aim in the year on Hopper's Hope, and even at this distance, she'd be able to sink a slinger bolt into the leader's chest.

She desperately wished he'd give her a reason. Clumped up like they were, she'd probably nail a few of the bastards.

But the trio descended the stairs into Elba Pool Station, leaving the cultists behind on the surface. Just like Nilah said, they were low-level nobodies, either too scared to approach—or with some other plan in mind. Inside the rail station, a throng of people stretched wall to wall, and tension squeezed Boots's muscles. It would be impossible to see any threats.

A slew of neon projections swam overhead, hawking the wares of local shops, filling the tunnel with uneven light. Thousands of reflective tiles gave the station an infinite feel, and Boots had trouble discerning details closer to the platform. A train silently swept into the docking cradle, its arrival covered over by the cacophonous voices of Aior commuters. At rush hour, crowds transformed the architectural marvel into a field of noise.

"You don't know who you're dealing with," came a voice behind them.

They spun to find a younger woman in a crisp suit, shouting into her comm. Boots's pulse hammered in her neck, and she glanced over to see Nilah take off her jacket and sling it over one arm. Aisha's hand rested upon the concealed butt of her pistol. All three of them backed away, trying to play it off as nonchalant.

"We need a security detail," mumbled Nilah as they made their way toward the platform. "This is ridiculous."

"These cultists are bold," said Aisha, watching their backs as she wound through the crowd. "It's shocking that someone thinks we shouldn't have stopped the *Harrow* conspiracy. That's just..."

"People are fools," said Boots. "Who knows? Let's get the hell out of this crowd."

"Nilah Brio!" came a woman's voice, and Nilah's tattoos strobed in surprise. When Boots gathered her wits, she found an older woman frantically searching her bag. Boots reached out and snatched the woman's arm with her metal hand, squeezing a little too tightly before Nilah stopped her.

"It's okay," Nilah whispered.

The woman, visibly shaken, withdrew an imager lens and meekly asked to take a picture.

Boots released the woman's hand and stepped back. She felt a hundred eyes on her, and the din of conversation quieted as bystanders became curious. She glanced at the nearest fellow, who'd stopped to gawk. "What are you looking at?"

"Are you really Nilah Brio?" he asked past Boots. Several other bystanders stopped and smiled, closing in to ask questions of the ex-racer.

Boots had never been one for attention, and with the cult members on the surface, it bothered her even more. She didn't know any of these people. Maybe one of them was an obsessive freak, a yahoo with a theory, an attention-seeker—or an agent of Henrick Witts.

"We shouldn't be down here," mumbled Boots, backing up to Nilah and Aisha as the flashes of imagers filled the tunnel.

"Steady on, old girl," said Nilah, smiling and waving. "This is what happens when people love you. Just follow my lead."

But Boots found herself ready to panic. Everywhere she looked, she found a smiling, excited face. They filled her every view, encircling her like vultures. She'd been fired upon in so many military engagements, whether in space or on the ground, but the level of dread this crowd conjured went way beyond battle jitters.

No clear threats. No clear allies.

"Don't call me 'old girl.'" Her throat was dry. "I'm not a horse."

Aisha posed for pictures with Nilah, signing them after with a finger. It suited the pilot, this worship. She was beautiful, after all, not like squat, boring Boots.

"Boots," said Nilah, placing a hand on her shoulder, "these are our adoring fans. You must find a way to smile, dearest."

Boots tried on a grin but knew she probably looked constipated. Nilah pulled her in, wrapping an arm around her hips, and sandwiched her with Aisha. Their warmth bled into her, and for the first time, Boots's desire to run away abated slightly. These were her sisters on either side, and they'd keep her safe.

"Nilah!" shouted a young woman in the front, leaping up and down with adulation. "Hey, Nilah!"

Boots tried to ignore her, but she was so much more insistent than the others. The woman's fingers curled into a fist, and Boots's gut churned with anxiety.

"The Children are watching you! You, too, dull-finger!"

The woman opened her hand, and a projection slithered out of a pocket-sized cube. Light twisted and bent around it, until the image became a warped, steel mask, deforming the air. The stone-cold face had no pity, no joy, no mirth or sadness—only a thin line where the mouth should be and two vertical slits for eyes. Carved into its forehead were the glowing lines of the usurer's mark.

"For we are myriad—" the woman began.

Boots bowled into her, slapping the projector box out of her hand. The cultist screamed in surprise as Boots's metal fingers wrapped around her throat. Boots was no hand-to-hand master, but she was deft enough to trip a surprised kid and throw her to the ground.

The woman couldn't have been more than twenty years old, her face uncreased by the worries of age. A bit of extra flesh lined her neck; her soft muscles spoke of a sedentary lifestyle. Boots had seen her kind before on the Link: the haters and doubters who'd hounded her during the days of the show.

"Whoa, whoa, whoa!" the cultist yelped in surprise.

"The Children are watching us, huh? Guess what, witch?" Boots snarled, smashing her metal knuckles against the tiles, cracking the stone. "We're watching right back!"

Boots drew back, and a flick of her fingers brought out her stiletto knife. It wasn't a fancy spell, but it was magic in its own way.

"I have a right to be here!" she cried out, but Boots scarcely heard her over the thundering blood in her ears.

Boots tightened up on the woman's collar as she straddled her. "I heard about you Children of the Singularity." Boots spat the name out like a ball of phlegm. "You're a bunch of cowards who worship Henrick Witts, aren't you? What do you know about Witts?"

"Boots!" came a voice, but she ignored it.

"I don't know him!" pleaded the woman. "Let me go!"

"Boots!" shouted Nilah once more, pulling her away from her target.

She knew not to resist Nilah, that the woman was fast enough to punch out springflies, and still Boots wished she'd taken a swipe at the cultist on the ground—given her something to think about.

"Let me go!" Boots snapped. She mustered the presence of mind to retract her knife, so she didn't accidentally show someone the wrong end of the blade. "They've got to arrest that lady!"

"For what?" shouted the woman, staggering to her feet. She leveled her finger at Boots, rage painting her face purple. "You're the one who took away our future!"

"You're only breathing because of me!" Boots roared, and the crowd took a step back, giving her the first space she'd had in what felt like hours.

She'd expected the good people of Taitu to tear this creep limb from limb, or at the very least spit on her. But instead, they donned stunned looks, their pleasant days disrupted with Boots's unexpected fury. Several of the bystanders exchanged glances, as though the path of righteousness wasn't obvious here.

"Boots," whispered Nilah. "You've got to stop talking. That's not how this works."

"Isn't this witch, like, a damned enemy of the state?" Boots's lips contorted into a scowl. "People like her are the reason our universe almost ended."

"Says you!" shouted the cultist, this time careful to take a step back. She rubbed the back of her neck where she'd hit the ground. "None of you know the truth! Those records were faked! Henrick Witts had big plans for us. Big Daddy Mandell would've saved Taitu!"

The train sighed into the nearby platform, now far more audible with the sudden silence of the crowd. Boots looked to her crewmates, expecting them to do something, say something, but the horror on their faces told her they wanted to disengage.

Boots thrust out a finger at the woman. "I saw the *Harrow*, you little piece of crap. I stood on his deck. It killed my planet before you were even born."

Then she turned away, not listening to any of the counterpoints, and strode down the ramp to their train. The lenses of imagers followed her the whole way, but the crowd stayed their distance, just the way Boots liked it.

The entryway of the Taitutian Special Branch Archives was smaller than Nilah had expected: just a well-guarded elevator in the center of a glass lobby. Nilah scanned their surroundings out of curiosity—she'd never been inside a secret government facility as a racer, but she'd seen plenty in the debriefing after the *Harrow*.

Each wall was made of thick, polychroic glass, with dispersers tastefully embedded in the accent lights. Surveillance imagers ringed the ceilings, all focused upon the elevator in the center of the room: a clear tube sunk into the floor like a well shaft.

Two guards flanked the entrance to the elevator, slingers holstered and ready. The trio of women checked their weapons at the door.

"All I'm saying is that you legally exposed yourself when you grabbed her," whispered Nilah, but her voice echoed across the marble floors. She hadn't wanted to lecture Boots, but the older woman wouldn't stop complaining about the cultists.

"So sue me," sighed Boots.

"Yes," said Nilah. "That's literally why you don't want legal exposure. I'm glad that you're back with the *Capricious*, but we need to teach you how to be famous."

"Ugh. Pass. How is it not legal, uh…exposure…to threaten us?" asked Boots.

"She didn't explicitly threaten us," said Aisha. "That's the awful part. She just called Nilah by name."

" 'Dull-finger' is hate speech," spat Boots, wrinkling her nose.

"Not technically illegal," said Aisha. "You can't assault someone for that."

"So it's bad if I scared her, but it's okay for her to take Witts's side and scare the hell out of us?" Boots spat. "Sounds like bunk to me."

Nilah sighed in exasperation, but she didn't have time to explain any more. She'd had stalkers in her past, people who took racing just a little too seriously. Her lawyer's advice had been simple: call the cops, don't engage. It wasn't fair, but Nilah couldn't seem to get that across to her companion.

The three women signed in with the guard, and Nilah traced her own sigil with a pang of pity as Boots rummaged in her bag for her paragon crystal—the small device that stored Boots's identity. Nilah's identity was linked to her magic and the tiny biometric variations in her glyph. Anyone with Boots's crystal could impersonate her.

"Must we do all of this? It's just gold-level access," Nilah complained to the nearest officer, but she shook her head, patting Boots down.

They let Aisha and Nilah through without any issue, but Boots was subjected to a lot of questions and two different scans. Nilah gulped as the images of Boots's arm spun out of the projectors above them, but the hidden slinger shell appeared opaque to basic scans. Wherever Boots had gotten the arm, the maker had done a damned fine job creating that compartment. Finally, the three women were allowed into the elevator, where they descended to the first sublevel—the least classified of all the areas in the installation.

Nilah glanced at Boots, whose eyes were downcast. She knew what her friend was thinking: somewhere in those archives, near the bottom levels, Kinnard's data cube lay dormant. Nilah chucked Boots's good shoulder and smiled, trying to distract her.

"Have you ever gotten into the Special Branch Archives before?" asked Nilah.

It seemed to work. Boots tongued the inside of her lip and replied, "Back during the *Finding Hana* days, I had all kinds of contacts. I never got in here per se, but I definitely had some records from here. Most of that was because..."

Aisha leaned in. "Your partner was an ex-cop, right? Stetson Giles?"

Nilah grimaced, her dermaluxes flaring green. She'd been trying to distract Boots, not plunge her into depression. "Okay," she said, grinning brightly. "I'm sure time is limited down here. What's the game plan?"

Boots shrugged. "Search for everything we can find on Maslin Durand, Izak Vraba, and the Children of the Singularity. Try to collate records and get a bead on what the hell we're dealing with."

The elevator passed below the thick layer of rock, and Nilah spied millions of spell-dampening shards—the whole place was made of urmurex stone, designed to withstand the spells from battleship slingers. Then the first sublevel of the Special Branch Archives opened up around the elevator shaft. Tens of thousands of data cubes lay glowing in the recessed shelves, their crystalline structures refracting centuries of accumulated knowledge. Much farther below, the very origins of Taitutian government rested, ensconced by autoturrets and devious traps.

Even at this weak level of classification, guns in the ceiling followed their progress until the elevator reached the base of the tube and the glass doors rotated aside.

Aisha scratched her cheek. "I can't help but feel like Armin would be better for this."

"He would," said Boots, stepping out into the maze of shelves. "That's why he's not allowed."

Nilah followed, looking around for the terminal. "What?"

"It's a military thing." Boots led them down the long corridor toward a nexus where several shelves came to meet, like the points of a compass. At her approach, a terminal rose out of the glossy floor. "Classification can be pretty stupid sometimes. Fact A is public knowledge, and fact B is public knowledge, but when you get fact A plus B, that's suddenly classified information. Can't bring Armin in here because his magic lets him instantly collate stuff."

Nilah nodded. "You're right. That's stupid."

"Bureaucrats will be bureaucrats," said Boots. "You want to fan out and see what we can see?"

Nilah did as she was asked, and they each took a research

topic: Aisha was in charge of hunting down more information on Maslin Durand, Boots would handle Izak Vraba, and Nilah would take active cases on the Children of the Singularity.

The first piece of information Nilah found was a tax record, of all things. The Taitutian government had granted nonprofit status to a group of the same name over thirty years ago. According to their forms, they were "dedicated to creating unity through transcendent thought." There were a number of redacted records attached to the entry: a Special Branch agent requesting the government look into the group, but it went nowhere, and Nilah was quickly stymied by blocked-out information.

A tittering spider drone clinked past her, hauling a set of cubes on its back, bound for a data sifter in the far corner. It paused before Nilah, looked her over, and continued along its merry way. She watched the drone's path until it arrived before the agent crewing the data sifter. She waved, and the man nodded but went on about his business. He had to be one of the official government datamancers.

Tired of reading bland, redacted records, she followed the drone.

"Hello," she greeted the man, smiling brightly.

He had to be in his late forties, with droopy jowls and a bit of extra belly underneath a drab suit. It wasn't hard to imagine that he had a few kids, the oldest of whom would be at university. He gave her a shy smile and returned the greeting. He blushed as recognition crossed his face.

"It's a pleasure, Miss Brio," said the agent, extending a gloved hand. "Hawkworth. What brings you here?"

"Research," said Nilah. "Slow going, though."

He demurred. "Isn't it always?"

"That depends. Are you an aggregator?"

"Aggregators are the devices we use to parse information. I'm a datamancer. Most government archivists are."

It was unsurprising that he'd get hung up on a technicality.

"Agent Hawkworth, I'm having a spot of bother with one of your cubes."

"Oh? May I see it?"

Nilah dutifully fetched him the cube. He inspected it, then slotted it into the sifter and traced his datamancer's mark, placing his palms against the contacts. His eyes rolled back in his head for a brief moment, then he came back to reality.

"It appears fine to me, Miss Brio. What seems to be the issue?"

Nilah scooted closer with a sheepish expression and white dermaluxes. "All of the good bits are ... you know ... missing."

"Redacted."

"Is there a way to ..." She let the question hang.

Hawkworth's expression flattened. "I can't wait to tell Clara I met you today. If you'll excuse me, I've a lot of work to do."

Nilah sighed. "Thanks, mate."

So much for shortcuts. She delved deeper into the archives, but the farther she went, the less intuitive the system got. A lot of records were improperly tagged or fragmented. She'd go to the alcove where a data cube should be only to find it missing, or swapped with the one next to it. She wasn't trained in this, and when she'd see Aisha, they exchanged pained looks. The only one in her element was Boots, who shuffled to and fro with real purpose.

She had no choice but to return to the financial records.

Most Children of the Singularity were spectacularly boring as far as Nilah could tell. They regularly filed their taxes, listing profits and losses as a wash. They had a few corporate holdings— small buildings here and there on backwater worlds, listed as their temples. Their expenses were so small as to lack itemization, so Nilah couldn't get a good picture of what went on inside, and reading tax form after tax form hurt her brain. Before long, she'd set up shop in one of the sifter cubicles, a pile of data crystals growing before her with each search.

She slotted another data cube and sighed, scrolling through the lists of articles containing the Children. She propped her chin up with one hand and glanced over in Boots's direction to find her sorting through a pile of cubes. The older woman looked happy, if a little intense. Loafing around in a library simply wasn't Nilah's game.

Until she saw an active case tag fly past out of the corner of her eye. She paused the projection.

Every other record had been bureaucratic, but this was a government surveillance operation dated back almost a year. From what Nilah could tell, the investigating agent had been delving into darkened communities on the Link, interacting with the Children through an encoded alias. His conclusion: official membership in the organization was almost nonexistent, but those identifying as Children had skyrocketed. The agent described a vast network of self-organizing, digital cells, each competing for the attentions of the official group. They spread their message across the Link through their own bizarre mythology—cryptic tales of solitary heroes through drug-addled dreamscapes. The official organization was silent in response.

So there were two factions: the secretive, tax-paying nonprofit, and the rabid communities of Witts lovers scattered across the Link.

She glanced back at Boots again, unable to help a tiny tingle of pleasure; she'd found valuable intel, even though she wasn't as versed in archives as the others. Judging from the frustration on Boots's face, she hadn't found anything yet. Nilah was about to share her coup with Boots when a picture of herself filled the cubicle.

Nilah was so accustomed to seeing reproductions of her likeness that, at first, she wasn't fazed. There were surely other images of her floating through the archives. This one, however, depicted her attacking Henrick Witts, while a strange arcane machine sputtered smoke in the background. It'd been made to look like the battle took place in a battleship, but it certainly wasn't the *Harrow*. And she recognized the expression she'd made in the picture—it was from the "Fierce Warrior" set of images she'd taken for *Glambot*.

Someone had drawn a blazing red ring around her and scratched the word "traitor" next to it. Her eyes flicked to the edge of the image, and she found a Special Branch serial number attached—when she touched it to see the rest of the images in the series, she found thousands. They'd twisted her defiant, cocksure smile into a malicious brand, depicting her attacking or harming the heroic members of Witts's crew. She swiped over to the case file header and found the words: ACTIVE INVESTIGATION: PSYPROP RB-14—PRO-WITTS DISRUPT OPS.

From the case header file, she had an easier time locating the agent's aims: to prove that the expensive, widespread pro-Witts propaganda originated within the Children of the Singularity…which meant they were evading taxes—no mention of protecting Taitutian interests or galactic security. Nilah let out a sigh. If tax law resulted in arresting the manky bastards, perhaps it wasn't so bad.

She called for a cup of water, and the spider drone delivered it while she perused the financial records related to the case. They came in one of three flavors: redacted and interesting, redacted and boring, and redacted with a side of redaction. With just a little more clearance, she could probably get the answers she needed. Nilah sunk a few hours down this rabbit hole, trying to figure out what new information the agent and the case worker had learned. She almost didn't notice when the overhead lights went out.

"Hello?" she called out without thinking, then immediately

regretted it. She checked the terminal; they had an hour before the archives closed, which meant the extinguishing of the light was unscheduled.

The muffled sounds of slinger fire rattled through the urmurex above, and her stomach flipped. Her slinger lay up there, as did Aisha's and Boots's. She didn't know what had become of the litigious men and women who'd let her into the archives, but she could guess. There'd be bodies upstairs.

Nilah dashed down the aisles, looking for Agent Hawkworth or the drone. She found the machine lying deactivated upon the ground, its legs curled under it like a dead bug. Hawkworth had disappeared, and she wasn't sure if she was sad or thankful for that. He didn't seem like the type to be prepared for an assault, but at least he was an authority figure.

"Boots," Nilah hissed. "Aisha!"

The two women emerged from the shadows. Aisha clutched a data cube, her grip unwavering through the magic of the marksman's mark. Nilah guessed that the pilot planned to throw the cube at anyone who attacked them—reasonable, since it was sharp and weighed half a kilo.

"Shots fired upstairs," muttered Boots.

"Get ready," said Aisha.

Nilah's dermaluxes radiated purple fear, but she suppressed them. "We're in it, loves. Any plans?"

The other two women shook their heads, and Nilah nodded.

"All right. You two are best with slingers," said Nilah. "Hang back."

The lamps in the shelving flickered and died. Emergency lights kicked on, painting the archives in bright whites and long shadows. Somehow, all the staff had disappeared. Nilah couldn't be sure whether they were victims or participants in whatever was about to go down. Nilah's enemies were resourceful, and someone in the Special Branch had planned to sell information to Aaron Forscythe. Sabotaging a small facility seemed well within their capabilities.

Loud klaxons sounded out, and the elevator rose, plugging the only exit they knew. The trio rushed to the far end of the shelves, seeking any cover from the long clear elevator shaft that they could find. Any second, that elevator would drop like a stone, and soldiers with heavy autoslingers would rappel down the tube.

"Where the hell are the cops?" Aisha whispered, her fingers tight around the data cube.

"We've got to fight like they're not coming," said Boots. "I've got nothing, except this arm."

Nilah nodded. It would be stupid to think they stood a chance. The memory of Prime Minister Mandell's strike team was still fresh in her mind. If the attackers upstairs were that good, the trio would be lucky to survive the first wave.

"Listen, I can punch things," said Nilah, forcing some of her racer swagger. She pointed to Boots. "You can stab things, and you"—to Aisha—"can throw things. We're armed to the bloody teeth."

"That seems kind of arbitrary," said Boots.

Nilah flexed her jaw. "I have Flicker, she's a sharpshooter, and you've got a knife that pops out of your finger. No more questions."

"Okay," said Aisha, renewing the glyph and grasping it with her palm. "Okay."

Except the elevator never dropped. No more shots pierced the air. The klaxon sounded its repetitive, binary alarm—on, off, on, off, and in the silent gaps, Nilah strained to listen for the sounds of onrushing doom.

What if the enemy had already breached the room, and she'd missed it somehow? Soldiers might be racing toward them that very second. After a minute, Nilah poked her head out, ready to duck backward if she saw even the slightest hint of fibron battle armor. A long, empty aisle filled her vision. The klaxons shut off, leaving only a ringing sound in their wake.

Then the ringing became a voice—a distant song, sad and slow, wandering from note to note.

"What in the name of—" Nilah began, but her heart started as something moved to her right. She ducked behind the shelving unit, expecting some blade to come at her head.

No black-clad assassins came for her, no murderbots, nothing. Only the queer voice broke the silence.

What had moved? She needed to look once more to be certain, and the shelves looked heavy enough to climb. Nilah removed a few data crystals and hoisted herself up, pausing before she crested the top; if she had been spotted, she didn't want to peer from the same place twice. Knuckles tight upon the edge of the shelf, she pulled herself over.

The place where she thought she'd seen the movement was a black rectangle, thrown into stark relief by the emergency lights. She narrowed her eyes and jutted her head forward, expecting to see a soldier, the reflection of a mask, the flash of a slinger, something.

But she found only hard tile, and the distinct impression of burbling. The song grew louder. The shadow across the floor wavered like the slow roiling of water.

And something reached out of it.

Nilah pushed off her perch, silently landing back between her compatriots. She hadn't been able to make out the exact form, but had glimpsed dripping blackness and a bony appendage, darker than any nanotube coating. She'd never seen a spell like that; it was like the old legends of ghosts and phantoms.

"There's a problem, loves," she whispered, keeping her voice as low as she could.

Boots eyed her. "Does it have anything to do with that creepy noise?"

The heavy shelf rocked behind them with the force of a massive blow, showering the trio with twinkling data cubes. Nilah ducked and covered her head, each crystal battering her back with sharp corners before bouncing harmlessly across the floor. Boots cried out as one of the crystals struck her. When the hail of cubes stopped, Nilah glanced up to find Boots clutching her hair, a rivulet of crimson running between her fingers.

Nilah backed away from the shelf, eyes darting from side to side, veins frigid with fear. With each step, she kicked crystals out of the way, almost stumbling. At the end of the aisle, long fingers, dripping with ink, wrapped around the endcap. A wicked claw tipped each finger, sharp enough to scar the metal shelving. It paused, as though sizing up a meal.

Lightning quick, it whipped itself around the corner and came at Nilah, gaunt arms spread wide like the wings of a bird of prey. She tried to leap out of the way, but her foot found purchase on a cube, and she went rolling to the ground.

A glimmering crystal thunked off the spot where the creature's head might've been, and Nilah looked back to see Aisha snatching up another cube to throw. Boots had gotten a few steps of distance and was wildly gesturing for her to join them.

The shade craned its head and opened impossibly wide jaws, its long, curved teeth sprouting and snapping into place. Smoky, pitch-black liquid flowed from its skin and dripped onto Nilah's legs.

She concentrated and cranked up her dermaluxes to full, sending blinding flashes in all directions. It recoiled from her visual assault, and she took the opportunity to kip up to her feet. This time, she watched her footing and found solid steps, dodging and weaving away from the creature.

It swung a claw at her, arms extending like a bullwhip crack, and Nilah leapt off one of the shelves to get clear. Her calf muscle seared with pain as knifelike claws grazed her skin, tearing her pant leg. She landed hard, but soundly, and dashed off after Boots and Aisha.

The song positively cooed with bloodlust.

"What the hell is that thing?" Boots huffed as they hurdled down aisle after aisle.

"I don't know," said Aisha, tracing another glyph, "but it didn't like your lights."

Nilah raced after them, not bothering to see how bad her leg might be. She could run on it, and that was good enough for her. "No, it didn't... Have you ever seen a spell like that?"

Both women shook their heads no.

"Could be an illusion," said Boots as they rounded another corner and tucked in, their backs flat against the wall.

Nilah crouched by her companions and reached down to touch the scratches on her leg. Her fingers came away wet with blood, a hard sensation to replicate with simple illusions. The shade was real, and it could really kill them with those talons. Taking a short breath, Nilah ducked out from behind cover.

She watched the shade slurp from shadow to shadow, pouring between them like carbon ink, its form flexing and changing with each leap, then she retreated.

"It can't walk in the light," she told the others, trying to keep her voice down.

"There are shadows everywhere," said Aisha.

Boots jutted out her jaw, nodding at the room beyond. "The place is lousy with them."

The emergency lights blinked over Nilah's head, illuminating an exit she couldn't use. Someone had shut off the power, knowing that the emergency lights would leave more shadows and make the spell work better.

Nilah gestured to a distant sifter workstation. "If I can hack one of these terminals, I can get the main lights back on."

Boots shook her head. "It's just going to sit there while you hack a classified terminal?"

"You'll have to distract it. Get on top of the shelves, closer to the lights. That's the brightest part of the room."

A smoky black skull peered around the corner, and a hundred bony hands snaked toward them. It lashed out after Aisha, taking hold of her neck, so Nilah plunged forward with her tattoos ablaze, smashing her fists into the darkness. She brought to bear years of training in Flicker, the Taitutian art of dermalux fighting. Using her tattoos, she could distract and strike with pinpoint precision. *Rising rocket.* Her uppercut connected smoothly with the skull, but where Nilah had expected to feel bone, she felt slick flesh. The arms released Aisha, but the skull wormed toward Nilah, jaws clacking. *Disrupted orbit.* A spinning kick sent the creature off course and crashing into the shelf while Nilah danced away. It surged upright, completely unfazed by the attacks.

"Run!" shouted Nilah, and they split up.

Chapter Five

Staccato

Nilah thanked her lucky stars for all the years spent keeping herself in tip-top shape. Before long, she was out of sight from the shade. She flattened herself into a nook between two sconces and waited, shutting off her blaring dermaluxes.

"Over here, bucko!" came Boots's shout over the mysterious song and the melodic crash of Aisha throwing data cubes.

The singing slowly diminished until it was barely audible, Boots and Aisha swearing loudly at the creature as they led it away. Instinct told Nilah to avoid the hard shadows, for fear that the thing could emerge beneath her at any moment. Then again, it appeared to see in the visible light spectrum, so maybe it was wiser to stick to the darkened areas.

On one of the endcaps, she spied her destination: an archive terminal with an open socket, its gold data contacts glimmering in the recess. It would be dangerous to hack a modern military system in the heart of Taitu's capital, which was not at all like the outdated defenses of the *Capricious*. In addition to the network defense AI, there was the risk that the shadow would find her while she was distracted with the attack.

It'd have to do. She traced her mechanist's glyph and crept toward the terminal.

When Nilah's fingertips brushed the exposed data contacts, she closed her eyes and concentrated, winding her magic into the terminal, slinking across network pathways and into the adaptive logic of the system.

She found a house in ruins. Shattered fragments of defensive code floated through the aether like feathers. Most of the system's core functions remained, but the defenses had been blown to bits. Judging from the clean wounds to the defense neurons, the attack had been swift and asymmetrical.

Nilah scanned the datascape for the strands that would lead her to the emergency lighting controls. A million darkened threads spread before her, and she sifted through for a glimmer of communication. At last, her queries touched upon a strong control signal.

At least, that's what she thought until she touched it.

Images of the archives flooded her mind from a thousand different vantage points—high, low, down each and every aisle. The data packets blasted through her in rapid succession, and the dozens of views scrambled into one another. These were the video feeds for all the imagers inside the archives.

Nilah summoned a filter snippet and sorted the threads until she found her physical body hunched over the terminal, eyes flitting under their lids. Switching the filter, she found her friends: across the room, Boots scrambled through the labyrinthine shelves as the hungry shadow slithered after. Aisha traced her glyph and tossed a data cube over her shoulder, landing it directly in the engorged jaws of the beast. The cube wedged into the creature's mouth, so it grew three more pairs of oozing mandibles. It bore down on her friends, drawing closer with each passing second.

Nilah traced the feed route to a connection to the outside

world. From the archives, the stream went to a government data center, then off into space to anyone with the right encryption codes. Someone out there was watching them—and perhaps controlling the shade.

Nilah summoned a spark of arcane energy and cut the data thread, burning out the external gateways to the world beyond so nothing else could connect. Without that connection, the facility would stop broadcasting video. If anyone wanted to watch them die, it'd have to be from inside the structure.

She reinitialized her filter, flipping through the imager feeds for her friends, but found nothing: no Boots, no Aisha, no shade.

"Nilah," said a woman, low and urgent, entering Nilah's mind through the dozen ears of the imagers. Was that Boots's voice?

She twisted the filter this way and that across the thread, searching for the source of the noise. Then a heavy hand fell across her shoulder.

Nilah broke contact with the terminal and leapt like a startled cat, slamming her head into the side of the alcove and slapping ineffectively at the walls. She tumbled onto her rump and clambered backward before finally getting her bearings. Boots and Aisha stood over her, panting.

"It's okay!" said Boots. "Just us."

Aisha helped her up, palms slick with sweat. "That thing disappeared. What did you do?"

Nilah took a moment to catch her breath. "I cut the video feeds. It was a spell—godlike magic—but the bastard still had to see where he was casting. No video, no eyes."

"Nick of time," said Aisha, rubbing her temple. "My cardioid was about to pop if I had to cast one more mark."

Nilah nodded. "We're not out of the woods yet."

Boots doubled over, hands on her knees. Sprinting wasn't her forte. "Still got those goons in the lobby."

"I've got a plan for that," said Nilah, tracing another glyph and pressing her fingers to the terminal contacts. "Just sit tight."

Once again, she delved into the damaged network, sifting through the strands for the lobby imagers. Connecting her filter, she was able to flip through the video feeds until she found a good overhead shot of the glass cube above. She wished she had Armin's power just then—she'd be able to view all the feeds at the same time and understand them.

At first glance, it appeared as though nothing was out of order. The security personnel were standing at their posts, automatic slingers strapped at their sides. Except Nilah spied a pair of legs sticking out from behind the scanning station desks. Judging from the make of the combat boots, the attackers had likely stashed the bodies of the real guards and taken their places.

Nilah sifted through the comm threads until she found the one that controlled the projections along the external glass of the building. She grabbed a few severed snippets of the decimated defense code and wove together a primitive motion-tracking algorithm.

She used the lobby's display glass to draw targets around the guards' heads and broadcasted a message: Hostages inside. Police snipers shoot here.

Nilah opened her eyes and looked to her companions. She called up a projection so they could watch the action above.

"What if the police think it's a trap?" asked Aisha. "They aren't going to just start shooting."

"Doesn't matter," said Nilah. "They'll still come and investigate. They can't ignore it."

"Nice," said Boots.

"You might want to cover your ears," said Nilah, and she triggered all the intruder alarms at maximum volume.

The police might not show up slingers blazing, but they

couldn't ignore a high-profile malfunction in the heart of the Justice District. A response team would be on them in under a minute.

When she broke away from the terminal, she found the archivist she'd met earlier, a tiny slinger in his trembling hands. At ten paces, he'd get off a shot before Nilah could ever close the gap to him.

"Oh, come on," sighed Nilah. "Is *everyone* a spy for Henrick Witts?"

"The Children have ways of getting where we need to be," he said with a weak smile.

Boots shook her head. "So the Children definitely work for Witts, then. Way to confirm a hunch, genius."

Hawkworth blanched but said nothing.

Nilah snapped her fingers. "What was your name again? Hank, uh…"

"Hawkworth. You should beg," said the agent, hands shaking. "I want to tell them you begged."

"Listen, mate," said Nilah, raising her hands. If she could get close enough, she might be able to take him down. "I hate to be the one to tell you this, but your bosses aren't going to help you. The Gods of the *Harrow* don't care one whit for you. Their original plan was to kill everyone in the galaxy, remember?"

"Only the weak," said Hawkworth, redoubling his grip on his slinger.

"No offense, buddy," said Boots, "but you probably shoot like an accountant. Your spell is datamancy and we're a couple of badasses. Maybe consider switching sides."

Hawkworth snarled. "Go to hell."

His finger tensed around the trigger, and Nilah leapt clear as a bolt sailed past her face. He lined up for another shot, but a glittering data cube smashed into his forehead, corner first. He stumbled back a few steps, eyes crossed, lips mouthing some unformed word, and toppled over like a tool chest. Blood dribbled from a nasty head wound.

Nilah rushed to his side and kicked away his slinger before turning to see Aisha straightening from her throw. The pilot let out a long sigh as the magic subsided from her system.

Boots's mechanical hand had ejected from her wrist, and Nilah spied the tip of the anti-ship slinger round locked into firing position. If she'd fired, Hawkworth would've been down, but so would most of one side of the archives.

"Okay, now I'm tapped out," said Aisha, brushing off her hands.

Boots sauntered over to their downed adversary and checked for a pulse. "Crap. He's flatlining."

"Sorry," said Aisha. "Wasn't trying to brain him."

Boots motioned to the projection, where the assassins were fleeing the premises. "At least Nilah spooked them. If we don't get this guy some medical attention soon, he's a goner."

Nilah traced another glyph, wincing with strain as she connected again to the network. The elevator controls were burned out. Whoever those killers were, they'd done a good job of locking the trio inside.

"Damn," she muttered, reconnecting to the exterior windows. "We're not getting out of here without the police."

She changed their message to read:

HELP. ALL TRAPPED INSIDE. SPECIAL BRANCH CASUALTIES LOBBY LEVEL.

"Why am I looking at you again?" asked Cedric Weathers as he surveyed the shelves upon shelves of scattered data cubes.

Boots smacked her lips and glanced to where Nilah and Aisha were being wrapped in blankets as they drank rich Taitutian tea.

The Special Branch agents were taking extra care of her camera-ready compatriots, but Boots was left out in the literal cold.

"Because your agency's internal security is a disgrace?" she mused, crossing her arms. She'd never gotten accustomed to the feeling of her prosthetic limb, but the gesture was complete, and she'd be damned if she showed discomfort in front of Cedric.

He clucked his tongue. "You've got some cheek for a woman detained at a crime scene."

"Oh, jeez, Agent Weathers, let me be the first to apologize for hurting your little feelings. Now that's out of the way. Do you know why a shadow monster tried to kill everyone and one of your men pulled a weapon on us?"

"For all we know, you people set this up somehow—so it looks like I should hold you three for questioning."

Boots grimaced. "Cut the crap. You've got the imager feeds from upstairs. You know we were stuck down here when those bastards shot the guards up top."

"The videos cut out after the assault was successful. There's no footage of the three of you after that."

"Yeah, but you know for a fact that we didn't shoot anyone, so forget your harebrained theories."

Cedric thrust his hands into his pockets. "We had this one case we trained on back at the academy—"

Boots waved him off. "Spare me. Are we being held or not? And before you answer, you might want to consult Prime Minister Bianchi."

Cedric shifted uncomfortably on his heels for a moment, weighing his options. Finally, he said, "One of these days, that little trick isn't going to work for you."

"Cool. Until then, why don't you try to remember that we did you, and the entire galaxy, a huge favor." Boots rested her hands on her hips. "We're the poor fools running down the leads you can't be bothered to chase."

"You're not government operatives. You have no jurisdiction of any kind."

Boots laughed. "That's true. We've got a lot more morals and a lot fewer leaks."

She pointed down at the anti-ship slinger round at Hawkworth's feet. "Not sure what he was going to do with that, but if it's as pleasant as he was..." Then she shrugged. "Have a nice day, Agent."

Boots made her way to Nilah and Aisha, this crowd of Special Branch personnel being far less enthusiastic for autographs than the ones at headquarters, and motioned for them to go. "Let's roll."

They went up through the elevator, out into the street, into a hired flier, and across town to the Port of Aior, where the *Capricious* lay docked.

Cordell awaited them at the ship's cargo loading ramp, a lit cigarette dangling from his mouth, its smoke crackling with eidolon dust. "Those government cats who stopped by were pissed, Bootsie," he called out as she approached.

"It was self-defense, sir, I swear," she said with less enthusiasm than the statement required. It'd been a long day, and it felt nice to trudge up the cargo ramp toward her warm bunk.

"I'm glad you three made it out okay. The others are waiting in the mess for a debrief." He took a drag and grasped her hand, clapping her on the shoulder.

"If you make my jacket stink of smoke, sir..." she said, ducking back a bit.

Cordell flicked the cigarette to the deck, where he crushed it underfoot. "The authorities had a lot of questions, but they weren't forthcoming with any answers. They were asking why you killed a government agent, Boots."

"Oh, I didn't kill him. Missus Aisha Jan had that honor."

Cordell cocked an eyebrow at the pilot, who smiled politely. He would've grilled Boots harder, but to Aisha, he said, "As always, thanks for looking out for them."

"She was working overtime today," said Nilah.

"Sir," said Boots, "I hate to rush the awards ceremony, but I'd like to get the ship buttoned up. I think it's time we got off this rock."

The captain gave her a quizzical look but complied, mashing the door closed. Boots watched the whining cargo ramp seal them off from the outside world.

Once they were safely inside the dock, Boots tapped her prosthetic arm and smiled at Cordell. "Maybe those Special Branch stooges didn't want to share info with you, but I've got a gift."

She popped off her hand and slid out three smaller data cubes, each twinkling with the bright lights of the cargo bay. They were the kind used for capturing and transferring records, and in plentiful supply at the archives storage.

"Your present is...exported classified data, I'm guessing?" asked Cordell.

"Bingo."

The captain shook his head. "The cops are going to have a field day with this. You know the forensic mechanists will figure out the theft eventually. I take it there are some good answers in here worth putting us in legal jeopardy?"

Nilah stepped forward. "Not exactly, sir. The records are heavily redacted, but with the help of a skilled datamancer..."

"It was a gamble," said Boots, and the captain's eyes lit up, though he tried to play it cool.

Cordell nodded. "All right, then. Let's convene in the ready room and discuss it."

The four of them joined the other crew in the mess. It still warmed Boots's heart to see the place once again packed to capacity, though if they took on any more crew at this point, they'd be stepping all over one another.

Aisha leaned into the crook of Malik's arm, and Orna held Nilah's hand. Boots smirked; the captain was going soft to allow those kinds of displays during a briefing. The fact that Armin hadn't complained meant there was a real policy shift going on— it was usually Armin's job as first mate to be the bad guy.

"I know all of you are anxious to find out what happened," said Cordell. "Miss Elsworth, you brought home the prize, why don't you fill us in?"

"First off," she began, handing Armin the three crystal cubes, "these are for you. Redacted records of Maslin Durand, the Children of the Singularity, and any bank transactions we could find that were blacked out at secret clearance. We copied everything as quickly as we could before the cops got there. Maybe you can make some progress."

He took the cubes without complaint.

"Also, you guys owe me a ship-to-ship lancer round," said Boots. "I left mine in the archives so I could fit the data cubes."

"Have Miss Sokol sort you out," Cordell replied.

Boots looked into the eyes of her compatriots one by one, not sure if she was excited or filled with dread by her news. "We've finally struck a nerve again. We were attacked by a powerful caster, maybe one of Henrick Witts's gods."

"How do we know that?" asked Armin.

"Just like a datamancer to ask for proof, sir," chuckled Boots. "First off, we were attacked by a huge, demonic shadow creature, which sliced open poor Miss Brio's leg."

"An unlucky scratch," said Nilah.

Boots rubbed her artificial wrist. The limb was too light without the lancer round in it. "The creature was fast and deadly, and we barely escaped with our lives."

"Just for argument's sake," said Armin, "what if it was an animal you haven't seen before, like the sirathica?"

"The spell cut out when I shut down the imagers," said Nilah, before hastily adding, "uh, sir. Someone was using the security system to scry on us and manifest the spell in our presence."

"Did you trace the signal?" asked Armin.

"Yes, sir. It went in a broadcast out to space."

Boots nodded in agreement. "Exactly. Whoever was casting those shadows wasn't even close to us, was capable of sending them across several light-years of distance. That's godlike magic if ever I've heard of it."

"So they can attack anyone they can see?" asked Cordell.

"Maybe," said Boots. "Don't do any live interviews anytime soon."

"We'd better come up with a countermeasure," said Orna. "I'll start working on a targeted disperser for puncturing those spells."

Armin scratched his head. "You think that would've knocked it down?"

Orna nodded. "With enough power, yes. But this rifle will have to be big...like, Charger's main cannon big. We've got the money—just need a few parts to get started. It'll be expensive."

The captain thought for a minute, pursing his lips. "Do it. This might've been retaliation for Maslin Durand. They didn't bother us when we were chasing down the midlevel flunkies, but they decided to go after you today."

"Someone in the Special Branch is working with them, sir," said Nilah. "The code they used to attack the archives exploited every single weakness like they knew the system in and out. There was a Special Branch bloke in there, too, ready to kill us. This took foreknowledge."

"We can't trust the Taitutians, sir," said Boots. "Present company excluded, of course."

Cordell and Armin gave each other grim looks.

Armin cleared his throat. "Since you've been away from the ship, there have been a few, ah, developments as well."

Boots's heart sank at his tone. This would be bad.

Armin gestured for a projection, and a screen appeared before him. He tapped in a query and flipped it to face the rest of the crew.

"This," he said.

Onscreen, Boots grabbed a woman's arm against the backdrop of Elba Pool Station. Then, she turned and threw one of the Children of the Singularity to the ground. The video couldn't have been more than a few hours old, but every news generator on the Link had boosted it to the top of their feeds.

A blink brought them a headshot interview with the cultist. "I had a right to be there. I have a right to my beliefs. She assaulted me."

Boots opened her mouth to shout at the projection, but thought better of it.

"They know the truth is coming out," said the cultist, "and they're afraid of everyone who knows it."

The projection froze as the story ended.

"I've been in touch with our colleagues at the Link data clearinghouse, and the ratings on this story are through the roof." Armin wiped away the projection and added a few more queries. "More troubling, all stories critical of us have been increasingly well-received over the past year."

"How many of these stories are there, sir?" asked Nilah.

Armin folded his hands behind his back. "The short answer is a steady trickle. The long answer..."

"It's a widespread psychological operation," said Nilah, and Armin gave her a surprised look. "My government is investigating. They knew about this and didn't tell us. It's part of what's on those data cubes, sir."

"That's probably why they need the Money Mill—paying for all of this crap they're throwing onto the Link," said Cordell. "Seems to me...there's a concerted effort among fringe news groups to discredit what happened with the *Harrow*, and it's working."

"Based on these ratings and projections from the clearinghouse," said Armin, "fully fifteen percent of civilized space may believe that the *Harrow* was faked. Thirty-two percent believe some part of it was faked. That's one in three. Based upon all previous intellectual upheavals, we've crossed the threshold for a catalytic event."

"I'm sorry, but what?" asked Boots.

Armin cleared his throat. "If people are exposed to a negative true story about us, we may see a large population calling for our heads. Essentially, the Children of the Singularity are hoping we'll screw up badly enough to lose governmental support."

"And I handed them ammunition," said Boots. "Why didn't I know about this?"

"It's easy to miss if you aren't media savvy," said Nilah. "Back when I was racing, I used to track the press religiously, and that was only the sports outlets."

"So what do we do, Captain?" asked Orna. "We're not exactly equipped to wage a war for hearts and minds."

"No. That would be fighting on their terms," said Cordell. "We don't have to worry about whether the public thinks we're right or wrong. If we can find this evil, maybe we can pull it out at the root. Everyone here knows exactly what happened. It's time to go back underground."

Murmurs went up among the crew. Most of them had friends and family. Boots had her distillery, but her employees would take care of it as long Ai paid them. The only true friends Boots had were in this room.

"I'm not asking," said Cordell. "This is for your own safety."

"Okay, sir," said Boots, "but how do you propose we disappear from one of the most guarded spaceports in the galaxy?"

Cordell smirked. "You start with a single-use, unlicensed jump drive, which we happen to have."

Boots frowned. "You put a jump dump on this ship? Our quartermaster approved this?"

Those boosters were the purview of smugglers and pirates—highly unstable and often damaging to the ship. They ran off tanks of impure eidolon crystals, which would vaporize in the transfer like an ancient flashbulb. Intergalactic authorities would often come upon pirate vessels with a failed drive, a spherical void in their ship where the engine room once was. The crew, of course, would be long dead.

Orna shrugged. "It's the captain's money. He wanted the ability to disappear at any time. I just had to certify its safety."

"Where did it come from?" asked Boots.

"Got it off an arms dealer in the Murphy Belt," said Orna. "It'll jump."

"There are probably a thousand imagers on us right now. If even one of those lenses catches us spinning up to jump, they can find us like we found the *Harrow*."

Cordell smiled. "That's true. That's why we're going to have to paint the satellites on our way out—a straight shot down the lens with our laser designator to blind them."

Boots pursed her lips. "Of course we are, sir. Why *not* sabotage Taitutian state property? This sounds like a fantastic idea."

"I'm so glad you're on board," said Cordell. "All crew to ready stations. We jump in two hours. If you've got messages to get to friends and family, get them out now."

Boots leaned against the wall of the engine room, watching Nilah and Orna scurry about checking connections. Charger handed them tools and buzzed loud complaints at Orna whenever he found something he didn't like—which was almost constantly.

Every time the bot winced, Boots's stress level doubled. She didn't fancy getting vaporized by a faulty crystal, or ending up sucking vacuum in near orbit. She'd done a lot of shady crap in her lifetime, but an unlicensed jump wasn't even remotely on the agenda.

The jump dump didn't look like it belonged in the *Capricious*'s well-maintained space. It reminded Boots of a waste compactor— a filthy aluminum cylinder, battered and pockmarked, attached to the main drive core.

"I hear you!" growled Orna, banging the spanner across Charger's forehead.

The bot snatched it out of her hand and tried to adjust one of the couplings.

"Charger, no!" shouted Orna. "Bad!"

"Listen to your mother, Charger," Nilah added absentmindedly. She was absorbed in her own tuning operation on the other side.

Nilah glanced up at Boots. "You don't have to stay here. Did you send out your messages?"

"Sure," said Boots. "Checked in on Ai. It said the stills are operating at seventy-eight percent efficiency. It was a touching moment for both of us."

"Har," said Orna, grabbing an arc-stylus from Charger's waiting claws.

Nilah frowned. "Boots, you know we might be underground for months. Maybe you should actually tell someone."

Boots laughed. "Who? Everyone I care about is on this ship. Who did you call?"

Nilah looked up, mentally checking people off a list. "Oh, Dad and Mum, Kristof, Lana—"

"Who's Lana?" asked Boots.

"Her Link agent," said Orna, in a tone so icy that Boots thought better of asking anything else about it.

"Okay. Who did you message?" Nilah asked Orna.

"Oh, I'm the same as Boots," said the quartermaster.

Boots snorted. "You're agreeing with me? Should I mark my calendar?"

Orna torqued down one of the cable connectors, grunting as she did. "No one to call, babe. Just you, and you're here with me."

Nilah stopped working. "That's really sad. You two need to make more friends."

Boots crossed her arms. "I take issue with that. I don't need to make friends for the sake of making friends. That's stupid. People from our world aren't exactly social butterflies."

"Well, excuse me," said Nilah, grimacing and returning to her job.

Boots and Orna exchanged meaningful glances.

"Okay, no," said Nilah. "See, that's exactly what I was talking about back when we were on the bridge, Boots."

"What?"

Nilah frowned. "You're doing that Fallen refugee thing again with my girlfriend, making me feel like I'm not one of you."

"You're overthinking it," said Orna.

"Don't tell me I'm imagining things," said Nilah, standing up straight. "I'm not from Clarkesfall, and you two are. Fine, I get it."

"It's just a connection we have," said Boots. "I wouldn't worry too much about it."

"I'm not worried about it. I just want to be included."

"You weren't 'included' in the Famine War, so count yourself lucky," said Orna. "Am I right, Boots?"

"Don't ask her to back you up," said Nilah.

"Okay," said Orna, throwing her arc-stylus at Charger, who caught it. "I'll ask *Lana*."

Nilah and the quartermaster stared each other down, sparking harder than the power couplings before them. Boots looked from one woman to the other, wide-eyed. Whatever was going on here, it was above her pay grade.

Orna's eyes darted to one side. "Charger!" she bellowed. "No!"

The bot had managed to get two of the bolts off its breastplate and was revving its ventral exhaust ports with obvious relish. Orna banged off in its direction, shouting obscenities and threatening to weld the plate in place.

Nilah stared into the mess of cables, not looking up at Boots.

"I'm going to be honest," said Boots, "no one should ask me for relationship advice."

"But I take it you have some?" Nilah asked, attaching a set of probes to one of the sockets.

"She needs to talk to you about this Lana thing. You need to talk to her about the refugee thing."

"Genius," Nilah replied, rolling her eyes. "Thanks, mate."

It'd been stupid to open her yap. In the past twenty years, she hadn't been rolling in men, and she'd never carried off a romantic relationship of any stripe. It simply stung her to see Nilah and Orna bicker.

"I'm pretty sure the captain needs me on the bridge," said Boots.

"Look, I'm sorry," said Nilah. "I've just—you know, never loved anyone before. It sucks."

"Since I'm older, I'd give you some sage advice, but we both know I'm a moron." She smiled at Nilah, who couldn't be moved to return the gesture, but nodded. Boots stepped out of the engine room and closed the door behind herself.

When she reached the mid-deck, she ran into Malik.

"Have you seen Nilah and Orna?" he asked.

Boots gave him a thin-lipped smile. "They're working super hard. Probably best to give them space until it's time to take off."

"We'll need one of them on the bridge. Surely the preparations are complete by now."

How could she warn him that he was walking into a raging conflagration between two lovers—without disrespecting Nilah and Orna's privacy? Those sorts of tiffs weren't supposed to occur on a military vessel, and the captain and first mate wouldn't want them to happen now. But it felt wrong to interrupt... whatever was going on.

"They're that way," said Boots, pointing toward the engine room. "Good luck."

Malik gave her a quizzical look but said nothing. He went his way and she went hers.

She looked in on the Ferrier twins, who were busy securing their quarters for launch. Every cabinet had to be closed, every loose object put away. They didn't have a place on the bridge, no launch duties to speak of, and so their job was simply to stay out of the way.

"You good?" she asked.

Alister sneered. "We'll miss this world, what with all the sight-seeing we got to do."

Jeannie shrugged. "Captain Lamarr wouldn't let us off the ship. Security, you know, ma'am."

"We're valuable assets," grumbled Alister. "Maybe one day, we'll be actual people in his eyes."

Stifling her annoyance, Boots nodded and took off. Was everyone in a terrible mood?

She arrived at the bridge for preflight checks with Cordell, Armin, and Aisha—her job was scramble readiness. The thought of a sortie during egress from Taitu was laughable. It was the heart of civilized space. If a fight did break out, they'd be surrounded by the Taitutian Planetary Defense within minutes.

Her combat spacesuit was hot and itchy, but she wore it out of protocol. She wouldn't be going out in the Midnight Runner. There wouldn't be an escort mission.

Then again, the archives weren't supposed to be full of shadow monsters. Maybe she'd been right to don her pilot's suit after all.

Orna arrived on the bridge with a brisk, "Brio wanted to watch the engine to make sure I did my job hooking up the jump dump."

Cordell eyed Boots. "O...kay. Let's get this show on the road, then. Missus Jan, take us up."

"Main drive priming, Captain. Ten seconds to launch."

Armin traced his datamancy glyph and placed his palms along the crystal sphere of the aggregator. "Captain, I'm getting a lot of comms chatter about us from STC."

"I don't like this." The captain sucked his teeth. "We've got state-granted emergency departure clearance until anyone says otherwise. Missus Jan, give us launch grav and let's boogie. Mister Vandevere, connect me to departure."

Armin twisted his hands over the sphere, opalescent colors shimmering under his skin. "You're on, Captain."

Cordell cleared his throat. "Aior STC Departure, this is Captain Cordell Lamarr of the *Capricious*. I'm invoking my unlimited port access privileges, state authorization code two-two-five-alpha-six-niner-four. For classified reasons, we are departing Taitu immediately."

A voice came over the speakers like a flat beer: sour and sad. "Departure copies, *Capricious*, but, ah... we're going to have to run that code. We'll need five minutes if you would just—"

"No," interrupted Cordell. "I won't just. We're leaving now, Departure. Get right with that, or be in violation of the directives of your new prime minister." He then made the cut motion.

Armin nodded. "Comms severed, Captain."

"They're stalling," said Cordell. "Either they want to haul Boots in for assault, or something worse is coming. We stay, we get arrested. Missus Jan, give us a countdown and engines to full."

"Ten..." Aisha began, the whine of the *Capricious*'s maneuvering thrusters resonating through the hull.

There was a sudden buckling of seat belts across the bridge, and Armin barked into his comm for everyone to strap in. Boots adjusted her own restraints, the fresh launch gravity momentarily swirling her guts.

"They're hailing us, Captain," said Armin.

"We've got thirty seconds to respond," said Cordell. "I want us clear of the atmos by then."

Someone in Space Traffic Control was trying to stall them after all. Boots craned her neck to look out the bridge windows, across the busy starport at the tower. Who was calling into that closed room, ordering them to detain the most decorated heroes of the galaxy? Was it a well-meaning police officer with the local authorities, following up on the assault charge? Was it Agent Weathers, with some new evidence that they were to blame for the attacks at the archives? Was it the newly minted prime minister, sensing the shifting tide of public opinion and willing to orchestrate their fall from grace to curry favor with the masses? How far up the chain did one have to go before they found the invisible hand of Henrick Witts?

A violent force slammed Boots back into her seat. Aisha had launched before the new gravity could take full effect, pancaking Boots's squishier parts to the chair.

"Tell me the path is clear!" grunted Cordell, knuckles tight against his armrests.

"We have a solid trajectory, Captain," said Aisha, yawing the ship slightly to adjust course.

"Let's hope it's just observation satellites up there when we break orbit," said Cordell.

Boots's body vibrated into the correct shape as the gravity drive reached full power. Clouds thinned into blue, which grew darker until open space twinkled before them—except one light was a little too large to be a distant star.

"It's the TPD *Magistrate*, Captain," said Armin. "They've got optics on us, and they're hailing."

Cordell leaned forward in his chair, scrutinizing the wide viewport of the bridge as if he could look right into the eyes of the *Magistrate*'s commander. "So we jump to another jump gate, then jump from there. We'll be gone before they can catch up."

"That's an interdictor-class vessel, sir," said Armin. "It's a jump hunter, designed to run down fleeing ships faster than they can get through the Flow. There are computers on there capable of—"

"I get it, Mister Vandevere." Cordell sighed and sat back.

That was it. They couldn't jump with a ship that size watching.

Hitting satellite lenses with a laser blinder was easy money. A shot down the barrel would paralyze them long enough for the jump to take place. Boots didn't know what kind of countersurveillance Orna had installed, but most jump protection systems could cover ten eyes staring at them. The *Magistrate* might have hundreds of imagers on them, had probably repurposed their day-to-day docking cameras to watch the jump.

"They're still hailing, sir," said Armin.

"Put them through," said Cordell, resignation on his face. He stood, straightening his collar.

A projection of a gaunt woman in Taitutian commander's blues spun into existence in the middle of the bridge. "Captain Cordell Lamarr," she said, inclining her chin. "This is Captain Neith Sadiq of the TPD *Magistrate*. I've been asked to detain you until we can sort out your launch clearances."

Cordell smirked. "I remember you, Captain; we met at the Armada Ball last year."

"It was my husband's great honor to shake your hand," said Sadiq, and she looked like she meant it.

"I don't mean to cut short the pleasantries, but we have emergency port access...and somewhere important to be."

"About that," said Sadiq, frown lines creasing her face. "The prime minister is conferring with special council about the status she's bestowed upon you. There seems to be some concern that your crew has been operating outside the law for too long. It's unlikely that we'll permit you to leave."

"And if we don't comply?" asked Cordell.

"That's an old ADF warship, Captain, and it's a long run to the jump gate. I wouldn't advise taking any actions that would cause us to consider you a threat. Please be patient while we investigate the matter."

Boots let out a breath. Of course these clowns were going to arrest them. The crew of the *Magistrate* were part of the Taitutian system, after all—the system where Henrick Witts had so successfully hidden his crimes, where bureaucrats had worked in the shadows to create the deadly PGRF racetracks.

"Captain," said Boots, "permission to speak to Captain Sadiq."

At first, Cordell looked at her as though she'd laid an egg. She held his gaze for pregnant seconds, until he had no choice but to answer her.

"What have you got to say to her?" asked Cordell.

This was a flagrant violation of rank, and Boots had no right to ask. In wartime, Cordell would've flayed her for even thinking the request, but he must've softened, because he merely stared daggers at her now.

Captain Sadiq cocked her head, able to hear Boots, but Boots's body wasn't being captured by the lenses on the bridge. Only someone in the captain's station could be seen on the other side of the transmission.

"I want to know," Boots said, speaking loudly enough for the bridge microphones to hear, "if she was commanding the *Magistrate* on the day we took down Dwight Mandell."

"Who's speaking?" asked Sadiq, looking at Cordell. "I'd like to address this person."

After a moment, he gestured her to come up to the captain's station so she could be captured by the imagers.

"Better be good," muttered Cordell.

"What are they going to do? Double arrest us?" she whispered. "Might as well try."

The projection of Captain Sadiq nodded at her. "You're Boots Elsworth. We heard you'd disappeared—the only hero I didn't get to thank."

"That's a bit dramatic, Captain," she said, the heat rising in your cheeks. "My duty had ended, and it was time to go home."

"But here you are," she said. "To answer your question: yes, I was the commanding officer of the *Magistrate* the day you brought the *Harrow* home."

Boots took a deep breath. "I know I don't need to remind you what happened to your strike team that boarded the *Harrow*. You may command a few thousand, but twelve deaths are still painful. I'm sure you wonder every day about how that could've been prevented."

Sadiq gave her a curt nod.

"They were murdered by a man operating inside the law, because…well…there are no laws capable of governing that amount of power and influence. And now there are people on your homeworld sympathetic to Mandell, people who believe your soldiers weren't actually killed—they're crying government conspiracy." She looked down at her feet, collecting her thoughts. "Look, ma'am, we know you have every right to detain us, just like those bastards have a right to shout at us for killing your old prime minister. Their opinions are protected."

Captain Sadiq shifted on her feet. "And your point, Miss Elsworth?"

"Maybe the problem is: people are confusing what's legal with what's right. Laws are predictable; they can be hacked."

The projected woman took a sharp breath. She understood the proposition Boots was about to make—insubordination and possibly treason. It'd be a career-ending move for Sadiq.

"We've got a good bead on the rot that's been infecting your planet. Now, you can do the legal thing and bring us in, let us face these people, and the chips will fall where they may." Boots chewed her lip for a moment. If she didn't convince Sadiq, she might be adding to their troubles. "Or…you can do the right thing, shut off your optics, and let us jump out of here without following us."

Sadiq smirked. " 'Shut off our optics'? Captain Lamarr, have you got an unregistered jump drive on your vessel?"

Cordell gave Boots a bug-eyed "what the hell" look. "We're capable of getting out of here, Captain Sadiq."

"You're high-profile," said Sadiq. "Even if our government *was*

121

still infested with conspirators, it's not as though they could just make you disappear from our custody."

Boots cocked an eyebrow. "They made the *Harrow* disappear, didn't they, ma'am?"

Deathly silence fell over the bridge, save for the soft beeping of scanners and proximity alarms. She stared into the eyes of the captain's projection, hazy and luminous, hardened by decades of making life-or-death decisions for a massive crew. Sadiq looked away.

"Captain Sadiq, don't do the legal thing," said Boots. "Do the right thing."

Sadiq worked her lips for a moment, then came to meet Boots's gaze. She nodded, then looked off toward someone not in her projection.

"Mister Drake," Sadiq barked. "Our optical array seems to be malfunctioning. I'm having trouble reading the registration numbers on the *Capricious*. This is unacceptable. Send a transmission to the Green Palace to confirm our problems."

She then turned to look at Cordell. "I'm afraid our optics will be offline for the next five minutes. The *Capricious* will remain in orbit while we diagnose our troubles."

Cordell's chest swelled and he nodded his assent. Boots lowered her eyes, not wanting to embarrass her commanding officer by gawking. Sadiq winked out.

"All crew to jump stations," called Armin. "Missus Jan, lay in a course for Harvest and let's get the hell out of here."

Boots rushed to her jump couch at the edge of the bridge and buckled in.

"Coordinates locked, Captain," called Aisha.

"Mister Jan and Miss Brio report jump ready," called Armin. "The Ferrier twins, as well."

Cordell surveyed the crew and smiled. "We're about to disobey a Taitutian warship in Taitutian space. Not how I pictured my day going. Let's make it count."

The ship whined with the energies of their temporary jump drive.

"Missus Jan, execute jump."

Chapter Six

Undercover

W elcome to Harvest!" Cordell stood by the exit to the cargo hold, addressing the fully assembled crew. "Kids, you're going on a field trip today."

Whatever they were doing on that rock, Boots knew it wouldn't be pleasant.

In a bygone era, Harvest was an eidolon crystal mining moon, its veins running pink with the universe's most precious resource. It had been a bulwark of incredible technology and economic development for a huge swath of colonized worlds, and had declared sovereignty at its height, holding its valuable energy source hostage from the rest of the universe.

Then they'd waged a half-dozen wars, and the eidolon ran out. Harvest faded to a backwater world, slowly burning its wick down into obsolescence. With the loss of its heavy industries, Harvest's power vacuum was filled by gangsters and thieves. It was possible for a crew to hide out there, to trade secrets or contraband in its serpentine tunnels, to buy powerful weapons from the many shady arms dealers living in its depths.

Boots guessed her captain was planning on all of the above.

"You are to report to the address provided to your comms," called Armin. "Miss Sokol has a chit with ten thousand argents for each member of the away team. You will protect her at all costs, and you will not engage with any of the local citizenry. Do not remove your rebreathers for any reason. Avoid all imagers and optics."

"May I ask what we're doing, sir?" said Boots.

"No," said Armin, then he gave her a thin smile. "You will all follow Miss Sokol's orders until you return to the ship."

"Yes, sir," said Boots.

"Mister Vandevere, Missus Jan, and I will remain here," said Cordell, taking his place by Armin and Aisha, "to oversee the alterations to the *Capricious*'s external geometry, as well as his paint and registration. I look forward to seeing you all again. Good luck out there."

"Let's go, folks!" shouted Orna, slamming the cargo ramp control. Everyone pulled up their rebreathers as the hissing whine filled the hold.

The dock they'd chosen was deep inside one of Harvest's gaping mine shafts, obscured from the outside world by a hard-shelled warehouse designed to store exotic sport fliers. The folks waiting outside the ship looked like the sort of gawky mechanists that'd strip anything down to a metal skeleton in seconds.

Charger clanked up beside Boots, sampling the new air flooding into the *Capricious*. Boots looked up at his bloodred carapace and knit her eyebrows together. Charger's lenses snapped onto her.

"Uh..." said Boots.

"What?" Orna called out from the base of the ramp.

Boots patted her bulky clothes. They were all dressed like maintenance techs in heavy protective gear, scuffed duraplast plates covering most of their bodies. Their rebreathers left only the tops of their heads visible, mops of hair sticking out around the headband. Even Nilah, one of the most famous women in the universe, was completely unrecognizable, save for the long mohawk.

"Your bot is kind of famous," said Boots. "Maybe you should leave him here?"

Charger's limbs curled inward, recoiling. She'd somehow hurt the bot's feelings.

Orna turned to Cordell. "Captain, thoughts?"

"Miss Elsworth is right. Can you have him patrol the dock?"

"Yes, sir," she said, with some disappointment. "My tool chests are locked. Could you make sure he stays out of them?"

"Miss Sokol," said Armin with a scowl. "Your captain is not in the habit of babysitting your creations."

Orna flushed around her rebreather, the scars on her forehead going stark white as she stiffened. "Yes, sir!" Then she turned to Boots and the others. "I said let's go, punks!"

As the cargo ramp closed behind them, Boots could swear she saw the bot wave goodbye.

The away team turned toward the assemblage of Harvest mechanics that had gathered outside the *Capricious*, a motley crew if ever Boots had seen one. She restrained a sigh; this was a harebrained scheme. The second they left, these bastards would be on the horn to the Taitutian authorities, giving away their location.

The closest one slapped a hand to his heart, the symbol of Arcan allegiance. "Sixty-eighth Infantry," he said. Boots knew the unit. They'd been wiped out in the Battle of Carmine Fjord.

"ADF *Sparrow*," said a woman. That ship had been rendered asunder in the last stand. How she'd survived was beyond Boots.

"Capitol Criers," said a third, referring to an insurgency group that had moved into the hole where the Arcan capitol had once been, a symbol of their resistance.

Each man or woman in the bay was a die-hard member of

the Arcan military, or a paramilitary adjunct. They'd lost everything in the last days of the Famine War. Some of them would be wanted for war crimes—sedition against the occupying forces, terrorism, and worse.

These were Boots's orphaned siblings, and she understood perfectly why Cordell had chosen this particular hole in the wall to resupply.

"Okay, enough gabbling," said Orna. "Everyone on me. We're out of here."

Beyond the docks, the streets of Harvest were a maze of bright lights and dazzling projections. Every pleasure of the flesh clotted their vision, swarming the crew, pressing in upon them.

Except Boots.

The majority of the drugs and magic available worked on the cardioid, something that Boots lacked, so very few temptations beckoned her, save for a shot of whiskey and a roll in the hay. Malik continued along with his classic stoicism—he had a knack for frustratingly clean living. Nilah, by contrast, pointed to each attraction in turn, noting for Orna the ones she'd done, the ones she'd shunned, and the ones she still had planned. The Ferrier twins were positively overcome, their eyes at once betraying exhilaration and disgust.

Harvest was the sort of place where one could get lost forever. It shouldn't have surprised Boots to find so many Clarkesfall refugees there. Everyone was either trying to be noticed—ultra-colorful feathered dancers—or trying not to be noticed—a hawk-nosed man, fearfully wrapped in a trench coat—and they all clustered together in the alleyways.

Boots sidled up to Orna. "Where are we headed, chief?"

"Where I say," the quartermaster replied. "That's all you need to know."

"Does 'where I say' have snacks?"

"No," said Orna with smiling eyes. "And you're not going to like it."

"Great."

Boots wrinkled up her nose and scoffed. The rebreather wasn't exactly choice for situational awareness, and she found herself scanning her surroundings over and over. Her vision was filled with armies of scantily clad people of all shapes, slick-suited executives, and that same hawk-nosed man.

Again.

Perhaps he was just headed in the same direction. Boots moseyed toward Orna; it was easy to disguise her alarm behind the thick filtration mask.

"We've picked up a tail," said Boots. "Maybe find somewhere quiet."

"Copy," muttered Orna, picking up speed and pushing ahead.

Now Boots felt bad about not including Charger. Orna could've sent the bot back to pick up old hawk-nose and bring him somewhere more private. Then again, Charger would make a scene no matter where he went.

Boots dropped back in the processional to Malik. "We've got a tail, and my slinger is loaded up for hole punching, not stunning. I'd prefer the latter."

"I understand," he replied in a low whisper and cut to one side of the thoroughfare, away from the group.

Before long, the ship's doctor disappeared into the crowd, and Boots breathed a little easier knowing he had their back. Ahead of Boots, Orna peered down alleys and through tunnels. Nilah immediately took note. The Ferriers were less observant.

Orna gestured for them to follow her down a side street. Boots and the others turned in behind her; by this point, Malik had faded from view entirely. Whether he'd ducked into one of the many shops or simply found an out-of-the-way alcove, she couldn't say. Boots hoped he could still see them.

This place was far less populous, lined with shabby dwellings and garbage businesses unable to afford the rent of the main thoroughfare. The number of drugs on offer grew exponentially more diverse, and infinitely more sketchy. There were sensory magi, capable of neurological stimuli so potent that addiction was a foregone conclusion. Once they'd gotten someone hooked, they'd coax away all of a person's passwords and bank data, then fry their brains with pure bliss. This side street reminded Boots of the place where she'd first gotten rolled for her paragon crystal—waking up with a throbbing head and an empty bank account.

Orna turned down another, darker blind alley.

Inside, they gathered into a group and waited. Boots could only hope Malik had found a way to sneak up on their pursuer. Their tail turned the corner, immediately saw he'd been made, and decided to run. A smoking purple hand landed on his shoulder, and arcane energies crackled into the hawk-nosed man. He opened his mouth as though to speak, but his eyes rolled back in his head, and he went slack.

Malik caught him, then dragged the fellow into the alley.

"Anyone got any bindings?" asked Orna.

"Fresh out," said Boots, and no one in the group offered anything up.

"Great," said the quartermaster. "Going to be tough to interrogate him."

Boots considered their options. On the one hand, they could leave hawk-nose sprawled out in the alley, unconscious. The only problem was that he'd awaken eventually, and he must've followed them because he knew who they were. They could try to drag him back to the other Fallen at the dock, but they might be spotted, and who knew what those desperate men and women might do to him.

Alister crept over to the sleeping man and peered over him before rummaging through his pockets.

"Careful," said Jeannie.

"He's *asleep*, sis," said Alister, patting his chest down. "He can't hurt us."

Boots was impressed by his frisking skills. Alister wasn't shy in any way with another person's body, and Jeannie joined in. They treated hawk-nose like a coroner would treat a corpse—or perhaps like a butcher would treat a piece of meat.

"Hello, there..." Alister pulled out a pocket slinger, one round, short range, from a hidden holster by the man's shoe.

"You think the Children have already spotted us?" asked Nilah.

Boots scowled down at the unconscious man. "If that's the case...we can't allow him to report back."

"Maybe," said Malik, "or maybe he's a petty criminal, or a journalist. We are people of note, you understand."

"With a hidden slinger?" she asked.

"It *is* kind of a crappy one, though," said Orna. "I'm all about some violence, but, you know...he could just be worried about getting jacked down here."

"We've got a lot of enemies," said Boots. "This guy could've been waiting to plug us. If he wakes up—"

"I was followed by journos all the time," urged Nilah. "You can't just murder him."

"Okay," said Boots. "If you're going to shoot down my idea, give me a better one."

"Well..." Nilah fumbled with a plan. "If we leave him here in the alley to sleep it off..."

"He wakes up and knows we came through here," said Orna. "We...can't afford that. I hate to say it, but I'm with Boots."

There was a flash of anger on Nilah's face, but it faded as she stared down at the fellow. She opened her mouth to make a case, but nothing came out.

"Doc?" Boots asked.

"We were followed in Harvest by an armed man," Malik replied, stroking his chin. "He might also work for the Taitutians. They want to keep tabs on us, too."

Boots crossed her arms. "Except they're full of leaks, and we're basically enemies of the state. But you're right—killing one of their agents would definitely provoke a response."

"Let's just read him," said Alister.

"No!" interjected Jeannie. "I mean, we don't have the right setup."

Alister rolled up his sleeves, straddling the man's body. "I'll rip the memories out of his head, then. Hold him down."

Jeannie put a hand on her brother's shoulder. "If he resists you, you won't be able to—"

He shot her an annoyed look. "I'm a lot more powerful than you. Quit treating me like we're back in... *Quit treating me like a child.*"

Jeannie took a step back, shaken at his sudden outburst.

So the two of you aren't perfectly synced after all.

Swallowing her trepidation, Boots knelt down, unsnapping her slinger holster in case she needed it in a hurry. She wrapped both hands around the man's right wrist, and Orna did the same on the other side. Malik and Nilah pinned his legs.

Alister traced his reader's mark, holding it in one hand. With the other, he gave the unconscious man a brutal backhand. Hawk-nose's eyes fluttered open in shock, then horror at seeing his restrained limbs. He bucked helplessly against Boots and the others, and Boots crushed his forearm to the ground with her knee.

"Why are you following us?" Alister growled, placing his spell against hawk-nose's forehead.

To Boots's surprise, the man began to speak. His voice came out hoarse and panicked.

"A mellow man lives near the graves, and five chairs at his table saves. From noon to noon and night to night, he hosts the ghosts to their delight."

"Mnemonics," Alister grunted, tracing a larger glyph, which sizzled with dark magenta light. He strained, pushing the spell into hawk-nose's head by grabbing a handful of hair. "Why were you following us?"

Hawk-nose writhed and began reciting faster and louder in a panic. Jeannie rushed to his side, speaking the man's poem back to him, a half-step behind his cadence. Her words echoed with his, and hawk-nose began to stutter with confusion.

"Why were you following us?" Alister demanded once more, sweat beading on his brow. He wrapped his hands around the man's throat, choking out his poem.

Hawk-nose looked up at Boots, terrified and red-faced.

Alister grinned madly. "Money. Of course it's money, but whose?"

"Let him speak," urged Jeannie. "I can't recite if—"

Tears rolled down hawk-nose's cheeks, and in a panic he recited, *"A m-mellow man l-lives—"*

Alister leaned into him, their eyes locked upon each other, touching foreheads, their lips close enough for a kiss, and whispered, "Your thoughts are mine."

Hawk-nose's eyes went even wider for a split second, then he subsided, shaking and sobbing. His lips began to move. "Don't—"

Then Alister yanked Boots's slinger free and blasted his brains into the pavement.

She jumped back, barely avoiding the splash of blood. "Whoa! Whoa! Whoa! What the everloving—"

The assembled party gasped in horror, backing away from the

shuddering corpse and the ginger perched atop it. Only Jeannie remained at his side, her disappointment palpable. After a moment, Alister stood, brushed himself off, and held out Boots's slinger for her, grip-first.

His whole body shook, his skin was pale, and fury clamped shut his jaw. Slowly, Boots leaned forward and took her weapon, clicking down the safety and returning it to her side.

With a shuddering breath, he said, "Thanks."

"Did you have to kill him?" Nilah breathed.

He affixed her with a stare so cold that Boots nearly stepped between them. "The short answer is: he was a Child of the Singularity."

"And the long answer?" asked Boots.

His lips pulled back in a snarl. "I didn't need the long answer."

Even Orna looked a bit stunned, but she composed herself and said, "Show's over. We've got to get to the surgeon, so fall in."

Nilah's blood had run even colder at the mention of a surgeon. She couldn't imagine a single medical procedure she'd want to have on Harvest. When they'd arrived at their destination, however, Nilah was surprised at the warmth and opulence of it all. They'd stepped off the dirty streets of Harvest and into sunbaked stucco and sparkling water features. Floating silver chimes whispered melodically across the ceiling as thick mahogany discs drifted into them. The lobby of this doctor's office was as pleasant as any treatment center on Taitu.

Nilah nudged her girlfriend. "What, uh, sort of doctor is this, love?"

Orna pulled off her rebreather and smiled back. "You're not going to like him."

The others shuffled in behind, pulling off their rebreathers and staring at the decor. Though everyone had been treated as heroes in the interposing year since they returned the *Harrow*, most of them would be unfamiliar with this level of luxury. A clean, woolen scent drifted past Nilah's nose, that of her mother's dresses on a Green Belt summer day. Only one magic cleaned while enchanting everything with nostalgic scents—the hotelier's mark. This surgeon must've been pretty rich to have one on call.

At the far end of the room, a pair of ornately carved wooden doors opened up, revealing a woman in a shimmering gown. Her smoky eyes overshadowed full, dark lips and black hair like crude oil, spilling down her alabaster shoulders. The entrance had an obvious theatrical quality to it—the newcomer wanted to be seen in her entirety. Nilah's heart leapt at the sight of her, a guilty little jump in the wake of her recent fights with Orna.

"Hey," said Orna, unfazed. "We're looking for Checo DosSantos."

"Did you have an appointment?" asked the woman, her voice smooth and sonorous, interweaving with the tones of the chimes.

"Yeah," said Orna, "and we've got his cash, so we'd like to get underway. Where is he?"

"I am they." The woman smiled. "I am Checo."

"Oh," said Orna. "How do you want us to talk to you?"

"I prefer they, them. Now, if you'll please follow."

Checo motioned the group to follow with a languid gesture from their long, slender arms. Nilah was accustomed to seeing beautiful people in her racing days, but Checo had a supernatural attractiveness that baffled her—and set her on edge. The graceful, musical person summoned their charges inside, like a light beckons prey into the belly of an anglerfish.

As Checo turned away, gliding ghostly down the hall, Nilah caught Orna's arm and held her back, away from the others. "Okay, babe, it was fun being coy, but I'm going to need you to tell me what kind of doctor this is."

"She's a sculptor," said Orna. "We're here to pick up a few disguises."

That explained the alien beauty, the strange length of Checo's bones, even the name. Checo had remade themself to be whatever they wanted, pulling and twisting their body into an artistic interpretation of a human. The sculptor's mark was one of the rarest of all.

"No! No bleeding way!" Nilah hissed. "You must be daft if you think I'm letting them muck about with my bones!"

"Babe," said Orna, "we're going to show up on facial geometry scanners all over the galaxy. We can't wear rebreathers forever. You're a rich kid from Taitu. Surely you've done some work."

"Yeah, but just a nose tweak or something! Nothing like a full disguise. They're going to mess up my face!"

Orna crossed her arms and frowned, obviously watching Checo's backside as they receded down the hall. "You literally gaped when you saw how pretty they were. You'll be fine."

Nilah shook her head. "No. You're new to this fame thing. You don't understand: our faces are worth money. We've got agents and publicity deals all tied up in our appearances."

Even as she said it, she knew it was silly. A new face would be invaluable if they were going to deal with the Children of the Singularity.

"Yeah. Our faces are going to be worth a lot more if we make the most-wanted list. Besides, we can put it back after we're done."

Nilah looked into Orna's eyes and bit her lip. She knew Orna was right, but she couldn't escape the feeling that she was about to make a terrible mistake. "Please, babe. I really, really can't do this."

Orna softened, taking Nilah by the shoulders and pulling her in close. Her voice was low, and Nilah rested her head against her girlfriend's chest. "This is for your own good. I don't know what Cap's plan is, but it's going to be dangerous." She pushed Nilah back. "I...look, uh...I know we've been snippy, but no matter what you look like, I'm still going to love you."

Nilah searched the face she'd fallen so hard for, memorizing the rifts of white scars dotting its surface, the blue eyes like liquid fire, the lips that had been so shockingly soft among Orna's hardened features. She ran a finger along Orna's cheek.

"I know...I just like waking up to this. Will you promise to put the scars back?"

Orna winked. "Only if you do."

"Everything okay?" asked Malik, leaning out the door. "Doctor DosSantos is waiting for you."

"Yeah," said Nilah. "Just jitters, mate. Let's go."

The interior of the office was even more peaceful, with low lighting and deep hues of pink washing the walls. Checo led them to a cozy waiting area filled with soft pillows and couches, as well as a low pulsing thrum. Sweet botanical scents filled the air, which was a little too warm for the maintenance gear Nilah was wearing. It all struck Nilah as very womb-like.

Checo went to a hidden panel in the wall and pulled out a pile of silken robes, handing one to each of them in turn.

As Nilah took her robe, she asked, "Can we, perhaps, turn up the aircon just a touch, love?"

Checo smiled politely, and up close, their face was disturbingly perfect. "I'm afraid this is the optimal temperature for molding flesh. You'll be more comfortable once you're in robes."

The doctor turned to the others. "For those with a need for modesty, there are dressing rooms to your right. Just press your palm to the wall, and they'll open up."

Boots and Orna took her up on the offer, disappearing into the hidden dressing rooms. Malik was quick to remove his maintenance gear, but the twins were even faster—startlingly comfortable with their bodies.

Nilah removed her clothes, and it was like cracking into a crate of old laundry. She'd grown sweaty in the maintenance garb, and she reluctantly donned the soft robe. It had a lovely feel, and she hated to soil it.

Checo stood stock-still, hands folded in front of themself. When everyone was robed and rejoined, the doctor cleared their throat.

"Right," said Orna, producing the chit with an unsigned bank account number in it. "There's a hundred large in there. Captain Lamarr sends his regards with the tip."

"Unexpected generosity," said Checo, taking the chit in their delicate fingers.

"Yeah, so, uh…let's do a good job today," said Orna.

Checo cocked their head. "My rates are usually ten times what your captain has paid. Frankly, I've taken you on as clients in gratitude and curiosity."

Nilah winced. *Great, darling. Insult the person who's going to be twisting us up like clay.*

"This is a transformative, safe place," said Checo. "Though you are here to disguise yourself, honesty is appreciated. If there is anything you desire, any way in which you are out of harmony with your visage, I urge you to request it of me. However, Captain Lamarr was quite explicit that you be made plain of face, so my more—exotic—services are off the table."

"I'd like a firmer butt," said Malik. "My wife would back me up if she was here."

"No body mods. Six faces will be quite taxing on my powers," Checo said. "Now, who's first?"

"I'll go," said Boots. "Already pretty plain, so you don't got much work, Doc."

"I disagree, but we'll see what we can do for you," said Checo. "Right this way."

Checo pressed their palm to the wall and it parted like a curtain, revealing a bright back room. They ushered Boots inside, and the wall closed behind the pair.

An hour passed, and Nilah did her best to relax, which should've been aided by the comfortable surroundings. They found a nook in the wall containing libations and food, which Orna ordered them not to touch, since they could be poisoned, and the ship wasn't paying for them. The Ferrier twins cruised the Link, watching a learning series on the history of the Prokarthic expeditions. Malik and Orna called up a game of knights from the projector, where he proceeded to crush her every ten minutes. Orna's lack of patience was anything but a tactical advantage.

Nilah searched out the replays of the latest Ultra F series to see how Kristof had done. His new drive wasn't the same marvel as the Lang Hyper 8, and his new team hadn't yet flourished under his ownership. Still, he had a few podiums this season, and they were on track to place third in the Constructor Crown, so it wasn't all bad. The rocky starts would go away, and he'd be dominating in a season or two.

Young teams were always a dicey proposition. For a galaxy-destroying monster, Claire Asby had done a bloody good job with Lang Autosport.

"All right, then," came Checo's voice, and Nilah looked up to see them pushing Boots out of the back room in a glider chair.

The first thing she noticed was Boots's hair, now shoulder-length and umber, with a slight curl to it. Boots's face stunned Nilah. She was at once familiar and foreign: her brow softened, her nose thinned, her cheeks full like the curves of an apple, her ears flattened.

"The drugs will wear off soon. She'll need to rest until then," said Checo as Malik helped them move Boots to one of the many cushioned couches.

"Drugs?" asked Nilah.

Checo nodded. "In spite of my considerable arcane skill, bones do not like to be pulled. Not to worry. I have a wide array of cocktails to suit your preferred method of relaxation. Next, please."

"I'll go," said Malik.

And so it went: Malik came out looking even younger, the Ferriers untwinned with freckles erased, and then Orna.

No amount of diversion could take Nilah's thoughts away from Orna. What if they never got their own faces back? What if Orna wanted to stay this way? What if she couldn't recognize her girlfriend anymore?

The rear walls parted, revealing Checo and Orna. The doctor pushed their subject over to Nilah for a closer look. Gone was Orna's midnight hair, replaced with a spiky mop of silver. The scars all over her face and arms had been massaged away, and the quartermaster's nose had been shaped to an upturned button. All clues to the many breaks and contusions over the years were wiped out in the span of an hour.

Without those beatings, Orna looked luminous, almost childlike.

Checo stretched a hand toward Nilah, and in their soft voice said, "Your turn, my dear."

Nilah looked to the others, in various states of recovery, and sighed. She had no one to hide behind now. She arose and followed the doctor inside.

The bright lights blinded her after so long in the peaceful antechamber. A rack of clear vials, silver caps shining, lined one of the walls. An operating chair filled the center of the room, with several lights on long, thin arms snaking toward Nilah for an eager embrace.

"I've wanted to meet you for some time, Nilah Brio," said the doctor, taking Nilah's robe from her shoulders and gesturing for her to sit.

Nilah gingerly settled into the chair, her stomach in knots. The lights stared at every inch of her body, bringing forth every hair, mole, and freckle on her dark skin. "A fan, are we?"

"An employee, I'm afraid," said Checo, drawing a sliding stool up under themself and moving close into Nilah. "I worked for the Fixers in another life."

"Oh, uh, sorry about your mates...you know...killing each other."

"No," said Checo, gently pawing at Nilah's cheeks, her chin, her neck. "I'm sorry we provided you such poor service. I hate that for you."

Nilah mustered a smile. "It's all right. If they'd gotten me off Gantry Station and delivered me to Lang like I asked, I'd be dead."

"Psychotropic or sleepy?"

"Sorry, love?"

Checo turned and took two vials from the wall. "The drugs. Preference?"

"Might be nice to have a bit of fun. Feeling a touch nervous," she replied, taking the proffered liquid and uncorking it. It smelled of cherries and warm sugar. Nilah downed it in one, and it hit her stomach with a surprising burn. "So you were a different person with the Fixers?"

"I always am," said Checo, wiping clean Nilah's skin with an antiseptic towel. "I'm afraid I've quite forgotten my own face. I've only kept the masculine name my parents gave me."

Horror crept into Nilah's heart. If Checo had lost their own identity...

"Don't worry, dear heart," said Checo. "We'll be making a backup."

With that, a bright flash filled the room, and Nilah knew she'd been scanned from head to toe.

"Now," said Checo, "let's get started. Any requests?"

Nilah considered it. "I can't lose my scars, please. Not the ones on my face."

"Ah. The diametric opposite of your girlfriend's request. She told me she wanted to be as beautiful as you."

"She already is," said Nilah, and little flutters caressed her flesh like the beating of birds' wings. The drugs had started to take hold.

"You two are so sweet. We'll see what we can do about those scars," said Checo, their face beginning to stretch, eyes moving apart, neck lengthening like a noble crane. Checo traced their glyph, round like a setting sun, and Nilah slipped into clouds.

"Have a wonderful flight, and I'll see you in an hour."

Nilah came to her senses to the fascinated stares of strangers. Her heart skipped a beat until she realized that these were her crewmates, and she was still in Checo's den.

"Projection," she mumbled through her dry mouth, "mirror, please."

Hidden lenses across the den focused in on her face and spun a copy into existence before her.

The woman depicted was pretty in the most traditional sense, plump lips, shadowed eyes, a pert nose—utterly, blandly consumable by marketing departments across all of space. Long plaits of blue hair spilled from her head, with a hard-cut line for bangs. The only exception: three short, blue brushstrokes on her right cheek, just under her eye. It was a tiny tattoo, barely noticeable, but it made a world of difference to Nilah.

She found Orna again and gave her a worried look. "Do I look bad?" she asked.

The newly youthful quartermaster smirked. "Doable. Let's get back to the ship."

"Oh, Nilah," called Checo, and Nilah turned to see the doctor standing in the open doorway to the operating room. "I've covered over your dermaluxes with a thin layer of skin. They were too distinctive. How strong are you with them?"

Nilah looked down at her arms, dismayed to find her signature tattoos completely obscured. A faint blue haze emanated from just under the flesh, and she shut them off. "I can push them pretty far into the infrared spectrum."

"Good," said Checo. "Then hopefully the opposite is true. If you need to get that skin off, ramp the light into the microwave spectrum."

Nilah's eyes widened. "That sounds...unpleasant."

Checo nodded. "It will be. Please show yourselves out, and do travel safely."

That night cycle, after they departed Harvest, Cordell and Armin called for Boots and Nilah to join them in the captain's quarters. He hadn't stopped giving Boots a double take since she'd returned with her new face, and it was getting unbearable.

When Boots arrived, she found the others seated around a small table, a half-full bottle of brandy on offer.

Cordell blinked at her again, and Boots snapped at him, "Would you stop that?"

He laughed. "I'm sorry, it's just that curly hair is a weird look on you."

"At least they didn't give me bangs like Nilah over here."

Nilah shook her head. "Please not today, darling. I've scarcely gotten over the shock of it, myself."

"Okay, Captain, this is the part where you tell us what we'll be doing with our new faces," said Boots.

Armin placed the stolen data cubes from the archives onto the captain's table. "With a lot of work, I was able to decrypt these. Sorry it took so long, but I'm nowhere near as powerful as Kinnard was."

Yeah, I miss him, too.

"We're looking at two substantial pieces of information, both of which have expiration dates," said Cordell. "Let's start with the Forscythe thread: the Children of the Singularity have been infiltrated, and Boots's stolen case files indicate the Special Branch is behind it. When Miss Sokol iced Forscythe, she killed the buyer, not the seller. That person might make contact with the Children and negotiate a second sale."

"If that happens," said Armin, "we can assume the double agent is dead. This person likely has lots of information on our adversary, and we want it."

Boots folded her arms and leaned back in her chair. "So what's 'Pinnacle'? That was in Forscythe's message, right?"

"In good time," said Cordell. "The other piece of intel pertains to Maslin Durand's case file. Turns out, unlike the other bagmen, Durand didn't just have unsigned bank accounts. He also maintained a small vault on Mercandatta Station."

Armin nodded. "The Special Branch has been surveilling him for some time. They know which box, how many times he visited, and that he was alone when he made whatever drops he made. That means he was likely the only one with access, because no one else has shown up yet."

"And Mercandatta is outside of Taitutian jurisdiction," said Cordell, "so the Special Branch can't beat us to it without creating an intergalactic incident with the IGF. If their intel is to be believed, the Children either don't know about it or can't get inside. There's a real chance that we can get to the contents before the Children figure out how."

"And you think these leads hold the keys to the Money Mill?" asked Nilah.

"The Children are bound to want both leads," said Cordell with a laugh, "so I want them first, damn it. Mister Vandevere, let's talk mission parameters."

Tapping a few buttons on the table, Armin dimmed the lights. "Miss Brio, your martial prowess is known and respected among this crew. That'll come in handy where you're going."

Nilah straightened. "To Pinnacle?"

"*The* Pinnacle, yes." Armin tapped a hidden switch on the table and the room's projectors spun a galaxy into being before them. "Straight into the mouth of the beast. Meta-analysis of the data cubes yielded seventeen long-range active Taitutian surveillance orders on this world here." He gestured to the projection, and a small planet in orbit around a gas giant lit up. "Hammerhead."

"Does it have a lot of sharks or something?" Boots chuckled, and Armin gave her a nasty look.

"I can tell you what it lacks, which is much daylight. There are thirty minutes of sun in each of its four-hour days. It's a homestead world," he continued. "No major jurisdiction, no registered residents, but there is a settlement on it." Armin pulled the planet closer and spun it, revealing a tiny red dot on one side.

"That's the Pinnacle?" asked Boots.

"The case file called it 'Point of Interest A,'" said Armin.

"Catchy," said Boots.

"We now know this is a training camp for the Children of the Singularity," said Cordell. "According to the case file, if you can find it, you can join up."

"That's it?" asked Nilah. "Hardly a secret."

"Not quite," said Armin. "In the time since I've started aggregating Link activity on the Children, I've never heard mention of this place or seen any other references to it. The closest thing I could find was their constant refrain of 'Only the strongest fighters can ascend the mountain.' It wasn't until I got this dossier from Boots's stolen data cubes that I was able to put a couple of clues together."

Nilah folded her arms. "What kinds of clues?"

"There are a ton of references hidden in their mythology," said Armin. "Different significant numbers that translated to galactic coordinates. You'd have to be obsessed to figure out that code."

"So we're going to smash up one of their bases?" asked Boots, hopeful.

"Don't be so bloodthirsty. Rescue op, remember?" said Cordell. "The insider was able to return some information before they were cut off: this settlement moves around every so often, holding ten 'ascensions' before disappearing to the next location. That's probably how they keep people from simply sharing the coordinates on the Link."

Boots frowned. "What's an ascension?"

"No clue," said Cordell, "but the intel report indicated that they might move soon, and it's already months old. We might get to Hammerhead and find nothing."

The projection pushed in on the landscape, the edges of the planet peeling away to show a topographical map of the settlement. There were two structures, one at the bottom of a mountain, and the other at the top.

"We believe the lower structure is the recruiting station," said Armin. "That's where we'll insert Miss Brio's team, undercover as recruits."

"And that's why you need my Flicker?" asked Nilah.

"We don't know what weapons you'd be allowed to keep, and you're the best martial artist on the crew," said Cordell. "In a worst-case scenario, you're not completely unarmed. You'll have Malik running control and the twins as backup. Your job will be to infiltrate the camp and get any information you can find, most importantly, keep your eyes on the double agent."

Malik nodded at her. "I'll be living in a blind near the base for observation. I'll also have contact with the ship, so you can report problems to me through a hidden transmitter."

"Looks cold," said Boots.

"The ambient temperature is below freezing," said Armin. "I don't imagine the good doctor will be taking in the sights. It'll be a long, boring surveillance, only suited to someone who can remain still for many hours at a time."

Malik smiled. "I can enter a trance, so I'm the ideal candidate."

"What about Orna?" asked Nilah.

Cordell shook his head. "I'm afraid we'll need her for Boots's mission."

Boots jammed her hands into her pockets. "And what might that be, sir?"

"We're going to break into a bank."

Chapter Seven

Discord

N ilah's quarters had become less than hospitable after hearing the captain's plans.

"Quit being a dumbass. I'm going to talk to him," said Orna, slamming down her conduit iron. Their shared workbench shook, and the meter-long disperser cannon nearly tumbled from its mounting bracket.

"You're going to burn yourself," said Nilah, "working in your skivvies like that."

"My quarters, my comfort. I do what I want." Then she pointed to the copious scars across her bare leg. "Not like they were pretty before. Wish Checo would've healed them."

The quartermaster had hit a snag in her designs; the disperser rifle still wasn't working. It'd put her in a foul mood for the past few hours, which hurt, since they'd be splitting up soon.

Nilah sat up in bed, hugging the sheets for warmth. "No, babes, let's not talk to the captain. It'll be all right. I'll have Malik working control, and the twins are supposed to have some kind of fighting experience. It's like the captain said, they'll probably take our weapons, but we won't be unarmed."

Orna stood up and snatched her pants from the nearby dresser, yanking them on over her legs. "That's crap! You've never seen them fight!"

"I haven't seen them—not—fight."

But in truth, Orna was right. Nilah knew next to nothing about the capabilities of the twins, and now she'd be relying upon them for life-or-death protection. It wasn't exactly ideal.

"I should be with you," said Orna. "That's that. We can do these missions one at a time, with the full support of the entire crew."

"It could take weeks for us to build up their trust, and we can't all go in there together or it'll be suspicious," said Nilah. "Besides, this is perishable intelligence—we don't know how long the Children will remain on Hammerhead. We've got two good leads, and we need to take them both."

"No. Unacceptable."

But when Orna returned an hour later, she was pale as a ghost, and it took Nilah a couple of tries to get her to open up about what was said. Cordell had ripped her a new one, and when Orna rose to meet his ire, he'd doubled down, threatening to eject the quartermaster from her longtime home. When Nilah scoffed that Cordell wouldn't do that, Orna simply replied, "You don't know him like I do."

Of course Nilah didn't. She wasn't a refugee, after all.

Orna was far colder than Nilah would've liked during their last few cycles together.

The ship came out of the Flow a day later above Hammerhead. Nilah regarded the world through the bridge windows, and cold fear crept into her stomach. A hard shadow cut across its surface, cast by the methane gas giant, churning beyond like an ocean. The shade creature of the archives came stalking back into her memories.

"Prepare for planetfall. Skids down in twenty," said Aisha.

"Mister Jan," said Cordell, "take Miss Brio and the twins and report to the cargo bay. I want this to be a seamless drop—down and up. It's a long way to the jump gate, and without the dump, we're going to need to get underway ASAP."

Malik nodded. "Yes, Captain."

They followed Malik to the bay, where Orna lay waiting with the portable shelter folded up in its transit case. It was a larger version of the ones they'd used on Blix, with full climate systems and pressurization. Nilah and Orna had spent the previous night cycle checking every seal and valve, making sure that Malik wouldn't freeze to death in there.

"There's atmosphere, but it's thin," said Orna. "So don't over-exert yourself."

Nilah nodded. "I won't, love."

"I wish I could leave Charger with you, but…once I'm out of range—"

Nilah stood on her tiptoes and kissed her girlfriend, silencing her. "You're worrying too much. Malik will tell you if we get in trouble."

Orna's lips curled into a frown, a rare moment of fear. "This sucks. You've got to come back, all right?"

The ship shook underfoot.

"Got some storm chop," came Aisha over the loudspeaker. "All crew strap in."

They made their way to the crash couches, where the turbulence gave their internal gravity drives a run for their money. The *Capricious* rattled and bucked, and Orna's tools banged like gongs inside their chests. And with a great thump, all motion stopped.

"Touchdown," came Armin's voice. "Mission crew disembark."

Orna dragged the transit case to the cargo bay door, where she mashed the button to open the belly of the ship. Freezing wind screamed into the bay, and Nilah was glad of her frost gear for this mission.

"Don't do anything I wouldn't do," Orna shouted over the gale.

Nilah slid her hands around Orna's hips. "Give us a smile, darling."

Orna gave her a weak grin, her confidence obviously fake.

Nilah kissed her once more. "That's the spirit, love. See you in two weeks."

She pulled up her muffler, donned her goggles, and stepped off the ship onto the ice of a night world. Behind her, Orna stared the whole time until the ramp closed. The four crew members took a knee and kept their heads down as the *Capricious* blasted off, rushing into the sky.

"Okay," shouted Malik, straining to be heard. His voice was so much less soothing when he yelled. "Let's get the station set up so you can get to the base camp."

They toiled through the short day into the frosty night, cold digging into Nilah's bones. She wasn't sure how much of this she'd be able to take, and Malik was supposed to live out in it.

At long last, they got the shelter operational and strapped down with its climate system running at full. They all piled inside, taking heavy breaths of the hot, oxygen-enriched air. Nilah shucked her jacket into one of the corners, letting her arms and chest thaw out.

There was scarcely enough room inside for one person, let alone four, and they rode out the brief night in exceptionally cozy quarters. Once the sun began to warm their front door, Nilah knew it was time to leave.

"I want reports once per cycle," said Malik. "Give me a heartbeat code, at least."

Nilah opened the case of concealed transmitters, a set of false-teeth retainers with a TX button on the roof, then mounted one inside her mouth. They were remarkably lifelike, though they made her look a little too smiley for her tastes.

She clicked the button with her tongue and spoke. "Echo echo one two three."

Malik tapped his comm. "We're good."

Nilah nodded. "Okay, then. Jeannie, Alister, what say you?"

"Just happy to be here," said Alister. "Ready to stick the knife in these bastards."

Jeannie's expression was one of worry as she pulled up her face mask to shield her nose from the cold.

The twins tested their mouthpieces, and everything worked as planned. Next came the ten-kilometer hike to the base camp. Nilah and the twins slogged through the snow for hours, coming into view of the station just as another sunset troubled Hammerhead's horizon. The building was a massive gray slab, windowless, save for a thick security door in the front.

She clicked her transmitter. "Hunter Two here. Come in Sleepy."

"Sleepy here," said Malik. "Go ahead."

"We're in sight of the base camp. Will transmit heartbeat once we're inside."

"Copy, Hunter Two. Good luck."

The three of them approached the structure with hands in full view, attempting to look as nonthreatening as possible.

In the coming sunset, the ice turned the same swirling azure as the gas giant filling their sky. No one emerged from the building to greet them. No drones or autoturrets showed up, slingers ablaze. There was only the howling wind, sparkling ice, and the flat, gray slab at the base of the mountain.

What if it wasn't a recruiting station, but an unmanned storage facility? The intelligence reports could be wrong, or outdated. Nilah's nerves went as cold as the air when she considered the possibility of freezing to death outside those thick doors.

When they were a hundred meters out, and night darkened the horizon, yellow warning flashers went off all over the front of the building. Servomotors on the thick warehouse door groaned, and it shook free the crust of ice. The open portal yawned before them, spilling white light across the ground, and Nilah doubled her speed. As cold as the day might be, the night was so much worse, and its frigid shadow fell across her back.

At last, they struggled inside, huffing. A half-dozen slingers leveled upon them, the *clink* of slides and bolts filling their ears. Nilah and the twins raised their hands and straightened up, looking over the assembled guards.

These weren't professional soldiers by any stretch. Their fire discipline was weak, and the closest one held her slinger so poorly that Nilah could have snatched it from her if she wanted. They wore plain gray work clothes, but had no patches on their uniforms or other identifying marks.

"Names," one of them barked.

"Hope," said Nilah. "Hope Aven."

"I'm Moira Connelly," said Jeannie, "and this is my brother, David."

The guard's finger wrapped around the trigger. Nilah hoped this amateur didn't blow her face off. "Why are you here?"

"Because we have a destiny," Nilah answered, parroting some of the Children's garbage she'd read.

"Handles?" asked the guard. She lowered her slinger, but the others didn't follow suit.

Nilah blinked. "What?"

"What do you call yourselves on the Link?"

There hadn't been enough time to build up any credibility in the various Link communities. Nilah's heart slammed at the request; she wished they'd orchestrated a better presence online.

There was nothing to be done for it. She'd just have to disguise herself with confidence and swagger.

"You know the difference between those losers on the Link and us?" asked Nilah, grinning. "We've made it here and they haven't, chum. We're not casuals. The Link is for pretenders."

"Check the database. Run their faces," said the lead guard, and one of her soldiers in the rear hustled away.

"Database?" Nilah asked.

"Of unwelcome faces," said the guard. "Pray you're not in it."

Tense minutes passed. Nilah glanced about at her surroundings. The walls were bare, save for the rivets and bolts, and the occasional control panel. Just around the corner, she spied a row of cots, as well as some curious onlookers, similarly dressed in drab gray uniforms.

The runner returned.

"They're clear," he muttered to the point woman.

The lead guard smiled. "Looks like you fared better than the last group."

Nilah quirked her lips. "Oh?"

"Yeah. Couple of Taitutian intel folks never made it home."

She forced herself to smile. They had a database of agents. Was it only Taitu, or were other governments compromised? Had they already taken out the double agent?

One of the guards holstered her slinger and fetched a few handheld devices from a nearby cabinet, passing them out to two others in the group. A flick of their thumbs later, buzzing filled the air.

The lead guard grinned. "Time for a shave, Children."

At least Nilah wouldn't have bangs anymore.

Boots stepped off the *Capricious* and into the urmurex maze of Mercandatta Station. Black streets striped the glass landscape, and even in the exhaust of the docks, the whole place carried the overly crisp scent of too-filtered air. They'd arrived at lunchtime, and suited people filed through the walkways like waddles of penguins.

Maslin Durand was a shady fellow, which meant he needed a shady series of bank accounts and a far shadier deposit box. There was nowhere better to store secrets than the Intergalactic Fiduciary Bank, the home of the unsigned fund. IGF was the de facto standard for everything from corporate crime to organized crime, but Boots could scarcely tell from the ultra-clean urban sprawl before her.

She already hated this place.

The Taitutians hadn't been able to get into Maslin's vault, despite their intel, because breaking in would constitute government-sponsored espionage, and the IGF was no joke. They'd come hard with tariffs, blockades, seizures, and account freezes. The *Capricious*, on the other hand, had no governmental concerns. If they were caught, they'd probably be executed instead of setting off a pan-galactic conflict.

"Get a move on," said Orna, coming abreast of her. "I want to get off this hulk and back to Hammerhead."

"Don't have to tell me twice," said Boots.

Orna touched her circlet. "Charger is on guard duty. Zipper as well."

Cargo pilots always hated being called zipperjocks, but Aisha seemed to relish the title. Boots couldn't figure her out. "Wish she'd had surgery, too. Could use the help. Boss and Prince will be fine."

She wouldn't use their names—had to assume there would be some microphones around the station.

"Nah. Pilot always needs to keep the ship hot."

"Ain't like we're going in there shooting, I guess."

They started down the pathway toward the great sprawl of corporate obelisks. The lower levels of the banking buildings were reserved for shops, and when Boots peered into the windows, she saw some of the top brands from all over the galaxy. Each outlet was like its own little world, consummately boutique and bespoke. They were the sort of places that sold exactly twelve items, each of which were displayed like works of art. Boots guessed they were similarly priced. Periodically, one of the shopkeeps would emerge into the thoroughfare to flag down a person.

"What's that about?" grumbled Orna.

"High-value targets," said Boots, jerking her head toward the corner of the nearest building. "Look at all the lenses around here. Ten to one odds: if we had our old faces, these salespeople would be all over us."

"Good riddance, then."

"Your new face is a good look for you, by the way, even if it makes you look like a child."

Orna snorted. "Yeah, my girl liked it. You ought to keep the brown hair."

"No way. I'll end up pinching it when I snap on my fishbowl." Boots mimed locking her flight-suit helmet into place.

They passed block after block, checking the signs as they went: One-A, One-B, Two-A, Two-B. Before long, Boots's legs were aching. Farmwork on Hopper's Hope had gotten her in better shape, but not by much. Their disguises were uncomfortable— the sort of clothes these stuck-up business folks would wear—and they did little to make the walk more pleasant. At least Mercandatta was chilly, so Boots could wear long sleeves and gloves to cover her arm. The metal prosthesis would've stuck out like a sore thumb: a shiny, silver sore thumb.

"Which block was it again?" Boots asked, trying not to sound winded.

"Maslin's vault is in Twenty-Six-D," said Orna.

"Let's grab a ride," said Boots, stopping before one of the Hansom Consoles and keying in their destination. It calculated the fare: 153 argents.

"That's robbery," said Orna.

"Everyone here is rich as hell," said Boots. "That's the price. I bet you're going to love signing the refuel receipt, Miss Quartermaster."

"I say we rebuild the jump dump and skip out on the bill."

"You can do that?"

"I mean, technically," said Orna. "But it's not a good idea. It'd almost certainly split the ship in half."

Boots ordered the taxi, and the service was quick. A sleek black flier touched down before them, its doors sliding open in total silence. The inside was unlike any cab Boots had ever taken, with calfskin seats and flamewood inlays. The console in the center of the cabin silently pulsed, awaiting payment before any service would be rendered. Boots pulled out her paragon crystal and twisted one of the facets until it was set to her unsigned account. The crystal flashed an acknowledgment, and she tapped it to the cash pad.

"Lucky you've got that thing," Orna said as the doors hissed closed behind her. "No glyphs to identify you."

Yeah. Lucky.

"I'll be expecting a reimbursement," grunted Boots, stashing it back in her pocket.

Boots was glad they'd flown to Twenty-Six-D. The roads of the Vault District were wider than those near the spaceport, to accommodate the numerous transport trucks. Though the vehicles were the same boring black as most of the other cars, they sported deadly autoturrets on top, and the pedestrians gave them a wide berth. The bank buildings went from being glass structures with inviting lobbies full of exotic textures to plain concrete or urmurex bunkers, hardened against all sorts of external attacks.

"What if we could do something to trigger a vault change for Maslin's stuff? If we could catch the contents in transit," Orna began, "I think Charger could take one of those armored cars out."

"Yeah, but those slingers look pretty scary. Besides, I'd bet you a cab fare that the other trucks would swarm us. This whole place is probably a hive of drones. We need a way to get in, get whatever is in Durand's box, and get out."

The cab settled onto the ground across from a set of luxury apartments. It had to be strange living next to a fortress, but then living on Mercandatta was probably odd all around. The pair hopped out and made their way into the lobby of Vault Storage Twenty-Six-D.

Inside, they found a lone desk, its duraplast surface faintly aglow, underlighting a smiling IGF employee. The fellow was thin and well-groomed, not a speck of dust tainting the jet-black of his suit. He stood and walked around the desk, each step clicking on the marble floor with a dancer's gait.

"Welcome," he called to them. "The Hansom Console told me you'd be coming, but they didn't provide a name, so you have me at a disadvantage. I'm John."

"The cab company called you?" asked Orna, obvious annoyance in her features. "Is everything around here networked?"

John laughed, his voice obnoxiously polished. "More or less. All of the businesses on Mercandatta are wholly owned subsidiaries of Intergalactic Fiduciary."

"Bad security," said Orna. "Sprawling networks are stupid. I don't want to find out that I lost all my crap because your vault was hacked through the cab company."

He gave a vigorous shake of his head, and Boots wondered if

IGF fed their employees drugs to keep them so chipper. "Oh, no, miss. All of our defenses are air-gapped for each building, and the alerts network is its own pipeline."

"We want to rent a box," said Boots, "and we'd like to know what's involved."

John's smile melted into theatrical concern. "Oh, so you don't have one yet? Well, that's a simple matter, really. You'll need to visit our main office in the Hub. I can bring another flier around for you, and—"

Boots cut him off. "What, you can't rent it to us here?"

"Well, it's not impossible, but it's not standard, either," he replied, folding his hands behind his back. "Normally, our clientele is assigned to a vault from the main office. This is a special vault, so I'll need a good reason to initiate your lease from here."

"We're looking at a rental property across the street, John. We'll be accessing this box on a fairly regular basis, and we don't want to walk far."

His smile returned. "I see. I see. And what sorts of items will we be storing in this box?"

Orna scoffed. "Sorry, John, but that's kind of the point of a secret box."

"Ah. I need to make you aware that we can't store any magical items at this location." A touch of nervousness showed through his veneer of customer service. They'd taken him off his script and made unorthodox requests. And they hadn't given names or occupations, which seemed to bother him immensely.

"I'm Elsie, by the way," said Boots, extending a hand to him. "And this is my partner, Bertha."

Orna was already scowling, so she couldn't scowl any harder at the name.

"Elsie, Bertha," said John. "It's a pleasure, and I think we can come to an acceptable arrangement. Would you like a tour of the vault, perhaps? I have a demo vault that I can show you."

"We'd love that," said Orna. "Got to know if our crap is going to be safe."

"Excellent!" John clicked his heels and spun, striding back to his desk and fetching an oversized brass key with a long red tassel. It was the sort of key someone with an Origin fetish might use: obviously ceremonial. He looked to both of them. "If you'll follow me."

They went with him toward the blank back wall: a marble edifice with no adornments, save for a golden keyhole. John placed the key inside, and a ripple of glowing energy passed through the veins of the rock. A chime filled the lobby, and the marble soundlessly parted, a perfect seam opening inside it. The hall that opened was at least two meters long, and the pair of stone slabs had to weigh many tons.

"First off," said John, "this may look like marble, but it's actually regraded, magic-resistant urmurex. Even *if* a first-rate lithomancer could get past our dispersers, they wouldn't be able to push this out of the way."

"What about folks with the porter's mark?" asked Boots. "They could just jump inside."

John shook his head no. "If this doorway is closed, and someone pops into the room beyond, I'd pity that person. I'll spare you the gory details, but we have a number of automated countermeasures."

"No need to spare me," said Orna. "I love that stuff. What have you got, like, sieve grids? Springflies?"

John looked from Boots to Orna, and Boots could see the wheels turning in his brain, trying to plan his sales strategy. Should he play up the gory details or demure?

"You could say we're in the defense industry," said Boots with a wink. "We like hearing that you take the appropriate measures to protect our work."

"Of course," he said. "We're quite sympathetic to customers like you. Tell me, are you familiar with our unsigned financial products?"

"Boy are we ever," Boots replied.

"To answer your question," said John, "we start with a full-spectrum stun charge: electrical and psychic. If the, uh, individual continues moving, we flood the chamber with indolence gas, and have a number of autoturrets with knock rounds."

"Weak," said Orna.

"Well," said John, "yes and no. We prefer to respond first with items that won't cause any cleanup, and leave us a chance of apprehension. After that, we employ a sieve grid with a five-millimeter aperture. That's a last resort, of course, because if they've gotten into one of our boxes, we don't want to dice the contents in the process. All items under our care are insured at a minimum of five million argents, with options and plans ranging into the billions."

Vivid images of her own demise came with his description as Boots reminded herself that she was there to steal. "Great," she said, stifling a gulp.

"Before we continue inside," he said, sliding open a hidden panel and removing a velvet-covered teakwood tray, "are either of you carrying any magical equipment on your person?"

"Yeah," said Orna. "Why?"

"Our sensors are incredibly sensitive," said John. "Any attempt to cast magic inside the vault will obviously be caught by our dispersers, but we also detect all arcane devices and medical grafts as an extra precaution. Anything more active than your cardioid will cause the defense systems to respond. Now you understand why our magical artifact storage is a separate facility."

Crap.

No matter what plan they assembled, it would almost certainly hinge on magic. Boots looked to Orna, who nodded and took off her circlet, gently placing it in the tray. Boots took out her paragon crystal and followed suit, then reached into her shirt collar and disconnected the eidolon power pack to her arm.

Even though this clown was just a random sales guy, it still embarrassed Boots to have her arm go slack as the power drained out of it. John flushed as he realized what was happening.

"I deeply apologize for the inconvenience, Elsie," he said, taking the tray and sliding it back into the wall, where he locked it with a fingerprint.

"Don't sweat it," she said.

They made their way into the vault proper, which was a high, cylindrical shaft of gleaming silver panels, each one with a number etched on its surface. A set of white sun panels above cast a natural light, removing all shadows across the floor. Two crawler bots stood guard, mounted on floor-to-ceiling rails, ready to retrieve any of the boxes at a moment's notice. A carrel took up one side of the room, with wood-paneled walls and a pair of stained-glass lamps atop a thick desk.

"Will it take long to get our stuff out of one of your vaults?" asked Orna.

"Not at all, Bertha!" said John, practically skipping over to the input console, which rose up out of the floor. "I'll call the sample vault we use for demonstration purposes. We occasionally get tours through here."

Orna rolled her eyes behind his back.

"It's a simple matter of putting in my access code," said John, "and..."

He tapped a few numbers into the glass pad, and the nearest crawler robot raced to life. Boots jumped at the sudden movement as it rocketed up.

"Not to worry, Elsie," said John, stepping over to the wall to stand directly in front of the rail. "They're perfectly safe."

A box ejected from the wall, and the crawler caught it before plummeting straight at John. It stopped centimeters from his scalp, buzzed a complaint, and waited patiently for him to step aside. It came level with him, and he took the box from its waiting forks.

"There's an inspection area over there, if you need privacy," he said, gesturing to the alcove. They followed him to the table, where he opened the box and retrieved a tray of truffles. "And our crawlers are capable of generating their own gravitational field, so none of the contents will be upset. Truffle?"

They both indulged. It was the best chocolate Boots had ever tasted.

John popped one into his mouth with a mock mischievous grin. "We get these from a chocolatier by the spaceport. I'd be lying if I said I didn't love these demos."

Boots turned to Orna. "Well, I think we've seen enough, Bertha. I'm impressed."

"Very impressed," said Orna.

John clasped his hands together. "So are we in business?"

"Absolutely," said Boots. "We'll take one."

John's grin widened, even though that shouldn't have been possible.

"Not even a question on price. I like that."

After shaving their heads, the guards took everyone's gear, issuing them identical gray uniforms. Nilah's had an ominous bloodstain just under the armpit. Her bed had no sheets, and she'd awoken shivering for the past three nights. They hadn't found her oral transmitter, but that'd been a stroke of luck.

The interior of the base camp was nothing more than sixty

cots, a few crates of rations, and a guard station where five armed individuals would watch over them. If this cult was somehow an important part of Henrick Witts's empire, Nilah failed to see it. People weren't eager to talk to them, and most avoided eye contact altogether. At her approach, conversations would shut down and disperse. If she was going to make this intel operation work, she'd have to crack their trust—which meant she couldn't appear overeager for answers. That meant three days of near silence.

Nilah had never realized how talkative she was before this mission.

Then the lead guard, whom Nilah had nicknamed "Shaver" for her enthusiastic clipping technique, gathered everyone around. She ordered Nilah, Jeannie, and Alister to the center of the crowd. Nilah's stomach lurched. What if they'd been discovered and this was to be an unmasking?

"Everyone, this is Hope and her two friends..." Shaver paused, looking to Jeannie.

"Moira and David," said Jeannie.

"Hope, Moira, and David," Shaver repeated. "They seek to join the Children during the next ascendancy. Their fates are strong to have carried them across the stars to us. After a full examination, our colleagues at the Pinnacle have determined that they're cleared to be supplicants like you. Show them respect."

Then Shaver turned to Nilah and added, "But the Laws of the Mountain still apply."

Nilah had been studying their mythology on the Link and recognized the reference instantly. It was a passage they constantly bandied about whenever someone complained.

Rise on your own strength,
For there is nothing upon which to rest.
There are no friends on your climb.
There is only weight.

"I'm not sure I understand," said Nilah.

"Resources can be a bit scarce," said Shaver, sporting a broad grin. "These people are your family, but in the end, we're all alone. If someone truly wants something—anything—from you, they may try to take it. Don't start any fights you can't win. This place can be a way station on your journey to greatness... or it can be your grave. It's up to your new family to decide whether or not they accept you."

A chill shot through Nilah, and she glanced around the room to see if anyone was sizing her up. If someone wanted to start a fight, she'd be ready for them. To her surprise, the other cultists just mumbled among themselves in small cliques. Either they had little interest in a challenge or were too taxed by their difficult environs to rise to the occasion.

Shaver clapped her hands. "Now to dedications! You've had days to recover. A powerful body is a gift to your future. Only the strong are chosen ones. Will you be joining us at the Pinnacle, or are you a mere side character in someone else's story?"

The others fell into neat lines, stretching weary frames and limbering up.

Nilah elbowed the nearest cultist, a fellow who looked like he probably ran marathons for charity. At the man's surprised reaction, Nilah whispered, "Help me out. What's a dedication?"

The cultist smirked. "It's a workout. Easy stuff if you're not a pushover."

"Let's go!" screamed the guard. "Fate waits for no one!"

Nilah found in the Children a measure of athleticism she hadn't expected. However, the two sleepless nights and poor nourishment caught up with her, and fatigue soon set into Nilah's limbs.

"You're not done!" Shaver bellowed into Nilah's ear. "Show me your real strength, Hope!"

She considered telling the guard where she could stick a slinger, but then the other supplicants joined in the encouragement.

"Let's go!"

"Come on!"

"It's our time!"

"Singularity!" This last was echoed by a chorus until it became a booming chant, filling the room with each repetition.

Nilah looked to Jeannie and Alister to find them sweating but otherwise keeping up. They screamed in time with the others, and Nilah joined in. Some of her strength returned, spurred on by the cultists. As the workout intensified with no breaks in between, Nilah realized it might seriously injure an average person. Novices need not apply to the Children of the Singularity, apparently.

She fell into a rhythm, pursuing each movement with a tunnel vision typically reserved for the track. Reaching her zone, every chant became a battle cry, every exertion a fight.

Then Shaver broke her flow by screaming, "Good! Dinner!"

They handed out the meals, and for the third day in a row, Nilah stared at her tiny protein ration, a fifth of a full bar. Her hunger had long been replaced by nausea during the "dedication."

"Down the hatch, then," she mumbled and placed it on her tongue. It had the taste and texture of a soggy cloth, but given the way they'd been starving her, she still swallowed it with relish. Then she clicked the transmitter on the roof of her mouth to send a heartbeat code to Malik.

In her misery, the utilitarian quarters of the *Capricious* seemed like a distant, luxurious dream. She closed her eyes and thought of Orna's warm skin, the scent of her breath in moments of passion.

Her fractional protein ration devoured, Nilah laid back on her squeaky cot. She'd never eaten something that simultaneously disgusted her and made her savor every swallow. As the milky flavor of the protein diluted into her saliva, she yearned for just one more bite.

"Give it over," came a woman's acidic voice, snapping Nilah out of her reverie.

Nilah looked up to find one of the other supplicants staring down the twins, who sat side by side on the cot nearest her. Jeannie had her cube of protein halfway to her mouth.

"You want my ration?" Jeannie soberly asked of the supplicant.

"You want a black eye, is what you want," spat Alister.

The woman standing over her shrugged. She had to be almost two hundred centimeters in height, with broad shoulders and rippling forearms. Nilah couldn't see her legs though the drab pants, but she got the sense they were thickly muscled. "Yeah, unless you've got something else."

Jeannie crooked an eyebrow. "Aren't we supposed to be your brothers and sisters?"

"Leave this one to me," said Alister, rising to his feet.

"You're weak, so you're weight," said the supplicant. "Give me your food or—"

"Oi," snapped Nilah. "Walk away, tosser."

The woman turned to face her, and Nilah recognized the aggressor instantly—Heather Ashburn, one of the up-and-comers in the rackets leagues. She'd done all right for herself until she got busted for amping her overhead smash with magical augmentation. Nilah rarely watched those sorts of sports—the thought of two people smacking a ball around was orders of magnitude less interesting than racing—but athletes often crossed paths. Nilah was altogether pleased not to be recognized.

Heather smirked and opened her mouth to talk.

"Nah, mate," said Nilah, coming to her feet. She barely rose to Heather's collarbone—racers were among the smallest athletes. "I know the script here. You're going to make a ham-fisted attempt at a threat, and then I'm going to remind you that you're already a has-been in your early twenties, *Heather*. So. Walk. Away."

"Better than a never-was," she shot back. "I doubt I'd know your name."

Solid confirmation the disguises were working.

Nilah sneered. "You're not going to know much else after I break your head open."

Heather shoved her hard enough to send her over her cot, and she went tumbling. It turned out the woman's smash wasn't all amp, after all. The haze of sleep deprivation and starvation evaporated with the rush of adrenaline, and Nilah rolled backward, getting her sore legs under her.

"I don't know why you thought you were worthy to be here," Heather growled, kicking the rickety cot aside, "but I've got a destiny."

"A destiny with my friend's protein ration?" Nilah balked. "The bards will sing of you one day."

A crowd seemed to materialize out of nowhere, drawn by the siren call of a forming fight. Nilah cut her eyes at the guard station, but they weren't interested in helping. Rather, they watched intently, smiles on their faces. They weren't there to protect the supplicants, only to stop them from leaving.

"You all know the rules!" Heather shouted to the gathering crowd. "To be elite is to take from others." Then she looked at Nilah. "And I'm going to take everything from you."

Nilah pulled a sour face. "Miss me with all of the monologue and come get your teeth rearranged."

Heather's fingers curled into a fist, and she took a long step into a swing, pivoting on her hips like a professional boxer. Nilah ducked away, feeling the wind and mass of her arm; getting hit by someone like Heather Ashburn would be like being clubbed.

Heather was quick on the courts, and she brought that speed to bear on Nilah with a wide right hook. Nilah raised her guard, and she plowed into it, pushing Nilah's arms aside and grazing her chin. Nilah returned fire, blasting Heather's kidney with all of her might, but her tense muscles absorbed the impact.

She was losing ground without her precious Flicker. Instinct screamed for her to burn off the fake flesh and take Heather apart, but sense stayed her magic. Heather pressed the attack, pushing Nilah toward the gathered, shouting crowd.

Nilah had to make up some headway, or she'd be dead. Heather raised her leg to launch a heavy kick, and Nilah's racer reflexes shot into high gear. She sidestepped and drove the point of her elbow into Heather's chest like a sledgehammer, stealing her breath. Then Nilah gouged Heather's widened eyes with needling fingers and slammed her palm into her throat.

"Never should've touched me, *Heather*," she growled as the woman stumbled back, choking, eyes watering. "Sit down."

She was giving Heather a chance, even though every fiber of her being screamed for blood. Nilah had beaten the springflies. This mere mortal never should've tried it.

"...kill you," Heather coughed, and lunged for her.

Again, Nilah skipped clear, bringing her heel down into the side of Heather's knee with a sickening crunch. She screamed, veins bulging on her reddened neck, and Nilah guided her head down into the metal corner of one of the cots.

"I said, *sit down*," she huffed, staggering upright and shaking out her fingers.

The guards muscled in between the cheering supplicants, stunsticks drawn and ready to do battle. Nilah's heart leapt into her throat, until she realized they weren't there for her. They dragged Heather away, her head thunking against the concrete floor.

Then, they opened the door and threw her outside in the ice, to the cheers of the crowd.

"Thank you," whispered Jeannie. "You didn't have to do that."

Nilah narrowed her eyes. "So you had it under control?"

A flash from Alister's hand caught her eye: he'd somehow fashioned a shiv.

"These cots come apart pretty easy, you know," he said with a smile before tucking the shiv into the back of his pants. "When you read the minds of murderers, you learn a few tricks."

"That was a thing of beauty," said a fellow behind her, and Nilah turned to find a pasty teenager, barely fifty-five kilos, looking like he'd put on his dad's cult costume.

Nilah shot him a look that would've vaporized most people. "Sod off." She made to walk away, but there really wasn't anywhere to go, so she awkwardly moseyed toward one of the corners.

"Okay, but no, like—you see, like...we should be friends," he said, completely undeterred. "My name is Courtney."

"Why would we be friends, Courtney?" Nilah asked, waving off Alister and Jeannie. If this punk was trouble, she had it managed. If he had information, maybe she could pump it out of him.

"Because I've got the murderer's mark."

The murderer's mark was a legend, and not a particularly reasonable one—supposedly, to see it was to die. It was the stuff of horror shows and children's tales, spawning characters from Black Beatrice to the Dead King. However, dealing with the Gods of the *Harrow* conspiracy somewhat altered Nilah's expectations of epic magic.

"Bollocks."

"No, it's true!" Courtney protested, almost begging. "It's real, I promise. It just, you know, doesn't work like everyone thinks it does."

"And why would I need the murderer's mark?"

Courtney leaned in close. "Because I heard the guards talking, and there's an ascendancy coming soon."

Nilah searched his face for some hint of meaning. She still wasn't sure what that entailed.

"You know," said Courtney. "An ascendancy? The reason we're here?"

She feigned comprehension. "I know. I'm just waiting for you to get to the bleeding point."

Courtney sat up straight. "We could team up. You could distract while I cast. Less competition. Just think about it."

For a prospective cultist, Courtney struck her as a well-adjusted, eager-to-please young man. Unlike Heather, he seemed to understand the rules of society, even outside of civilized space.

"I've got to ask," she said. "Why are you here?"

"Talking to you?"

"Why are you trying to join the Children, you daft git?" The cultists seemed to like it when she was mean, so she added on a little extra nastiness.

He leaned against the wall next to her. "Because I'm supposed to be somebody. I've got a destiny. We're the chosen ones, and like, uh, there's always somebody trying to like—stop us from getting that."

How very poetic you are.

"Like," Courtney began, "we're held back in all kinds of ways. My mom is actually a big deal on Taitu. Or at least, she was. She was one of the senior vice presidents of Audian Logistics. We were, like, stupid rich. Lived in Verdance and everything."

Nilah knew that neighborhood of Taitu's capital well. More than a few politicians, lobbyists, and heads of major syndicates made the great forest their home, and they all threw parties when the grand prix was in town.

She shrugged. "Sounds like you were rich, and now you wear rags and live on a cot. Not the wisest trade I've heard."

His eyes narrowed. "You think I gave it up? Do you have any idea what happened to Audian Logistics?"

"I'm guessing the answer isn't 'They continued shipping goods across the galaxy for a fair and equitable price.'"

"You're damned right they didn't. When those bastards from the *Capricious* overthrew the prime minister, there were all kinds of inquests from the new puppet state. My mom was indicted by the Office of the Special Prosecutor!" Courtney's hands shook, and Nilah half wondered if he'd turn on her in rage.

"Was your mother part of the conspiracy?"

"What conspiracy? You mean the one the new prime minister made up so she could throw all of her enemies in jail? They said my mom helped orchestrate the barges to supply the *Harrow*. They put her in prison, and she's rotting there still. Like, I'm never going to forget the day they pulled me out of class at Wilkinson University, saying the bill wasn't paid. The dean didn't care that my grades were great. He didn't care that I had nowhere else to go! The Special Branch froze our assets and left me to starve!"

It'd be pointless to ask if his mother was innocent. The courts might have an ironclad case, and little Courtney would never believe it.

"And that's when I finally understood the way the galaxy works," said Courtney. "There's no one out there looking out for you. There's just you, the mountain you have to climb, and your prize waiting at the top. I thought I had everything, but they took it from me in a heartbeat. Worse still, they gave my family fortune to those Clarkie washouts as part of the Restitution Fund. The prime minister needed an excuse to drain the fortunes of the most influential people on Taitu, and she found it."

"I'm guessing you don't believe the Winnower Fleet destroyed Clarkesfall."

"Oh, please! Like, I know you're just testing my faith, but that's ridiculous. Who would ever believe something like that? The 'Fallen'—or whatever—are just a bunch of losers from a dead world coming begging for handouts. They screwed up their own planet. They should have to fix it."

His words put tiny little holes in Nilah's heart—as stupid and stumbling as he was, she'd spoken similarly back when she was a racer, relentlessly pursuing the Driver's Crown. She never would've denied the genocide, but she hadn't shown an abundance of empathy. When Mother killed Cyril Clowe on the track, Nilah had considered the murder an inconvenience, costing her points in her race for the championship against Kristof Kater. When Nilah had been forced to land on Carré with the crew of the *Capricious*, she hadn't appealed to Duke Thiollier to spare his people the indignities of indentured servitude and slavery. She'd been single-minded, aiming only for her future as queen of the Pan-Galactic Racing Federation. If Mother hadn't tried to kill her, would Nilah ever have stuck her neck out for someone else?

"Yeah," said Nilah. "They think they ought to get a free ride just because their planet was destroyed."

Courtney gave a bitter laugh. "*Allegedly* destroyed. But I get what you mean. Like the rest of us have problems, too. I basically don't have a mark at all. It's not like running around murdering people is a job."

"I think that's called an assassin."

"Okay, no, though, because I..." He grimaced as he struggled for a counterpoint, then gave up with a sigh. "No one wants me for that. It's like being a freaking dull-finger, but you don't see me complaining about it."

Nilah restrained herself from slapping him. Boots must've been rubbing off on her. "You're a scholar, Courtney."

"Thanks," he said, smiling. "You get me."

That I do, mate. That I do.

She watched a cadre of guards making their way through the

crowd, shoving supplicants out of the way. "And what is our strategy for the ascendancy?"

But before he could answer, one of the guards pointed to her, and all five turned in her direction.

"Hello, hello," said Nilah, her throat tightening. She didn't want to admit it, but her brawl with Heather Ashburn left her with a few bruises, and she'd be extra sore tomorrow. "What have we here?"

"Maybe they're pissed off?"

"Maybe I need to kick their asses, too," muttered Nilah, watching them close the gap to her. In truth, she'd never be able to take all five without her Flicker, and the other supplicants and guards might join in.

Shaver stopped in front of her. "Hope," she said.

She held out her fist, and Nilah didn't know what to do. In fighting, touching knuckles meant it was time to start the match. If she did nothing, maybe she'd take that as a sign she relented.

Eventually, Shaver shook her fist and said, "Hold out your damned hand."

Nilah cupped her hands beneath the guard's, and she dropped a half ration into her palms.

"It would've been Heather's," said the guard, grinning from ear to ear.

Nilah took the morsel into her mouth; unlike the other rations, this one was fresh, like a cookie straight out of the oven. The taste conjured a distant night cycle aboard the *Capricious*, sharing Boots's ration bar and talking into the late hours. It took all of Nilah's restraint not to give a little groan of pleasure as she exhaled.

When she'd finished chewing, the guard nodded. "It appears you have a destiny."

Nilah gave Shaver her most menacing smile. "Too right, chum. Too right."

Was it night? Nilah couldn't remember. They kept the lights on inside the recruitment station at all times, and she began to have strange dreams. But on the fourth cycle, she dreamed only of blackness, running across her skin like rivulets of oil, and the strange ululation of the shadow spell.

Night pooled in the corners, spilling over the floor, the cots, and the other supplicants. It rose underneath her, lifting her body free of the worn mattress. The wandering voice became a dirge.

When someone shrieked, Nilah realized she wasn't dreaming.

A sea of shadows churned inside the barracks, tumbling supplicants' bodies against one another, sweeping the cots aside. The cultists' shrieks reflected off every wall, and Nilah's fearful cries escaped her throat, unbidden. Then someone shouted, "He comes!" and the screams dimmed. More of them shouted for their "Lord," abandoning their panicked cries. Nilah joined them, half out of hope, half out of fear. Maybe they could appease him.

The shadows became a still pond in which the supplicants floated, only their heads above the ink. She churned her arms as though swimming, but it made little difference—the shadows pushed her to the surface like a saltwater lake.

A deep growl emanated through the space, like the low, smooth drone of a maneuvering thruster through a ship's hull. Words took shape from its depths.

"You must not fear. Know only desire."

"Yes!" shouted someone in the back, and the ink drained a few centimeters. The others cried out for him, as well.

"Bide your time, for even when you are paralyzed . . ."

The blackness congealed around Nilah, freezing her limbs in place, and she spied panic on the faces around her. She strained against her prison, but it wouldn't part. Pressure built inside her limbs and her head grew light as her surroundings constricted.

The archives had been full of gnashing teeth and grasping claws, thousands of wild blades eager for flesh. Now the shadow held her helpless. It could drive a spike through her heart or tear her spine from her body.

Was this the ascension? Had she already screwed up?

She clicked the transmitter in the top of her mouth and wheezed out the word "Help."

"*. . . you must be ready to strike.*"

With a disorienting swirl, darkness drained away, leaving nearly a hundred supplicants on their rumps, as well as a matching lupine shadow creature for each. Nilah's black dog loomed over her, spikes of matted fur covering an unknowable hide. Snarling echoed through the room, coming from everywhere at once. The beast took a step toward her, and she scrambled backward.

Ten paces away, one of the animals latched onto another cultist, and he screamed, blood pouring from the bite marks on his arm. The beast shook its head, menacing the wound with jagged teeth, which seemed to multiply with each passing second.

"*Be ready to strike.*"

Nilah swallowed her fear and launched for the creature, slamming her knee into its snout. The shadow went scrabbling back and splashed across the ground into a pool of night. The other cultists followed suit, attacking the animals and crushing them in a single blow. They banded together until all of the creatures were nothing more than black puddles.

"Well done, my Children of the Singularity," came the deep voice, and Nilah realized that speakers were pumping him into every corner of the room. "The dogs are circling, and you have chosen to stand against them."

The puddles oozed into the shape of a man, his flesh eating the light around him.

"I am Lord Vraba, the right hand of our master," came the voice.

Some of them gasped. Others shook with joyful laughter. A roaring applause suffused the barracks, drowning out all other noise. The shadow raised its hand for silence.

And they all took a knee.

The shadow man leapt, becoming a spherical arrangement of continents. Nilah recognized the silhouette of her homeworld, Taitu, in them.

"Our world," said Vraba, "was the greatest power this galaxy has ever known. We were the seat of wealth…" Cheers rang out. "…of beauty…" More cheers. "…of power." Vraba became a man-sized sword, whose blade slammed into the concrete ground, taking root in the floor with eager tendrils. The closest supplicants reached down to touch them, and the shadows quested out to caress them in turn.

Nilah glanced around to find the cultists' eyes wide with elation. This was the man they'd all come to see. She tried to copy their expressions, clapping when they clapped, whooping when they whooped, but she knew Vraba's display to be nothing more than a show, his voice conveyed by a nice sound system. If he'd wanted to show his real power, he would've chewed someone to pieces.

Across the barracks, Alister backed into a far corner, awe on his face, and Nilah spotted a tiny flash in his hand. Had he cast a glyph? He began to inch toward the nearest guard.

Nilah looked for Jeannie, finding her only a few paces away. Inching through the crowd, she reached Jeannie and whispered, "Moira, your friend needs to pay better attention to our lord."

Jeannie jumped, but noted the direction of Nilah's gaze. She immediately began pushing toward Alister.

"But Taitu has been *infected*," hissed Vraba, his avatar shaking and crumbling at the edges, "with weakness and doubt. Our leaders seek to sell our interests through galactic treaties. We welcome tens of thousands of criminals, wastrels, and undesirables to our world, polluting our noble soil. Our prime minister is nothing more than a GATO puppet, spinning lies about the greatest military leader of our age."

"Kill her!" screeched one of the supplicants, and the others joined in with a host of reprehensible punishments. Nilah added her own voice to the mix, watching with trepidation as Alister brushed past the first guard. He must have read the man's mind, but not found what he was looking for.

Alister locked eyes with Nilah, gesturing toward Shaver. Nilah shook her head no, but she could see the defiance in his eyes.

"Taitu is doomed." Vraba became a man, his silhouette growing a full five meters, so tall he could brush the ceiling. "Grand Admiral Henrick Witts understood and created the Winnower Fleet to give us a final chance. And instead, our world spurned him."

Alister cast his glyph again, hiding the flash as best he could with a half turn of his body. He was going to get himself killed. Spell in hand, he took another step toward Shaver. Jeannie was closing on him, but she might not reach him in time.

"But we are the inheritors of that stolen planet," said Vraba, "and we will take what fate has denied us. In your faces, I see commitment and the will to forge your destiny alone. If you succeed in reaching the Pinnacle, you'll have the honor of serving at the Grand Admiral's pleasure. You will be more than a Taitutian, more than a human, more than mere meat; you'll be a vessel of everlasting glory at our side. In a week, I shall appear in person to take you from this world into the vast night, your futures unabridged by the false comforts of civilization."

Nilah did the mental calculations. If she made it to the Pinnacle, and Vraba took her away…she'd lose her chance to rendezvous with the *Capricious*. She might never make contact without getting caught.

Perhaps the Special Branch agent had already been extradited in the same fashion. Perhaps the whole mission was a deadly waste of time. Her eyes darted back to Alister.

His hand was a centimeter from Shaver's back when Vraba's shadow roared through the crowd, bowling into him. The blackness smashed him into the wall, pouring up his neck in long drips. Alister made to scream, but the darkness slurped into his mouth, tugging at his lips.

"A mind reader," growled Vraba, "reading my devotees. I should crush you."

Jeannie froze. Nilah couldn't help him, either. She was going to have to watch Alister be ground into nothingness.

The shadows withdrew from Alister's mouth long enough for Vraba to ask, "You have one chance at redemption. What were you doing?"

Alister's ragged breath carried flecks of spit, but panic must've stayed his tongue. The black web around him constricted, eliciting a pained squeal from him, then loosened.

"Answer me," said Vraba.

"Advantage," coughed Alister. "I must take every advantage I can...as a Child of the Singularity."

A black hand reached out of the mass and pinned Alister's head against the wall with a thunk. Nilah wanted to rush in, tattoos ablaze, but she would only die alongside him.

"Is that so?" asked Vraba. "And what did you *think* you'd learn?"

"The secrets of the ascension," huffed Alister. "But—but I did find out that one"—he nodded at the first guard he'd touched— "is afraid you'd learn he was asleep during last night's watch."

Another arm grew from the black mask, its clawed finger pointed at Shaver. "Check the recordings."

Nilah and Jeannie exchanged glances, and Nilah understood the look on her face. If Alister had signed his death warrant, Jeannie would go down with him.

When Shaver returned, her face was grim. She nodded to the shadow.

"I see," said Vraba.

It washed over the guard, pinning him to the ground, burrowing its tendrils into his flesh, his ears, his nose, his eyes. The man's hands were free to claw and scratch, his legs free to kick, but nothing would pull Vraba's spell from his skin. Only tiny droplets of blood emerged from the wounds, and his cries were choked out by the roots rushing down his throat. The shadow scooped his eyes from his head and peeled the muscles from his bones before snapping every joint in his body.

Then Vraba evaporated, and the hideous song vanished with him.

"Well played, little mind reader," said Vraba. "You'll do well in the ascension."

Alister collapsed, panting, looking for all the world like he was choking back vomit.

"But don't do it again," said Vraba. "Clean up this mess."

Once Nilah was clear, she transmitted a whispering, "I'm okay." She wished she could hear Malik's reply.

For the rest of the night, Alister had to carry the remains outside and scrub the blood free from the stone. No one would touch him, but they didn't hate him. They seemed to Nilah as though they were in awe.

Alister, for his part, wasn't upset at all.

Chapter Eight

Safecracking

"L et's go over this one more time," said Armin before taking a swig out of his coffee mug.

Boots noticed the accumulated rings lining its interior and wondered if he ever washed it.

"We *have* the serial number of Durand's box from the Special Branch investigation," said Aisha. "We *need* the access code, or some way to drill the box out of the wall."

The night cycle on Mercandatta was slowly warming to a sunrise. Boots, Orna, Aisha, Cordell, and Armin sat on the bridge, where they'd been calculating plans through the evening with the aid of some overpriced delivery food.

"We already went through it, sir," Boots groaned. Her eyes were so dry that it was like rubbing two strips of leather together when she blinked. "It's impenetrable."

"Nothing is impenetrable or unhackable," said Cordell, but his usual swagger had been softened by the hours of debate. "Quartermaster, how much is our resupply and refuel bill?"

"A hundred large, easy," sighed Orna. "And we're supposedly robbing *them*."

"Are you serious?" asked Aisha. "That's quadruple what we paid on Carré!"

"That's why we're not leaving here empty-handed," said Cordell. "Now go over it again, Boots."

Boots gave herself a moment to stare at the ceiling. It was so nice to lean back in her chair and fantasize about the cool pillow in her bunk.

"Are you waiting for a 'please,' Miss Elsworth?" asked Armin.

That was like a shot of coffee. "No, sir. I'm sorry, sir. Like I said, if the vault doors are closed, there are life-sensing traps. Security ranges from nonlethal to splattered. That rules out drilling the box out with no one watching."

"Hard to see any weaknesses there," said Cordell.

"Maybe," said Armin. "Maybe not. Life sensors are very effective in space because there are no bacteria, viruses, pollen, and so forth floating through the air. In atmosphere, sensor sweeps are harder to calibrate. There have to be microbes in the vault, if not from the visitors, from the contents of the safe-deposit boxes—documents, money, et cetera."

"What are you getting at, Mister Vandevere?" asked Cordell.

Armin folded his fingers under his chin. "Perhaps we can trick the life sensor array in the sealed room by gradually adding microbes until it's overloaded—flood the signal with noise. Of course, that all depends on how clean they keep the interior chamber. If it's perfectly clean, then the presence of any life inside, no matter how small, will trigger an alarm. Did the whole place smell like antiseptic?"

Boots thought on that. "No. It smelled like polished saltwood."

"Crap. I smelled milled metal," said Orna. "Hoteliers. That means the inner chamber is as lifeless as the core of a star."

Boots nodded. Hoteliers were sought after by the finest establishments in the galaxy, as well as medical and science research labs, since their magical cleanings would perfectly sterilize any surface.

Armin held up his hands. "Let's not rule out the idea of sneaking something biological into a safe-deposit box. If it could get out..."

"We covered that, sir," said Orna. "Even if we had something, it won't be able to interface with their security until it gets out of the box. Any halfway intelligent vault designer will make sure those boxes have no computer contacts on the inside."

"So we have to hack it while the vault proper is open," said Boots, "but if Orna casts the mechanist's mark inside there, the defenses come on and beat the hell out of us."

"Maybe you could shield yourself somehow?" asked Aisha. "Do a really quick hack into the dispersers and turrets?"

"It takes time to hack something that complex," said Orna. "I'd be down before I could even lay hands on the console."

"Any way to use that expensive disperser cannon you've been working on?" asked Cordell. "You could puncture some of their defensive spells."

Orna sighed. "No, sir. Haven't gotten it working yet, and the thing is big: most of your height, all of your weight. We'd never be able to sneak it inside."

"So we really need to hack," said Cordell. "While you were outside, you could cast and carry."

"Hold a stable spell in my hand—undetected—for the three minutes it takes to get through security?" asked Orna, reaching over to Boots's station and grabbing a handful of crispy noodles. "I'm good, but I'm not that good. I think I could go at most one minute without connecting to something."

Armin rubbed his eyes, then stopped. "What about a barnacle?"

"A what?" asked Aisha.

Orna looked at her sidelong, crunching away at her snack. "It's like a cheap version of the circlet I use to control Charger. I cast my mark and connect to him when I wake up, and the connection stays stable. That's a good idea, sir"—Orna wrinkled her nose—"except we'd never be able to sneak it into the vault."

The first mate steepled his fingers. "Yeah, but what about the extremely low-powered ones?"

"Not a chance," said Orna. "Those sensors are calibrated so carefully they'll trigger security on anything bigger than a cardioid. That means I can't carry even the smallest barnacle in there."

Boots froze, her soda halfway to her mouth. Her eyes darted to Cordell, and she could tell from the look on his face that he had the same idea.

"What am I missing here?" asked Orna. "Why are you making that face?"

"Arcana dystocia. I don't have a cardioid," said Boots. "That means I can carry a barnacle into the vault."

The barracks were unkind to Nilah. Even though a year of ship life had toughened her up, she still had trouble sleeping without the creeping fingers of frost sinking into her bones. The thin blankets they provided were scarcely enough to provide modesty, much less comfort.

"What are you owed?" screamed Shaver. Her voice was like a cup of hot tea—if someone threw it in Nilah's face.

Nilah scrambled to her feet to find Shaver standing directly over her and stammered an unintelligible reply. It was too early for this crap. Or was it too late? They never let any natural light into the compound.

Shaver scowled and spun to face the rest of the room. "Wake up, people! I asked you a question!"

Exhausted cultists struggled to consciousness, malnourished and fatigued from regular physical devotions. Shaver pulled out a remote and triggered a deafening alarm that rattled Nilah's teeth. That got everyone moving.

"What—are—we—owed?" bellowed Shaver, enunciating each word.

"Nothing, except what we can take!" came a tentative call from the far corner of the room.

Shaver took Nilah by the shoulders and looked her in the eyes. The guard had developed an affinity for her, and took obvious pleasure in asking, "Why so timid, Hope?"

"We're owed nothing," said Nilah, giving her a dark look, "save what we can take."

"And what can you take?" asked Shaver, clapping her on the shoulder.

She mustered some of the old fire that dominated the racing press conferences. "All that fate has set aside for me."

Shaver picked up Nilah's blanket, and Nilah's gut churned at the thought of losing it. "Can you take this blanket?"

Beating the hell out of Heather Ashburn had been an easy decision. Striking a guard would be another proposition entirely.

"It was granted to me," Nilah replied, which seemed like the most diplomatic answer.

The look of sanctimonious shock on Shaver's face made Nilah want to retch. "Did I ask if we gave it to you?" She stepped in close, getting nose to nose with Nilah, then drew a slinger out of her waistband, holding it at her side. "I asked if you could take it."

Nilah stared into Shaver's green-gold eyes, ready to headbutt her if things went awry. Was this a game? Were they planning to make an example out of her? If she surrendered her blanket, was it a sign of piety and deference to the guards? If she took it, was she demonstrating her willingness to risk harm for what she desired?

"We both know that I can," Nilah growled, "so I dare you

to raise a finger to stop me." She slowly removed the cloth from Shaver's possession, never breaking eye contact.

The guard's look of righteous indignation melted to a broad smile. "They're going to love you at the Pinnacle," she whispered, then stepped back and turned to address the crowd.

"This," Shaver cried, pointing to Nilah, "is exactly what you must be! You must show no fear of seizing your power. If you're worthy to serve Lord Vraba and our gods, everything will be yours. You're owed what you can take. Let our sister Hope serve as your example! To Hope!"

"To Hope!" roared the assemblage, and Nilah's heart skipped a beat. She despised herself for it.

When Shaver departed, others came to Nilah to share their approval with restrained respect. Their adoration was unlike the thunderstruck racing fans of her old life. Those people had been vapid, clamoring for the chance to be close to a driver. They sat at home or on the side of the track, fantasizing about what it was like in Nilah's shoes. The Children of the Singularity, though heinous, were driven to excellence in one another's presence. They didn't want to watch their heroes; they wanted to be their heroes.

More devotions passed, more paltry meals, another sleepless night, and the cultists grew closer to Nilah. Shaver and the other guards regularly used Nilah as their example. They debated the meaning of beauty and the need for death. They memorized winding passages of contrived heroes' journeys. The barracks began to fill up as new supplicants trickled inside, two or three a day, then five or ten. They arrived from all over the galaxy, but they all came from nice families and had decent educations.

The ninth morning, Nilah shook herself awake shivering hard. The rear loading doors were open, and the guards had their slingers drawn.

"Wakey wakey!" called Shaver. "You don't have to go home, but you can't stay here!"

Nilah wrapped her arms around herself and stood, looking for Jeannie and Alister, but they were nowhere to be found amid the crush of bodies. Courtney, on the other hand, was jumping in place to limber up. Nilah clicked the transmitter on the roof of her mouth and pushed through the crowd toward him.

"What's happening?" she asked, nodding toward the guards.

"Ascendancy," said Courtney, with a big smile on his face. "Today's the day. Going to prove my destiny. Just remember: let's be friends."

"Have you figured out what the hell ascendancy is?"

"No one knows exactly, but it's how we get to the Pinnacle. Just be ready to fight. I am. I was being serious when I said I had the murderer's mark. Don't look at it."

"Trust me," said Nilah, "I won't."

He cocked an eyebrow. "*Destinies are never given…*"

"*They're taken,*" Nilah replied, completing the phrase she'd seen floating around dozens of Link communities. "See you at the Pinnacle."

She had to get private word to Jeannie and Alister about Courtney, and this would be her best chance. It took her a tense minute to find them; she still wasn't accustomed to their new faces.

They startled as she placed a hand on their shoulders. "Listen, kids," she whispered, pointing out Courtney. "I don't know if that bloke is telling the truth or not, but he's saying he's got the murderer's mark."

Jeannie and Alister exchanged glances, and Nilah expected them to laugh, but they were deadly serious.

"What did he tell you?" asked Alister.

"Not to look at it," said Nilah. "I doubt he's—"

"The murderer's mark isn't a myth," said Jeannie. "If he casts, put your head down."

"Keep your wits about you," said Nilah, "and for god's sake, *don't read the guards, David Connelly.*"

"Best way to find out how they felt about our Lord Vraba," he replied, voice low. "And I did find a traitor, after all."

The commotion of evacuating supplicants would scramble most listening devices, but she couldn't take a chance that her lips would be read by imagers. Nilah had been wanting to have a private moment with him for a while.

She grabbed the back of his neck and yanked his head close, almost pressing her lips into the cup of his ear. "Mark me, chum. Your stunt almost killed your sister. You're not the only life at stake, so choose your targets more carefully."

She released him, and Alister gave her an indignant look before opening his foolish mouth. "I'm not here to take orders from—"

Nilah's palm whipped across Alister's face before she even realized what she'd done. He clutched his cheek, seething anger in his eyes, but that was all she could see before Jeannie stepped between them like a cold stone wall.

"See you at the Pinnacle," she said. "Don't touch him again."

And they shuffled away for the open door. Nilah watched them leave, wondering how long she had before Alister blew their cover. He couldn't be controlled, and now her fate was tied to his.

Sharp pain tore across Nilah's shoulder as the butt of a slinger came crashing down into her. She stumbled away and turned to face her attacker: one of the guards.

"We said outside," he said, chambering a round. "We meant outside."

Nilah eased through the open loading door and her breath caught in her lungs. The initial shock of wind blew through Nilah's thin uniform like she was stark naked. The icy ground burned the soles of her feet through ratty shoes. Her shoulder would be bruised, but it was eminently less important than the freezing temperature.

"Oh, stuff this," she mumbled through chattering teeth as she looked around at the assemblage of miserable supplicants.

Jeannie stood abreast of Alister, trying to shield him from the wind as much as her willowy frame allowed. She looked to Nilah and nodded. If something went wrong, they could signal Malik, but he wouldn't be able to do much.

"Spread out a bit!" called Shaver, and the group of supplicants thinned in the middle. The men and women on the edges of the informal circle looked around nervously—pack animals away from the herd.

Shaver pointed up to the dark fortress at the top of the snowy crag. Its windows reflected the rolling, icy landscape below, and Nilah got the keen sense that whoever was up there, they were watching.

"That's your destination," Shaver called out over the wailing wind. "The Pinnacle. It's two kilometers away at a thirty-degree grade. You're all in good shape! That's basically a brisk jog."

Nilah could sprint that distance, even at that incline, even in that cold, because of the harsh training regimen of a racer. Even though she'd been on the *Capricious* for a year, she could still take on a distance like that. Heather Ashburn would've made it easily, too, had they not murdered her. Glancing around, Nilah saw a lot of candidates that could make the hike—and that fact brought cold fear into her gut.

Shaver clapped her hands together, as if announcing her favorite theatrical act. "Now, some of you may have been counting, and there are about a hundred people trying to get to the top. That's a problem, because our master has ten beds for the latest class of recruits."

Oh, no.

"You have sacrificed to be here!" screamed Shaver, burning zeal

188

in her eyes. "You've given up your families! You've given up your fortunes! Through that Pinnacle lies your path to greatness. The training you receive there will give you a place among the gods themselves!"

The guards by the barracks leveled their slingers at the crowd of supplicants, who flinched and gasped.

Shaver raised a finger to the heavens and shouted, "So we'll make you a deal: those doors will open up when we've got ten recruits. *Destinies are never given, they're taken.*"

Shaver lowered her hand and pushed through the crowd, shouldering people out of the way. Murmurs rose above the howling wind as supplicants looked to one another for some kind of social cue. Out of the corner of her eye, Nilah saw Jeannie and Alister cast the reader's mark and touch hands.

Upon reaching the doors back to the barracks, Shaver took out her slinger and said, "I have one more lesson to teach you. Always be ready for anything,"

She fired a lancer round straight into the crowd, skewering a man and a woman. She collapsed dead, a hole through her torso. He went down screaming with a mauled shoulder.

Nilah didn't wait to see what happened next, launching for the distant gates of the Pinnacle. Slow, methodical pops filled the air, along with the whizzing of spells overhead. The guards weren't aiming directly at the cultists, but if Nilah stopped, they wouldn't hesitate to shoot her. She sprinted along the ice as fast as her legs would carry her, cold air ragged in her throat.

The slinger fire died away behind them. Either the guards had stopped shooting, or they were reloading. She wasn't about to turn and find out. Despite her fitness, Nilah was nowhere near the front of the pack. A lanky boy far out front took that honor, and Nilah had little doubt that he'd be the first to the gates. That was all right. It left nine spots for Nilah and the Ferriers.

Then a screaming bolt of fire struck the lanky boy, sending him to the ground in a pile of flailing, smoky bones.

It'd come from another supplicant near the front of the pack. Nilah spun just in time to catch a fist from a husky fellow. It wasn't enough to break anything, not enough to even hurt, but it put her off balance, and she went tumbling across the hard-packed snow.

She rolled onto her back to find an all-out battle developing behind her. Magical bolts arced back and forth, elemental energies blistering the landscape. One supplicant impaled a woman on a spear made from light. Another released a noxious gray cloud from a glyph, sweeping down the hill, choking the others. Still more fought with their bare fists—strong bodies but weak cardioids. While these people weren't the best of the best, they certainly killed each other with wild abandon.

The man with the light spear came barreling toward Nilah, and she rolled backward onto her feet, avoiding a swift end. No sooner had she caught her balance than she had to bend over backward to avoid a wide swipe of the sizzling staff, which opened him to a disrupted orbit attack. Nilah swept her hands inward and went to shoulder check him, only for him to deftly step aside. Without the stunning flash of Flicker, he saw her coming a klick away.

If she used her dermaluxes, she might make it to the top, but she'd be murdered where she stood. They'd know her as Nilah Brio in a heartbeat.

Two more stabs of the light spear forced her back, and he made to lunge a third time when an invisible force sliced his throat clean open. He clutched at his gushing neck, furious to be felled, struggling to contain his life's blood. As he collapsed, Nilah spied the caster, the air around her fingertips glimmering like shards of broken glass.

Nilah spun and hiked up the hill, the icy shell of snow breaking underfoot. One of the invisible shards whizzed by her head, and she ran a serpentine pattern to get some distance. Ahead of her, Courtney caught her eye, his fingers afire with an inky spell, strain wrinkling his boyish face.

Bloody hell. He wasn't lying.

Nilah frantically searched the crowd for the Ferriers—she had to warn them, but all she found were knots of cultists in furious combat. Her heart thumped so hard against her ribs she thought her chest might break. Two figures leapt, hand in hand, crashing facedown against the frost. Had to be the twins—they were the only ones who'd be such close allies in the melee. More to the point, they were the only supplicants that would dare hold hands.

Nilah closed her eyes and hit the deck as a bone-rattling scream filled the air. Her joints seized up like she'd torn every muscle in her body, and her teeth chattered in her head. Her blood leapt in her veins, trying to burst from every vessel. For a horrifying moment, she thought Courtney might've lied to her, meant to catch her off her guard. Maybe this was what it was like to die.

Then blissful relaxation fell upon her, leaving only the blistering cold. She looked behind her, where the shard-casting throat-cutter once stood.

Two dozen men and women stood motionless, their eyes rolled back in their heads. Fingers clasped and unclasped the air before them, clutching uselessly at ghosts. Tears of blood streamed from whitened eyes, and they collapsed.

A glance at the Ferriers found them climbing to their feet, brushing away the ice. Nilah scrambled upright and looked up to Courtney, who pumped his fist and whooped.

With one fell swoop, he'd killed many of the supplicants behind them, leaving only the men and women farther up the hill. The guards at the barracks shielded their eyes, and from this distance, Nilah thought she could make out a smile. Had they known about him? Seen it before? If they'd had surveillance devices in the barracks, they could've heard the fool plotting to use it.

"Come on!" Courtney shouted down at Nilah, and turned just in time to catch a brutal tackle from a woman twice his size. Nilah surged to her feet, dashing toward the tangle of Courtney and attacker. She couldn't use Flicker, but it was derived from Taitutian Ghost Fist, and she still knew the forms.

The woman rolled Courtney onto his back and raised a fist, the flesh of her hand transmuting into jagged rock. Nilah closed the gap and leapt, coming across the woman's face with a flying knee. Nilah tumbled clear of the tangling limbs, then dashed back into the fray, seizing her dazed target by her hair and smashing her face against her elbow.

"Kill her!" shouted Courtney, but Nilah let the woman go the second she fell slack.

She helped Courtney slough off his would-be murderer and rise to his feet. Her breath came in ragged huffs. "Come on, mate. Halfway there."

Courtney kicked the woman onto her back and crushed her throat with a vicious stomp. "Ten spots, Hope. Ten."

She never should've bothered to save Courtney. Nilah turned and took the path at a brisk jog, ready to leap clear if anything happened.

Ahead, a pair of supplicants hurled spells at Alister, who crouched behind an outcropping of glittering black rock. Nilah watched in horror as they advanced on his position, pinning him down. Jeannie came creeping up behind the attackers like a mountain lion, her shiv at the ready. She pounced, sinking her jagged blade deep into the neck of the first attacker. Alister fled his cover in perfect synchronicity, charging straight for the surprised second man. Jeannie ripped free her shiv and flanked Alister's target, and they dispatched him with little difficulty. They weren't great fighters, but they moved as a single body, surrounding, yanking, and stabbing.

The bedlam continued near the top, brilliant sparks and deadly magic flying in all directions. Each of the remaining supplicants were powerful magi in their own right, nothing like the average scribbler. Spears of ice collided with smoking meteors. Glowing shields clashed with the fangs of a ravening, scaly beast. Men and women fell by the dozen, torn to shreds by the rages of arcane combat.

Nilah was just a simple mechanist. Without tools or a car or a slinger, what chance did she stand against these powerful glyphs?

The crackle of magical combat began to die down as more bodies hit the ice. The closer they got to the top, the harder the shell of snow became, until it was a thick, slippery crust. It was slow going, even for a former star athlete like Nilah. By the time she got within a hundred meters of the Pinnacle, exhausted wizards grappled together on the ground, desperate to thin the herd enough to get inside.

Less than twenty remained.

"Get ready," said Courtney. "And if you get a chance to kill someone, you do it. I'm not going to die on account of your weakness."

"Shut up, and focus on getting to that door," Nilah shot back. "What's the plan?"

"I'm kicking it in," she said, watching another supplicant fall to an ice spike through the chest.

"The rules say only ten can get in," Courtney hissed.

Nilah bored into him with her eyes and spouted another phrase she'd heard the Children say on the Link. "There are no rules, Courtney. We're owed what we can take! Now give me a distraction."

Courtney balked. "I'm not sure I've got another one of those in me! I already took out half the playing field! Pull your own weight!"

Nilah lashed out, slapping the hell out of his cold-reddened cheek, then smashed a fist into his teeth. She wanted to do much worse to him, this monster so proud of killing.

"Do it," she growled, "or die here."

"Okay," he said, touching the blood on his lip.

"Moira, David," Nilah began as Jeannie and Alister jogged along-side. "Courtney here is going to cast a murderer's mark, the biggest one he can muster, and we're going to muscle through to the door. I need you to get people out of my way and stay right on my tail."

As they approached, the fighters gathering near the Pinnacle took notice. They battled one another with tentative attention, keeping their eyes on the newcomers. Those who'd felled their opponents turned to face Nilah and crew, sensing some sort of plan. She counted over a dozen battle-worn faces.

Nilah set her feet and prepared for an awkward charge across the ice. "Now, Courtney!"

Once more, he began his glyph, hideous black energies gathering at his fingertips. The other combatants readied their spells as well, eager to target the most deadly threat in their midst, but Nilah surprised them by breaking into a full-on sprint.

Their shock at her brazen maneuver resulted in missed marks and fizzled spells as magic flew far and wide. She dodged a guillotine of solid ice and hurdled a bolt of fire as she dashed for the door access panel. She strained her ears to hear the completion of Courtney's deadly spell, but she needn't have worried.

Those in her path turned away, shielding their eyes after what'd happened to those below. The magic of the murderer's mark crawled up Nilah's spine like a needle-footed spider. As long as she didn't look at it, she'd be fine.

What if Jeannie and Alister weren't behind her? She couldn't hazard a single glance. She could only have faith: in her friends, in her abilities, in Courtney's dark talent.

Nilah dropped to one leg and skidded into the wall below the access panel, tracing out her glyph as she did. The others might have meteors and light spears, but they could never force the

Pinnacle to open its doors. She slapped her palm against the keys, pushing her magic inside.

Security was rudimentary. Nilah couldn't be sure if the ease of access was a trap, or if they truly didn't expect someone to simply try and pick the lock. Either way, she was none too keen on wading back into the chaos and breaking some necks. They might've been evil, genocidal bastards, but she didn't much feel like taking out the trash herself.

A twist here, a turn there as Nilah picked apart their electronic defense network. In the maze of wires and data points, she began to sense the shape of their anti-aircraft grid—a trio of muscular cannons with more than enough punch to take down the *Capricious*. She desperately wanted to disable it, then send an emergency message to her ship, but there was no time.

She broke open the lock security, splitting its code into jagged chunks. The doors flew open before her, and she took to her feet.

Inside stood three guards, each holding a slinger. They leveled their weapons at Nilah, fury in their expressions.

In the blink of an eye, Jeannie and Alister fell upon either side of the watch, stabbing and shrieking. The third guard had just enough time to register her shock before Nilah closed the gap and sacked her, landing astride her chest with fists clenched and rage on her lips. She screamed in her face as she broke her teeth and ripped her slinger rifle from her grasp. That guard was lucky. Jeannie and Alister had made short work of the other two.

When Nilah rose to her feet, she found a squat, withered old man standing before her, an excited smile on his face.

In a rasping voice, he said, "No more than ten may enter the Pinnacle."

Nilah looked behind herself and found the access panel, striding past the twins, who'd gathered by her side. She traced her glyph, knit together a short security code, and slammed the door shut, leaving Courtney outside with the other killers. It was cruel to let them freeze to death, but what were her other options? Wait for the other cultists to rush in and kill them in an effort to pare down the numbers? Nilah straightened herself, puffing out her chest as the Pinnacle's warmth seeped into her skin.

"No more than ten have, my friend."

"Ready to do something stupid?" grumbled Boots as their taxi set down across from the entrance to Twenty-Six-D.

"Ready as I always am," answered Orna, adjusting her sunglasses with a smirk. "This won't be half as hard as taking the *Harrow*."

Boots narrowed her eyes. "Speak for yourself. At least we had a head start that time. Security is going to be on point today. We screw this up, we'll be a fine red mist all over everyone else's stuff."

Orna polished her glasses for what seemed like the fiftieth time. "I still think it's ridiculous to wear sunglasses."

"Gives them something to complain about. Vaults never allow sunglasses, so they'll be looking at our faces," said Boots, "instead of paying attention to the barnacle on my neck."

"Whatever." Orna smoothed down her spiky hair. "Just get over here and let's get linked up."

She traced her mechanist's mark, then reached behind Boots's head to touch the flesh-colored sticker they'd attached beneath her hairline; underneath it lay the barnacle. A sharp warmth permeated the device, almost hot enough to burn Boots, and she flinched. Orna gave her a gentle slap and pointed at her nose.

"No. No flinching," said the quartermaster. "I don't care if you're catching fire in there, I don't want to see you even wince."

Boots gritted her teeth. "It's like I have a hot bug crawling on my neck. Couldn't we have done my palm or something?"

"You want the scanners to mistake it for a cardioid, don't you?" Orna closed her eyes. "I've got a good link to the barnacle.

Remember the plan: we go in there to access our box, you stick down the barnacle on the console, then block the guard's view while I get access to the warehouse controls."

Boots continued for her, "We take what we need out of Durand's box, put everything back where we found it, and get the hell out of there. Easy peasy, right?"

"The easiest of peasies," said Orna with a nod. "Just don't forget the barnacle when we leave. I can't walk out with it or the scanners will dice me."

"Okay," said Boots. "Let's rock."

They climbed out of the cab onto the busy street of the Vault District, bustling with the armored strongbox transports. Boots watched the parade of autoturrets and wondered just how networked the defenses of Mercandatta were. If she tripped an alarm, would the armored cars stop to blow her apart?

They crossed the street into the lobby, and where once Boots had felt welcomed, she felt only the chill of a mausoleum. Everything was the exact same as last time: the single desk, the rock walls and floors, the overly friendly salesman/attendant, but entering the hallowed halls of commerce with larcenous intent changed the temperature a bit.

"Elsie! Bertha! How lovely to see you today," said John, clapping his hands together. "Visiting our new box already?"

"We're making some additions," said Orna, holding up a small carrying case. It was mostly empty, but that was none of John's business.

"Fantastic." John nodded at Boots's awkwardly tied folder of papers. "Do you need a moment to sort your affairs before we go into the vault? Can I get you anything to drink or eat in the meantime? I can pop you up a workstation, and we have the best coffee service in—"

"John," said Boots, "calm down. We're already renting a box. You're selling past the close, buddy."

He drew up short and an embarrassed smile spread across his face. "That I am, that I am." He fetched his key from behind his desk and gestured for them to follow. "You know, I just get so darn excited. We've got these terrific cookies, and the staff can't really eat them unless our clientele indulges." With that last, he winked.

Boots clapped him on the shoulder. "Tell them we had cookies then, John, and spoil yourself. You deserve it."

John placed his key into the hole and winked at Boots. "Oh, you are so bad."

You have no idea, John.

He almost turned, but stopped short, looking the both of them over. Could he see her pulse thumping in her neck? No, his eyes were on Orna.

"I'm so sorry," he began, and Boots braced for some kind of denial, "but eyewear off, please."

It took every ounce of Boots's control not to smile as Orna removed her glasses and tucked them into her collar. John turned the key, and magic flooded the veins of the marble wall, parting it before them. John walked to the interior corridor and pressed the hidden recess, bringing forth the tray for magical items. He held it out for them.

Orna took off her circlet and placed it into the tray. Boots did the same with her paragon crystal. John held the tray steadfastly, his face expectant.

"Now are we sure that's everything?" he asked, and Boots briefly wondered if he knew, if he was warning them not to try anything.

"That's all," said Boots. "Bertha, you got some magical items I don't know about?"

Orna shook her head no, but John refused to close the box, his face growing concerned. He stared intently at Boots, like he could see right through her, all the way to the cheap barnacle flesh-taped to the base of her skull.

"I don't have anything else," said Boots.

"I'm afraid you do," said John. "I'm really sorry about this."

Boots balled her hands into fists, ready to punch him if he did something to trigger an alarm. Maybe she could get halfway down the block before the drones mowed her down. Her fingers clinked.

John nodded at her shoulder. "Your, um, arm battery, miss."

"Oh, for crying out loud, John!" Boots guffawed. "Am I ever glad for you! If you hadn't stopped me from going in there..."

John cocked his head with a sunbeam smile. "I do like to see my clients in one piece! I simply don't like bringing up someone else's amputation. Seems a bit uncouth."

Boots reached under her collar and pulled the battery loose, her arm going slack as she did. "Too right, John. Too right. Have an extra cookie on me."

He turned and slid the box into the wall. "And now I'll leave you to your good works. I'll be in the lobby when you're ready for me to close up."

Boots and Orna walked down the trio of stairs into the sunny vault proper. Gleaming, polished boxes greeted them, reflecting light onto the central console. Boots circled it once.

"How do you work this thing again?" she asked, pretending to scratch the back of her neck. She dug her fingernails up under the sticker and peeled it away as nonchalantly as she could. Once she had the barnacle in hand, she palmed it and pressed it to the side of the glassy console opposite the door.

"Just put your access code in." Orna came and pushed her aside, leaning against the console and placing her fingers over the barnacle. Once she had bare skin against the machine, she could reconnect to her spell. The quartermaster let out a soft sigh, and Boots recognized that look on her face—mechanists loved to interface with machines, maybe a little too much.

Boots crossed around to put her body between the open door and the console. "Oh, yeah. This thing is so fancy."

"Yep," said Orna, but she clearly wasn't listening. Her eyes flitted back and forth, skimming through some data that Boots couldn't see.

"We should get something like this for the ship. It'd be real nice."

"Yep."

She glanced at Orna, waiting for her to crack the system, but instead found a cold sweat on the quartermaster's brow. Orna bit her lip, and a vein bulged on the side of her forehead.

They'd chosen their crew incorrectly. Nilah was the hacker. Orna was the fighter. If she couldn't hack the system, their whole adventure would come to an end, and Nilah would be left dangling at the end of a rope on Hammerhead.

"Everything okay, ladies?" John called from the entryway to the lobby.

Boots cleared her throat, trying to muster a bit of confidence. "Fine! We're fine. Just forgot our access code."

"Oh, no!" He clasped his hands together and wrung them. "I'm afraid I can't give you that information from here. You'll have to go to the main office."

Orna's skin drained of color. Whatever security was inside the console was eating her lunch. Boots had heard tell of systems that would fry a hacker, and wondered if she should pull Orna free and cancel the op.

Boots shifted, to better hide Orna's face from John. "No, uh, I think we can remember it. Can't we?"

John cocked his head. "It's not such a long trip to the main office. I can call you a Hansom Cab and let them know you're coming. In and out, as they say."

He took a step down the stairs, and Boots's mind raced for some way to get rid of him. John was polite, polished, and, most of all, professional. Time to test that.

Boots's face darkened. "John, I'm going to need a minute alone with my business partner. I'm concerned that she isn't doing what she's supposed to, *like remembering the damned combination.*" With this, Boots turned theatrically to Orna and gripped the sides of the console in anger. "We're expecting to stash the goods today, Bertha, and I hope you understand the consequences of failure here."

Orna's lips quivered with her efforts. "I'm... trying to remember..."

"You had better, or it's your job!" Boots barked.

John went pink with embarrassment, nodded, and retreated to the lobby.

As soon as he was out of sight, Boots relaxed her anger. Orna's eyes had rolled back in her head, and her lips parted. Any second, Boots expected to see a strand of drool trickle out.

She glanced back at the door, just to make sure John was gone, and whispered, "You okay, kid?"

Orna blinked, her eyes focusing on Boots's, and smiled. "We're in."

The crawler bot spun its rails around the room, then rocketed toward the distant roof, disappearing into the light of the sun panels.

"We're VIPs now," whispered Orna.

Servos echoed through the cavernous space as the crawler snatched a box somewhere above.

"What does that mean?" asked Boots.

"I don't know," said Orna. "I saw a flag in the database and I flipped it. Figured it would be good to be important."

The bot plummeted down the rails before stopping suddenly above the ground and jutting out its pincers, box attached.

"You don't know for sure that's what VIP stands for!" Boots hissed. "It might mean they consider us suspicious."

"Who'd use VIP for that?"

"Spaceport security! Back in my day, 'VIP' was code for 'customs is going to search your ship and take your smuggled whiskey,'" said Boots, heading over and grabbing the box from the pincers. The crawler chimed once and then shot away. "You're supposed to know this, *quartermaster*."

"'Back in your day' was about a billion years ago, so stop complaining."

They hauled the box to the carrel and placed it on the desk. Glowing spheres arose from the lamps to give them more even light. Boots's hand came to rest on the latch and she took a deep breath.

"I swear to god if this thing is empty…" she muttered.

"Why would it be empty?"

Boots gave Orna a dire look. "Durand is dead. Maybe our intel is bad and the Children already looted it."

"Hurry up and open it, then."

Boots pulled back the lid and set it aside in a fitted recess on the desk. The first layer was a tray of brassy chits, meticulously laid out in a grid. Boots counted the rows and columns, then multiplied out the result.

"Looks like a hundred and ten data chits," she said.

Orna lifted one to her eye, turning it over. "Software?"

"Each one probably has an unsigned account," said Boots. "These are untraceable cash for bagmen."

"Wasn't expecting a payday," said Orna, pulling a shopping bag out of her coat pocket and shaking it open. "By now, they know Durand is compromised, so there's no harm in taking it."

"Every argent in our hands is one they can't spend killing us," muttered Boots, then nearly shrieked when John appeared inside the vault.

"I apologize," he said, "but another one of our clients has some urgent business and needs to access the vault. If you need the privacy screen, the button is right there. And I'm going to turn on a bit of music to cover your conversations."

"Nothing too frumpy," said Boots, giving him a thin smile. Then she tapped the privacy control as the electric strings of a soaring concerto filled the vault. A screen slid across the opening of the carrel, and through its mesh, Boots saw another hidden room open up across the way. How many other surprises and secrets were folded into the vault?

"Let's get this done and scram," said Boots, lifting the tray and dumping the chits into Orna's sack. She set the tray to one side and peered into the rest of the box, disappointed to find only leather-bound papers awaiting her.

She glanced away to see the newcomer enter the vault and found what she expected: a tall woman with slicked-back hair and an expertly cut suit. She nodded in greeting at them through the mesh before entering her code into the console. The system beeped in error.

"Elsie," whispered Orna, but Boots didn't want to look away.

The woman didn't look like the sort to enter her code incorrectly. She shook her head as if a fool and began to type it once more.

"Elsie!" Orna punched Boots on the arm.

The error beep filled the vaults once more.

"What?" Boots said through clenched teeth.

Orna tapped the title of the leather folio: A Promissory Letter of Deeds and Services Rendered in Exchange for Certain Compensation.

"So?" Boots shrugged and glanced over her shoulder at the stranger once more. She pressed each key with maximum deliberation, making certain not to miss.

"So look, you jackass!" Orna pulled her chin to drag Boots's gaze to the folio. She held it up and pointed to an embossed seal at the bottom.

Boots's mouth went dry as her mind deciphered the shapes of the letters, rendering them into four words, transmuting into meaning.

"Hereby Witnesseth, Stetson Giles."

Boots's mind raced back through the mists of years to find a derelict starship, the *Saint of Flowers*. She saw a chalice, a corpse, and her old partner, Stetson Giles, with a smoking slinger. She remembered her own screaming and the stab of his betrayal at their moment of triumph.

He'd ruined her.

It couldn't be him, but there was no other explanation.

The error code sounded one last time, and Boots looked out through the mesh curtain.

The stranger was staring at them.

Chapter Nine

Reverse

At first, the elder had said nothing to Nilah and the twins. When more guards showed up, bristling at the murder of the gatekeepers, he stayed their attack and told them to prepare quarters for the new initiates. He also ordered them to mow down everyone still outside.

At long last, he looked at Nilah with elated eyes and clapped his hands together. "We've proven who was strongest. No need to be cruel about it." Then, to the guards, he said, "Treat the new-comers with care. They're the most exciting batch in such a long time! I'm Elder Osmond, and it is my most, most, most distinct pleasure to welcome you to the Pinnacle."

Much to Nilah's surprise, the guards' anger dissolved, and they introduced themselves in a friendly enough fashion. They weren't full-time members of the watch, but initiates in the Children of the Singularity, just like Nilah, Jeannie, and Alister. They were all clad in black uniforms of varying cuts—some in robes, some in pants and mag-snap shirts. Elder Osmond wore a long red sash, embroidered with interweaving geometric patterns, the only sig-nifier of his office.

One of the guards bore a small, silver shield badge upon his right breast, emblazoned with the same blank mask Nilah had seen in Elba Pool Station. The perfect cut and tasteful design of his uniform annoyed her—Nilah preferred her fanatics to be less put together.

"Sharp," he said, extending a hand to each of them in turn. "Head of security here."

Nilah accepted his greeting, and it was like shaking hands with a statue.

The elder gave Nilah a quick pat on the shoulder. "I'm off to help the lads clean up the stragglers outside. Mister Sharp will get you settled in. Save me a cookie, will you?"

Nilah gave him a tight smirk to mask her confusion, then followed Sharp deeper into the stone halls of the Pinnacle.

The scent of freshly baked, buttery bread snaked through Nilah's nostrils to yank on her stomach. Other smells emerged: herbs and spices, roasting vegetables, frying onions. Then came the fat and salt of cooked animals, souring her appetite.

At least, she wanted it to sour her appetite.

In truth, her torture-by-protein-bar stay at the base camp had softened her vegetarian's resolve, but she'd never eaten an animal before and wasn't about to start. Taitutians didn't eat meat—unless they wanted to spend the next five cycles farting.

When she turned the corner to the main dining hall, her eyes nearly fell out of her head.

A feast spread before them across a long, stone banquet table, a host of delicacies from across the galaxy: Blixish olives and caviar, salt-crusted bass from the streams of Yearling, meaty orchid petals from the jungles of Taitu. While she didn't eat flesh, she'd attended enough state dinners on different planets to know the rarity of this regal spread.

"Please," said Sharp. "Help yourselves. Apparently, we made too much."

Nilah gave him a nonplussed look. "Sorry?"

Sharp quirked his lips and replied, "We were expecting a party of ten."

Nilah wanted to trust in the food, to thrust her hands deep into the plentiful dishes and gorge herself by the fistful, but it made little sense. If this was some sort of extreme monastery, they shouldn't be indulging in such extravagance. What if it was a test?

"You should join us, then," said Nilah. "It'd be a shame for all of this to go to waste."

He shook his head, though he took a moment to decline. "We're not into sharing here. You earned it, you eat it. This is your achievement."

She glanced at the twins, who'd already sat down and begun to stuff their faces. She couldn't blame them; after all, she'd been getting double their rations every day after beating Heather Ashburn. It was a wonder they hadn't collapsed from exhaustion.

"I'm not sharing," said Nilah. "I'm buying. I earned this meal. You can tell me how to keep my edge in a place like the Pinnacle. Let me trade for information."

Sharp smirked and pulled up a chair. He then ladled out a pair of golden filets of arrowfish onto his plate—the most expensive item on the table behind the caviar. To it, he added rare cheeses from the farming worlds, some of the fish eggs, and a dollop of crème fraîche. Nilah took note of his plating skills. This wasn't his first experience with such wealth. Jeannie and Alister, on the other hand, made Nilah want to slap their hands and teach them how to properly eat. They'd always been overeager with the food on the *Capricious*, but this was even worse.

"What would you like to know?" asked Sharp.

Nilah helped herself to one of every vegetable there, scoring a double serving of the jewel-toned bean curd. "What will we do here?"

He took a bite of the arrowfish, savoring every moment. "You'll become greater than you could've imagined. You'll take back your destiny from mediocrity."

She popped a bit of succulent orchid into her mouth and chewed away the sweetness. "That sounds great in the abstract, but I'd like to know the real scoop."

He shrugged. "Training. Preparation. Some of us will go on to fight in the most important war ever waged. Others of us will be writing the rules of the very near future. It starts with taking back our homeworld from the interlopers."

Nilah had heard enough of their conspiracy theories to know where this was going. "You want to overthrow the prime minister of Taitu?"

Sharp grimaced. "That's only the start. We'll have to work on your ambition."

A much younger-looking woman entered with a jug of wine, pouring generous servings for the four diners. A small light blinked under her hairline, just at the base of her skull, and Nilah craned her head for a closer look.

"Those who fail will stay on and serve," said Sharp. "We can't exactly send them home, considering what they know. I'm sure you understand."

The woman leaned across her to pour her wine, and Nilah restrained a gasp. She knew the device implanted in the waiter's spinal column—illegal on almost every world: the neural spike. She'd follow any orders given her, but remove it, and she'd die of shock.

Nilah tried to play it cool, but her insides burned with righteous fury. "You've...enslaved her? Why not simply kill her? Aren't you risking execution if you're caught by the authorities?"

Sharp carved off another flake of arrowfish, admiring its sheen before savoring the meat. He patted the waiter on the shoulder. "Fritz here arrived at the Pinnacle because of her substantial talents. She might not be much of a free thinker nowadays, but don't let that fool you—she's a teleporter of the highest order. She could probably go from one side of this moon to the other in a single leap. We basically have the greatest anti-invasion force possible: a bunch of talented magi with no fear of death."

With that, Fritz's lips curled into a forced smile.

Sharp toasted her as she walked away. "Fritz was a commodities trader until she beat someone to death in a drunken haze. She came to us and thought she could get a new start. From the moment she set foot on Hammerhead, she consigned her body to whatever fate we decided. She wasn't good enough, and now she pours wine. But don't let that bother you. For the moment, you're an elite—a true Child of the Singularity. You made it up here."

Nilah glanced at the twins, who continued to devour their food. Since arriving, they'd seemed a little too much at home with all of the atrocity. Whatever they'd seen in their old lives, it must've been horrid.

"No one forced Fritz to challenge Elder Osmond," said Sharp, "but she was so eager for what comes next."

"And what's that?" asked Nilah, hiding her scowl behind a wine cup.

He shrugged. "Heaven. A sampling of pure bliss. Your true destiny. Whatever you want to call it. Everyone calls this the Pinnacle, but the truth is that it's more like a diving board."

"Oh?"

"From here, you leap off into the real universe," said Sharp. "No boundaries, no limits, no rules, no safeties. Just you and your ultimate fate, traveling through the stars."

Nilah sliced apart a perfectly tender honey dill carrot and

winced, imagining the person who cooked it was a slave, living in a nightmare. "Isn't ultimate fate the one thing all of us have? Why would we need to come here to get it?"

"Because you're part of a system," said Sharp, helping himself to more caviar and toast points. "You don't know how freeing it is to live outside of that."

Of course I do, you git. Try going on the run for a few months.

"So any tips for survival? I did, after all, ply you with my share of the feast."

Sharp gave her a wolfish grin. "Learn to be cruel. Learn to eat meat. I watched you out there, and you didn't harm a soul, save for a light beating."

Nilah spread her palms over her plate as if blessing it. "I'm sitting here, aren't I, mate? I'm cruel enough."

But her blustering lie became truth as it left her mouth. She'd told Courtney to kill all those people. She'd tricked the sad, forgotten boy and closed the door in his face, so he and sixteen others could die. In the pursuit of her goals—the promise of secret knowledge of Henrick Witts's organization—she'd led a person to slaughter. Nilah couldn't be certain she'd find the infiltrator in this place, so was there a reason to kill those people?

But the cultists were going to die anyway, weren't they? Most of them would've fallen to one another's wrath on the hillside. Then a thought stole into her head so subtly that she almost missed it: ninety of them would've been murdered. She'd only bumped up the total to ninety-seven. The difference between those two numbers wasn't so great, was it? They were all killers.

But then, she didn't personally know the seven extra dead. There could've been another among the supplicants like her, someone trying their hardest to stop the Children and the other *Harrow* conspirators. Maybe there was a police officer or spy dead on that icy hill, eyes frozen open, their last thoughts of a family they'd never see again. Or maybe, those seven dead would've realized the error of their ways and quit the cult to help the side of justice. Seven extra corpses were too many; one extra corpse was too many.

Nilah had done exactly as the Children of the Singularity wished—she'd let people die without question in pursuit of her own goals. Were they getting to her? She hadn't personally killed anyone. The Children orchestrated the murders.

She'd only acted as they wished, which was cold comfort.

Blinking, Nilah realized Sharp was talking to her.

"I'm sorry?" she asked.

"Tired from your battle?" he asked. "I can only imagine. I've seen at least a thousand men and women pass through here. I was one of them, you know, a pilgrim, but I can't beat Elder Osmond, and I know it." Sharp took a bite of caviar, obviously relishing the feeling of popping the eggs against the roof of his mouth. "Better to remain a guard than to have a spike in my neck."

"That depends," said Jeannie, and Nilah nearly dropped her fork with surprise.

Sharp cocked his head. "On what, my dear?"

Jeannie took a bite of bloody marpo, its skin fried tight and crispy. "Whether or not you're the folks we shanked at the gate. They were guards, too, weren't they?"

Sharp nodded. "Yes, they were, and I'll be sure to keep my eye on you." Then he said to Nilah, "My statement stands: the only way out is up, and the only way up is to defeat Elder Osmond in a challenge. You lose? You get the spike."

"We won't lose," said Alister between bites. "Came too far."

Nilah took a large gulp of wine. "You're gathering a lot of people up just to kill them. Not particularly efficient."

Looking her in the eye, Sharp said, "Only a precious few are worthy to join us, and they must have absolute resolve and incredible talent. Our ranks contain only the most ruthless strategists and deadliest fighters. Of course most of them die, but no one forced them to join. People die climbing the highest peaks in the galaxy, but the ones who reach the top are heroes."

The stranger's face distorted with rage and she rushed to the privacy screen, sweeping it aside. The carrel gave an angry beep at her intrusion, but did nothing else to protect them. Her eyes darted from Boots, to Orna, to the open deposit box—to the unique serial number etched on its side.

She'd been trying to enter Maslin Durand's access code into the central console.

She was there to collect his things.

Boots raised her hands to calm her. "Listen, lady, this is a secure vault. You've got no slinger and no spells, so let's talk. Who are you?"

The woman drew a palm-sized handle from her suit pocket and flipped it, ejecting a razor blade almost as long as her forearm. Weapons were allowed in the vault, of course, because the IGF didn't give a damn if their clients shanked one another.

Boots went to eject her finger blade—no arm battery. "Oh, uh..."

Orna swept up the metal tray and hurled it at the woman's head, and she ducked clear. Orna leapt the table and tried to sink a kick into her gut, but the woman caught her foot and swept the ultra-sharp blade toward her neck. Orna seized the woman's wrist, but she turned her momentum into a throw, hurling the quartermaster out against the console like she was a child.

The suit turned on Boots like a wolf ready to tear out her throat.

"Let's think about this," said Boots, lunging to keep the table between them. "You don't know who I am. I could have valuable intel."

She swung her blade across at Boots, and as she ducked back, it extended another few centimeters, whipping across her nose with a thunk. It didn't hurt much, but it bled like a river.

Boots staggered back, clutching her face, shocked at the amount of crimson pouring between her fingers. The stranger came rushing around one side of the table in a flurry of swings, and Boots retaliated with the first thing that came to mind—she slung her blood-soaked hand at her attacker's face. A slash of her blood hit the stranger's eyes, and she shook her head, trying to wipe it away. Boots seized the opportunity to grab the folio out of the box and bolted for the entrance of the carrel.

Before she could make it clear, something crashed against the back of her head and she rolled to the ground in a daze. Shaking away the dancing lights, she spotted pieces of one of the desk lamps on the ground around her. She pulled herself across the tile, trying to get to the vault entrance—if she called for help, she might be arrested. If she didn't, she might die.

She'd almost made it to Orna when she glanced back to see the stranger striding to the edge of the carrel, adjusting her cuffs. She stepped one foot into the open vault—

And a crawler smashed a vault box into her body, folding her in half for a quick end.

Boots looked back at Orna to find her hand against the barnacle, her eyes rolled back in her head. She blinked, her icy eyes coming to focus on Boots.

"Got the cash," she said, hefting the sack of chits.

"Got the contract," said Boots, and they both rushed for the vault exit.

"Is everything okay in he—" John appeared before them, and his tray of steaming cookies clattered to the floor. Boots couldn't smell them through her blood, but they looked heavenly. "Oh, my god, your nose!" He peered past them. "Oh, my god, that woman!"

"We were attacked," said Boots. "We have to get back to our ship, because—"

Silhouettes crowded the lobby exit to the outside, and Boots gulped. Coming in from the street, there had to be a half-dozen other goons ready to succeed where the first of them had failed.

Slinger fire perforated the room, and John, Boots, and Orna hit the deck. John yanked back his sleeve and checked something on his watch.

"Apologies, ladies!" he shouted over the thump of armored transports outside spinning up their autoturrets. "I didn't realize you were VIPs!" He tapped the watch face and a set of duraplast shutters slammed down in front of the assailants.

"Now," said John. "Let's let security handle all that, shall we? Fetch your things."

They rushed to the hidden recess, where John drew out the velvet-lined box with their personal effects. Orna donned her silver circlet and closed her eyes, contacting Charger. Boots pocketed her paragon crystal and plugged in her battery, happy to have her arm back. As a precaution, she tested the stiletto knife in her finger, glad to have it working.

"What all comes with VIP service, John?" Boots asked, trying not to sound too frantic.

"Occasionally, we have clientele with exceptional enemies." The attendant pounded another hidden panel, which unfolded to dispense a tripod and an assault slinger with a massive drum magazine. "Those designated VIPs will have a priority escort from the station in the event of an attack. Pardon me a moment."

John grabbed a staff from its clips next to the tripod and slammed it down, where it branched out like a tree, each limb webbed with layers of shield magic. He snapped the barrel of the assault rifle into the mount and took aim at the front doors. Then he raised his watch to his lips.

"This is John Buppert, auth code seven-five-two-two-four, requesting access control lockdown on my location. Give me a two-block clear zone."

Explosions rocked the street outside, melting the duraplast windows like popping bubbles. Through the raging blaze, Boots could make out the shapes of armored transports on fire. Whoever these people were, they'd taken out a veritable motorcade of armored trucks.

"Stay behind the shield, if you please!" John called out with a smile, then spun up his heavy slinger, filling the entrance with knock rounds. They exploded against assailants, the interior walls, the street outside, and the skeletons of armored transports. The air thundered with each impact, and he held down the trigger until the magazine ran dry.

Boots took her hands from her ears and stared at the carnage in disbelief.

John gestured to the open panel where he'd gotten the assault rifle. "Just to be on the safe side, you shouldn't go out the front door. There's a lever in that cabinet. Would you mind pulling it?" Then, into his watch, "I'm going to need support for two VIPs. Yes, they are. No, I'm looking right at them."

Boots scrambled to the cabinet and yanked down the switch as another volley of fire crackled across the back wall beside her head. Then she nearly fell over as a two-meter square of the floor began to sink.

"Orna!" Boots called out, and the quartermaster raced to her side, sliding into the opening.

Crap.

At the mention of Orna's real name, John glanced back at them, a venom in his expression that Boots never could've expected. He might not know how or why, but he knew he'd been betrayed. Then a lance round caught him by the leg, and they sank out of sight.

The elevator opened into a wide electrical shaft full of conveyors and maintenance bots zooming along conduits. The hallway thrummed with power. Steam hissed from gratings in sudden spurts. The elevator sealed above them, magic shaping the rock into a solid face.

Boots looked around for an obvious way out, but the maze of tunnels extended in all directions. "If John reports us, we're screwed. The station's automated defense network will track us anywhere we go."

Orna scoured the wall of conduit, jumping out of the way of a crawler bot. "Maybe those bastards outside will kill him before he can get a message out."

"Don't say that. I like John. Can't you hack us some station credentials or something? Make it so we can get past all of the cameras without getting blasted?"

"It's not that easy. I was only able to designate us VIPs within the vault because it was local security. Central security would fry my brain in a heartbeat. There's another solution, though," said Orna, tracing her glyph and grabbing one of the duct maintenance bots. It stopped with an angry beep as she forced her magic inside. Then it let go of the conduit pipe, and she placed it on the ground.

"I'm listening," said Boots.

"This place is huge, so they can't lock down the whole thing, just the protected structures. Buildings, vaults, that kind of stuff." She grabbed another bot off the rails and paralyzed it. "It's hard to shut down an alarm, but it's easy to set one off."

"Yeah. Alarms are the problem."

Orna grabbed another. "No, alarms are the *solution*." Then another. "I'm going to send these bots throughout the station underground, and they're going to start drilling."

"Did you hit your head back there? You're going to bring security down on us like a tidal wave!"

"Wrong," said Orna, hooking the bots to all different conduits. "The exit to the tunnels is right there. They're going to think there are hundreds of hackers drilling into the data cables down here and put every building on lockdown."

"Then we get topside while security is spread thin. Okay. What about those guys that shot at us?"

Orna clicked a fingernail against her circlet. "Working on that. Charger is en route."

One by one, she tapped the bots with her spell, and they raced off down the tunnels. Orna grabbed Boots's hand and dragged her toward the nearest ladder before climbing up and cautiously opening the door.

"Looks clear," she called down to Boots. "Let's go."

They emerged onto the street level to find an abandoned thoroughfare. It hadn't been crowded before, but the commotion outside Twenty-Six-D had cleared everyone out. Deafening klaxons blared at two-second intervals. Between the alarms, Boots made out the sound of an approaching security drone.

"Drone!" whispered Boots. "Back to the tunnels!"

Orna grabbed her by the collar, hauling her away from the ladder. "When those crawlers start drilling, the underground will be a death trap." She slammed Boots up against the back wall of Twenty-Six-D and said, "Flatten out as much as you can."

"What the hell? We're sitting ducks out here! That drone is going to shoot us!"

The drone came buzzing around the corner, a pair of slingers on either side spinning up at the sight of them. Boots braced herself to be beaten unconscious by knock rounds, but instead, it made a pleasant chime, swooping down to guard them.

"We're still VIPs inside the vault," said Orna. "Looks like the immediate surroundings are zoned vault, too."

"So as long as we don't leave this area, we're okay?"

"Yeah. If I can get my hands on this little guy, he can give us an escort back to the ship." Orna traced her mechanist's glyph and slapped at the drone, trying to catch it. The bot swooped out of the way with little trouble and gave her an angry chirp. If they left the side of the vault and lost their VIP status, it'd almost certainly shoot them for trying to hack it.

Boots watched with mounting fear. "Grab it!"

"What do you think I'm trying to do?" Orna jumped for it and stumbled away from the wall. Boots caught her and yanked her backward.

"If we don't get out of here before the human security shows up—" Boots started, but was cut off when a trio in suits rounded the corner, slingers in hand. She couldn't be sure if they were cultists or guards.

Then they blasted the defense drone.

"Run!" shouted Boots, and they hotfooted it for the far end of the clean, featureless alley.

Slinger bolts sizzled past them, and Boots counted the distance to the end of the alleyway. Thirty paces—it felt so unbearably far. Twenty paces—rock shrapnel sliced the side of Boots's face as a round struck the wall beside her. Ten paces—Orna surged ahead of her.

A glowing bolt of energy punctured the quartermaster's hip with a puff of bloody mist.

Orna screamed in pain and stumbled to the ground. Boots slowed up enough to clasp hands with her and began dragging her backward toward the corner.

"Crap, crap, crap," Boots repeated as Orna groaned in agony. Five paces—she needed a distraction. Boots shouted, "If you shoot us, you'll never find the papers we stole!"

Their attackers loomed large in her view, taking confident aim at Boots's head. One of them signaled the others to hold fire, and they closed in on the pair like trained mercenaries.

"Give us the folio, now, and you can walk away," called the lead, just a few meters down the corridor. He wore a similarly crisp suit to the woman in the vault, his features polished and fashionable. He'd probably bought his visage—few people were born with that unnatural beauty.

"What folio?" feigned Boots.

The leader fired a slinger bolt right past her ear, stealing the breath from Boots as it passed. It had come so close that she felt a light sunburn on her cheek. "Answer incorrectly again, and we'll just search your corpse."

Orna clutched her bleeding side and laughed, just a chuckle but strange all the same.

"Shut her up," said another one of the suits.

Boots looked to her comrade, who must've been delirious with blood loss. "Buddy, I've been trying for over a year."

The quartermaster only cackled louder. The leader kept his slinger trained on Boots, but cut a glance over to the laughing woman. His slinger shifted ever so slightly toward the quartermaster. If she was trying to stall them, it seemed to be working.

"Whoa, now! Let's be reasonable," said Boots, drawing out the leather-bound pages and holding them in front of herself like body armor. "Shock can do nasty things to a person. I've got your folio right here."

"You have no idea what's coming," said Orna, baring her teeth.

His slinger barrel snapped to Orna's head. "Shut her up, or I will. Three."

The quartermaster was almost wheezing with laughter.

Boots gave him a pained smile. "I'm sorry, can I just have a word with my friend?"

His grip tightened. "Two."

Boots turned to Orna and gave her a "what gives" look, but the woman kept on laughing. Her stalling tactics were only going to buy them three seconds.

"Knock it off, Orna!" Boots considered slapping her.

"One."

Orna sat up with madness in her eyes and a wild grin. "Here comes my special boy!"

She wrapped her arms around Boots and threw her to the ground. Charger bounded around the corner at the end of the alleyway and flooded the corridor with discus rounds, slicing the attackers at odd, spinning angles. Boots shut her eyes and held on to Orna as the projectiles hissed overhead, sailing into the vault across the street.

In the silence that followed, Boots surveyed the damage. A couple of dead goons and shallow, smoking slashes in Twenty-Seven-E: barely even scratches on the massive structure. Servo screams and lightning crackle brought Charger to them, where it loomed over the pair of women.

Gone were the slick, regraded steel plates and duraplex guarding his torso. Arcane fires roared from his chest like souls in a demonic smelting furnace. Skeletal supports jutted out of him like bones, and he held out one claw to help Orna up.

Boots stared at the machine wide-eyed. "Holy..."

"Charger!" Orna slapped his claw away. "Why are you naked?"

Charger recoiled and pointed to its open chest, making a case only Orna could hear.

She rolled onto one side and pushed herself upright, doing a terrible job of stanching the blood pouring from her wound. "No, I don't care if you're faster! Keep those chest plates on and—"

Orna passed out into his arms.

"Damn it!" Boots rushed forward, but Charger backed away,

popping open his chest plate and stuffing Orna inside like a rescue bot—except he wasn't. He was Orna's original creation. "No,
Charger! She's wounded!"

It held up a hand to Boots, giving her the wait finger. She considered giving it a finger of her own, but thought better of it. Then
she saw the styptifoam filling Orna's wounds and the duraplex
mesh erupting from spinnerets in Charger's cushions.

She'd redesigned Charger to handle her massive blood loss after
Mother had punched a hole through Ranger.

Charger leaned forward to Boots, and a young boy's voice said,
"Nominal oxy sat. Blood pressure envelope okay. Pulse okay."

Boots blinked. Was that little thing really the voice package
Orna had installed? It totally ruined its badass aesthetic.

More alarms sounded across the station's expanse, and Boots
looked over the freshly departed corpses littering the alleyway.
She grabbed the leg of their leader and turned him onto his side to
search his pockets. His top half didn't turn with the rest of him.

Boots held down her lunch, but only because she'd been to
some dark places in her day. She didn't find an ID, access cards, or
anything of the like. Holding her breath, she attempted the same
search on his mangled blazer and found a portable drive with a
built-in imager. She also (unfortunately) learned he'd had a significant number of organ modifications done, from the sparkling
silver bits in the ocean of blood.

"What were you doing with this imager, buddy?" she mumbled
to herself, inspecting it.

A red light flashed across its surface; it took her a moment to
realize it was a dying heartbeat. These men were transmitting
imagery to something off-station—

—just like the imagers in the archives.

The eerie song of Izak Vraba's spell filled her ears.

"Crap!" Boots yelped, throwing the imager to the far end of

the alleyway as shadows poured forth from the walls around her. They danced wildly to the flipping of the lens as it bounced across the concrete. It came to rest at an odd angle against the far wall, still able to see her.

Charger buzzed loudly to get her attention, and Boots bolted for him as fast as her stocky legs would carry her.

"Okay, uh, boy. Let's go!"

The bot reached behind its head and unslung the ammo canister from its back, hefting the tub under its arm like a beach ball. Charger nodded and turned around, so Boots could see a mounting handle and a couple of brackets she could ride.

"You want me to hang on with my bare hands? You know I'm forty-three, right?"

A score of shadowy vipers, pouring toward her with fangs outstretched, cut short the discussion. High alert was rolling through Mercandatta like an earthquake, and the first place they'd send security forces was the epicenter. Charger knelt down so she'd have an easier time and chimed.

She mounted him as best she could. This wouldn't work. It'd buck her off in seconds if it mustered even half the speed she'd seen from it.

She was about to tell Charger so when it leapt thirty meters through the air, jammed its toe-claws into the facade of one of the buildings, and bounded off onto the opposing roof. She tried to shout for it to stop, but all that came out was an unformed scream and a vibrant stream of swears. It launched again and again. The shadows surged toward her, grasping for her feet, to no avail.

This was nothing like the rocket rung in the *Capricious*'s cargo bay; this was raw power, like trying to keep her mitts screwed to the hull of a launching starship. If she hadn't had a metal hand with the grip strength of a gorilla, she would've been ripped free in midair. Boots gave up on the foot mounts and wrapped her legs around him, getting more acquainted with the bot than half of her former boyfriends.

When at long last, she was certain of her fate as a splatter across Mercandatta's steely landscape, Charger slammed down at the docks.

She threw up all over its neck and slid off, a gasping wreck.

"Sorry," she mumbled, wiping away her drool and clutching her forehead. If she lived through this, she'd have one hell of a migraine.

To her surprise, the other starship captains had deployed tons of their own security. Turned out that a banking station fueled by off-the-books transactions had a lot of criminals on board, and all of them were eager to defend their ships. Charger scarcely looked out of place, considering the other military hardware on hand.

Boots spun to find the *Capricious* in its mooring, engines thrumming and ready to go, its bay wide open. Alongside Charger, she rushed up the cargo ramp, fearful of what she might find. What if the Children or someone else had come and taken out her crew while she'd been cracking the vault with Orna?

Instead, she found Armin just inside the door with slinger at the ready.

He looked at her aghast and shouted, "What did you do?"

Boots pinched the sick and blood from her nose and coughed. "Doesn't matter. Tell you in the air."

Armin punched the close button with a sour look and called out over the comms. "All aboard, Captain. Good to go."

Cordell's voice flooded the bay in return. "Copy that. Get strapped in and let's boogie."

Snow filtered in through the vents, piling into corners of the Pinnacle's central courtyard. The room would've been a freezer, save for the lit fires belching heat along every wall.

Nilah wanted them to stop the fight. She wanted so badly to intervene on behalf of her friend, but that might blow her cover and kill all three of them.

"Come on, then!" the big fellow shouted at Alister. "Come hit me!"

Alister panted on the cobblestones of the outdoor arena, wiping the blood from his lips. His opponent was an ogre of a woman, towering close to two meters tall. With Jeannie at his side, Alister was a ruthless fighter. Alone, he was mincemeat.

He spat out a mouthful of blood and mumbled, "I'll do worse than hit you, you overgrown..."

He rose to his feet and popped his neck, striking a pose awfully similar to Nilah's fighting stance. But Nilah could easily suss out the cracks in his posture, his poor attentiveness, his distracted glances at his sister.

Alister Ferrier was no fighter.

The big woman came charging at him, pulling together a vibrating glyph of sunlight. She landed a punch, and Alister went flying backward into a snow drift, coming to rest against the wall in a white puff. Alister had been lucky to strike the snowy ground; a little to the left, and he might've been shattered against the stones.

The mission wasn't going well.

Alister and Jeannie had spent two days casually reading other cultists, sneaking spell castings and asking people why they were there with a handshake or pat on the back. All the while, Nilah had swallowed her nerves and been ready to support them any way she could.

They didn't get caught, but they didn't find the double agent, either. And Alister was getting sloppy, trying to do more than one read at a time, or ask more than one question.

Then, the elder had summoned them for combat training. The result was an unconscious mind reader with a probable concussion.

"What the hell, Sharp?" bellowed the ogre. "I thought you had some new recruits!"

"If you'd let us fight together," shouted Jeannie from the sidelines, "you wouldn't be so lucky!"

Sharp crossed his arms and lit a cigarette. "That kind of defeats the purpose of one-on-one matches...Moira, was it? These trials are designed to prepare you to face Elder Osmond." He pointed to the big lady. "And you're not supposed to be killing each other, Georgina! It's inefficient!"

"We killed each other plenty getting up here," said Nilah, trying to hide her worry for Alister.

"Yes," said Sharp, "and now that we've skimmed the cream off the top of the recruits, we're not going to simply throw it away."

Georgina shrugged those mountainous shoulders of hers. "He yet lives, doesn't he? Who's next? I'm bored."

Sharp looked at Jeannie, but she'd already gone to Alister's side to try and rouse him. Sharp sighed and glanced at Nilah, then pointed to Georgina. "Why don't you give it a shot?"

Nilah rested her hands on her hips. "Fighting all the time is well and good, but how does that make us the best Children we can be? Are we supposed to punch our way to the eternal truths of the galaxy?"

"You're here to be disassembled and rebuilt as an elite force. A Child of the Singularity is all things: a fighter, a diplomat, a saboteur, a spy. Forget your old life. Forget whatever you think you are." Sharp sighed out a cloud of smoke. "To be one of us, you have to be better than the rest, and that starts with physical discipline. You'll be bruised. You'll be broken. We're going to pull away your cocky veneer and teach you how to wield true power."

"Uh-huh," said Nilah. "And when do I get to do the diplomacy and espionage stuff?"

"The Pinnacle is the first rung on your climb. If you defeat the elder in combat, then you'll join Lord Vraba for the rest of your training. Eventually, you'll earn the power to take all that you desire."

" 'First rung'? Then the Pinnacle is kind of a misnomer, isn't it?"

Sharp flicked his cigarette at her. "You're far too arrogant. We'll help you with that."

Nilah cracked her knuckles. "It's only arrogance if I can't back it up, mate."

She walked toward the center of the ring, eyes fixed upon Georgina's. Nilah's abdomen ached at the very thought of the giant's fight-ending punch, and she wondered if Georgina would try to make an example of her. The woman was a kineticist, able to impart tremendous energy into an object, or person—and she was a bloody quick caster. If Nilah wanted to win, she'd have to keep Georgina's hands busy and get in close.

When Nilah came within ten paces of Georgina, she broke into an all-out sprint. The giant guffawed and wound up for a huge backhand, sparks of arcane light reflecting off the snow behind her.

It was an obvious feint—attack with a jab, deliver a spell with her cross. Nilah dropped into a slide, slamming her heel into the side of Georgina's knee. The giant's fighting instincts were excellent, and she twisted away, sparing herself from a crippling injury. Nilah lashed out at Georgina's groin, but she danced backward from Nilah's kick with surprising dexterity. Nilah scarcely rolled clear as the giant's spell blasted the ground where her head would've been.

A blistering explosion of snow erupted from the impact point, swirling into Nilah's eyes and blinding her. She scrambled upright, but Georgina's knee sunk into her gut like a rolling boulder. She was lifted bodily off the ground with the force of the blow, only to come down on her feet with stolen breath. Then a hook rocked her cheek, dazzling her. Then another into her temple, and she found herself sitting down on the soft concrete, icy water melting onto her rump.

"Stop!" called Sharp. "That's enough! If you kill her, the elder is going to be furious!"

Come on, then, love. Shake it off.

"Why?" asked Georgina. "You've got three new ones. Surely you can spare an initiate."

Nilah fixated on one of the guttering torches in the wall sconces, snapping her eyes to it every time it drifted away. Each drift got shorter and shorter until her vision returned, along with a splitting headache.

She'd been blinded. Georgina had taken advantage and struck her, unguarded. In many ways, the assault wasn't that different from Flicker. Georgina interrupted her meditations by seizing her by the collar, and Nilah palmed a handful of snow.

"Let's see how valuable you are to them," she growled into Nilah's ear, her fist whining with a charge as she traced a glyph. At this range, she'd snap Nilah's neck with a single punch.

Unless Nilah tossed a snowball into her spell.

The ball struck Georgina's fist and exploded with a sound like a fuse blowing next to her head. Nilah closed her eyes against the shower of ice and leaned back, kicking out at the giant's throat. She felt a solid connection, and Georgina stumbled back, choking out a set of nasty comments.

Rising rocket. Nilah ascended, throwing a spray of snow forward in a milky cloud. She watched for Georgina's predictable attack and ducked under it, smashing her throat once again with her elbow.

Accretion's pull. She reached down and grabbed two handfuls of snow, pinwheeling and hurling them in arcs before leaping up to come down on top of the giant's head with an elbow.

Disrupted orbit. She hooked her foot behind Georgina's knee and shoulder checked her, loosening the ogre's stance before rushing in to pummel chest, kidneys, and groin. This time, Nilah's crushing blows struck home over and over again, and Georgina's guard dropped to cover her torso.

Cold star. A scoop of snow into the giant's snout to turn up her chin, and Nilah struck the woman's eyes with a claw hardened by years of fingertip push-ups. Nilah dug in deep, listening to the screams of her opponent.

Singularity. Another wheel of powder blinded her target, not that she needed the help, and Nilah stepped in with an elbow straight for her nose. Nilah put every ounce of force she could muster into the blow, and Georgina's scream was cut short by a hard snap—then she fell over, shaking.

Nilah stepped backward and relaxed her stance, to find all eyes in the room wide and fixed upon her. She looked over Georgina once to make sure she wasn't getting up; the giant moaned hoarsely, cupping her nethers and eyes. She wouldn't be fighting any day soon without serious medical help.

Just to put a fine point on it, Nilah turned to Sharp and said, "Don't ever intervene on my behalf again, sport. I won my entry to the Pinnacle, and it's far from the last stop on my journey."

Except they weren't looking directly at her, but at something behind her. A set of thin claps echoed through the space from one set of small hands. Nilah turned around to see the old man from the gate, his black robes trailing in his wake.

"Elder Osmond," said Sharp. "Honored that you'd join us."

"Ha! How could I stay away with such a promising young woman in my temple?" cackled the elder. "Oh, I love it! I love it! How did you fell Georgina? She's killed so many, you see, and she always claims it's an accident." He waggled his finger theatrically at the downed ogre. "But we know better, don't we?"

Georgina moaned a few curses, and the elder seated his fists on his hips. "Now, now. We're the Children of the Singularity, not the Children of the Vulgarity. I shall have to punish that wicked,

wicked mouth of yours. This brilliant fighter took you down fair and square, didn't you, dear?"

Nilah realized he was addressing her and stammered. "It... was nothing."

The old man crooked an eyebrow at Nilah. "That's Flicker, isn't it?"

A bomb went off in Nilah's stomach. "Ah, well, uh... It's Taitutian Ghost Fist, and—"

"Modesty is for the sheep, but they always get shorn anyway," interrupted Osmond, sweeping across the arena to her. He had a way of moving that reminded Nilah of Mother. He held up her arm as though it were a piece of cooked meat and let it drop. "Why have you no dermaluxes?"

"Because I'd rather use the environment to my advantage," she said, eyeing Jeannie and Alister recovering in the corner. If Osmond tried anything, they wouldn't be able to help. "It's a more natural approach, Elder."

Osmond laughed, his voice smooth and jovial. "A *natural* approach? Oh, that's richer than a fried marpo pie. A mechanist, vegetarian naturalist. You young Taitutians never remember the old days when we ate meat. You know this is a new thing, right? Only the last two hundred years or so."

Sharp perked up like a wolf about to be released from his cage, and Osmond waved him off.

"Walk with me," said Osmond, then pointed to Jeannie and Alister. "You two, as well, children, assuming that boy *can* walk."

"I'm good," grunted Alister.

Nilah did as the elder bade her, following him down one of the side passages. They came to a heavy bulkhead, then Osmond traced a glyph and placed his hand against the access plate. It registered his identity and the door yawned open.

As they ascended a flight of stairs, the passages changed: from the bare stone and steel of the Pinnacle initiate quarters to wood and gilding, reminding Nilah of Claire's old office, and of Alpha. Stuffed animal heads covered the walls, their faces forever frozen in surprise. Before uncovering the *Harrow* conspiracy, Nilah would've seen this place as luxurious, if a little overwrought. Now, she could only think of the corpses suspended in the ice beneath the Wartenberg Mining Colony.

Then they emerged into a majestic rotunda, a place clearly designed for giving lectures. Statuary lined the edges, perched atop marble plinths. A series of columns punctuated the expanse at even intervals, and in the center, there was a raised dais, upon which a speaker might deliver an address. More of the taxidermied heads ringed the ceiling. An alcove on one side held a buffet, tables, and chairs, as well as a wine service.

"So I hear you three have been asking questions of my friendly little initiates," said Osmond. "A few of my people have told me that one"—he pointed to Alister—"is making them uncomfortable."

Nilah restrained a gulp. "Are we at the Pinnacle to be comfortable, elder?"

Osmond filled a glass of wine from a nearby decanter, waving with his free hand as though swatting flies on a summer day. "No, my dear, I shouldn't say so. Though, if we're being honest, I've got a pretty cushy job." He took a long slug of the wine, holding up a finger for them to wait. He gave a gratified sigh and wiped his lips on the back of his sleeve. "Honey, where else can you day drink and plot treason at the same time?"

Nodding, Nilah said, "The Pinnacle truly is a marvel."

"So I'm going to ask you what you three have been asking everyone around," said Osmond. "Why are you here?"

Nilah touched her mouth with the pad of her thumb. Georgina had split it, so Nilah had red on her lips, too. "Because I want to take what's mine. I want to be one of the elites. I was told that with your training, I can become one of the masters of our galaxy."

Osmond inspected the twins, though their new faces rendered them unique to his eyes. "And you two?"

"The same," said Jeannie.

"Tired of taking orders," added Alister.

"Who's giving you orders, kiddo?" asked Osmond, turning to walk onward without offering them anything to drink. "If you're anything like the other little bastards around here, you grew up with a silver spoon stuck up your ass."

"Anyone, sir," said Alister with a nervous glance at his sister. "I don't want to take orders from anyone."

Osmond stopped. "Do you know what the word 'sir' is, young man? That's you, taking orders. From me, from any of your elders, simply because we're *old*. It's an appeal to tradition, you see—we survived the longest, and so we're deserving of your respect. I can't eat spicy foods without wanting to crap myself. How do you respect me now?"

"Perhaps I'm just paying lip service, Elder Osmond," said Alister, hands balling at his sides.

"Paying lip service is following orders, too," said the old man, turning and walking onward. They ascended another flight of stairs and he gave Alister a disappointed look. "If you're waiting to stab someone in the back, it's because you don't have the stones to stab them in the front. Subterfuge is a form of supplication, lying to compensate for a lack of dominance. You say you came here because you're tired of taking orders, but I told you to walk up some stairs and you're following like a hungry puppy."

"Downstairs," said Alister, "they all were afraid of you. Showed you deference."

Osmond smiled, and there was something askew in his rictus, like his face didn't fit correctly. "That's because they know what I'll do to them, should they draw the ire from my good-natured heart. They're not lying to bide their time. They're afraid. We're honest here. We don't hide behind pretense. We want something and we learn to take it, or we learn to keep our mouths shut. You want a life like that, or do you want to call me 'sir' one more time?"

Alister looked to his sister, then to Nilah. "I want what's mine, then."

Osmond raised his hands, and projections formed around them. He called forth a series of texts from his computer terminal, paging through them in the center of the chamber. "Then look at why we gather into herds in the first place. There was an ancient philosopher, Tariq the Younger, who said the herd was an effort to create humanity in inhumane conditions, to better the treatment of the sick, the elderly, and the people who lived on the fringes of society. He said that's why we bloomed everywhere we set foot, how we could experience new ideas and spread across the stars."

Tariq's face formed from the aether. Nilah recognized him— the Children loved to post about him on the Link, spouting theories about his book, *Foundations of Life.* He was one of the originators of Taitu, assassinated by his own people and later venerated in Taitutian law. The Children claimed the first Taitutians, the ones who murdered Tariq, were in the right, and the planet never would've thrived if they hadn't killed him.

"Tariq ruined our gorgeous planet, and what could've been the seed of an even greater empire." Osmond took a swig and contemplated the man's face with a bitter swallow. "He sought to ensure the lives of those who should be dead. To live outside that system is to chase true freedom. There is no virtue greater than following the natural law, taking what you can, surrendering what you can't. And when you are too old to lift a finger, too frail to carry on, you either become meat for the circling wolves"—and with this, he crept toward Nilah—"or snatch your own life from death itself."

He straightened up, his theatrics draining from his body. The twinkle faded from his eye, his pupils shrinking to pinpricks. "But I think you already know that, don't you, dearie?"

She took a half step back, shifting her weight closer to a fighting stance.

"You understand what's required to win. To take everything from your competition, no matter the cost." And with particular relish, Osmond said, "To be a champion, Nilah Brio."

No.

He couldn't have called her by her name. A million possibilities shot through her mind, all of them nullified by his hungry gaze. With those last two words from his mouth, he'd gone from being an old man to an active threat. Had he told the others? Could she silence him now and say it was an accident? A few dozen highly motivated killers lurked in the facility below, eager for a reason to erase the hated Nilah Brio from the fabric of existence.

In the blink of an eye, Elder Osmond's glyph bloomed from his hand, masterfully drawn. Nilah tried to leap away, but viscous tendrils of energy compelled her knees toward the floor. She looked on in horror as Jeannie and Alister tried to escape, but a rolling wave of shimmering space knocked them over.

"Alist—" Jeannie tried to call for her brother and was silenced by a crushing, invisible force. Alister clawed at the ground, his face contorted in agony.

More drips of wavering air fell upon Nilah's shoulders, dragging her down, wrapping around her wrists like lead weights. Nilah clicked the transmitter on the roof of her mouth and opened her jaw. If this was going to be her final moment, she wanted someone to hear it.

The old man chuckled and pulled a long steel spike from his robe, pressing a button near its base. As it began to spin like a drill head, Nilah knew it must be a neural spike. "They call my magic 'the spinner's mark,' because it's like a spider. I like to think of it more like being crushed by a boa constrictor, but it just doesn't have the same ring, does it?"

"No!" she gasped, struggling to pull away, but the tendrils wrenched her arms aside and yanked her forehead against the marble floor, exposing the back of her neck. Osmond brought the spike close to her ear, its high-pitched whine grating against her bones. He moved it to her other ear, as though dubbing her for knighthood. She wanted to look up, to plead with him, but the tendrils redoubled their grip on her head.

"They say you can still think with one of these in your brain, that you can still be yourself," he whispered, his awful breath tickling the back of her neck. "I could make you serve in my retinue."

Orna, I love you. I'm so sorry. Nilah struggled against her restraints, but with every kilogram of pressure she generated, the weights upon her doubled. She cut her eyes to the twins, seeing them flattened in her periphery, their mouths locked in silent screams as Osmond's spell crushed the breath from them.

"From the top of the podium to the bottom of my order... It's a good look for you." Osmond positioned himself for the kill, enjoying every second. The neural spike pinched the hairs at the base of Nilah's skull, ripping them free, eager to dive into her spinal column and subvert her nervous system. "You'll be part of the herd forever, Miss Brio."

She brought one of her feet underneath herself, pushing as hard as she could, and she felt Osmond's spell give slightly. Straining to raise her head, Nilah gave a vicious roar. Osmond's tendrils couldn't hold her forever.

"If you're going to kill me, do it!"

And the spell released. Jeannie and Alister rolled on the ground, gasping, and Nilah's muscles burned from the exertion, but she refused to let Elder Osmond see her weakness. Osmond stood before them, another spell in his hand, his face stony with a lack of exertion. He could easily crush them if he cast again.

"But that's not in the cards, I'm afraid," said the old man, taking a short step back and pointing to his brain. "Spike thralls can't be double agents. Can't pass as one of us, you know."

A thousand insults swarmed her mind like stinging insects, but Nilah kept them all inside. She couldn't attack him again, not while he'd be ready for it. His glyph pulsed in his palm, ready to pour over her again if she stepped out of line.

"I'll die before I join you."

Elder Osmond regarded his hands for a long moment, as though he were only just noticing the liver spots and bony knuckles. "Join? I wouldn't let you join my Wednesday night card game, much less the Children of the Singularity. No, honey, we're going to crack open that little skull of yours and pull every trick out of your head. We'll get your hideouts, your bank codes, and everything else you know. Then, we'll make you turn on your friends and carve them up in the night."

Nilah stepped backward, rubbing her sore shoulder joints and neck. "And how do you propose to do that?"

Osmond grinned. "You know the barrister's mark, don't you?"

That mark was the foundation of intergalactic treaties and slave contracts alike. It compelled those under its thrall to perform all agreed-upon services.

Nilah's jaw tensed. "Those spells can be broken."

"Not this one, dear." Osmond shut down the neural spike and replaced it within his robes. "Why would we have a mindless drone, when we could have you, body and soul? My Lord Vraba will be here in three days, and he's going to take you to the best barrister in the galaxy."

Nilah balled her fists. She'd never felt so weak in her life. "I'll break any contract. My friends—"

Osmond laughed so hard he wheezed. "You think that's what this is about? Sure, those boys and girls downstairs are pissed at you, but the upper echelons couldn't care less. You're a flea, my sweet, but you've got *access*. I bet we could even have you snap that new prime minister's neck if we wanted, in the cold light of day."

He pulled back the sleeve of his robe and tapped his watch. In response, Sharp rushed out of the stairwell with a cadre of armed spike thralls in tow. Osmond flicked his arms, straightening his sleeves.

"Miss Brio," he began, "we're not accustomed to taking prisoners at the Pinnacle, so we don't have a brig for you. You three be good and stay here until Lord Vraba arrives."

Then, to Sharp, he said, "Drug them."

The last thing Nilah felt before the warm embrace of sleep was the sting of a fléchette.

Chapter Ten

Escape Clause

"heir cover is blown, but they're not dead," said Malik, and Orna sucked in a breath before wincing at her injuries.

Boots and the others stood around the bridge. Malik's glowing face filled the central projector, where battle plans were usually displayed, giving Boots the odd feeling of talking to a giant.

"Hunter Two still hasn't given me a direct report. She was searched, and they discovered the transmitter," he said, his voice close and a bit muffled by the survival tent. "Here's her last communication..."

An old man's voice filled their speakers, promising a horrid fate to the three crew members. Boots looked to Cordell and Armin to find their expressions grim.

Orna pounded the console next to her, and it squawked a warning. "We've got to exfiltrate them before then, Cap."

Cordell tapped his chin. "I'm inclined to agree. What do we know about the defenses of the Pinnacle?"

"They've got some anti-air slingers—large lancers and all," said Malik. "But they're also using neural spikes to control some of their initiates. We have to assume they've got a hodgepodge of talented casters ready to battle."

Boots blanched. "Neural spikes? Are you serious? Whose territory is that?"

"Doesn't matter," said Armin. "Hammerhead has no major jurisdiction."

"No," said Boots, "but it does have citizens of other planets stuck there. Any government with a person on Hammerhead would want to intervene."

"So you're suggesting we call the cops?" said Orna. "News flash, Boots, we don't know which cops are the bad guys!"

"What did the old-timer mean about 'an unbreakable contract'?" asked Cordell.

"Stetson Giles, sir," said Boots. "We haven't had time to review the intel, but we know he's involved. If they coerce Nilah into signing a contract, and Stetson hits her with the barrister's mark, she's as good as gone. She'll have to do whatever they say."

"So we drop in there, gun everyone down, pick up Nilah and the twins, and go," said Orna. "She was supposed to collect the double agent, but there's no chance of that now."

"We'll need someone to sabotage their anti-air," said Aisha, gesturing to change the projection to an aerial view of the Pinnacle. "And it'd be good to shut down their network of spikes."

"I can do that," said Malik. "I've been encamped on this glacier for too long. Now that they've found the transmitter, we can assume they'll come looking for me. May as well work on shutting them down in the meantime."

"No, you can't," Aisha cut him off, then cleared her throat. "I mean, you're not a hacker."

"What about an aerial insertion?" asked Orna.

"What about your hip?" asked Boots. Her own hips were sore

after that escape, and she hadn't even been shot. Orna's right side bore a faintly glowing duraplex cast, visible through her shirt.

Orna shook her head. "Charger's emergency med systems took good care of me. I've been through worse."

"I remember," Boots replied, thinking of Mother's claw going clean through Ranger's—and Orna's—abdomen.

The quartermaster gave her a poisonous look. "You drop me with Malik and we clear out the resistance on the ground. If we blow a hole in the side of the Pinnacle, you can use it as an extraction point." She pointed to the sheer cliff on one side of the installation. "See? We'll be shielded from the guards in the barracks."

Armin measured the distance with his finger, the projector noting ten-meter increments to the gaping chasm at the bottom. "That's quite a drop on the other side, Miss Sokol. If Miss Brio or the twins are substantially injured—"

Orna's nostrils flared. "We can make it, sir."

"There are a lot of assumptions in this plan," said Cordell, pacing around the console. "One: we're not a hundred percent on their air defenses. Two: we have essentially no intel about the interior of the Pinnacle. Three: we don't know the location of our crew members," he said, ticking each point off on his fingers as Orna's face grew redder and redder. He turned to her, halting the coming objection. "And four: we can't be certain they're alive."

Orna slicked back her hair. "But you heard that elder guy—"

"Yes," interrupted Cordell, "and he may have been counting on us listening in, Sokol, so sit your butt down and let's use our damned heads. Wounding a soldier so you can attack their rescuers is the oldest trick in the book."

"What we need is eyes-on surveillance, Captain," said Malik. "Even if I can't get inside, I may be able to see something with a passive sensor kit. There's a ridgeline opposite the cliff. My computer has a path for me, but it's a dangerous hike. I can be there in two of your days."

"I don't think that's a good idea, Captain," said Aisha.

Malik shook his disembodied head. "I have to move anyway, hon. I may as well move somewhere useful. If Nilah can get me a signal, that'll be something."

Boots swallowed, her skin growing prickly with her next thought. "If Stetson Giles is casting the barrister's mark, I know where he's going to be…"

The curse kicked in immediately, sending stabbing pains up her spine. That fateful day aboard the *Saint of Flowers*, Stetson had made Boots promise never to say where he was or even give a single clue. Welts formed on her arm as though she'd been whipped, and she clutched her tortured flesh. Fresh rage blossomed inside her as she remembered him drinking confidently from the chalice, Gemma lying dead at his feet with a hole in her head.

Cordell eyed her new marks. "First time I've ever seen that. You okay?"

"Yeah," Boots said through clenched teeth as the fire dissipated from her skin. "Just felt like it had to be mentioned."

"So we could pick up Malik and intercept them at the next location," said Aisha, "if we could break Stetson's curse."

"Except you can't," Orna spat. "Boots can't tell us, so we'd have to read her mind, and guess what? Our two readers are on the ground with my girlfriend!"

"You're going to control yourself, Miss Sokol," snapped Armin, "or you won't be part of these discussions."

Cordell placed a cigarette between his lips, but he didn't light it. It was a sure sign he was ready to go stress out in private. "Look, we're not going to leave any of our folks on Hammerhead, okay? But we're not going off half-cocked. It's a two-day jump, and I expect us to be ready the second we exit the Flow. If we don't have a signal by then..."

His expression darkened. "We may just have to pick up Malik and leave."

"Captain!" Orna snarled, but Cordell interrupted her.

"Enough! You know the risks! You all knew them when you stayed on the ship and kicked Witts's anthill. I'm not saying Miss Brio and the Ferriers are dead, but we have to consider the living crew first."

"So you're just giving up on her?" said Orna, face bright red.

"Absolutely not," said Cordell, "but unless we can be sure there's a reason, we will not assault the Pinnacle. And before you open your mouth to say something foolish, Miss Sokol, they have a few days to get us a signal. Any signal at all."

"If you intend to leave without her," said Orna, "I'm staying behind."

Boots had never seen Orna look at her captain that way.

Cordell shook his head. "You do what you have to do, but I aim to keep everyone alive." He waved the map up to full. "Malik, you're to go wait along the far ridgeline. We have to know if any shuttles arrive or depart, and if possible, who's on board. Nilah and the twins have had some amount of military training on our vessel. If they've absorbed enough, they'll know it's their duty to get a signal to us."

Cordell turned to Armin. "Mister Vandevere, I want you running scenarios of all possible air defense, as well as infantry magic tactics...in the event that the rescue mission is a go. I want to know where the most scanner-opaque place is to set Miss Sokol and Charger down. If we can weave through their sensors, they won't see us coming."

"I'll get right on that," said Armin.

"Mister Jan, when you rendezvous with Miss Sokol, you two

are to create as much chaos in that base as possible. When I'm satisfied their air defenses are shattered, we'll launch Miss Elsworth in the Midnight Runner and hammer that guard post with everything we can."

Everyone nodded their assent, but no one looked particularly pleased with the plan.

"And since there's a possibility we'll encounter a shadow god..." Cordell began, giving Orna a meaningful look.

Orna leaned back against a console, her icy glare fixed on the captain. "The disperser rifle will probably work, if I cannibalize some of the parts from Charger's main slinger. That's going to leave me up close and personal during any fighting."

"Are you complaining about that?" he asked.

Her lips curled in a snarl. "No. I'm looking forward to it."

"Dismissed. Missus Jan, lay in a course for Hammerhead."

"She's going to signal us, Captain," said Orna.

He put his hands on his hips and huffed through his nose. "I know she will."

Orna took off, no doubt headed for her bench in the cargo bay, where she could start prepping, and Armin followed shortly after, bound for the datamancer's throne in his quarters. Aisha said her goodbyes to Malik and retreated to the pilot's chair. Boots turned away from the married couple's conversation, feeling as though she was intruding on a private moment. Cordell tapped her on the shoulder.

"Everyone is getting down to business," he said. "That means it's up to you and me to look through the contents of Durand's box in my office."

"And I'm guessing you want to smoke, sir."

"Head down to the mess, grab us enough coffee to wake the dead and some snacks. Maybe I'll be done by then."

Boots scoffed. "Yeah. I'll take my time."

*   *   *

Nilah had spent a few hours in a daze, wandering around the Pinnacle's rotunda like a buffoon. But when she ate again, the food tasted strangely bitter—and the cloying sensation of the cultists' drugs fled her system.

Someone had fed her an antidote, but who? Maybe the double agent was still around. Maybe it was a mind game.

The twins both regained their awareness in tandem with her, and with a brief but meaningful stare, they agreed to continue the ruse of being drugged.

The Children had taken Nilah's oral transmitter, but left her and the twins relatively intact, aside from a rough search. The three of them had been shut onto the top floor of the Pinnacle, though Nilah doubted she'd have trouble breaking the locks. The problem was: where was she going to go? The guards had burned all their cold-weather gear. She didn't have a slinger, and there were no vehicles at the Pinnacle—at least none that she knew.

Imagers and other recording devices dotted the Pinnacle, embedded into sconces, statuary, stuffed animal heads, and anything else complex enough to confuse the eye. It'd taken Nilah a while to find the first one, but once she did, she couldn't stop unearthing new lenses. Even if she wanted to try to hack the door open, the imagers would alert security before she could do anything.

They'd taken shifts resting on the various luxurious furnishings throughout the upper level. There were no bedrooms this high in the structure, only the rotunda and its accompanying study. Everything was ornate and gilded; almost nothing was comfortable. Soon, every bone in Nilah's body began to ache from the many trials she'd suffered the day before.

"Do you think we should try to shoot our way out?" whispered Jeannie, picking up an apple from a serving platter shaped like a wolf's head. The pair of women kept their backs to the known imagers, mumbling what little communication they could muster.

"With what?" Nilah sighed. "We're not exactly armed here. They even took your shivs. And have you seen a slinger up here?"

"I won't be taken alive," said Jeannie as Alister wandered to her side, pantomiming the drunken stupor of the drugs. "Not again."

Jeannie looked at Nilah with pleading eyes, and Nilah restrained a flinch. She'd helped them get out of one of Witts's most disturbing installations, and she understood exactly why they wouldn't go back.

"Then find something sharp," said Nilah, her blood running ice-cold. "I'll be the last to go down, if it comes to that."

The twins shook their heads in unison. Nilah wished they'd be subtler about that. They might've pegged Nilah for the famous racer who brought home the *Harrow*, but they'd failed to recognize the pair of science experiments.

"Do you think the others are coming for us?" asked Jeannie.

Nilah's heart sank. "Maybe. They might assume we're dead."

And there was no way to get a signal out to them.

The chunky growl of the stairwell doorway opening shook Nilah from her thoughts. The twins stood up and spread out, not eager to be caught in one of Osmond's spiderwebs again. Instead, Sharp entered, followed by a retinue of dead-eyed spike thralls carrying steaming trays of food. The bastards may not have stocked the base with slingers and escape craft, but they certainly had knives in the kitchen, and maybe a few accelerators or radiators, too.

"Elder Osmond thought you'd be hungry," said Sharp.

They filed into a small dining hall, where thralls placed the trays upon a mahogany table. A tableau of slaughter had been carved into the wood along the sides of the furnishing: predators of various planets, chasing down and consuming their prey. When the servants whipped away the silver shells covering the plates, there were three thick, bloody marpo steaks with pats of herb butter across the top.

Sharp took in Nilah's disgust with an impassive expression. "The elder said you need to enjoy the kill."

Nilah spoke slowly, with eyes hooded to emulate the stupor of a drugged target. "No . . . no animals to eat."

The twins tucked into their meat.

The thralls left Sharp seated at the table and retreated to the exit, where they dutifully flanked the door, ready to attack any-one who tried something stupid. Nilah reminded herself that her entire mission qualified as something stupid.

"Are you really Nilah Brio?" asked Sharp, his expression unreadable.

Hiding her ire for the meddlesome captain of the guard was the second most exhausting part about getting to the Pinnacle. He watched her with folded arms and an obnoxious smirk.

"Go 'way," she grumbled.

"The network is down for maintenance," he said. "No imagers. You can stop pretending to be drugged."

The twins both sat up straight, their expressions alert and wary. Instead of answering, Nilah strode to the nearest hidden lens and connected to it with her magic. He wasn't lying—the whole net-work was down.

"What's your game?" she asked, slowly turning to face him.

Sharp shrugged. "You look nothing like yourself. Judging from the images on the Link, I thought you'd be prettier."

"Sodding hell, do you want an autograph?" she snapped at him. "It's called a disguise."

He was still staring at her.

"Don't look at me like that. Why would you even ask such a stupid question?"

His eyes traveled to her arms. "I just wonder where your dermaluxes are. You're supposed to be famous for them."

"They're also disguised, you twit." She instinctively rubbed her forearm. "They're in there, and if you don't want me using them on you, you'll back off."

He scoffed. "Okay. Keep your disguise after your cover is blown, *Nilah*." He said her name with such annoyance that it may as well have been a mouthful of salt. "Seems like a waste to me."

Sharp was right. Hiding her dermaluxes wasn't doing Nilah any favors, and they knew exactly who she was. She'd been foolish not to think of it before. But why give her any advantage?

Nilah rolled back her sleeves and focused on her forearms. When she'd fought the springflies, she'd forced the wavelengths of light in her arm into longer and longer frequencies to fool their infrared sensors. To clear away the veneer of skin from Doctor DosSantos, she needed to go in the opposite direction.

She traced her glyph, connecting to the nanomachines and reigniting them. They appeared at first as a dim, reddish orange—the color of sunlight through her eyelids. She shortened the wavelength, driving them upward through the colors of the rainbow, to arrive at the blurry violet. Then, she cycled the intensity, unburying the functions like stretching a muscle after a long time cooped up in a small place.

She began flipping the dermaluxes on and off, her skin flashing in slow beats, growing faster. She reoriented the nanoscale plates inside her arms to reflect outward, shaping the light. After a trial ramp, she closed her eyes and drove her dermaluxes past violet.

Her arms itched. *Faster.* Then came the burning as she crossed out of the visible light spectrum. *Brighter.* The neural circuit complained at the magic load, and still she forced more inside. Patches of light desynchronized from her arms in mosaic patterns as the system failed to keep up. The dermaluxes weren't designed for this, but she was still a tuner, damn it all. Her eyes watered.

Burn.

Nilah threw her arms out wide and pushed a jolt of magic through them so severe, she thought she'd short out the nanomachines for sure. The skin on the surface of her forearms went up like flash paper, erupting from her in patches.

Alister put down his fork and clapped softly at the impressive light show. Jeannie gagged as the scent of burning arm hair hit her. For her part, Nilah coughed and swatted away the ashen flakes of skin that peeled from her body. Her arms would be disgusting for a while, and she could do with some lotion, but at least she had her tattoos back. Her pleasure radiated from her in golden waves.

She shut them off and pulled her sleeves back down. At least she wasn't unarmed now.

"How long is the network down?" she asked.

He cut his eyes to the thralls. "Sixty more seconds. Your friends have to know you're here. Do you have a rescue coming?"

She considered the question. It was entirely possible that they'd already isolated or killed the double agent, and Sharp was just there to mess with her head. If she answered honestly, it might help lure her friends into a trap. She'd only been their captive for a short while, and her friends' exfiltration schedule would be a valuable piece of intelligence.

Then again, what if he was the double agent, and he'd just exposed his secrets to them? If a rescue wasn't incoming, she'd be nothing more than a potentially deadly liability to him. He could fake an escape attempt and blast her on the spot.

The truth might kill her friends. A lie might kill her then and there.

She waited out the clock, watching sweat form on his brow.

"No rescue if they think I'm dead," she said at the last second, allowing her features to go slack.

Sharp growled and seized her by the arm, whispering in her ear. She very nearly clocked him, but that would've given her away. "I'll be back the next time the system goes down. Be ready to talk."

Then he took a few steps back, his smirk returning. "Don't be naive about meat, little Miss Brio. Before long, you'll get hungry enough to lick the steam from the plate covers." He pointed to the silver domes, his eyes lingering on hers overlong.

Then he left, taking the thralls with him and securing the stairwell door.

Nilah eyed the marpo, gray lumps of fat congealing as it cooled, and her stomach churned. She'd never keep it down. If she'd known she'd spend this whole mission starving to death, she would've at least had a feast before departing.

You'll be hungry enough to lick the steam from the plate covers.

It struck her as a stupid taunt, out of character for the security officer. But there had to be more to it than that. Nilah crossed toward the table, pretending at the last second to drunkenly stumble on the leg of one of the expensive chairs. As she did, she flailed her arms, knocking one of the lids to the floor, where it rolled underneath the table.

She muttered a curse, leaning under the table to where the lid had rolled bowl-up. It hummed like a bell, and she pushed a chair out of the way to get at it. Stuck in the direct center, molded like a piece of modeling clay, was a full-sized mycoprotein ration.

She might not know Sharp's game for certain, but it seemed he was another player on the field.

The contract investigations had put a pall over the captain's quarters.

"I need a lawyer," grumbled Cordell, his smoky breath coming out in irritated little puffs. "What do ancient trees have to do with anything? This is like reading another language."

"It *is* another language," corrected Boots, taking a sip of her dark Morthan coffee. Its musky notes were an acquired taste, but at least it covered up the stench of tobacco flecked with eidolon crystals. "Why don't you know programmatic contracts?"

He set the sheaf he'd been inspecting down across the top of the stack. "Because I'm not a doddering archivist. I'm a dashing starship captain."

"You should try doddering sometime. At least then you'd finally be acting your age."

Boots sighed and massaged the bridge of her nose, adjusting the bandage. She'd been having sinus trouble ever since raiding the med bay for supplies, which meant she'd probably done something incorrectly. She missed Malik.

Once she'd gotten over the shock of Stetson Giles's signature—and the fury at touching something he'd held—Boots had dived in full force only to find a brick wall. The terms of the contract were deliberately obscured and encrypted. There were seemingly thousands of moving parts to it: escrows, money transfers, conditional terminations, severances, actions and reactions. Each paragraph was a coded function in legal speak, and instead of the variables having names like "Henrick Witts" and "Children of the Singularity," they had names like "Succulent" and "Ice Peak."

Armin would make better sense of it, but he was too busy working on the calculations for Orna's stealth drop. Boots would have to go on her deductive abilities alone, just as she had done back in her Gantry Station apartment.

Every programmatic contract held a key somewhere inside it, and if she could just find a thread to pull, the rest of it would quickly unravel. She found a fee schedule for something large, something that might correspond to the "Ladder" variable class, but her brain ached as she tried to grasp the whole picture.

Cordell interrupted her train of thought for the thousandth time. "So you can't tell me anything about where Giles might be hiding?"

She smacked her forehead against the desk. "You know the terms of the curse, sir. I can't tell you his whereabouts. I can't help you find him."

He looked away. "Sorry, Bootsie."

Boots put down the "Ladder.repeat" page and regarded him sidelong. He'd sprouted a few gray hairs since she'd gone to Hopper's Hope and returned, and the crow's-feet under his eyes had grown more pronounced. Maybe he'd always looked that much older and she'd only just noticed. Maybe he'd seen some things in her absence.

"You want to tell me what's on your mind?" she asked.

He gave her a look like she'd reached out and booped his nose. Crew didn't ask their captains to confide in them, and he'd never do it. Any fear he showed could damage morale. Any damage to morale could get people killed. The burden of an officer was to never share, and they both knew it.

He took a drag. "Can't stop thinking about Nilah and the twins, is all."

Boots blinked. She hadn't meant it seriously. The galaxy was upside down if he was confiding in her. "They'll, uh... they'll be fine."

"It's just that, when I think of the magnitude of evil that we're facing, I can't even wrap my head around it. Sending twenty-year-olds into battle when you're thirty is one thing." He stubbed out his cigarette and the vacuum disposal on his desk sucked it down with a pop. "But in my fifties, it's even worse. And those twins... they've been fighting long enough."

Boots leaned back in her chair and took another sip of coffee, clearing the last of the smoke from her sinuses. She set down her cup and crossed her arms, suddenly awakened by Cordell's worried revelations.

"How about you level with me, sir? What's their deal?"

A characteristic smirk tugged at the corner of his mouth, but he couldn't even muster that. "When the *Harrow* came home, there were a lot of good intel hits. A lot of work to do."

"Yeah. I figured after I left, there would be some action. I, uh..."

Feel bad for disappearing, but I did my part.

"It's okay," he said. "You had your thing for the first time ever, and I was happy for you. But the Taitutians were in a rare sharing mood, and Armin and me, we found some stuff. Well...mostly Armin."

"What kind of stuff?"

Cordell reached under his desk and fetched a bottle of cheap whiskey, the kind he liked in his coffee, and splashed a bit into his mug. He held it out for Boots, who took it and added some to her own. She wasn't looking forward to the warm nap the whiskey would shove onto her, but she doubted they'd make any more headway on the contract during the night cycle.

He swirled his mug around to thoroughly mix it. "You know how unlikely it is that the twins would both have the same marks?"

"It's a genetic impossibility," said Boots. "The closer the gene pool, the more mutations in the cardioid."

"Right," said Cordell, "which means you basically can't pick your mark...except Witts was working on a way to do that. The VanHoutens were some of the financiers of the *Harrow*, and when the Taitutians let us evaluate some of their holdings, we found a school on Blix, nestled into the mountains. At first, we didn't think anything of the place, but the clan executor got his underwear all bunched when we started talking about it."

"So you decided to check it out?" asked Boots.

"Yeah," said Cordell. "Without the Taitutians. I've never fully trusted them. Nice people, but their intel services leak like a used jump dump. We thought about calling, but you were, you know, retired, and we wanted to get to the chalet before the VanHoutens could close up shop."

"And you found the twins there?"

"We busted in. It was a lab, but in total chaos. Most of the techs were dead—burned to bits by spellfire. We found a bunch of unconscious...uh...subjects." He downed the rest of his beverage and refilled the whiskey, sans the coffee. "It was a breeding ground for spies. Puppeteer's marks, reader's marks, eyebreakers, jumpers, you name it. Every spell that could be used to infiltrate a place was on display. These people were genetic donors, spiked and forced to...I don't know. But Jeannie and Alister's, uh, parents had to be among their number."

"Wait, the twins were spiked?"

"No. I'm getting to that."

Cordell's military history was the same as Boots's: he'd seen so many soldiers die, the weak and elderly starve, witnessed all of the evils a war could inflict. So when he got that haunted look in his eye, her heart stumbled over its next few beats.

"They'd grown kids with accelerators and all kinds of dangerous crap. You couldn't call these experiments, though, Bootsie. That would've been way too generous to these children. We got into the security archives and saw what they were doing to the 'failures.' They'd cut out the cardioids and test on the severed organs...before throwing the bodies in the incinerator."

He reached over to his roller and withdrew another cigarette. The device clicked and whirred, depositing another stick into the newly vacated spot. He lit up, smoke drifting across his eyes, and sighed out a plume.

"The worst ones were the side projects—the attempts to graft a second cardioid onto a child. We called them banshees, just because they wouldn't stop screaming at us. They roamed the halls like hollow-eyed ghosts, coming after anyone they saw, magic streaming off their fingers in long, sputtering wisps. We... we had to shoot them. Couldn't save them. Don't think they wanted to be saved."

She couldn't stop her mind from rendering his words in stark detail.

"Then we got to central holding and found our twins, bags packed, blood-spattered, standing cool as cold iron—no spikes in their heads, not even superficial damage. They were waiting for us. When we asked where the blood came from, they pointed to this...this lady on the ground. They'd sliced her up something fierce, Boots. Judging from the look on her face, she hadn't known to put up a fight. Or maybe she hadn't wanted to. Considering all the awful things we found in that chalet, she might not have meant to live. And those twins...they were the only success of that godforsaken project. They'd been bred like a couple of animals to have identical marks."

Boots took a long pull of her coffee and gulped it down. "How did the twins survive in there?"

Cordell laughed. "Survive? They'd been reading their nanny's mind without her knowledge. When the *Harrow* came home, a mole in the Taitutian Ministry of Defense called the chalet. Told the nanny to get ready. Jeannie found out with one of her regular mind readings. Opened all the cells. Set the banshees loose on unsuspecting scientists. Boots, I'm telling you, those two created a bloodbath."

A drop of whiskeyed coffee went down the wrong pipe, and she coughed hard. "So you brought them onto the ship? Why?"

The captain looked away, his gaze distant as he finished the last of his cigarette. He stubbed it out and licked his lips. "Because they reminded me of a little kid I picked up on Clarkesfall once. Sokol grew up on this ship, and she's a damned sight better for it."

Boots smirked. "You got a bad habit for picking up strays, Captain."

"Let me tell you about the worst one. This ungrateful Elsworth woman won't stay on my dang boat."

They laughed, but fell silent a little too quickly, lost in thought. What if the Ferriers weren't the only successes? There had to be hidden projects across the galaxy. Henrick Witts couldn't just up and destroy the universe in a day, not without research and maneuvering on a level never seen before.

His life's work had already gone beyond the *Harrow*, to the PGRF racetracks, and now the Blixish chalet. Boots's gaze fell to the stack of contracts before her as she swirled her cup.

Her eye snagged on the word "cedar."

"What did you say earlier, sir? Before you needed a lawyer?" she asked.

"What?"

"You said something about trees."

His eyes had grown bleary with the story he had told her. "I did?"

"Yeah, you mentioned some kind of exotic tree."

"Ancient tree," he corrected. "The contract mentioned a cedar tree. Like in some of the old pictures from Origin."

Boots held out her hand. "Show me the page?"

Cordell shuffled through the unruly stack, searching out the sheaf he'd cast aside. Eventually, he found it and handed it over. Boots scanned down the page, searching through the dozens of archaic terms, function calls, and conditional objects until she found the word "cedar."

It described an intense, branching root structure, dipping into thousands of encrypted entities. She grabbed the other page where she'd seen the word and found a lengthy programming loop that triggered until a cedar was fully grown. She couldn't wrap her brain all the way around the complexities of the code—it held entirely too many different interlinked conditions and references to local weather at the branch level—but she understood the gist of it.

She stood up. "I get it. Or, at least, part of it."

"What are we talking here?"

"I think these might be payments," she said. "This is a fee schedule. These roots could be galactic exchanges—thousands and thousands, if not millions, of different stocks."

Cordell shrugged. "Okay, so someone is earning from the stock market."

"No, these are repetitive triggering clauses for companies and stocks on a stock exchange, but I'm not sure which ones. The code takes percentage points off holdings, with the ability to dig deeper anywhere there's fallow ground, like a set of tree roots seeking out more nutrients. Like...okay..." She searched for the best way to illustrate scale. "Let's say each of these roots is a market model, generating one argent. The successful ones get stronger, the weaker ones die off to limit financial exposure to debt. At that scale..."

She spent the next five minutes tracing down single variables back to their definitions. She waved up a calculator projection and rigged a weak simulation, glad that Armin wasn't there to see her sloppy work. She played everything as conservatively as possible, only adding to the simulation when she was sure of what she was doing.

As she tapped in the final numbers, the computer spit out a result into the air. "In a worst, worst, worst-case scenario, this is generating...uh...a hundred and eighty argents per cycle."

Cordell laughed. "Oh. Okay. Well, that's not so bad. What's the cycle time?"

"Uh..." She shuffled through the papers to find any semblance of an answer, but it was too complex to get all at once. Then she caught a break—a shorthand reference that should've been deleted. She plugged it into the rest of the sim.

The objects before them multiplied exponentially, exploding into glowing fractal root systems too multitudinous for the human eye. Boots swallowed hard and looked down at her captain, who regarded the curling sim like an all-devouring star about to consume his ship. He gripped his armrests and gritted his teeth.

"What's the cycle time, Boots?"

"Nanoseconds."

"That's..." Cordell looked on, thunderstruck. "But the gods are already rich. They're all from major banking families, so this doesn't change anything."

"No..." Boots stared into the dancing simulation, her jaw clenched. "You don't understand the kind of capital we're talking about here."

The sim spat out an astronomical figure, and they both regarded it as though it was a venomous snake in their midst.

"This is it..." said Cordell. "This is the engine that runs the Money Mill."

Boots shook her head. "That's enough money to finance a project beyond anything we've ever seen, Captain."

"What do you think they're doing with it?"

"Whatever they're building," she said, "it's going to make the *Harrow* look like a toy."

Boots let that sink in as Cordell worried his lip.

"Okay," he breathed, clearing his throat. "How do we shut it down? Destroy the contract?"

"No. There could be duplicates. We need to figure out who the players are, but, Captain—this contract is incomplete." She hefted the sheaf of papers. "It's signed and functioning, but only the parties involved know the terms. We can't decipher it, so we'll never know the real names of all the businesses and brokerages involved in it. As much as I'd love to out all of these people for helping Henrick Witts, we can't know who they are with this document alone."

"How do you know that?"

"Because I took a course in contract law. I was trying to start a business, remember?"

"No, I mean how do you know we can't decipher it?"

She pointed to the list of "includes" in the contract header. "Because we need a special document called the 'index' to sort everything out. It'll contain the real names of all the entities in here. It's the part that makes the contract binding for a barrister's mark. According to this section, if there was no index, this document would be unenforceable."

"So you're thinking…"

Boots crossed her arms. "Imagine you're Stetson Giles, and you've just negotiated an unbreakable contract for the biggest, baddest people in the galaxy. Because you're the contract executor, you already know too much. They're primed to kill you the second they get the chance. How do you keep them from turning on you?"

Cordell sat up. "You build a clause in the contract that renders it null if the index is destroyed!"

"Exactly! And where would you store the index?"

"In…a box?"

"No. You'd keep it wherever you were, so that if they decided to blow you up, it'd leave their financial masterpiece in ruins."

Cordell drained the contents of his glass and slammed it onto the table. "So all we have to do is find Giles. With the index in hand, we can release a list of names to the galaxy: all of Witts's current conspirators."

Boots grinned. "Then we destroy it and void the contract."

"And all we have to do is find Stetson Giles."

The sharp sting of Boots's curse from Stetson was still fresh in her memory. Cordell's excited expression wilted when he saw the look on her face.

She nodded. "And I really hope you do, but I can't help you."

Chapter Eleven

Frequency

Nilah couldn't stop thinking about how to get a signal to the others.

She'd tried hacking the network through one of the security cameras, but found the cameras were only connected to one another and projectors, as well as a monitoring station somewhere below. She couldn't get to anything external to the room: no door access, no power, nothing—and that meant it'd be hard to get a signal out while she was trapped inside. Frustrated, she began to secretly implant malicious code in anything she could touch. As a matter of course, she hacked the lights, electrical switching, climate control, and any other exposed systems. She introduced so many flaws that they'd never know exactly what she'd done until they reinstalled everything.

But she had one real goal: she programmed the cameras to scramble when they received the right series of light pulses from her arms. She'd keep that bit of sabotage ready for later.

Sharp returned a day later with food, but he left the thralls outside behind the thick bulkhead. He turned from the food cart and said, "Security is down for the time—"

"Get him!" Nilah cried, pushing back her sleeves and charging straight for him.

Without missing a beat, Sharp hunkered low, his hands outstretched and eyes narrowed. His fingers curled and uncurled, as though massaging the air. It wouldn't matter, because he couldn't grab what he couldn't see.

Nilah went in for a quick flurry of blows, fanning her left arm to dazzle Sharp's eyes. Instead of trying to make sense of the pulses, he seized her lit arm with a rock-hard grip and twisted. She popped him in the jaw, but her balance was thrown, and she couldn't put much power into her punch.

The world spun on the wrong axis, and she found herself flying toward the stone floor, face-first. At the last second, he stopped her from breaking her neck by cushioning her fall—but then he twisted her up like a Harvest pastry. He yanked her arm in a direction it shouldn't go, and she slapped the ground with a shout of surprise. He didn't immediately release her, but pulled a little harder.

"Read his mind, Alister!" she grunted, but when he rushed in with a lit glyph in his hand, Sharp ducked out of the way, releasing his grip on her.

"Stop!" he shouted, but she wasn't going to do this on his terms.

Nilah sprang to her feet and switched both arms to a deep, throbbing violet, flowing through the forms with a dancer's grace. *Flow in and out, as inexorable as the tide,* her teacher had once told her. She'd take her time on the approach, confusing him, blurring the lines of her limbs with exploits of his visual cortex. She flashed her dermaluxes white with each extension of her arms, creating a skeletal effect known as the Solar Storm.

And, at first, it worked. She sank a punch into his unprepared gut, winding him, and blasted him across the nose with a surprise kick. On instinct, she flowed into the next form, rising rocket, shifting her dermaluxes to pounding white.

He laid hands on her, and she knew it was all over before he even threw her. An eyeblink later, she lay on the ground, her shoulder aching and lips pressed into the gritty tile.

The punk was sitting on her.

Despite their viciousness on the fields of ice outside, the twins were about as helpful as a flat tire against a masterful combatant like Sharp.

"Stop," Sharp commanded. "I'm not going to let you hold me down. If you want to read my mind, let's just get this out of the way."

"Do it, Alister," Nilah grunted, her cheek pressed to the stone.

The twins closed ranks with Sharp, tracing their glyphs and placing their hands to the crown of his head.

"He's not hiding anything from us," said Jeannie. "He's the double agent."

"We'll see," said Alister. "What's your real name, Mister Sharp?"

The captain of the guard twisted free and hurled Alister against the stone with blinding speed before plopping back down onto Nilah.

"I don't think so," he said. "You know what you need to know."

"Get off me, you stupid oaf!" Nilah wheezed, and he let her scramble free. Once she'd put a respectable distance between them, she added, "Never seen moves like those."

Rubbing his hands together, Sharp replied, "Galaxy-class grappler, so you strobe, I grab. Being able to snap a neck helps me get where I'm going—quietly."

"Yeah," Nilah spat. "Except out the front door."

The captain of the guard checked his wrist display and grimaced. "Eighty seconds left before the imagers come online. Do you have a rescue coming or not?"

Nilah nodded. "Yeah, mate. But if we don't get them a signal, they might assume we're dead. Connect me to the radios, and we'll call for help."

"Too dangerous. You'll be detected, then I'll get caught, too," he said, offering her a tiny metal object. "I can plug this drive into the Pinnacle's building management system and you can cause a disturbance. Put whatever code you want on it. Now when your ship comes, I want a ticket out of here."

"Of course you have a place on board, you sodding fool. You're the reason we came!"

He narrowed his eyes. "What?"

"We intercepted a Child of the Singularity named Aaron Forscythe above Taitu. He had orders to buy the identity of a double agent at the Pinnacle. They know about you."

"Damn." He checked the time once more. "Well, here I am. Don't forget me when the ship comes in."

"Wait," she said. "What's the point of the Pinnacle? What are they doing here?"

"Training recruits for Bastion."

She wrinkled her nose. " 'Bastion'? What's that?"

"No time," he said. "I've got a list of every Child of the Singularity in active service. You get me out of here, you get the document."

Nilah's mind raced through the possibilities of how she could get a message to her friends. It'd need to be more detailed than a mere malfunction, or an observer might mistake it for a system on the blink.

Still, it wasn't the worst opportunity. She could code and appear drugged. Hell, she already looked stoned when she connected to networks.

"Come back in an hour," she said. "I'll slip you the drive. Plug it into the lighting grid."

Sharp turned to leave. "I hope your friends are as solid as they say."

She smiled. "Could be a lot worse, chum. At least we're not as inept as the Special Branch."

*   *   *

Dread settled into every corner of the ship over the next two days. Boots had to pass the twins' quarters every time she walked to her room. Their door wasn't open, but she knew she'd find their things just the way they'd left them, frozen in time. Orna couldn't have been much better, sharing quarters with Nilah. The quartermaster must've been drowning in worry when everywhere she looked contained a memento of her girlfriend.

Boots couldn't be sure if she was happy or sad when Malik's call came in, and they were summoned to the bridge. Walking down the corridor toward the ship's nerve center felt like walking toward a morgue to identify a loved one. She'd done enough of that in the Famine War.

Orna muscled past her in the hallway, and Boots couldn't blame her. When they entered the bridge, they found Cordell and Armin talking to Malik's huge disembodied head on the projectors.

"I've arrived at the rendezvous point, and something strange is happening at the Pinnacle," said Malik.

"But you're safe?" asked Aisha.

"So far so good, dear."

"Any sign of Nilah?" Orna cut in, and Boots looked down to find the quartermaster's hands in tight fists at her sides.

"No," he said. "Not yet."

Orna nodded. "She'll get us a sign before the extraction."

"And the weird thing you mentioned is...?" Boots began.

"The lights aren't working properly," said Malik, a shiver in his voice.

Boots crossed her arms and squinted at Malik's projection of the Pinnacle. Just as he'd been instructed, he'd hiked across frozen tundra and crossed a deadly chasm just to get level with the Pinnacle on a distant peak. His scope was powerful enough to see fine detail on the installation, the best view the crew of the *Capricious* had been granted yet.

"Help me understand what that means," said Cordell, hooking his thumbs into his belt loops as he stretched. "We're coming out of the Flow in six hours, and I'd prefer to have some intel."

The projection blurred and shifted as Malik turned his imager around in his hands to face himself. The lens magnified his nose, giving them a three-dimensional projection of a pair of colossal nasal cavities.

"I was up on the ridgeline, as instructed, observing," said Malik. "And then the lights suddenly dimmed. All of the external floodlights are at half-capacity."

He turned the imager to face the facility again and zoomed in, pointing out the ring of lights around its perimeter with a huge, blurry hand.

"These," said Malik, "perimeter lights have been on the fritz. I think it's safe to say that someone is interfering with them."

"It's Nilah," said Orna, stepping closer to the projection to peer at the white dots of the spotlights. "That's our sign that she's alive."

Cordell raised his eyebrows. "Lights on the blink? That's a long shot, don't you think?"

Orna's nostrils flared. "No, sir. That's Nilah's doing, I'm sure of it."

The captain shook his head and looked to Armin. "Any thoughts on what we're looking at, Mister Vandevere?"

As they spoke, all Boots could think of was the captain's words, "on the blink." It was such an ancient expression, from the days of Origin, and Boots had seen more than a few old journals of engineers and scientists using the phrase. Originally, it meant a light bulb that blinked because of a short circuit.

"Malik," Boots interrupted the debate, "does your scope have a shutter adjustment on it?"

"Uh"—the view shook nauseatingly as Malik prodded his device for a menu—"I, uh...yeah, just a...just a second. Okay, it does. It's set to full analog capture."

Boots stepped closer to inspect one of the lights. "Can you slow it down?"

The view shook, but nothing happened. "This is one thirty-thousandth."

Boots tried to drum up her memories of an ancient machine language she'd once read about. Supposedly, the first automated factory in the colonies had gone insane and killed all its workers. She'd read the specs before cobbling together a legend about artifact storage and some other garbage. She'd used a shipping manifest and a single technical manual as her source, and they'd calibrated the ancient cameras to some shutter speed...

"Going to have to be much slower, Malik. And make sure you're set to capture photons, not light fields. Like one sixtieth."

The image of the Pinnacle grew brighter and dimmer as the imager's internal processors compensated for the drastically increased light hitting the prisms.

"This is one sixtieth," said Malik, but the building appeared no different.

"Not light fields. Capture photons?" asked Boots.

With the flip of a switch, the floodlights became shimmering sets of stripes along their lengths. The stripes alternated and jumped every half second, creating a vibrating effect around the perimeter of the installation.

"What the hell?" Cordell breathed.

"Son of a... Those stripes are binary data codes!" Armin's voice broke into a shout, and he rushed to his bridge aggregator console to record the feed. "Keep the shot steady, Mister Jan!"

The projection stiffened, as though Malik were sitting up a little straighter on the other side. Armin twisted his data sphere this way and that, aligning disparate sources and simulation models. Boots had no idea how he did it, but she'd done her part in discovering the encryption.

A sentence appeared beside each of the lights:

THIS IS HUNTER TWO

I AM STILL ALIVE

MY COMPANIONS STILL ALIVE

LOCATION 43/0572950N BY 64/2020562W 435 ASL

IZAK VRABA ARRIVING IN [VAR SYSCLOCK INVALID REFERENCE]

"So my girlfriend isn't the best programmer," said Orna, a massive smile on her face, "but she's a damned genius."

"What? What do you see?" asked Malik. "I can't see your overlays on my end."

The captain ascended his dais and plopped down into his chair with a sigh. Boots watched in awe as all the stiffness melted from his muscles, transforming him back into the lithe man she'd grown accustomed to.

Cordell grinned. "Everything we need to mount a hell of a rescue. Mister Jan, I want you to hang back. Plan on providing exfil support. Miss Sokol, how do you feel about the prospect of an orbital drop?"

Orna inclined her head. "Never better, Cap. I need to build a shell for Charger, but he'll be in fighting shape soon enough."

"Then, Boots," said the captain, "get rested up. I want a sortie in six hours. Let's just hope Miss Brio can rescue some intel from their clutches before we drag her out of there."

Every minute that Nilah wasn't thinking of Elder Osmond, she was thinking of Sharp and his roster of the active Children. Getting the twins and herself out of the installation would be a hell of a trick. Getting Sharp out would be so much harder. She kept trying to formulate a plan around the coming rescue from the *Capricious*, assuming they'd show up at all. There was no way to know if they'd gotten her signal. When would they arrive? Where would she be? Would the twins be there? Would Sharp be nearby?

All of her plans came to: *Step one—the crew arrives; step two—explosions happen; step three . . . step three goes here.*

And if a rescue wasn't inbound, she had to find a way to get out of the Pinnacle and survive in the frozen wastes of Hammerhead. For the first time in her life, she contemplated how she might need to commit suicide if everything else failed.

She pondered this, as she had for the past day and a half, by walking around the rotunda in total silence. She was on the far side of the room when the bulkhead ground open, revealing Elder Osmond and a retinue of dead-eyed thralls.

"Well, hello, hello!" he called to her as his servants furnished the table with yet another meal of sizzling meat—precut, of course. They'd never leave sharp objects to be used in an escape attempt.

Nilah pantomimed a groan and turned away from him, wandering back toward the couch.

Osmond caught up with her quickly and spun her around to face him. Every muscle in Nilah's body urged her to smash his nose, then break him in half—but the thought of the coming rescue stayed her hand.

"You know, sweetheart, I just had to see you for myself, one last time," he chuckled. "I don't think I've ever been so lucky in my life."

She grunted and slapped at his hands with limp arms. He brushed away her flimsy attacks and shoved her to the ground. Stone bit into her backside, but she controlled her emotions.

"Lord Vraba is so very, very pleased, you see," he cooed, looming over her. He crouched down. "And with my lord's favor comes another infusion of magic."

Nilah bit back a question. She'd assumed Henrick Witts had divvied out all of his ill-gotten spoils from the *Harrow*, but what if he hadn't? What if he could grant power to his cronies whenever he chose?

Osmond jutted out his lower lip and pinched her cheek, speaking as he would to a baby. "That's why I came to check on my little race car driver. Wanted to make sure she was in one piece before I personally delivered her. You are in one piece, aren't you, dear?"

She slapped at him again, her ruse twice as hard to maintain. "Kill…you…" she mumbled, and he guffawed in her face, his breath foul like a stinking animal carcass.

"Sure, sweetie," he said, patting her on the head. Then he stood and added, "I'll leave you four alone. He likes to work in silence."

It was only as Osmond left that she heard the song.

She couldn't quite work out the wandering melody that warbled through the hall. It might've been a woman singing, or the tune of some ancient flute.

When a man-shaped void of light walked toward her, she knew it was Izak Vraba. She stifled a shiver and regarded his approach, dead-eyed.

"Nilah Brio," said the shadow, voice washing through the cavernous hall like shifting waves. "Not the specimen I was expecting."

Five more shadows slithered from behind the arcade of columns to join the first, like a set of reflections between two mirrors. Their fingers dripped in unison, becoming long talons. The song intensified, rising and falling faster, though it refused to make any musical sense.

"When you brought back the *Harrow*, you were"—the shadow craned its head—"larger than life."

His voice emerged from everywhere at once, booming through the massive chamber.

Two of the figures erupted toward her, enveloping her in tenebrous goo, while a third plowed into her gut like a crashing transport. Nilah buckled backward, wheezing, while the twins receded into whatever corners they could find.

She couldn't restrain the scream that clawed out of her mouth, nor the presence in her expression.

"How feisty. And here the elder told me you'd been drugged." Vraba laughed. "He'll have to be punished for his oversight."

"Which drugs, mate?" she gasped. "I do a lot of them so you'll have to get more specific."

"I don't have time for jokes. I have a ship to command. I see you've found our errant twins."

Jeannie and Alister exchanged glances—they must've wanted to help, but the shadow kept them at a distance. Nilah tried to give them a reassuring look, but her eyes watered from Vraba's devastating hit.

The shadows craned their heads, and those hands that held Nilah faded away. "Don't look so surprised, Theta and Sigma. How many times have you cast your marks within my little palace? It was only a matter of time before we guessed. Two readers in perfect sync? Your mannerisms betrayed you."

"Go to hell," said Alister.

"But isn't that where you were born, Theta?" asked Vraba and the shadow melody shivered like a chorus of violins. "In hell? You've escaped, so why not claim your reward in heaven? We could care for you. Talk some sense into him, Sigma."

"I slit the throat of the last woman you had caring for us," said Jeannie.

"Yes," Vraba sighed. "I saw the videos. I'm impressed by your resourcefulness."

Alister stood defiantly before one of the shadows. "Why don't you show up in person? I'd love to get my hands on you."

The silhouette talking to Alister bent and stretched into a long talon. "Be careful what you wish for." Vraba's intrigued voice was like the drawing of a cello's string.

"Oi," said Nilah, pointing to her eyes, "you're talking to me, Vraba. I'm over here."

The shadows squared up against her, multiplying across the

room, peeling out of every crack like swarms of spiders. The melodic warble became discordant noise. "It's been a long time since someone failed to call me 'Lord Vraba.'"

Nilah snorted. "Why? Are you landed nobility? How did you come by your peerage?"

The hail of blows that fell upon her from all sides brought Nilah to her knees. In the Special Branch Archives, he'd been all teeth and blades, but here, his blunt instruments played her rib cage with all the skill of an orchestral percussionist.

The Pinnacle's camera network had no long-range transmitters. She'd checked when she hacked it, because she would've used them to call for help. Vraba's ship had to be close—just a short jump away, if not already in-system. She needed to keep him talking, to learn what she could.

When Vraba had attacked her in the archives, he'd relied on distant cameras to orient himself. The real spellcaster was on a battleship somewhere, guiding his magic through the images before him.

"Look, mate: I'll get straight to the point," coughed Nilah as the shadows let her stand. "Surrender to the authorities and help us hunt down the rest of your kind. If you're lucky, they'll just break your connection to magic."

The shadows froze in place, like pieces of software suddenly unattended. The amount of concentration and magic Vraba employed to keep them going was impressive.

"You're grasping at straws, Miss Brio," said the shadows.

"I mean, if it was up to me, I'd put a single lancer through your skull, but I'm not exactly a war crimes prosecutor."

"There is no crime in taking what's rightfully yours," Vraba replied. "We don't prosecute the lion who eats the lamb."

"No, but we bloody well put people in jail who eat other people. Isn't that what you did to Clarkesfall? Cannibalize it to increase your own power?"

The shadows pondered the question, placing their taloned thumbs to their chins. "I prefer to think of it like a salvage operation: taking something derelict and extracting the only remaining value from it."

It was so strange to hear him proud of being one of the worst mass murderers in history.

"That's some sorry logic," she spat.

"I have a proposition for you," said Vraba. "And before you speak, you should know that I have held the lives of millions in the palm of my hand. I have ended so many. I command thousands more with unquestioned loyalty. There is nothing sacred about a human life; we have entirely too many of them." The shadows receded, giving her a tiny amount of space. "So know my mind when I say that you are worthy to join us...by contract, of course."

Nilah coughed once, her body singing from Vraba's punishment. "There's more to life than magic power."

The shadows dripped together in mercurial strands, forming a titanic humanoid, rising over her like a statue in an ancient temple. "Indeed there is. There's more to life than life itself. There is an existence beyond this flawed, delicate shell." He ran one of his massive claws over the top of her head, and she felt like a mouse about to be smashed.

"The afterlife?" asked Nilah. "Your assholes on the Link were prattling on about that, too."

"How naive," he chortled, his voice distorting and chorusing to the symphony of his magic. "The quintessential distraction of the human experiment... 'What happens after we die?'" Vraba straightened, his head almost touching the distant roof. "Humans seek to control the time and place of their demise, or whether it happens at all, but blithely accept all the rules attached to the game—that death must inevitably come for us all."

Her easy breath had finally returned, and looking at Vraba's mass, he'd been gentle with her. "So what? You want to be immortal? Big deal. Lots of usurers basically live forever, and—"

The shadow's giant hand reached down and Nilah dodged out of the way as it flicked at her. When it missed once more, it melted into a wall and slammed into her, sending Nilah sprawling with the coppery taste of blood in her mouth. When she rolled onto her back, she found herself pinned by a nightmarish silhouette, its head a split row of long teeth.

"Human immortality is a fool's endeavor. How can sentience be limited to this disgusting arrangement of cells? No matter how brave, your history will disappear. No matter how immortal, your mind will break. No matter what you do, the universe will one day plunge into utter darkness, freezing away everything that ever was in the march of entropy." With each word, Vraba's voice rose higher and louder, until his toothy maw pressed against her cheek, huffing. "You have no answers. You cannot save the best of humanity from the coming tide of oblivion."

"Everything dies one day," Nilah grunted.

The grip of the beasts loosened. "You're accepting the rules of the game again."

"And you're a genocidal monster, so your opinion is worth bollocks."

A flash erupted from behind the shadow, and Nilah peered around its form to find Jeannie with her hands against the blackness. She'd cast her mark while he'd been distracted, though Nilah had no idea if it'd work. The manifestation of a spell was far from a real person.

"Naughty," said Vraba, dissolving into a giant hand and striking her to the ground with a vicious slap.

Nilah waved her arms to get his attention. "Over here, you overgrown puppet!"

Vraba's form went through several tortured metamorphoses before returning to an array of shadow men. "You'll come around, Miss Brio...which reminds me of what I was here to do."

Once more, the shadows fanned out to flank her on every side, and Nilah responded in kind by ramping up her dermaluxes to full blast. Unlike at the archives, however, these shadows showed only tiny signs of erosion at her light. The frightful dirge that accompanied them became a hurricane howl.

"I'd rather not risk any...incidents when I meet you in person," said Vraba, closing the circle, "so I'll be separating your cervical vertebrae, as well as your spinal cord. If you're useful, we'll fix that later."

The shadows lunged, and Nilah whipped her arms about in a frenzy, punching anything she could. The viscous darkness closed around her forearms, but couldn't secure a proper grip through the pulsing lights. Nilah ripped her arms free and spun to flee, but found a rising tidal wave of singing black sludge.

With a running leap, she vaulted it, only to come down on unsteady feet on the other side. The beatings, the starvation, and the cold had all taken their toll on her, but with her life on the line, Nilah would muster every ounce of strength she could.

"Run!" she called to the twins, and Vraba's laughter barked through the cavernous rotunda.

"To where?" the shadow bellowed, swelling to fill the center of the room and sloshing outward.

He was right. The exits were all locked. Jeannie had scarcely picked herself up before the roaring darkness bowled her over once again. A lash of ink caught Alister, knocking him to the stones. Hundreds of tiny claws latched onto his legs, pulling him deeper into their depths. Only Nilah was spry enough to remain free, and that couldn't last.

She needed to get back to the center of the rotunda, where she could be seen by all the imagers and trigger her hack—except Vraba's titanic spell was occupying her spot.

The shadows distorted and bloated, bursting into sticky threads like syrup. Nilah dashed between them, calling on every ounce of her reflexes to carry her through the net. She swept aside the thinnest strands with her strobing forearms, and to her delight, she sheared right through them.

Jeannie's and Alister's screams were silenced as the shadows poured into their open noses and mouths. They surfaced once like drowning victims, then disappeared into the ink.

"Over here!" Nilah shouted, and he lunged for her with his tremendous mass, splitting into a dozen thick roots.

She weaved through the web of his body, bound for the center of the room, where she could flash her pulse code and shut down the imagers. She was so close—

—and then something wrapped around her leg and threw her to the ground.

Darkness poured over her, coating every inch of skin like tar, and even her dermaluxes couldn't free her from the rising tide. Her head spun from the hit, and she tried to get her bearings, but the world refused to reorient.

"Let's get a better look. Wouldn't want to be a careless surgeon," mumbled Vraba, barely audible over the haunting cries of his spell. He lifted her toward the nearest imager and pulled her collar from the nape of her neck.

From there, Nilah wouldn't hit all of the cameras with her pulse code, but it'd have to do. She flashed her arms in a precise pattern, triggering the hack she'd installed in the imagers. The shadow shifted abruptly to the left, its coordinates confused by the partial loss of imaging.

But there were other cameras, and a sea of darkness enveloped her like a crushing fist.

"Maybe you're more trouble than you're worth," came Vraba's voice, shouting over the sound of Nilah's screams. "Better to simply end it."

Her voice left her. She couldn't take another breath. Eyes bulged. Muscles burned. This was how she would die—crushed like a rat under a boot. Everything dimmed out.

Distant thunder filled her ears. Was it a precursor to the crackle of crushed bone? The roar grew louder, rattling Nilah's teeth until it was the only sound left. Then came a colossal crack and the splitting of stone.

A sine wave tore through all other sounds, reverberating in Nilah's chest with a heavy bass thud. Light flooded her eyes as the shadows tore asunder, but she saw only white.

Cold wind blew across her skin. The chemical stenches of ozone and sulfur filled her nose. Baked metal tick-ticked away as it cooled. She tested her limbs to find they still worked.

Charger's body came into focus, bloodred armor shining like the evening sun, completed disperser rifle in its hand. Behind it, an orbital drop capsule hung open like a bent-up sarcophagus. Smoke poured from the capsule's exterior, and pockmarks marred the sides from hostile spellfire.

The robot extended a hand to Nilah and, in Orna's gorgeous voice, said, "Hey, babe. How's it going?"

Behind Charger, the Ferriers rose to their feet, dusting themselves off and checking for damage. And behind them, Nilah spied a spell forming, like a little black flame waiting to consume them all.

"Destroy the imagers!" shouted Nilah.

Charger's shoulders sagged. "That's it? That was, like, the single greatest entrance of all time, and you're making demands already?"

The black flame sprouted into a spindly, blade-footed spider and charged at the battle armor. It leapt, its ultra-sharp knives bound straight for Charger's back plates.

"Look out!" shouted Nilah, and Orna spun, planting a shot from her disperser into the dead center of the spell. The shadow exploded into gossamer webs of energy, dissipating.

"Nilah!" bellowed Charger, resting its hands on its hips. "I was worried sick about you, and you need to say hello!"

Nilah raced to the armor and hugged it just above the waist. "I love you, babe. I'm sorry. Can we please destroy the imagers?"

"Thank you," said Orna, and Charger's chest popped open, allowing her to jump out. She wore a formfitting cold-weather suit, a bandolier of heavy rounds, and her personal slinger at the ready in its holster. "Charger, scan and lock onto all imager lenses, then destroy them."

Charger's head spun in place, stuttering at intervals as it noted the locations of cameras. Then it leapt, bounding about the rotunda and smashing its claws into hidden recesses to rip out imagers Nilah hadn't even seen.

She watched in awe of the robot until Orna's warm arms wrapped around her. Nilah sighed and kissed her girlfriend deeply before pulling away.

"Listen," said Nilah, "there's this guy. Sharp. We've got to get him, too."

Orna glanced about. "Where is he? Can we even get to him?"

"He's the insider! He knows more about this operation than anyone."

"We're glad to see you, Miss Sokol," Jeannie huffed, limping over with Alister.

He'd gone pale. One of his eyes was closed, leaking blood, and he held on to his sister with a death grip. Nilah couldn't shake the feeling of the bristling roots on her skin and could only imagine how bad the damage to his eye would be.

Its work done, Charger returned to Orna and dumped a canister at her feet. She popped it open and pulled out three cold-weather suits.

"We'll guard the door," Orna said, drawing her slinger and checking the safety. "Get dressed."

"We're going outside?" mumbled Alister.

Orna smiled. "We're going home."

Before they could so much as contemplate the frost gear, the door buckled inward, sending shards of regraded steel into the nearby stone.

A hulking mech burst through the frame, flanked by a swarm of thralls, their expressions locked in aimless rage. Blue shield bubbles bristled from its exterior, covering its eidolon core and all its most vulnerable parts. Its head resembled one of the drawings of ancient elephants from Origin, with a pair of sizzling red eyes.

It leveled a pair of cannons at them and, in Elder Osmond's voice, bellowed, "Welcome, Orna Sokol!"

Chapter Twelve

Desperate Measures

We've hit a snag, Boss!" Orna's thin voice came over Boots's comm as she waited in the cockpit of the Midnight Runner. Heavy slinger fire crackled over the connection, and the quartermaster shouted something unintelligible.

Boots understood one word: "Trap."

Well, they'd have to be stupid not to lay a trap.

"Boots," said Armin. "Stand by to sortie."

She gave all her controls a last preflight check, the familiar ball of nerves forming in her gut. "Departure, no offense, but let's go."

"Boots, it's Boss," said Cordell. "I think we're looking at a worst-case scenario here."

"Anti-air in place?" she asked.

"Yep."

"No clear exfil path?"

"Yep."

Boots took a deep breath and steadied her hand over the throttle. "All right, then. Let's light these punks up."

"Departure," said Armin as the flashing yellow lights popped out around the opening cargo bay door. "You are cleared for launch, weapons free. Good hunting."

"You've got this," Cordell added, failing to say the phrase he'd told her during every sortie of the Famine War.

She placed her index finger over the mag-clamp switch. "Aw, Boss. Am I not your only wing anymore?"

"No need to stay on the bird this time," the captain replied. "Just bring our folks home."

The *Capricious* pulled straight up, and Boots launched out the back, her stomach flipping with each rise of the horizon. She fired her maneuvering thrusters in the old familiar pattern before leveling out and blasting for the Pinnacle.

"Priority one," said Armin, "take out any air towers and clear us a path for approach."

"Copy."

The engines shoved her back in her seat, and threat warning indicators spread out across her HUD. She couldn't believe she was jealous of Orna's jarring orbital drop, but at least a capsule was too fast to be targeted by the towers. The Midnight Runner was another story.

She dipped low and skimmed the ice, angling her dispersers forward; maybe she could avoid a lancer smashing through her keel. Maybe her defenses would hold. The target calculator counted down, possibly a timer for her fiery demise.

The anti-air towers opened up on her right on time, and she had to peel off to avoid their initial volleys. They'd fired in a spread pattern to prevent any break off, and her dispersers smashed the first anti-air spell. They continued filling the sky with sizzling death until she was forced to bank away.

"Damn it! Prince, I can't even get close!"

"Sleepy here. Maybe I can help," said Malik, his smooth voice filling her ears. "Any chance you can pick me up?"

"In an MRX-20?" laughed Boots. "Are you insane?"

"Boss here. What's your plan?"

"I've got a few explosive charges and a grappling hook," said Malik. "If you can pick me up and drop me in the canyon by the Pinnacle, I'll put a hole in their active defenses."

"No time to get you up into the cockpit, buddy," Boots grunted, angling her dispersers to zap the shots coming up her backside.

"I'll hang on to the skids. Orna did it."

"In Ranger!" said Aisha, breaking radio protocols.

"So did Mother!" was his reply.

Boots grunted in annoyance. A normal fighter jock might've felt more like a taxi service, given the circumstances.

"Boss, that's a suicide mission," Aisha spat.

"Combat simulations aren't good with those towers in play, Boss," said Armin. "I give Boots a ten percent chance of survival."

"I want my crew back," said Cordell. "You're to execute Sleepy's plan."

"Copy that," said Boots. "Sleepy, get ready for the least comfortable ride of your life."

She ripped back the flight stick and hammered the thrusters, rocketing in the direction of Malik's mountain hideout. If she was too slow picking him up, mortar rounds would zero in on her location, blowing her future package to smithereens. Strafing across the ice, she set her dispersers to cover her ninety, bobbing up and down to prevent the computers from leading her craft with their targeting.

"Let's get some cover in here!" shouted Boots, flinching as a blinding round passed too close to her canopy.

The *Capricious* roared into view, its keel slinger pounding the Pinnacle, but the installation's defensive measures tore the spells into bits of glowing glyphs. If the marauder came in range of the lancers, they'd be cut down. The *Capricious*'s covering fire distracted their anti-air towers, but not enough.

"Prince, I need an approach vector to the canyon by the Pinnacle. I'd rather not get perforated dropping him off."

"Copy, Boots. Calculating now."

Her distance to target fell by the thousands. "You'd better be ready with bells on, Doc!"

"Leave it to me," Malik replied.

She raced up the mountain and came in hot on his campsite, deploying her landing skids. With the gear down, she'd lose 20 percent of her maneuvering, and Malik would be outside of the inertial dampers, so the more extreme maneuvers would be out of the question.

The ice crunched under her ship, and she spotted a prone figure in the snow, hanging on to a rock for dear life. Malik rose and sprinted for her craft. The hillside exploded with an off-target mortar round, and she winced. The opposition force would walk the next one right onto the canopy of the Midnight Runner.

"Let's go, let's go!" she barked, watching the keel gun camera.

Malik's tiny figure rushed up under the craft and wrapped his arms around the skid pylon, and Boots rotated the image to make sure he was latched.

"I'm on!"

Boots fired her maneuvering thrusters, lifting off the ice. "Brace for incoming, Sleepy. I guarantee another mortar strike in the next five seconds."

Pulling away, she took care not to rise above the lee of the mountain—any exposure could mean instant puncture of her cockpit by anti-air.

Another mortar slammed the mountainside, ravaging what was left of Malik's campsite. The Runner listed to one side, and the keel slinger camera depicted Malik barely hanging on in the wake of the explosion. Another strike would knock him clean off into a hail of rocks, fire, and ice.

"Where's my vector, Prince?" Boots demanded, hurtling down the back of the mountain.

"Hold tight," said Armin. "I'm relaying the targeting envelopes to your HUD now."

The entire landscape lit up red, save for a small tunnel scarcely larger than the Midnight Runner itself. Boots's gaze slid along the translucent projection, finding altogether too many kinks and turns for her liking.

"You're not going to like this, Doc," she breathed.

"Doesn't matter what I like," he grunted. "We're in it together now!"

"Hang on!"

Boots weaved through the rocky landscape, dashing from cover to cover before the slinger turrets could lock on to her. Mortars crashed down before her, rattling her cockpit with stray rocks. Every time one landed too close, she checked her displays, expecting to see Malik plummeting to his doom. Despite everything, the doctor held on with an ironclad grip, teeth gritted below his frosty goggles.

"Distance to drop, fifteen hundred, Doc! Just—"

She'd climbed too high, and her HUD screamed warnings at her. A stray lance round cut through the rock face before her, and her disperser blew it apart, but the burning spell threads cut into Malik's arms and back. He wailed over the comm and buckled, sliding down the landing skid and catching himself at the last second. His legs dangled precariously above the stony ground—a meat grinder at this speed.

"Oh god, Boots, land!" he shouted.

"If I set you down here, a mortar will end you," she said. "You have to hold tight."

"I'm going to fall!"

She checked her distance to target—seven hundred meters. Just a few seconds. "Use your grapple gun."

"I can't reach it," he groaned.

Her eyes darted between his dangling form and the approach envelope. She couldn't get careless again.

"Four hundred meters, Sleepy. Stay with me."

An ominous rusty stain began to spread across one side of his parka. "I think I'm hit," he said.

She dropped the Runner closer to the trench floor, just in case he let go of the skid, but to her amazement, he held fast. "Just a stray rock, buddy. One hundred meters."

She eased off the throttle, firing her maneuvering thrusters as she edged closer to the landing point.

"I'm a doctor, Boots," he growled, the effort consuming every ounce of his being. "You have to set me down, right now. I'm—"

And he let go.

To land directly onto the snow. She watched through the slinger cam as he fell to his knees and kissed the snow, the nasty wound on his back bright red.

"Okay, you are hit. Didn't want to tell you," she said, spinning the craft and pulling off the way she came. "Might want to take care of that."

"Boots!" snapped Aisha.

"This is Boss. Can you still complete your mission, Sleepy?"

"Yeah. The others are counting on me," he replied, a little unsteady. "Still got some styptifoam. Going to apply that now."

Boots's heart sank as he whimpered into her comm. Her carelessness had put him in that position, and when he got to the Pinnacle, it might cost him his life.

Armin's voice interrupted her thoughts. "Back off, Boots, and let the man do his job. We'll provide topsight from here."

"Copy, Prince. Good luck, Doc."

"I'll open a hole for you," said Malik. "Be ready."

*   *   *

The whine of the hulk's autoslingers filled the air as they hunkered down behind what was left of a stone plinth. Each spell tore away more chunks of the statue above, and Nilah pulled her limbs in close, huddling next to Orna and the twins.

The slinger fire stopped, and metal screeches wailed in Nilah's ears. She poked her head around the corner just in time to see Charger leap onto the giant mech.

"Gotcha," Orna muttered, smirking.

The battle armor whipped out a short handle and flicked it, ejecting a flaming blade so bright it could've seared Nilah's retinas. White light washed the room like a supernova, and she had to squint to see the battle.

Charger swiped its blade across the hulk's arm, cleanly severing one of the autoslingers. Only the glowing cross section of the weapon's internal components remained, like a technical drawing. Wild magic oozed from the ruptured shells, forming a makeshift, prismatic flamethrower, and the hulk brought this new weapon to bear on Charger.

Orna's battle armor retreated, an enraged tiger circling its opponent. It lunged and swiped but couldn't quite get the angle of attack it sought.

Meanwhile, the thralls fanned out through the room, their poisonous glyphs throbbing with malice. The hulk's preoccupation with Charger got the fire off Nilah's cover, but Orna couldn't spare the concentration to do anything about the minor combatants.

Nilah leaned over and kissed her on the cheek, lifting the quartermaster's slinger out of its holster and checking the clip—six shots, glowing with a light she hadn't seen before.

"Thanks, babe," Nilah whispered before ducking around the corner to snap off a round at a howling thrall.

A bright flash blinded Nilah, and then all that remained of the thrall was a smeared shadow across the floor.

"Shadowflash," said Orna. "It's not perfect though—"

"Bloody fantastic," Nilah interrupted, before taking aim at another target and vaporizing her.

One of the dead-eyed thralls approximated rage before ripping the summoner's mark out of the air. A portal opened before her and a pack of ravening wolves rushed out. They tore across the stone toward Nilah in a swarm of teeth while another thrall carved out some unknown spell. The strange glyph completed, it began to strobe with a cold light, coating the rotunda in a deathly pallor.

She'd never seen the effect before, but she felt her downfall coming in the pit of her stomach. Crushing dread filled Nilah's bones, and she understood the hopelessness of her battle. The phrase *We're all going to die here* began to play on repeat in her mind. After the first surprise cut, the hulk easily batted aside Charger's assaults with its glowing shields. Jeannie and Alister waited their turn to be useful—a turn that would never come.

They were doomed. The thrall's spell had only shown her the truth.

"Nilah!" Orna's voice sliced through the fog of alien thoughts. "You have to shoot!"

Stumbling backward, Nilah jerked the trigger at the wolves, vaporizing two of them. The beasts broke off, but again came waves of nauseating despair. Suicidal thoughts invaded her mind, and she considered offering herself up to whatever fate would give her.

Charger gestured to the thrall holding the cold glyph. "Shoot that one! Now!" it bellowed in Orna's voice. "Also, don't use the shadowflash on—"

The hulk took advantage of the momentary distraction to bat Charger across the hall, where it skidded across the floor with a furrow of sparks. It rolled backward, catching its talons in the stones and springing upright. With a flourish, it sliced one of the thralls in half, and the devastating depression vanished like smoke on the wind.

"Pesky," rumbled Osmond, and the hulk's amps fired, projecting his hideous glyph across their surface.

He'd tie them down, break them, liquify their brains with neural spikes. As he cast, Nilah could almost hear the whine of the drill, millimeters away from the nape of her neck.

"Spread out!" Nilah shouted to the others, and they dashed from their cover behind the plinth, finding new sanctuaries behind half-demolished columns. Nilah fired twice more, burning away another thrall. She took aim at the hulk and pulled the trigger. Osmond raised the bot's arm to cover the cockpit and—

—the shadowflash did nothing.

"Bollocks."

Nilah checked the slinger and clicked the trigger again, but she'd used all six shots.

"Yeah, sorry, babe," called Orna. "Organic matter only."

Osmond's spell seized Nilah, ten times more powerful than before. The air went viscous around her and a force lifted her up, only to slam her down on the stone. The wavering force swept her out from behind the column into the center of the room, along with all the others, and the barrels of the hulk's remaining autoslinger whined with delight.

"Nope," Orna barked through Charger, firing its disperser cannon into Osmond's spell, shutting it down.

Nilah got free just in time to avoid the barrage of rounds, scrambling out of the way for the nearest cover. The percussive blasts of spells addled her balance, and she scarcely made it to safety. Thankfully, Osmond's attention refocused on Charger; the bot's flaming sword and disperser rifle meant it couldn't be ignored.

Shrugging away her dizziness, Nilah realized she was crouched beside the hulk with an empty slinger and no body armor. The others had bolted in a different direction.

Osmond began to cast once more. With another "Nope," Charger skidded out of cover and planted a shot from the disperser into the heart of the spell to deflate it. In retaliation, armor plates popped free of the hulk's shoulders, revealing a sinister array of missiles—which Osmond let fly at Charger.

Gouts of flame and pressure battered Nilah as she flattened against the floor. The roof blew open like a cracked egg, considerably widening the hole made by Charger's orbital drop pod. Nilah's ears rang in the silent wake of the explosion, and she checked her person to ensure she'd not been hit.

Lightning quick, Osmond cast his spell, yanking Charger out of cover and snatching his disperser rifle as though it was a doll's accessory. Charger's servos whined as it tried to resist the force, but amplified by the hulk, Osmond's magic couldn't be opposed. First, it spun Charger's right hand, snapping it off at the wrist.

"I like your armor, Miss Sokol," Osmond said. "It's so dainty."

The elbow joint was the next to go, crumpling in on itself. Charger squealed errors, kicking out at the wavering spell. Without him, they were as good as dead, though it could've been worse. At least Orna had jumped out before the fight started. From her vantage point near the hulk, Nilah could almost make out Orna's face—teeth gritted, cheeks flushed with anger. She hadn't seen Ranger die, but she'd have to watch Osmond destroy version two.

The hulk stomped forward, its foot coming down hard beside Nilah's hiding spot. Either Osmond didn't see her, or he didn't care.

"Shame we can't get you under contract, Miss Sokol," said Osmond. "I'd just love a suit like this."

Another step brought the hulk so close Nilah could almost

reach out and touch it. If it wanted, it could simply stomp her into jam, or kick her hard enough to break every bone in her body.

But it didn't.

Wasn't it looking at her? A machine of that size should've had active target tracking on every surface, cross-referenced between visible light, ultrasonic, and infrared. The computer should've rendered Nilah a bright spot on his viewports, crouched and cowering. But then, what if Osmond's attention was on her friends?

More viscous tendrils of air sucked Orna and the twins into the open.

"Lord Vraba will take care of all resistance soon enough," Osmond crowed, rotating out the canisters in his remaining autoslinger for a fresh charge. "Why don't we dispose of one of you to make clear the consequences of defiance?"

Osmond was within spitting distance for the first time in their battle. It was now or never.

Her breath caught in her chest. Nilah drew the mechanist's mark, praying that his trackers wouldn't point her out as a threat. Mustering every gram of strength she possessed, she reached out and placed her palm against the toe of the hulk's boot, forging a psychic connection with its circuitry. A labyrinth of cybersecurity gates spread through her mind. She blasted through the outer loop with little trouble, but the inner sanctum of the hulk's data processor closed in upon itself.

"I don't think so, dear," growled Osmond, bringing his rotating cannons to bear on her.

Nilah briefly saw herself through his gun imager before she managed to zip through his servo network and knock his aim wide. A blast of slinger fire demolished the walls near the shattered roof, expanding the gap even farther. Bitter-cold wind suffused the room, racing around the rotunda like a banshee.

"Precious. But too little!" barked Osmond, and his heavy swing came far too quick for her to dodge.

Nilah tasted metal; then the lights went out.

"We're catching a lot of activity there!" Cordell said over Boots's radio. "Two of the Pinnacle walls just went up. Something just blew from the inside."

Boots swiveled her keel imager to view the collapsed wall, finding a smoking hole. "This is Boots. I've got eyes on the hunting party." As a gust of wind tore away the gray curtain, she found a massive bot lumbering toward her trapped friends. She'd seen that model in the Famine War, embedded with the enemy infantry. "Boss, looking at a Carrétan 225 Demolisher pinning down Orna and the twins. Do we have a status on Hunter Two?"

"Hunter Two is hit!" cried Orna.

"Boots," said Armin. "That Demolisher needs to go down, now."

Boots scoured her glass for any weaknesses. "Not happening, Prince. Not while their anti-air defenses are in play."

Malik sighed theatrically over the comm. "Please stop nagging me. I've been shot."

"ETA, Sleepy," said Cordell.

"Twenty seconds," Malik replied. "I've crested the cliff and I'm arming the first charge now. Going to take down the central disperser."

"Line up your strafing run, Boots," Armin said. "You've got enough time. With the disperser down, we'll take out the closest air tower."

A chill ran through her gut, but she banked hard to face the Pinnacle and gunned the thrusters. "And if he doesn't make a big enough hole?"

"If you go down fighting," said Cordell, "we will, too. I'm not leaving this planet without my crew."

"Copy."

Through the Midnight Runner's computer-enhanced imagers, Boots could make out Malik's tiny figure. She wasn't that far out of range of the anti-air turrets, and they were coming up on her like a brick wall.

"Reduce thrust twenty percent," said Armin. "Maintain the slower airspeed."

She eased off the throttle, supplementing her altitude with maneuvering thrusters. "I'm not going to be able to dodge when they start shooting!"

The turrets swelled in her view, ready to burst with volleys of deadly light.

"Arrive late, risk getting shot. Arrive early, definitely get shot," said Armin. "I'm projecting the reactions of the other air towers to your HUD."

Long stalks of laser light spread before her in a forest, the potential shot patterns. It'd take some fancy stick work not to get sliced in half. She eyed the anti-air turret in front of the Pinnacle's smoking hole, hoping she wasn't blocking Aisha's shot. Keying the Demolisher on her screens, she leveled off and readied to fire.

She crossed into the range of the anti-air towers. No explosion on the central disperser yet. Pops of heavy fire dotted her horizon in the same spread pattern as before. If she didn't break off, she'd be toast.

The *Capricious* fired its keel slinger, the force round sailing past Boots's cockpit toward the Pinnacle. In perfect synchronicity, Malik's explosive charge blew the disperser tower and the force round slammed into the anti-air slinger, clearing the way for Boots.

But the other anti-air towers had still gotten off a volley.

Boots fired her keel, maneuvering thrusters at maximum, shoving her downward in her seat as her dispersers zapped the nearest round, leaving a web of hot spell threads directly in front of her cockpit.

She threw her hands in front of her face and gritted her teeth. Errant shards of magic came slicing through her cockpit, shattering her windscreen, binding to her rubberized suit, eating through sections of her helmet. Her shattered canopy glass ripped away in a heartbeat, and wind roared in her ears as bright strands chewed on her visor.

Boots shoved her fingers into her broken helmet and yanked the face plate away, flooding her lungs with frosty air. She squinted at her target, trying to line up the shot through freezing tears. Her flight suit glove smoked where burning magic struck it, but she couldn't feel it through her metal arm.

"Boots!" came Cordell's voice, and she tried to transmit, but they'd never hear her over the gale-force winds buffeting her cheeks. "Boots, what's your status?"

No instruments, no imagers, not even iron sights like the ancient pilots of Origin—visual only.

Another force round from the *Capricious* streaked past her, smashing the next anti-air tower, opening up a larger gap in their defenses. She dipped low and raced across the snow, enemy lancers chewing up the ice in front of her.

Wait for it.

This close, she could make out Malik, collapsed in the snow, a red stain around his form. Then the gaping hole in the wall, then the Demolisher. She squeezed her eyes against the blistering cold and leveled off, her finger twitching around the trigger.

Now.

Boots sprayed a line of glowing fire up and down the hole, splashing across the Demolisher's shields, through chinks in its armor, over the wall behind it, into the decorations, and all around the edges of the hole in the Pinnacle.

The Midnight Runner zipped past the structure, banking hard in the atmosphere to avoid the fire of the remaining anti-air towers. Boots tapped her comm package, screaming that she wanted a status from the *Capricious.*

"Say again, Boots," said Armin. "We couldn't make out your last."

"Give me a goddamned status on the Demolisher!" she yelled into the shrieking wind.

"Are you asking about the Demolisher?" said Armin.

She tried covering the mic with her smoldering metal hand. "Yes!"

"What?"

"Affirmative!"

Her cheeks had stopped hurting, instead going completely numb from the cold. If she didn't already have frostbite, she would soon enough. The Runner sailed clear of the Pinnacle, rocketing over the guard depot toward the uninhabited wastes beyond.

"Confirm hit," said Armin. "Good kill."

"Tell Boots I said thank you," Orna gasped over the comm. "Hunter Two is unconscious but breathing."

"Aisha, take us in," said Cordell, "and mow down anyone who dares to poke their heads out. We need to grab that husband of yours."

"Yes, Captain" was Aisha's curt reply.

She tapped her comm package again in predictable intervals, attempting to make them understand that her cockpit was blown and she needed to dock. She repeated the pattern twice, and Armin finally understood.

"Boots, return to the mothership," he said. "Repeat, return to the mothership."

Thank god, she wanted to say, but her mouthpiece would never transmit over the cacophonous howl. She ripped into another anti-air tower, reducing it to detritus, and the *Capricious* iced the last one. They were free to approach.

Boots raced toward the ship, her face so cold she was sure her skin would slough right off, and angled to dock. She brought the Midnight Runner home and flipped on the magnetic locks on the landing skids.

"Approach, this is Boots. I've set him down onto the floor of the cargo bay. Requesting gravitational compensation."

"Approach acknowledges. Glad to have you back," said Armin. "Aisha, adjust cargo bay gravity to Origin point one."

Boots's gut churned with the dimming of gravity, and she unbuckled her belts to float out of the cockpit. Kicking off the side of her ship, she sailed over to the powerjack and yanked an energy cable out of the wall. She plugged in her ship, snapping the charging hook into place.

Only then did her face begin to burn. Boots raised her shaking hands and inspected the damage: several painful lacerations, third-degree burns, and puffy, irritated flesh. Bits of duraplex had melted to her metal hand. She wiped her stinging eyes, swearing.

"You okay, Boots?" asked Cordell.

The Runner's canopy was nothing more than a jagged lining of glass around its cockpit. Twisting curls of magic had stitched scorch marks across the hull. Without a doubt, she should've died.

She sighed, letting the lack of gravity take a load off her. "No, sir. I'm hit."

"Okay, copy. Can you make it to the med bay?"

"I'd like to stay here until everyone is aboard, sir."

"Sometimes we don't deserve you," said Cordell.

She snorted. " 'Sometimes'?"

Boots kicked over to the crew locker and replaced her flight helmet, happy to have a shield against the cold. Her hands would have to wait—there was no time to change her whole suit. She clipped the cargo tether to her belt and walked to the edge of the ramp with her mag boots.

The *Capricious* was descending, its keel slinger pounding anyone foolish enough to emerge and fight. With no dispersers and no anti-air, Aisha's ultra-precise shots could strike even the smallest soft targets. On the distant snow, Malik had curled into a ball, probably trying to keep warm after losing so much blood. Orna and the others were fighting for their lives inside the stronghold of the enemy.

"Contact!" called Armin. "Bogey spades, Hatchet five-seven-three, one thousand kilometers, twenty thousand ASL."

"What is it?" asked Cordell, but Boots already knew the answer. They'd cut it too close, and now they'd pay the price.

"It's a dreadnought, sir," said Armin. "It...I believe it's Vraba's ship."

Chapter Thirteen

Breakbeat

Nilah's eyes lolled in her head, fixing on features of the rotunda, only to have her vision slide to the left every time she focused up. Hard metal smacked against her stomach in regular time, and her hands and feet prickled with blood. Charger carried her over his shoulder.

She retched, then vomited across his armor, bits of protein sizzling on his open chest vents.

Orna moaned. "How much puke am I going to have to clean out of this guy?"

The smoke brought on more retching, and Nilah choked out the words, "Oh god, put me down!"

The world spun, and she found herself against the cold stone, the black plume of the exploded hulk filling her view. Every surface of her body was a bruise. Broken ribs stabbed into her sides with each inhalation.

Orna rushed to her side, pushing a comm into her ear. "You're going to be okay. Captain, this is Hunter One. Package secured."

"I've been in crashes before, babes," Nilah murmured, mustering a confident smile. "'S just I was backhanded by a big robot."

"Glad to have you back, Hunter Two," said Cordell. "We've got some new dimensions to the mission. No easy way to say this. Vraba is here. Malik is bleeding out by tower two. If you don't get on board right this second, we're all dead. If we go now—and go full burn—we can keep that dreadnought at bay until we hit the jump gate to somewhere more private."

Vraba's monstrous shadows crept into the edges of her mind, momentarily pushing away the fog of Nilah's concussion. And in it all came the face of Sharp—the man who knew everything about the Children of the Singularity. He had the master list of their active agents.

She'd killed supplicants on her ascent to the Pinnacle. If Nilah could just save one deserving life on this mission, the sacrifices might've been worth it.

"Hunters acknowledge," said Orna, pulling a small canister from her belt and twisting. It blinked, projecting a flare into the sky as she hurled it against the far wall. "Knock down the rest of that wall, and we'll come to you."

"Prince here. Be advised, danger close."

The twins joined Nilah, and Charger loomed over the four of them like a protective parent.

Orna tapped her comm. "Acknowledge danger close. Blow it."

The sound of the *Capricious*'s heavy slinger impact deafened them. Shrapnel filled the rotunda as one half collapsed into rubble. Charger knocked away a stone slab before it could crush them.

"Time to go," said Orna, and Charger's good claw gently scooped Nilah up.

"No," Nilah murmured. "We've got to get Sharp."

Orna looked to the twins.

"Bad luck for him, babe," said Orna, and Charger hefted Nilah into a cradled position. "We're leaving now. The mission failed."

Except Sharp hadn't been allowed to leave. He'd been trapped here for over a year, forced to play along for fear of death, or worse. He would have advanced training to defeat enemy readers and mnemonimancers alike. He'd have an extensive network of underground contacts, and the goods on hundreds of highly placed members of the Henrick Witts organization.

"No!" said Nilah, pushing off Charger to jump to the floor. Every neuron in her brain lit up with agony as her foot hit the ground—her ankle had been twisted in the fight.

"Nilah!" Orna cried, rushing to stop her from standing. "That's it! You can't walk. You can't fight. This op is finished!"

Nilah gripped Orna's collar to hoist herself off the floor. "No. We didn't come out here to be beaten and abused just so we could walk away without a prize. We have to get Sharp!" She tapped her own comm. "Captain, I know who the double agent is. If we don't grab him, he's dead."

Orna gritted her teeth, the engine wash of the incoming *Capricious* ruffling her hair. "She's delirious, Cap, and she can't even walk. There's no time."

The marauder's searchlights blinded Nilah. Her exit was right there; all she needed was to be carried away.

"Boss here. As much as I hate to agree," said Cordell, "we can't win them all, Hunter Two."

"No," said Nilah. "I always win. I know how we do this."

Orna pushed her off to reload the slinger. "Captain—"

"Let's hear it," came Cordell's reply, and Orna flushed pink with anger.

She took a knee to keep the weight off her ankle. "The twins grab Malik and get him to the med bay. I can ride in Charger to go find Sharp, and Orna can provide fire support."

She glanced at Orna, who looked as though she'd been slapped. Not once in their year-long relationship had Nilah ever ridden inside the battle armor, and she understood why—that bot was

Orna's sense of security. Ranger had been her only salvation since childhood, and she'd be just as protective of Charger. It'd be like reading her girlfriend's diary.

"If we don't leave now, that dreadnought will catch up. Prince, how much time do we have to get loaded up?"

"Two minutes thirty seconds," said Armin.

"No time for a rescue op," Orna spat. "Now let's go."

"What if we reload the jump dump and fire it again?" Nilah asked, and silence came over the line.

"With what?" Orna shouted. "Besides, there's no guarantee it'd work! Captain, this is stupid!"

"Boots here. The Runner's canopy is shredded and his systems are all jacked up. He ain't flying again any time soon. We could gut his eidolon core." Then, after a pause: "I want this Sharp guy, too."

"Two minutes," said Armin. "The estimates are good, but we need a decision, Boss."

Nilah, Orna, and the twins watched the stairwell for any incoming. The quartermaster's arms shook with rage, but she held her tongue in wait for the order.

"Do it," said Cordell. "I want the twins on board yesterday, with Sleepy in the med bay, you hear me? Boots, can you get the core out of the Runner?"

"I've got the Rook jacket, remember?" asked Boots. "Pretty sure I'm a certified mechanic now."

"Stow the stupid jokes, Boots," Orna snarled. "Just don't drop anything."

Orna reached up and removed her circlet with uneasy fingers before settling it across Nilah's brow. Her lips locked into a scowl.

Nilah looked into her eyes, searching for any kind of sympathy. "This is the only way," she whispered, but her girlfriend said nothing to comfort her, instead rattling off a list of mechanical peculiarities and quirks of Charger's systems.

"This isn't a damned race car, Nilah. Don't drive it like an asshole."

Nilah traced her mechanist's mark and connected to Charger's circlet. Inside, she found a confused animal, frightened and searching for its master. She smoothed her authentications over its core, assuring it that everything would be all right. Charger knelt, and its breastplate popped open to reveal the scuffed cushioned cockpit inside.

"Hello, Nilah Brio," the voice of a young boy spoke directly into her mind.

"No questions now," said Orna, preempting Nilah's curious glance.

Carefully, Nilah reached out and grasped its waiting talon. She pulled herself upright despite her agonizing ankle and hobbled into the cockpit.

"Don't break him," Orna said.

As the armor plates closed around Nilah, she said, "I'll be careful."

It smelled of Orna in the best and worst ways. An array of heads-up displays sprang to life around Nilah's eyes, showing her a world of detail she'd never seen before. It was overwhelming, like trying to count every grain of sand on the beach, and she shook her head, trying to comprehend all the features of the scene before her. Pneumatic cushions swelled around her injured leg, the sensors tuning actuators to baby her wound. A pair of pinpricks stung her calf muscle, then her ankle went cold and numb.

"Charger is helping," the boy said, his voice cheery.

"With the new plan, you've got five minutes to get back," Armin said, "then another five to secure the jump dump to the main core."

Nilah grasped Charger's blade and channeled magic into it, igniting it with brilliant energy. She turned to face Orna, who held her slinger at the ready.

"You loaded up?" Nilah asked.

"Let's get this clown and get out of here."

Together, they raced into the bowels of the Pinnacle, where the rest of the cultists surely laid in wait.

Orna crept through the halls, caution in every step, but Charger was considerably louder.

"Turn on walk assist," Orna hissed, "unless you'd rather just shout our location to everyone."

Nilah dove through the ambulation menus until she found the AI balancing assistant, connecting the relay.

"Charger will be quiet," said the boy.

The bot sank low around her, creeping in the direction Nilah wanted, with movements not her own. Actuators doubled in power, taut with menace, never whining. Its silent slink through the darkening corridors both unnerved and exhilarated her, like inhabiting the soul of a great cat.

The battle armor wasn't simply an extension of her skin, but a transformation into another being entirely. On instinct, she flexed her remaining claw, savoring the clink of regraded steel against fibron.

Nilah could get addicted to this.

Her enhanced hearing detected enemy footsteps. She stopped Charger, halting Orna with a fist.

She gestured to the edge of the corner, holding her claw and stump apart to indicate distance. Orna removed a grenade from her belt and twisted the primer to one second before clicking the button and hurling it down the hall. It bounced down the corridor and exploded in a ball of flame. Cooked flesh and blood rushed into Charger's olfactory sensors, and Nilah had to stop herself from gagging.

For the universe to live, the Children had to die. Still, Nilah had never wanted to kill anyone.

"Check the body," said Orna. "Better not be Sharp."

Creeping to the corner, Nilah kicked over the charred corpse and winced. He didn't look remotely like Sharp, though it was hard to tell. She was already beginning to regret volunteering for this mission.

With a flash of blue light, two cultists stepped from a tear in space. Lightning crackled from the first man's fingers, raking over the armor in agonizing jolts. The other cast his teleportation spell, reaching for Charger to drag it away to some distant location— maybe space, maybe solid rock.

Nilah whipped Charger's blade across the pair, cleanly dividing them in two before staggering away. They toppled like toys, and sickening breath caught in her throat. They hadn't left her a choice. It was one thing to lock the initiates out in the cold. That had been distant, unfeeling. She'd sensed the blade passing through their bodies like a hot knife through butter.

Orna placed a firm hand on Charger's back plate, pushing it forward.

"Keep going. Don't think. Just live," whispered the quartermaster, a crack of mercy in her tone.

"R... right," Nilah whispered, pushing onward into the complex.

They came to a junction, and Nilah fired up her active scanners, searching for heat signatures: five in one direction, one in the other. Would Sharp attempt to hide among his false confederates, or would he try to be alone in the hopes of a rescue? She gestured for Orna to follow her toward the single signature.

It was a faint blur behind several layers of rock, and it could've been anything—a generator, an eidolon crystal reserve, a roaring fire. As they crept through the maze, Nilah let out a sigh of relief when it resolved into the shape of a man. They stopped outside a closed door, Nilah gesturing for Orna to take cover against the wall.

She sliced a glowing, molten X through the door frame and kicked the panels into the far interior wall.

She rushed inside and shoved her target against his bed frame. Charger's stump pinned his neck, and the blade came to rest millimeters away from his bobbing throat.

"Please don't, please don't, please don't," came Sharp's frantic cries. He tried on instinct to wrestle her away, but even his champion grappler's strength was nothing compared to Charger's motors.

Nilah let him stand, and Orna pushed into the room behind them, sweeping for any hostiles. The quartermaster let her finger off the trigger when she saw him.

"You must be Sharp," she said. "If you want to get out of here, you come with us right now. Try anything, and you'll be a carbon paste faster that you can say 'scumbag cultist.'"

"Charmed," Sharp replied, dusting himself off. "Did you bring me a slinger, too?"

"We brought you a rescue, so keep your mouth shut and let's go," said Orna.

"We've got to move," said Nilah, her voice filtering through Charger's speakers to make ripples and eddies over the scene. "Vraba's ship is in-system."

"How close?" asked Sharp, eyes widening.

"In orbit," said Nilah.

Sharp poked his head into the corridor before returning in a panic. "He could flood this base with shadows and butcher everyone inside. His powers are—"

"Shut up. What's the fastest way out?" asked Orna.

"Up top," said Sharp. "Or the front door."

Nilah detected a faint howling on the other side of his bedroom wall. "Or through there," she said, pointing to a blank patch of rock. She sliced apart his wall, along with his bed, a writing desk, and all his clothes, and it fell away into the wailing wind beyond.

On the other side was the canyon: a sheer drop of a thousand feet.

"Prince, you see that new hole in the side of the Pinnacle?" Nilah asked, swallowing hard.

"We see it," said Armin.

Charger's powerful hearing detected another noise, too: the shadow song of Izak Vraba.

"He's coming!" Sharp called, peering down the corridor, and Nilah saw writhing shadows extinguishing all the lights.

She yanked her companions back under her arms. "You've got two seconds to get the ship in front of that hole, Prince. I'm jumping."

"What?" Orna cried, but Nilah was already setting up her leap into the great, open space beyond.

"There's nothing out there!" Sharp protested.

Charger's heads-up display lined up the angle, and Nilah swallowed hard.

"No. No. No. No!" cried Orna, struggling in Charger's grip.

Charger bounded twice and leapt through the blast hole, and for an oddly serene moment, the only sounds were the wind and Orna's sustained scream. They sailed out into the night, the distant floor of the ice canyon ready to swallow them whole.

Then came the thundering engines of the *Capricious*, searchlights and solid hull under Charger's feet.

Charger's claws hit the ship wrong, and the trio of them bounced across the roof, sliding toward a deadly fall. Nilah lost her grip on both of her passengers, and they went rolling off in different directions, both struggling for any handholds—Sharp toward the comms array, Orna toward the hot wash of the main drive.

Nilah's claws caught purchase, and she jerked to a halt for just long enough to register her girlfriend's trajectory. "Aisha, pitch forward now!"

The ship swelled under her feet as the thrusters roared to double output, and Orna was launched into the air like a ball from a racket. Charger snatched the quartermaster to the deck, using its prehensile toes to secure purchase on the dish from the wide-scanning array.

Nilah looked down the ship's length to find Sharp, white knuckles around the comms antennae. She had trouble making sense of what she was seeing, but he screamed as something attacked him. Charger's sensors grasped the shape of a long tentacle, stretched thin from where it'd followed them out of the hole in the Pinnacle. It stabbed at Sharp with a dozen knives, and his leg was already a wet mess.

"We need shields up here!" she cried.

"Stay low," said Cordell. "Don't want to knock you off!"

A dome of soft blue light swept over them like a sunrise, slamming into the tentacle and severing it. The shadows coming from the Pinnacle reared back in a massive spike and assailed the shields with sparking attacks. Each strike resounded like a tuning fork.

"Hunter Two, is everyone aboard?" Armin demanded.

If you can count hanging on for dear life while you're bleeding to death. The shadow hammered the shields hard enough to shove the ship off course.

"Just get us out of here!" was Nilah's response, and the thrusters roared around them, rocketing the *Capricious* upward.

At this altitude, the moon stretched before her, and Vraba's ship was a distant glimmer of light. Its dozen engines fired in pops to control its approach to the moon's gravity well. Shadows tore through the Pinnacle, prying it apart, destroying everything inside for a mad grasp at Nilah and her friends.

The blue shields rushed away, swinging under the ship to protect its belly. The *Capricious* swelled under their feet as spike after spike lashed out from the surface like ferrofluid, smashing into their defenses. Nilah made sure Orna was secure, then staggered toward Sharp across the bucking *Capricious*.

She reached him as his strength failed, and he slipped free of his purchase, sliding toward the void below.

"Gotcha!" she said, grasping his hand with her manipulator. He was ragged, but conscious for the moment.

"Hey!" Orna called to them. She'd gotten the roof hatch open, and Jeannie poked her head out, ready to assist.

The ship yawed violently to avoid a cataclysmic strike from the growing shadow creature. The *Capricious* fired pinpoint barrages at its spikes, blowing them off course. The shadows were now at least a hundred meters in height, swinging hungrily for the ship.

Nilah stumbled over the roof with Sharp in tow, praying with each step that the ship wouldn't be struck hard enough to fling them into the great beyond. Upon reaching Orna, she shoved her charge into the hatch, where Jeannie caught him, then she dove in after.

"We're in," Orna said, then looked to Nilah. "We've got a lot of work to do. Jeannie, can you get him to the med bay?"

"On it," she replied, and Alister came to help her carry Sharp deeper into the ship.

Nilah popped open Charger's armor and hopped out, handing the circlet back to Orna before she was even asked. The quartermaster wordlessly donned the circlet before marching in the direction of the cargo bay, Nilah following after.

The pair bounced along in the weak combat gravity, leaping down entire flights of stairs.

"We're going to harvest the electricals from the jump dump, but nothing else," said Orna. "The battery chamber is just going to be melted crystal."

"We can wrap the core from the Runner in spare shielding panels. That'll—"

"Hang on to the railings when we're in combat grav."

Right on cue, the ship took a hit, and it was like the wall jumped out and smashed Nilah's nose. It wasn't a catastrophic blow, but when she brought away her hand, she had the slow drip of blood.

"Keep going," said Orna. "We'll deal with it after."

They reached the engine room, where Boots awaited them with a mag-locked dolly and a glowing pink core. They all three paused a moment to look over their potential salvation: an antique fuel cell from an old fighter, unhooked and delivered by a totally unqualified technician.

Nilah traced her mechanist's glyph and laid a palm across the safety housing on the top. She closed her eyes, feeling her way through the system distributors and link cables.

"This looks good," she said. "Shall we get to work, darlings?"

Boots was out of her depth. The mechanics popped up tiny diagnostic spells left and right, linking with their tools, speaking to each other in a language that sounded like Standard, but with a lot more numbers and acronyms.

There was a strange iciness over Orna when she'd arrived, but as long as they could get the jump dump working, it didn't matter. The two mechanists swarmed over it like a pair of Arcan lemurs, so it was as under control as it could be.

"Boots," said the captain over the intercom, "you're needed on the bridge, now."

"On my way."

Boots launched down the hallway and onto the bridge, where she saw explosions across their bow.

"I need help down here!" Aisha shouted over her shoulder, slamming the stick to one side to force the ship into a hard, dipping bank.

Boots maneuvered down the terrace, past Armin with his face locked in concentration, to arrive at the pilot's side. "What do you want me to do?"

"They're launching long-range missiles," said Cordell. "Missus Jan can shoot them down, but she'll need all of her concentration."

Aisha gave her a brief smile. "You're going to be taking my seat, ace. Guess we'll see if you're cut out to be a zipperjock like me."

She jumped up from the controls, and Boots had no choice but to scoot in and grab the stick.

"This is a terrible idea," Boots grumbled, eyes frantically scanning the controls for familiar surfaces. "I ain't even close to certified on this thing."

Nothing immediately jumped out at her other than the throttle and the joystick—and the lock alert light flashing by her side.

"Incoming!" shouted Armin.

Aisha reached over Boots and trimmed the two-seventy, sending the ship into an off-axis roll. On the projector, a single red missile glanced against Cordell's shield and smeared a flaming comet across the sky.

"I've got this!" said Boots. "Focus on the heavy slinger!"

"You sure?" Aisha asked.

"I'd better be."

Boots throttled up, and much to her disappointment, the *Capricious* didn't go rocketing away like the Midnight Runner. He was a sluggish boat, and his maneuvers were less about grace and more about throwing weight around.

"Multiple contacts. They're scrambling fighters!" said Armin. "Six bandits. Hatchet five-seven-zero, eight hundred fifty, sixteen thousand ASL."

"We don't need to respond," said Cordell. "Just keep that throttle open, Boots."

Boots shoved the throttle to full, hoping that was the right way to handle a marauder. "Yes, sir!"

"How are we coming on that jump dump?" asked Cordell, swiveling his shields back into the firing solution.

"We'll shout for you when it's done, Cap," Orna's voice echoed through the bridge. "That's the only status we've got."

"Missile inbound! Tigershark multi-warhead seeker. We're dead to rights in two seconds," said Armin, and Aisha rushed to the dedicated weapons controls, tracing her glyph.

"Tracking..." said Aisha, swiveling the keel slinger on the projection.

Boots pitched the ship down to give the gunner more horizon to work with. The model ship flashed as its slinger discharged a lance round, which led the distant missile by a wide margin. The two projectiles collided, blooming into fiery flowers in the sky.

"Good kill!" said Cordell. "If you keep that up, we can hold them off for a few more—"

"We've got to disconnect the main power," Nilah interrupted over the intercom.

"That'll put us in free fall over a moon with no shields, amps, or gravity," Cordell responded. "Any other options?"

Vraba's warship launched fifty missiles, each speeding toward the *Capricious* like a rabid dog. Boots checked the readouts; they were already at full throttle. Aisha frantically traced her glyphs, blasting at the projectiles, but she'd never hit all of them.

Then the lights went out, and Boots's stomach contents rose into her throat. The breezy combat gravity disappeared, replaced by the sickening spin of free fall. The roars of the *Capricious*'s three engines fell completely silent, replaced by unsettling rattles.

Standby power gave them two things: emergency lights, and a depressingly accurate altimeter. Boots watched the numbers plummet, each second dragging them closer to an icy demise.

The lights returned along with the main drive. Boots shoved the throttle wide open, and nearly blacked out from the sudden pull of gravity. She glanced back to find Cordell on the ground, trying to get back to his feet. The gravity drive toggled back on, and he nearly leapt from the deck with his newfound weightlessness.

"Jump dump connected," said Orna. "Sealing the engine room."

"Missiles closing fast!" said Armin. "Time to jump!"

"The warship can see us! They'll be able to follow us!" Boots called back.

"It'll take them time to analyze our trail," said Cordell. "Jump to the Harvest gate now."

Boots tapped away at her console, loading in the prearranged coordinates—and hoped she'd done it right. It'd been a long time since astrogation school. "Ready to jump, Captain."

Aisha blasted two more missiles, but she could barely keep herself upright with all the spells she was casting. "I can't hold them off much longer—"

The long trails of missiles inched toward the projection of the *Capricious*, ready to harpoon its hull. A heartbeat later, they'd all be salvage.

"Jump!"

Boots slammed down the all-discharge button, and the ship compressed around her, pushing its distances into two dimensions, folding into the shape of the Flow. She'd never made a jump from inside atmosphere, but she knew what they'd left behind: a massive fireball of fusing oxygen, dissipating into a hot glow. The missiles would be thrown off course by the transmuting gravity well of the fleeing ship, hurling the warheads in a half-dozen random directions at almost the speed of light.

When at last the smear of stars in the Flow came drifting past, Boots dared to hope they had escaped. The projection indicated the whole ship had made it, not just the bridge, so that was promising. When they arrived at Harvest, they'd jump straightaway to a hidden location. There'd be witnesses, but Vraba would have to get that information, too.

Boots let go of the controls. She'd just flown a sortie in a cargo ship, and it was the single most unnerving experience of her career. It handled like an overgrown hog, and Aisha regularly whipped it through space with unparalleled grace.

Aisha's hand came heavy on Boots's shoulder. "Nice going, zipperjock. You keep flying. I'm going to check on my fool of a husband."

Chapter Fourteen

Airlock

Boots was impressed.

To say that Sharp had been a good score would've undersold good scores everywhere. The man was an ultra-fast healer, metabolizing Malik's protein therapies like a champ. The second he was well enough for long conversations, he'd started briefing everyone on the inner workings of the Children. He said he'd been holding back for months after he was cut off from his handler, and he was all too happy to share with the *Capricious* crew.

The doctor was in decent spirits, despite getting pretty sliced up by hot, exploding rocks. Most of the wounds had been cauterized by the process, and the bad cuts required simple closures. If she'd taken that beating, Boots would've been lying low, but the doctor had too much to do, checking on everyone else's wounds.

She'd only just finished her shift when Armin and Cordell called her up to the captain's quarters.

Boots arrived disheveled—she hadn't had any decent sleep for two days—to find Sharp seated at the captain's table eating stuffed cabbages and fresh-baked bread. It was Armin's family recipe, something the first mate prepared on a regular basis.

Cordell had already tucked in to his meal, and he held a bite halfway to his mouth as she entered.

"Here she is," said the captain. "Tell her what you told us, Mister Sharp."

The man looked Boots up and down before extending a hand. "I don't think we've formally met, Miss Elsworth. I was barely conscious when you came through the infirmary."

"It's all good. Boots Elsworth."

"You may as well call me Sharp."

"What happened to you?" asked Boots. "Why were you stuck out there?"

"I think they killed my handler," said Sharp. "Not a hundred percent on that, but I stopped getting messages, and I couldn't ask for extradition without a trusted contact. I thought I'd have made it out by now, but... the opportunity never came."

"Now tell her the other thing," said Cordell, smiling.

Sharp nodded to Boots. "I think your, uh, gods are building a space palace... on a level never attempted before."

It jived with what they'd seen from the Money Mill's engine. The massive amount of capital required to build such a structure would bankrupt a planet. Boots kept those observations to herself, since they hadn't properly vetted their new passenger.

"A 'space palace,'" Boots repeated. "Nice. What makes you think that?"

"The Pinnacle wasn't a cathedral, or a holy site. It was a recruitment office. Those who could defeat Osmond would be periodically lifted away by shuttle. The initiates talked about their coming rewards, about living in the stars with the most powerful people in the galaxy. They called it 'Bastion.'"

Boots narrowed her eyes. "How would you know where they went?"

Sharp's expression darkened. "Because one of them was my friend."

She waited for him to finish explaining, but he didn't continue. Whatever had happened to this friend of his couldn't have been good. She needed him to keep talking. "Maybe she just forgot to call?"

He shook his head, casting off a bad memory. "Her name was Clara. She was able to pass the test, but once she arrived at their base, she couldn't handle it. Said she just…wanted to hear my voice again. Sent me the one message from Bastion, then went dark forever."

"What do you think happened to her?" asked Cordell.

"I hope she's dead," Sharp replied. "If she was caught doubting the mission, they wouldn't hesitate to…It wouldn't be good. The other option is that she renewed her faith, and I hope to kill every last one of Henrick Witts's cultists."

Boots leaned against the liquor console. "You came to the right place, buddy. How do we find Bastion?"

Sharp took another bite and chewed it thoughtfully. "That's the thing. I was able to get off Hammerhead once or twice while under deep cover. They brought me along on recruitment missions to pick up specialists and contractors—some of the galaxy's best talent. If people agreed to work for us, we took them on the spot and delivered them to Vraba."

"Where were these recruitment missions?" asked Cordell.

"Taitutian colonies across the galaxies. We recruited from a lot of private academies." After a long sip of wine, Sharp sighed and put down his fork, leaving little on his plate.

Crossing her arms, Boots said, "What did Vraba do with them?"

"He'd take them away in his warship to be signed to unbreakable contracts," said Sharp. "The good news is that the recruitment missions gave me access to Vraba's servers, where I could download their agent roster."

"Unbreakable contracts… Why not just sign everyone?" asked Armin. "Why aren't you under contract?"

Boots snorted. "Maybe he is."

Awkward silence settled over the table, and Boots's stomach decided to break her posturing by grumbling loudly.

Cordell laughed. "Have a seat and dig in, Bootsie. It's hard enough to talk without your gut being part of the conversation."

Sharp leaned back in his chair, steepling his fingers. "Can I get some wine? This is the first time I've been off duty in almost a year."

Boots poured him a glass, then sat down beside him at the table. "I feel like I already know the answer, but humor me. Why aren't you under contract already? Some kind of compulsion?"

Sharp took a grateful swig from his glass and swallowed. "Because these aren't ordinary contracts. They'll last through anything. Regular barrister's marks have their limits—loopholes like obeying the wording instead of the spirit of the agreement. They can be sued away. The kinds of contracts Vraba signs… he could make you kill your own kids."

"Thankfully, none of us have any children," said Boots. "And let me guess: the barrister in question probably charges a fortune for his services, which are both perfect and everlasting."

"I didn't get that far," said Sharp, "but I'd imagine that you're right."

Boots looked to Cordell and Armin. "Well, we know who that is."

"No surprises there," said Cordell.

Boots served herself a cabbage roll and sliced into it—a little overdone. Armin wasn't half the cook that Didier had been. "Stetson Giles… I owe that guy a hot slinger round right between the eyes."

Sharp nodded. "The guy from *Finding Hana*?"

"You watched it?" Boots asked.

His embarrassed look gave her all the answers she needed. "Nah. But everyone in intel reviewed your case after you parked the *Harrow* in our stratosphere. He's the guy who shot your partner."

"More importantly," said Boots, "he's the guy with the—"

Blinding pain pushed in through her eyelids, eliminating all thoughts of finishing that sentence. It was the old curse, as familiar as an abscessed tooth, coming to shut down the conversation. How many times had she felt it during the press junkets after her show went belly-up? When she'd talked of Stetson before, it'd been idle speculation. Now, she intended to implicate him, to help her friends catch him, and the contract she'd signed wouldn't abide that.

Between the thrumming beats of her heart, she could still feel the cold steel of Stetson's slinger against her temple, his wicked laugh as he forced her to agree to his terms. The pain brought her low, and if she had to endure it forever, she'd sooner kill herself.

"Boots!" said Armin, breaking through the haze.

Sharp had jumped out of his chair, backing away as though she was contagious. "What's with her?"

"She can't help us find Stetson," said Cordell. "He bound her to a contract."

"Are those the only terms?" asked Sharp, and Boots gave him a weak nod.

She sipped at the air, its safe coolness returning in the wake of her wave of flaming agony. "I know where he is. Just can't tell you."

Sharp folded his arms and began to laugh. Boots could've slapped him if she could've mustered the coordination.

He gave her an ominous smile. "It's a good thing you have two readers, then. You don't have to tell anyone anything."

The jump to Harvest had taken a single cycle, but in all that time, Nilah and Orna barely spoke. Once the energy charge was expended from the jump dump, they set about quietly dismantling the system and removing its glassy remains from the main drive. The big cylinder was more char than steel and eidolon, and the crystals inside had melted to black slag.

The quartermaster remained tense throughout the procedure and, when they completed it, wiped her forehead and said, "Going to bed."

"Why don't we grab a shower together?" asked Nilah, trying to brighten things despite their wounded ship. "It's...been a while since we saw each other."

Orna exhaled through her nose. "Shower, yes. Anything else, no. Got to sack out, since the Runner is going to need serious repairs."

Something in the way she said it told Nilah her coldness was more than simple work stress.

"Oh. Okay."

Orna made her way to the engineering hatch and pushed it open, the groan of the old hinge piercing in the cramped main drive compartment.

"Hey," Nilah said, stopping her as she climbed out.

"Yeah?"

"I love you."

"You, too," Orna said, and left her alone in the small workspace to clean up the tools.

For the rest of their voyage through the Flow, Nilah scarcely saw her girlfriend. Orna was either in their quarters, asleep, or working on the Runner. When Nilah finally found her way into bed, the quartermaster moved to the edge of the mattress, putting as much distance as she could between them. After the harshness of the Pinnacle, the gulf of cold sheets was almost more than Nilah could bear.

They lay there for hours, and she stared at Orna's scarred back, watching the rise and fall of her breath. She wanted to wake her, to kiss her, but was too afraid of what she might find out if she tried. Was Orna mad because Nilah forced them to rescue Sharp? Was she mad because Nilah had ridden in Charger? By the time she could work up the nerve to ask Orna what was wrong, Aisha's voice came over the intercom.

"All crew, ready stations. Dropping out of the Flow in ten minutes. Planetfall at Harvest in fifteen."

Orna was on her feet in seconds, yanking on her trousers and buckling her belt. She turned to Nilah, who gave her a smile.

Nilah sat up. "Good morning, babe. Sleep well?"

"Yeah," she replied, pulling on her bra and tank top. "Not too bad. You need to get ready. Cap will be pissed if you're late."

Just ask her.

But that was too hard for Nilah. She could race a hundred grand prix, fight a horde of robots, and face down a god, but she'd never loved anyone as much as Orna. The quartermaster's cool demeanor frightened her more than anything.

She rose and donned her own clothes, and before she'd finished dressing, Orna left. Outside the door, Charger's footfalls banged closer as he met his master to head to the mess.

"See you down in the cargo bay," Nilah called, but Orna had already left.

As the engines spun down to normal space, she tensed, half expecting an ambush planetside, but none came. Docking calls were made. The *Capricious* descended to the surface without incident, and all crew gathered in the cargo bay, along with Sharp.

The cargo ramp whined open, and behind it, the shipyards of Harvest. Nilah spotted the familiar faces of the Arcan mechanics, and was happy to dock among friends. She'd had a lot of fans in her time as a racer, but they could be strange and unpredictable. The men and women who worked the Harvest docks had suffered untold horrors at Henrick Witts's hands, and she couldn't imagine them betraying the crew of the *Capricious*.

Sharp stood at the top of the ramp, hands in his pockets, and Nilah clapped his shoulder.

"Those ladies and gents are all ex–Arcan military," said Nilah. "They may look like inmates, but you can trust them. Still, you sure you don't want us to drop you somewhere more remote?"

He shook his head. "To be honest, I'm pretty eager to get back to work. For that, I need a modicum of civilization. I should be able to coordinate some things from here."

"About that: how will you know who to trust back home? Any one of those people could've sold you out."

He worried his lip. "Well, I've been thinking about that. If the operation was scrapped, but I wasn't killed... that probably means my handler is dead. He was a good guy—would've taken my name to the grave sooner than blow my cover."

"What are you going to do?"

He gave her a dangerous smile. "I'm going to kill every last mole I can get my hands on. Might want to steer clear of Taitu for a bit, because some people are going to start disappearing."

Cordell came clomping down the decking in his captain's boots, hands in his pockets. "Well, Mister Sharp, it's been interesting having you on board. We certainly do appreciate you letting us debrief you for hours on end."

The agent shrugged. "Least I could do after Miss Brio rescued me. If it wasn't for her, I'd have been chewed to bits. I'm just sorry

318

I didn't have any more data cubes to give you. That has to be frustrating for your datamancer."

"He'll live," Cordell said. "Now if you'll pardon us, we've got urgent business to attend to."

Sharp parted ways with the rest of the crew, shaking hands with each of them in turn, until he got to Nilah and the twins. "You three are some of the most resourceful people I've ever met. I hope we'll meet again, but if not, I'll always say I got to ride on board the *Capricious*."

"You'd be the first one to be proud of this rusty tub," Boots said, striding past them and into the waiting autocab.

"Maybe the captain ought to have you clean the rust off with a hand laser," Aisha called after her, face sour.

Nilah grinned. "Take care, Sharp."

He waved goodbye, and made his way toward the serpentine roads of Harvest. Nilah watched him go, certain she hadn't seen the last of him. When she turned back to the cargo hold, she found Malik, Aisha, the Ferriers, and Orna ready to go.

Cordell folded his hands behind his back and squared his shoulders. "They'll be analyzing any security footage from Pinnacle and Mercandatta, so your covers are blown. Let's get rid of those stupid faces, shall we?"

"Gladly," said Nilah. "The new look isn't for me."

"Miss Sokol," said Cordell, "you and Missus Jan will go first, then return to the ship together. You'll need to oversee the purchase of all our supplies. Mister Vandevere will be here handling comms while you're out."

Orna nodded. "Sir."

"Dismissed," said Cordell. "No shore leave. I want us airborne the second we've got everything on board. They'll be following us, and I want to be long gone by then."

*   *   *

It was good to have her old face back. Nilah had enjoyed her exotic fling with an old lover sporting a new look, but the shine had worn off since her time in the Pinnacle. Judging from the rest of the crew, they felt the same way.

They loaded up and made a short jump to one of the uninhabited sectors, one with few eyes on it and fewer police. The Gate Cartel never disclosed details of those using the jump gates, and the *Capricious* passed through unmolested. It felt like forever since Nilah had enjoyed the comforts of civilized space, but the thought of returning to Taitu, with all manner of secret intrigues brewing, churned her stomach. They wouldn't welcome her back, anyway, after the way she'd left.

Once they'd safely entered the Flow again, Cordell summoned her to help extract Stetson Giles's whereabouts from Boots. They'd convened in the mess, where they all took their places around Boots like a surgical team about to operate.

Nilah watched Boots sit in her chair in the middle of the mess hall, tapping her foot to some quick, unheard beat. She knew her part in the plan—distract Boots, let the twins come up and do their thing while she was surprised. It'd be just like Maslin Durand, except they'd be doing it to a friend.

"Is it going to be bad?" asked Boots.

"They just have to throw your defenses," said Nilah.

"Even if I'm fully willing to collaborate?"

"What happens if you think about telling us where Stetson is?"

Boots winced and touched her forehead. "Yeah, that makes sense..."

"Just try and relax. Think about home."

Boots shut her eyes, and Nilah knew exactly what was going through her mind: *Try not to see the twins sneaking up on you.*

Fried leeks and roasting chicken tainted the air, a traditional fare from Clarkesfall. There could be no questioning Alister and Jeannie's plan.

Cordell strode over to Boots and whispered a few encouraging words in her ear. She looked up at him like he was a doctor giving her terrible news. Stetson's curse had trained her to fear.

Nilah had been briefed on the script for Boots and awaited her cue. She'd ask a few disarming questions, then Jeannie would sneak up and hit her with a big one—and finally, Alister would ask the thing on everyone's minds.

Where is Stetson Giles?

From the kitchen, Jeannie nodded for them to begin.

"Boots," Nilah began, hesitantly, "I want you to concentrate on the sound of my voice. Are you ready?"

The pilot nodded, her lips pursed white. "I'm kind of nervous."

"Don't be. Remember what Alister said? He can get into anyone's mind."

"Yeah," said Boots. "And I can tell he doesn't like doing it."

"You once said you had a cactus, back on Gantry Station," said Nilah. "Did you name it?"

Boots narrowed her eyes. "What kind of a lonely spinster names a cactus?" Then she looked around at the assembled crew, their eyes expectant, and said, "Oh. Well, yeah. His name was Kevin."

"Okay," said Nilah. "What's your favorite food?"

"Spatchcock, ale-roasted chicken, and fingerling potatoes," said Boots. "What you're cooking now."

Time to up the ante. "How many, uh, sexual partners have you had?"

Boots grimaced. "Are you serious right now?"

Nilah nodded, gesturing to Cordell, Armin, and the twins. "It's just essential crew right now. Please answer the question."

She looked as though she was chewing a bitter kamaroot. "Five."

Jeannie tiptoed toward Boots, carving out the first mark that would stun her.

Nilah took a deep breath. The questions had to get more personal, so they could throw off any accidental mental defenses. "Are you attracted to any members of the crew of the *Capricious*?"

Boots's hearty laugh fell over the mess hall like a warm blanket. "No. God, no. One of you lot? I don't think so."

Cordell smiled. "That hurts, Bootsie. No love for a man in uniform?"

"Least of all you!" she laughed.

Then Jeannie grabbed her shoulder and said, "What was the happiest moment of your life?"

Boots's eyes went wide, and Jeannie gave her a reassuring look.

"Come on, don't tell them that," the fighter pilot begged.

Nilah leaned in closer. As Boots's friend, she was supposed to tease out the rest of the answers with Jeannie. "Tell us what, Boots?"

"Yeah, tell us what?" Cordell added, a long smile working its way across his face. If she was embarrassed, he was there to pile on and push her further off balance.

"Aw, come on, Jeannie, not him," Boots begged. "Please not him. Captain, get out."

"Oh, is it about me?" he crooned in response, resting an elbow on the table. "This ought to be rich."

Jeannie had been right about Boots: with her intensely private personality, she was far more embarrassed by joy than shame. She rocked in her chair, unaccustomed to being the center of attention.

Nilah looked to Jeannie. "What did you see?"

"You were flying," began the mind reader.

Boots shot her a murderous look. "And I do love to fly, so I guess that's one mystery solved. Anyway, case closed."

"What kind of ship?" asked Cordell.

"It was one just like the one in the hold. The, um, MRX...
fifty?" Jeannie said.

"Twenty," Boots corrected.

"And you only flew those under Captain Lamarr's command,
right?" asked Nilah.

"That's right," said Cordell.

"There were brown hills," said Jeannie, "wide and rolling. You
were flying over them as fast as the ship would take you. And
then, you pulled back on the sticks and began to rise."

Boots eyed her sidelong, but stopped interrupting, perhaps out
of curiosity, perhaps out of acceptance of the experiment.

Jeannie continued. "The atmosphere began to thin, going from
cerulean, to navy, to star-studded black. You heard alarms in the
cockpit. And then there was a voice in your ear saying—"

"'You're leaving the patrol area, Boots,'" interrupted Cordell.
"'Turn around before you get the Kandis' attention'...but you
didn't hear me."

"She deliberately keyed off something called the 'alternate band
hopper comm,'" said Jeannie, and Cordell scoffed. "You just kept
climbing higher and higher, the thrusters at your back and the
heavens ahead of you. And when the gravity indicator hit point
two, you angled your cockpit to the planet and switched off your
ship."

Cordell stood up straight. "Are you kidding me? We were on
the ground in the command center going wild, trying to figure
out how we were going to rescue you! We were worried sick! Kinnard thought you were going AWOL!"

Boots nodded angrily. "Well, I wasn't, Captain. We were flying three patrols a day waiting for a Kandamili assault and I was
damned sick of it."

Jeannie waited for them to finish. "You let your arms fall to your
side, and took long breaths in and out, letting the weightlessness

of space take your body. That's when you saw it—a tiny speck of green island on the mirror of the ocean."

Boots leaned forward in her chair, resting her elbows on her knees with a distant look in her eye. "Up there, I was just a piece of junk, you know? I wasn't part of some stupid war. I didn't kill anyone. I was just... at rest."

Her gaze fell upon Nilah, then Cordell, as if looking for some kind of absolution. Nilah nodded, but said nothing.

"And there was, like... this oasis down below me, and everything in between was blood and fire and guts and fear, but"—Boots wiped her nose—"the ship and I weren't in it for a minute. It was like dying. For a split second, I didn't owe anyone anything. Didn't have to shoot anything. Didn't have any friends to think about. It didn't feel like my brother and my parents were dead."

"It's just like you," said Nilah, and Boots perked up. "Your happiest moment was disobeying orders."

The pilot shook her head. "There was peace beyond measure out there. I don't think I ever could've felt so free if I hadn't been so trapped."

Nilah could feel it—the grace of a pure moment in a dying world—and she almost missed Alister creeping up behind Boots, fingers charged with his spell.

He placed his hand atop her scalp and said, "Where is Stetson Giles hiding?"

They both screamed, clutching their eyes like they'd been blinded. Boots fell from her chair, banging her head against a nearby table, groping for any purchase to keep herself upright. Alister stumbled to his knees, dry heaving and pouring with cold sweat.

Of course it'd been too easy. Nilah rushed to their sides while Cordell called for Malik. The screaming wouldn't stop. She rolled Boots over to the recovery position, cradling the woman's head in her lap. Boots went still and her eyes flickered, but the agony returned, curling her into an even tighter ball.

"Think about the stars, Boots," Nilah urged, stroking her hair. "Find that little green island in the ocean."

Boots's breath came in shorter and shorter bursts as she began to hyperventilate. Nilah mopped her brow and glanced at the door to find Malik rushing inside, carving his purple glyph out of the air. He was in a bad state, limping, bandages wrapped around his bare chest and shoulders. First, he laid his hands on the wailing Alister, who went slack under his touch.

Malik affixed Nilah with his piercing, golden-brown stare. "Please back away, Miss Brio."

Nilah did as she was asked, though as she tried to gently push Boots to the floor, the older woman clawed at her to get her to stay.

"It's all right, Boots," said Malik, tracing another humming glyph. "No dreams for now."

He pressed his palm to her cheek, and Boots's eyes rolled back in her head. She let out a long sigh and fell still. At last, Malik winced and rested a hand upon his chest wound, sinking into Boots's abandoned chair. Jeannie glared at all present, holding her brother down as his agony subsided.

"Is Boots okay?" Nilah asked Malik.

"She'll be fine," he reassured her, "just a little bruised."

When no one else spoke, Jeannie shattered the silence with a sternness Nilah had never heard before.

"And how about Alister? Hm?" she said, lips white with anger. "You know, you're all so quick to use him, but you don't have to pick up the pieces after!"

Malik raised his hands. "Miss Ferrier, you do not want to wake them up right now."

"I'm tired of seeing my brother hurt on your account," she

hissed, bringing down the volume, but all the malice remained. "He's not just some tool to pull out every time you need an expendable—"

"That's enough!" said Cordell, taking slow, deliberate steps toward her. "No one on this crew is expendable, and if I ever hear you say that again, you'll be on your own." He squared up to her. "We do what has to be done for the good of the galaxy and the survival of this ship. You want to protect him? Fine. I expect to see you jump into his place the next time I ask for volunteers."

No one else dared to chime in.

"I've been briefed on every away mission, Miss Ferrier," Cordell continued, his brow shadowing his furious eyes, "and not once have you taken a risk or performed a reading in hostile conditions. Yet, you gladly sliced your nanny's throat to protect your brother. So where's that backbone, huh? Where's the fire in you?"

Jeannie's lips curled into a snarl, but she drew her limbs in close, like she was expecting to be struck. A pang of guilt coursed through Nilah; at the chalet, they'd probably tortured her. Cordell's tactics might've been appropriate for soldiers, but abuse victims—it was hard to watch.

"He's my only family," she spoke through bared teeth.

"Wrong," said Cordell, looming over her. "*We're* your family now. Take some time to get right with that or get the hell off my ship."

To Jeannie's credit, she didn't back down until he added, "Dismissed."

She left the mess like a receding storm, leaving only wreckage behind.

Once her footfalls quieted, Cordell deflated and said, "Well, this plan didn't work worth a damn."

Armin brought some gurneys and helped Malik take Boots and Alister to the med bay, leaving Nilah and Cordell alone together.

He gave her a defeated glance and drew out his silvered cigarette case. Nilah wasn't a fan of the captain's habits, but at least it would cut through the smell of that poor, roasted chicken.

"Don't tell Boots," he said.

"Wouldn't dare."

"You know," Cordell sighed, exhaling a burst of smoke, "I really thought we had that one in the bag."

Nilah's arm still smarted from where Boots's fingernails had etched angry welts. "It was a decent plan, Captain. I think we just underestimated how strong that bleeding curse is. It's not like we can disperse it. The barrister's mark gets into your bones... into your mind."

"You don't have to worry about all that 'captain' stuff when it's just us." He blew a pair of rings into the air. They intertwined, dancing in helical turbulence. "That mark from the Chalice of Hana is powerful. I can see why everyone wants this Giles guy."

"Just think: that could've been Boots writing the greatest contracts in the galaxy."

Cordell smirked. "She'd have the whole place getting on like a house on fire by now."

"Between the chalice and the *Harrow*, she's something special."

"You don't have to convince me." The cherry lit his face, and Nilah noticed a pair of sharp crow's-feet around his eyes. Had he always been that old? "I feel like the twins are integral to getting the info from Boots. She'll never be able to spit the words out on her own, not after years of paralytic pain when she tries. I just wish there was some way to suppress that damned spell. Maybe indolence gas?"

Nilah thought about it and shook her head. "I don't think that'll be enough. According to everything I've found on the Link, the barrister's mark trains your mind to follow the spirit of the contract, so she'll never be able to speak the words. We need the twins to read her mind, but they can't be exposed to the gas when they do."

Cordell looked around for a place to stub out his cigarette and, finding none, went behind the bar to wash his used stick down the drain. "So we can't use dispersers," he called over the running water, "because there's no active spell to puncture. And we can't use indolence gas, because then the twins can't cast." He shook his hands into the basin and flashed them in the dryer. "So... none of the tech out there will help us, unless you know some tech to suppress magic that I don't."

Nilah shot him a playful side eye, and started to make a joke— but she pulled up short.

She did know a way.

It was not a pleasant way; it would require careful positioning, split-second teamwork, and naked exposure to the vacuum of space.

"Captain Lamarr," she began. "There's a place where magic doesn't work quite right. Remember?"

His eyes widened as recognition dawned. "You're not suggesting..."

She wordlessly nodded her head.

"Holy hell. I'm going to need another cigarette."

Boots awoke to a buzzing at the door to her quarters and blinked hard. She wasn't sure how long she'd been out, but one minute she'd been sitting in the mess, and the next—

Had they questioned her? How had it ended?

"Boots," came Cordell's voice. "Open up, I want to talk to you."

She looked down at herself, expecting to be anything but decent, but she was still wearing the same clothes as when they'd tried to extract Stetson's location from her mind. How had she gotten to her quarters? Who'd tucked her in?

"Boots, come on. You've slept for a good long time."

"Yeah," she grunted. "Uh, come in."

The door unlocked with her voice authorization, sliding aside to reveal Cordell with a plate of food. She'd never known him to do anything like that in his life. He certainly hadn't cooked it. He held it out to her—a plate of spatchcock chicken and golden-brown fingerling potatoes.

"How long was I out?" she asked.

"Two days. You had a traumatic event. Malik came by and made sure you got some fluids, helped you with some stuff and put you back under."

She narrowed her eyes. "That's not the same chicken they were making during the interrogation, is it?"

Cordell laughed. "We ate that one. Figured you'd want your favorite before I give you some bad news."

Her stomach churned when he said that. Cordell had never been one for cushioning things, and she didn't exactly want him to start. Her appetite returned, a gift from the hot steam and browned skin of the chicken. The honey dill carrots didn't look that bad, either.

"Did you, uh, bring a fork?" she asked.

He sucked his teeth. "I forgot."

Boots snorted. "Room service is lousy here."

Cordell put his hands on his hips and grimaced. "I'm your captain, not your butler. Let's get this over with so you can get your own damned fork."

Boots put the plate aside, though she certainly wouldn't leave it untouched when they were done talking. "So what's the news?"

Cordell sat down on the chair by her bed, an oddly intimate gesture for him. He'd always been the type to stand, or sit behind the desk in his captain's quarters—making it clear there was distance between them. "We know how to break the curse on you."

She sat up straight, suddenly invigorated. "How sure are you?"

"While you were under, we ran some simulations, did some research, talked with a few experts over the Link."

"That's supposed to be my job, Captain."

"Had to be sure before we shared our plan. It's dangerous as hell."

Tired of waiting, Boots picked up a piece of chicken and popped it into her mouth, savoring the salty brine and yeast of the ale. "Whatever gets me a shot at Stetson, I'm in."

"So...we were thinking..." Cordell leaned forward, massaging his weathered hands. He chewed the inside of his lip and squinted, having trouble getting the words out. "Uh...that binary star system where we found the *Harrow* has a pretty decent magic suppression field. Basically all of our unshielded tech didn't work, like, you know...the sensor arrays."

For a moment, Boots stared at him, wondering why he would bring that up. Then, the pieces clicked into place, and she nearly slapped him.

"You're going to toss me out the airlock!"

Shaking his head, the captain said, "No, it's nothing so informal. We've got—"

"'Unshielded.' You specifically said that! You want me out there without a suit on!"

"Now, Boots, I think you're being a little bit unreasonable here. We've got the best doctor around and a legendary group of explorers. It's not like we're winging this."

She stood up, her plate clattering to the ground. "We wing everything! It's what we do! Oh, my god, you're going to get me killed!"

Malik peeked around the door frame, looking considerably haler than he had on Hammerhead. "Boots, may I come in?"

"Yes!" she said. "As a medical professional, please explain to my captain that space is bad for you."

"I told you to let me break the news, Captain." The doctor ran a hand through his hair and sat down on the bed beside her with a sigh. "You're technically correct, and as the ship's medical officer, I wouldn't recommend being outside without a suit. However, with planning, we can mitigate those factors. Every year, hundreds of people are involved in airlock accidents, and most of them live."

"Yeah," Boots said, "but not over Chaparral Two. Not with weird, antimagic binary stars! You're not even sure this will work! Do I get to be part of the planning, or just the frozen meat?"

"Are you an expert on decompression and arcane nullification?" asked Malik. "I am, and we have a battery of experts ready to assist you. Miss Brio and Miss Sokol are working on technology to help the twins cast over a distance. Mister Vandevere is running umbral and orbital simulations. I'll be taking care of your physical health."

"The plan is good," said Cordell. "The real question is: do you want to get Stetson Giles or not?"

She stared long and hard into her captain's eyes while her mind wrestled with Giles's location. She desperately wanted to just spit it out and skip the whole "naked in the vacuum of space" thing, but Cordell was right. She couldn't go after Giles. She couldn't send someone after him. No one said anything about trying to break her contract.

She'd put everything on the line for longer shots than this one.

"Okay," she breathed. "Okay. Yes. When do we do this?"

Red lights flashed in the corridors, and Aisha's voice echoed through the halls. "All crew to ready stations; we're coming out of the Flow in the Chaparral binary star system. Normal space in five minutes."

"About that..." Cordell began. "We were thinking in an hour."

The cargo bay airlock was cramped with four people inside: Malik, Alister, Jeannie, and lastly, Boots. Of course, they were all in spacesuits, and she was in a set of loose-fitting pajamas she'd brought with her from Hopper's Hope. If she was to be cast out into the great beyond, comfy pj's were preferable. Malik had fitted her with a plain fall restraint harness and anchored her to a tether point inside the closet-sized room.

For some reason, Jeannie insisted on standing next to Boots, which didn't hurt her feelings much. Alister could be a little creepy at times.

Nilah and Orna had stripped all the orichalcum out of the resuscitation bot in the med bay and fashioned a conductive wire, which they'd woven into the tether with a long, barbed tail on Boots's end. It wouldn't be useful to her if she started dying, anyway. Without a cardioid to respark, the bot would likely just watch her life ebb away.

Malik turned to her, his helmet lights blaring in her face, and she shielded her eyes. He took the barb and fished it up the back of her shirt before swabbing her neck with antiseptic.

"A quick stick," he said through his tinny speaker, then pressed the barb into her skin below the base of her skull. "This is going to let Jeannie cast her mark on you from the shelter of the airlock. If she fails, Alister will try. Then, we'll pull you back."

"I'll do better this time," said Alister. "Better odds."

"You won't need to," said Jeannie, flatly. "I've got you, Boots."

Boots tried to feel the wound, but Malik brushed her hand away and taped the wire down.

"A human can maintain consciousness for fifteen seconds in a vacuum," Malik said. "After that, you'll pass out and begin to asphyxiate. I'm going to cast my mark on you so you can retain some higher brain functions even through an unconscious mind. Think only of Stetson's location. You can go three to five minutes out there without any air before we're looking at permanent brain damage."

"I've seen the safety videos," said Boots, trying not to think of the vets she'd met with tremors and cognitive impairments from violent decompression.

"Good," Malik continued, "then you know to blow out as hard as you can before we open the airlock. Plug your ears when you decompress. It should help the air escape a little more slowly so we're not repairing hearing damage. I don't care if you've heard it before, I'll say it again: if you have any air in your lungs, it could cause your tissues to rupture and you'll perish from an air embolism. Am I clear?"

"Yeah, Doc."

"Explain to me what I just said."

She did, and he rewarded her with another swab and a jab in the neck from an automatic syringe. "Damn it, Doc!"

"That's Hemaflexin. Takes two minutes and improves the solubility of your blood gasses. We want to reduce the impact of the bends on your body."

"The shadow of the umbra basically ends fifteen meters out," said Jeannie. "We're going to push you as hard as we can when that door opens. Once we're certain you're in the solar rays, I'll cast my mark, which will be transmitted up the orichalcum line."

"Best be fast," said Boots.

The intercom chimed and Cordell said, "You have a moment if you want to say anything to the crew before we get underway."

Boots narrowed her eyes and thought about it.

"You guys are a bunch of assholes."

No one laughed.

"But..." she began, "I guess that's why I fit in so well. Don't let me die out there."

"That's it?" She could hear the grin in the captain's voice.

"Yeah. Now leave me alone. I need to reflect on my life or whatever."

"One minute thirty to mission start," said Armin. "Mission crew, check in."

"Spyglass, standing by," said Jeannie.

"Pensive, standing by," said Alister.

"Sleepy. Ready to execute," said Malik.

The mission clock ticked down, with Armin calling the intervals. When he reached the ten-second mark, Boots fixed her gaze on the airlock door like it was a rabid dog.

"Mission execute," said Cordell. "Kill the gravity, Missus Jan."

Her weight fell away. Boots plugged her ears.

"This will keep your conscious mind active during the minutes it takes to asphyxiate," said Malik, casting a glyph and touching her bare forehead through his spacesuit. "Breathe out, right now."

She blew out as hard as she could until her eyes bulged. Malik yanked the emergency override before mashing the release.

Then all sound vanished as the door opened.

The cold that greeted her was beyond anything she'd ever felt in her life—worse than the icy caverns of Wartenberg, worse than an open cockpit on Hammerhead. She wanted to scream, but drew in nothing to help her. She shook uncontrollably, and rough gloves gave her a hard shove into the great black beyond. The pajamas did nothing to shield her from the bone-deep frost creeping into her.

Close your eyes. Her eyelids stuck partway as the corneas froze, and she pushed her palms against them, trying to salvage what warmth she could and melt her tears long enough to get them shut. Dancing sparkles filled her periphery, a sure sign she was about to lose consciousness, maybe from pain, maybe from asphyxiation.

And then heat covered her over, filling her frostbitten skin with a painful itch. Except it got hotter—

And hotter.

She was like a coin—one side boiling, the other side frosty.

The tether snapped taut, jerking her palms away from her eyelids, and sunlight filtered in, bright and bloodred. She no longer had the strength to protect her face. Everything hurt. Before her, hell; behind her, oblivion.

But the queer dissolution of thought that followed unconsciousness never came, and so she filled her mind with the one thing that could possibly give her comfort:

An impossible gala. A never-ending dance.

Stetson Giles and the coordinates to the Masquerade.

Chapter Fifteen

Solo

Boots convulsed in the medical bay gurney.

"I need those numbers, Nilah!" Malik shouted.

Nilah had never heard him shout before. Now that she'd thought about it, she'd never seen him in a management role at all.

She and Orna had been stationed in the med bay to help operate the equipment they'd gutted by stripping out all the orichalcum. The various machines couldn't use the rare metal probes, so Malik had to call out Boots's vitals, and the mechanists would psychically feed the data back into the systems. Nilah closed her eyes and sifted through the system architecture, looking for a tiny strip of code in a sea of variables.

"Numbers!" Malik repeated.

"Proteins, twenty-eight percent! Synthesis drivers holding steady," Nilah replied.

He glanced to Orna before threading a needle into a vein on Boots's arm. "How's the dermax coming?"

"It's cooking," said Orna. "Fifteen more seconds."

Nilah fished out the sedative Malik had requested and passed it over, then Orna gave him the skin regeneration spray. The poor woman's body was a bright pink color, as though she'd been attacked with sandpaper, and drool bubbled up around the bite guard Malik had slipped into her mouth.

"Be ready with that sedative," said Malik. "This should rebuild a lot of the epidermis, along with some pain nerves. The shock could prove too much."

Nilah gaped. "Uh, where do you want me to inject her?"

"Any fatty areas," said the doctor. "The radiation and frost have sterilized most of her surface, and the dermax ought to do the rest."

He clicked the nozzle trigger on the pressurized bottle of dermax, spraying Boots down. Her pink skin grew veiny and black as nanites burrowed into her flesh. The room stank of sulfur and eidolon powder, like burning rubber on a racetrack.

Boots began to choke, and her eyes rolled back in her head.

"Sedative now," said Malik, guiding Nilah's injector down to the soft flesh of Boots's thigh.

She clicked down the trigger, and the older woman fell still. The powdery dermax faded from black to gray ash, then flaked away like snow onto the table. The nanites continued crawling over Boots's flesh, knitting her cells back together to build a protective layer.

Once the alarms subsided and Boots appeared stable, Malik turned to the pair and said, "I think we've got everything under control. If you can get those monitors working, that's most of what I'll need. Can you get the orichalcum back out of Boots's tether?"

"We've got it, Doc," said Orna, and the pair of women silently set about repairing the circuits on the vital monitors with the metals they'd stolen.

Malik was fast asleep when they finally got the last component online, and the night cycle had worn thin. Aisha had come to give Malik some food, and she rested in the corner bed with her head on his shoulder, a thick blanket covering the pair of them.

Jealousy tugged at Nilah's heart as she looked on them. Orna's short hair had matted to her head, and Nilah hardly felt fresh after crawling behind the drug compounding console to do repairs, but she wanted what Malik and Aisha had. Every cold moment with Orna was a needle of ice in her chest, and she desperately wanted to talk things out.

"I'm going to bed," Orna said, rising and walking out of the med bay with little notice.

"I'll come with you," Nilah said, but Orna waved her off.

"It's fine. Why don't you get some breakfast?"

Instead, she followed her girlfriend back to their quarters and shut the door behind them.

"Okay. What is your problem?" Nilah asked, and Orna just looked at her with a flat expression, pausing midway through pulling off her sweaty top.

That could mean anything. Nilah had seen that look from Orna when she didn't care at all, when she cared deeply and was pretending not to, and when she was about to break into her signature killing grin.

When Orna didn't speak, Nilah repeated herself, adding, "You've been acting weird since Pinnacle. You've been...well... bloody cold, and you're pissing me off!"

"Is that how you want to start this?"

Nilah narrowed her eyes. "Listen, darling, we've got to start somewhere, and it might as well be with your bloody attitude."

Orna nodded, pulling her top back on and slicking back her hair. "All right, then. You know what's so annoying about you? You're just assuming that I'm the problem!"

"You *are* the problem! We're supposed to be in love, and you're giving me the cold shoulder every five minutes!"

"And why do you think that is, *Nilah*?" Orna put a nasty inflection on her name that she'd never heard before. No one talked to her like that. "You figure I just woke up one morning and thought, 'I'm going to piss off my girlfriend today'? No! You've been treating me like crap, and I'm tired of it!"

"Before this mission, I have wined and dined you across the blighted galaxy. Don't you—"

"You did rich people stuff, and that cost you basically nothing. Don't act like fancy gifts matter."

Nilah spread her arms wide in a "fight me" pose. "Yeah? So gifts are only worth something if they severely cost me? Is that how you measure love? In suffering?"

Orna rubbed her brow. "That's not what I'm getting at."

"That's what it sounds like you're saying!"

"Okay," said Orna, crossing her arms tightly. "We're not doing this right now. I'm tired, you're tired—"

Nilah's eyes should've caught fire from the glare she shot Orna. "I don't give a damn about how tired you are. You may not keep running away from me, Orna Sokol."

"You think you can just walk all over me, huh? I'm not one of your fans, and I'm certainly not Lana, bowing and scraping to keep you happy. I can do whatever the hell I want, Nilah Brio, and right now, I'm going to take my crap and sack out in the cargo bay! Don't think you can tell me what to do any more than you can go prancing off on some suicide mission in *my robot*!"

Nilah's chest puffed out. "Is that what this is about? Your stupid robot? We needed him to rescue—"

" 'Stupid'? How dare you? He's a replacement for the one you killed!" With that, Orna yanked the blankets free of their bed and spun on her heel, dragging them into the hall with her.

Nilah's cheeks burned like she'd been slapped. Standing in the middle of the bedroom, she couldn't quite believe what'd just happened.

Orna couldn't have been that mad about her little jaunt inside of Charger, could she? It hadn't been Nilah's fault; it was simply an operational parameter.

Simultaneously dazed and furious, Nilah wandered into the hallway to watch Orna leave. Instead, she found Armin standing around with a pair of teacups.

"What?" she asked, annoyed with herself for blinking back tears.

"I saw Orna dragging a comforter through here, so I guess it happened."

"What happened?"

"You two had a fight," he said. "The data points line up."

She puffed out her chest. "Yeah? Well then a bloke like you ought to know not to talk to a lady after—"

"I made Taitutian Royal Pearl tea," he interrupted. "It's your favorite. My simulations indicated I should've been worried, and I was correct."

She scowled. "And what makes you think you know my favorite tea?"

"Oh, let's not be silly, Miss Brio," he said, his voice almost singsong. "There's more information about you on the Link than any other member of the crew, and that's saying something. Of course I know it."

She sneered. "Well good job, mate."

"That's first mate to you," he said, but his voice lacked the characteristic severity that accompanied reminders of his title. "Let's chat."

Armin's quarters were messy, but they were a safer place to meet than Nilah's, with the possibility of Orna bursting back in at any moment. He'd never bothered to clean up his cables, which were routed this way and that in long tangles across his floor. Twice, she'd nearly tripped over the arrangement on the way to her seat at his meager dining area. He settled in across from her in his datamancer's throne—the one she'd helped him construct during the end of the *Harrow* mission.

"You're remarkably easy to decipher," he said.

Nilah took a sip of her warm drink. It wasn't well brewed, but Royal Pearl wasn't a mixture for novices. "I take it from your offering that you're trying to make me feel better."

"Not at all," said Armin. "I'm merely attempting to improve my own emotional intelligence, and you make an ideal test case."

"Oh," she grumbled, sitting back in her chair and taking another greedy swig.

"Or," he began, resting the cup on the arm of his chair, "I said I was practicing emotional intelligence so you'd mentally categorize this conversation as low impact, and be more willing to stick around."

"You're such a filthy cheat, Armin. You should've taken up cards."

"You know casinos won't allow my kind inside," he said. "Not unless I work there."

"At least we're happy to put up with you."

"You pushed Orna too hard on your last mission, and now you're paying the price."

The old Nilah, the one who stood on podiums, might've thrown her mug at him for such brazen familiarity, but the new Nilah was simply shocked at the first mate's utterance. Fresh anger boiled inside her, and if he was going to abandon his officer's rank to comment on her relationship, she'd show him the minefield he'd entered.

"So this is my fault?" she shot back, all trace of playfulness gone from her voice.

"Nilah," he said, "there's a difference between 'your doing' and 'your fault.' The problems in your interactions can rarely ever be chalked up to a single party." He stood from his throne and went to lean on the edge of his workbench. "I'm concerned that if you two don't reach some kind of parity, you could lose a good thing."

"Do you have a girlfriend?"

He blinked at her with a strange look, like he was trying to work out a puzzle. "I wouldn't suffer a woman my company."

"Boyfriend?"

"Not interested." He raised a hand. "And before you keep going, I don't care for sex or romance at all. Never have."

Nilah shrugged. "Then why would you have any advice about Orna?"

"Because we're all just data points, and from those, I can create information, and from that, I create insights. You did something that Orna can't abide, and I'm here to tell you what that is. Think of it as keeping our engines lubricated."

Arching an eyebrow, she said, "You don't lubricate arcdrive engines. They don't have moving—"

"Try to bear with me," he interrupted. "On a normal military vessel, your relationship—as well as Malik and Aisha's—would be forbidden, and for good reason. You'd be vulnerable to nasty lapses in judgment that could cause people to get hurt or killed. You might favor one another over the other members of the crew, handing out preferential treatment such as promotions or even rescues."

His face hardened, and she spied some of his famed shrewdness coming through. "And I promise, if that was the case, I'd have harangued the captain until one of you was dismissed."

Nilah leaned back in her chair and set her saucer to one side. "But it's not."

"Correct. Military doctrine is largely based upon two cognitive biases: confirmation and survivorship. However, the data don't lie: the couples on our ship are more productive and brave than we could've predicted, and the *Capricious* has survived far more encounters than he ought to have."

Nilah swallowed a bitter look. "So...what? I should keep shagging Miss Sokol for the good of the ship?"

The first mate stood, tapped his console, and summoned a couple of trend lines into effect around their heads. "I hadn't wanted to put it so succinctly, but I'm glad you grasp my thoughts."

"You said that I'd done something to her."

He raised a finger. "And I could tell you what that is, but you're statistically more likely to accept my conclusion if you arrive at it yourself. So we need to start with your greatest fear."

"Sirathica?" she snorted. "Because those bat things on Blix were—"

"Impotence," he countered, tracing his glyph and slapping his palm to his personal aggregator crystal ball. Thousands of luminous particles filled the air, and when Nilah looked closer, she could see her own head and torso, clad in a racing fire suit. They were frames from her tons of trackside interviews.

"These," he began, and most of the heads grouped into a tight, glowing cluster, "are the times you said you worried about technical difficulties before a race."

Frowning, she made a quick survey of the remaining heads—not a lot. "Of course. Engine failures are ridiculously common, so we're all afraid of that."

"Compared to the remainder of the league in the last season, you mentioned car failure twenty-six percent more than the average racer. You were most afraid that circumstances beyond your control would cause you to lose sight of the car in front of you."

"Did you know I fired my last sports psychiatrist?" she asked, her voice flat with annoyance.

"I wouldn't doubt it. They probably suggested that your mind was currently beyond your control. That plays right into your worst fear." He raised a hand to stop her speaking. "Those fears have enabled you to do incredible things. You broke out of your cell and took over our ship. You fought off a horde of springflies. You volunteered to remain on our mission to destroy the Gods of the *Harrow*, a charter deadly beyond measure. So fear is nothing to be afraid of, so to speak."

She stood, peering through the interviews, trying to conjure up the memories of each one, but without context, it was hard to remember anything she'd said. "If you're about to tell me I'm motivated by fear, and Orna is motivated by love—or any other flavor of the fear-love dichotomy—I'm about to tell you to stuff it."

Armin waved away the face-shaped snowflakes, and they disappeared into nothingness. He picked up his tea and took a sip, pulling a face. "I didn't do a very good job on this. Already bitter."

Nodding at her own cup, she said, "It takes a lot of ceremonial training. It's not for foreigners."

"Orna has fought so hard to have a family of any stripe. Security and safety are—"

"Safety!" Nilah repeated incredulously.

"Yes. That's important to her."

"We reused a jump dump! She dropped into the Pinnacle in a crash pod!"

"Oh, don't get me wrong," said Armin. "Her view of what constitutes safety is light-years away from what anyone else would find acceptable."

He twisted his hands over the crystal ball and the image of a grubby adolescent materialized, clothes tattered, face twisted in anger. Nilah realized with a pang of sadness that the kid stood hand in hand with Ranger.

This early on in its life, Ranger's origins were easy to spot. It still bore the battered paint of an emergency rescue armor, designed to extricate humans from extreme conditions. Those kinds of suits weren't without some intelligence—if they sensed a threat to someone's life, they'd charge in there and jam that person into the body cavity, whether they wanted to come along or not.

It was so easy to imagine what'd happened in the Arcan war-zone: Ranger rescued Orna, and she hacked it so she could stay alive.

"Orna had to endure more than most of us could bear," said Armin. "She doesn't talk about her origins, but it's easy for a data-mancer to connect the dots. She lost a sibling, both parents, and last year, the most faithful friend she ever had."

Nilah swallowed. Despite the fury her girlfriend had engen-dered, that smoldering anger couldn't survive this picture of young Orna. Nilah wanted to reach out and hold the projection, kiss her forehead, tell her that everything was going to work out.

Armin interrupted her thoughts. "So now you need to under-stand what you did. Several times, you've . . . disagreed about the best ways to pursue a mission. In the Pinnacle, she wanted to cut and run, and you insisted on rescuing Sharp."

She scoffed. "And on the *Harrow*, she wanted me to go on without her. If I'd listened to her, we'd both be dead."

Nodding, Armin said, "I know. We're talking about what you did, not what you did wrong. Despite not having a fixed chain of command, our unit cohesion remains excellent because of our exceptional crew. I wouldn't change it for the largest, purest eido-lon crystal out there. You need to understand, however, that Orna worries that she'll lose you, and with good reason. She's lost every-thing else."

Nilah rolled that thought over in her mind as she stood and grabbed a cube of soda out of Armin's food locker. She got one for him, too, and placed them both into cups, where they melted. She handed his over with a smile. "Sorry about the tea, chum."

Armin thanked her and put the cup aside. "You like to go it alone, striking out whenever you want, and that's hard for her. She thinks she's going to watch you die . . . or leave. She's distanc-ing herself from you, getting ready for the blow."

Looking Nilah dead in the eyes, he added, "Don't let her. Show her how much you love her and get this worked out. For the good of this ship."

Orna never much spoke about the early days on the ship, no matter how much Nilah had pressed her. Armin's image of the young woman distorted and disappeared, leaving only empty space where there was once something beautiful.

Boots awoke with the taste of copper in her mouth, and the accent lights of the med bay faded up. She smacked her lips and licked them, her tongue catching on dry skin. A pleasant chime signaled her consciousness, and Malik sat up in a nearby bed, yawning.

"How are you feeling?" he asked, tracing his purple glyph and placing his hand to her shoulder.

"Bleh," she replied, but the drowsiness drained from her system, replaced with an acute sense of her own body—not too shabby, considering she'd done a space walk in her pajamas.

He charged his spell again and touched his own chest, his eyes lighting up. "The Hemaflexin will do that."

Boots frowned. "Your glyph can wake people up?"

"Don't tell anyone," said Malik, winking. "I'll have half the crew down here any time they have a hangover." He passed her a pile of her clothes and added, "You'll want to get dressed."

Boots nodded, testing her unsteady feet on the floor. They seemed to function just fine, so she stood and pulled on her clothes over her skivvies. After a moment, Malik crossed to the intercom and called the captain to inform him she was awake.

"Good. Have her report to the bridge," was the captain's only reply.

Taking his finger off the transmit button, Malik said, "Don't let him push you too hard. Doctor's orders."

Boots finished fastening the clips on her shirt and smiled. "Oh, then I've got about twenty years of complaints to file."

Malik chortled, and she took her leave. The corridors of the ship were deserted, and the quarters Boots passed were buttoned up tight. Whatever was going on, the crew were already at ready stations.

She made her way to the bridge and found Cordell, Armin, Aisha, and the twins at the orienteering console once occupied by Didier, patiently watching the projection in the center of the room.

"Glad you decided to join us!" said Cordell. "Sleep okay, or did you want another nap?"

Boots gave him a lackadaisical salute. "You ever stepped out an airlock, sir?"

Running his fingers over his curly hair, Cordell said, "Not after watching that, I won't. I felt awful just looking at you."

"Just tell me you got the intel, Captain."

His eyes remained affixed to hers for a good long while, face stern, brow furrowed. She could see in his posture that they'd failed, and she'd jumped into space for nothing.

Then he cracked a smile.

Then burst out laughing.

"I'm just jerking you, Bootsie! We've got him!"

Armin nodded with a jovial grin that fit him like a cheap mask, then keyed on the projector, and the image of a space station scrambled into focus along with the word "Congratulations!" The twins clapped. Aisha raised her fist.

The barrister's mark uncoiled within her, and the melting of that vast, unseen burden nearly toppled her over. Warmth suffused her body, like relaxing a muscle she hadn't known was tense.

She'd told others what she knew, so her contract was void. She was free.

"I keyed in the coordinates from your memory, but what are we looking at?" said Armin, gesturing to the large, if plain, space station depicted on the projector. "This place is totally unregistered."

"That's the Masquerade," said Boots. "The ultimate neutral

ground. No fights. All organizations welcome. Identities are protected. That's why the gods can't just take the chalice from Stetson."

"Who runs it?" asked Armin.

"It's independent," said Boots. "Funded by a trust. They make a point of not working for anyone at all, and it's one of the best-kept secrets in the galaxy."

"Well, that's neat." Cordell hooked his thumbs into his pockets and sauntered over to her. "I've got to admit, Bootsie, this is going to make a sweet story when we finally kill old Henrick Witts."

Armin raised a finger. "And I can finally say we tossed you out of an airlock."

Boots chuckled. "Good god, sir. Now that you've accomplished that dream, what are you going to do with yourself?"

"Maybe I can focus on throwing the gods out of airlocks," he said, turning to face Jeannie. "Any word from the *Prism*?"

"Not yet, sir," she replied. "We'll keep listening."

"The *Prism*?" asked Boots.

Cordell nodded to the blue sphere of Chaparral, broken by cracks of volcanic activity. "This is an uninhabited system. No Gate Cartel presence, which means no jump gates, so we're doing the next best thing."

"We hired a Flow freighter," said Armin.

That couldn't be right. Those ships had a dozen personnel and were carefully controlled by galactic logistics companies. Someone like Cordell couldn't simply reroute one off its shipping lane.

"That sounds...expensive?" Boots ventured.

"It was," said Cordell. "I don't have the contacts to make something like that happen. Lucky for us, we know an ex-Fixer we can trust with our lives. Checo DosSantos may be a plastic surgeon now, but Fixers can get anything."

"Miss Brio might disagree—" But a bright flash lit up the bridge and sucked away the rest of Boots's sentence.

"Contact!" called Aisha.

As the shock wore off, Boots spied a massive cargo vessel at least half the size of the *Harrow* looming in their view. It had a used, industrial look, like it'd scraped across half the ports in the galaxy, and scarred paint down one side read *Prism*. With a vessel of that size, they could move half a city from world to world.

"Looks like our boy," said Armin.

Boots frowned. "Sir, uh... how... did you get a ship this size to come to us?"

"When she made disguises for everyone, Doctor DosSantos said she owed Nilah," said Armin, "so she handled all the procurement and secrecy."

That made sense, but it still didn't explain how they'd moved a ship like the *Prism*. It wasn't like he could be rerouted on a simple favor. "What about fuel, personnel, all that stuff?"

Cordell sniffed and looked away. "Remember all of those argent chits you recovered on Mercandatta?"

"You mean the only cash we've made on this haul?"

"We're rich, Boots!" said Cordell. "We don't need more money!"

"We won't be if you keep throwing away all our loot!"

"Look..." said Cordell. "We expensed the *Prism* against everyone's shares, so there isn't much left."

So even though they'd robbed one of the best-protected vaults around, probably getting onto a few most-wanted lists, they had no argents for it. "How much have we got?"

With a grimace, Cordell said, "We could probably pay your bar tab for one week."

"The *Prism* is hailing us, sir," said Aisha.

"Patch them through."

A squat, imposing fellow with a bushy beard and brow lines like layers of sedimentary rock filled their projection, standing before Cordell.

"Captain Lamarr. This is Checo DosSantos."

Not the lithe paragon of beauty they'd seen on Harvest, then. Boots liked their style—a gorgeous creature when they wanted to sell new disguises, a cantankerous old coot when they wanted to captain a jump freighter. Judging from Aisha's reaction, she was similarly impressed.

"Glad to see you. Mind if we come aboard?" he asked. "We've got places to be."

Checo turned off image and called to someone, "Marshall, let's make this pickup and get paid, shall we?"

As they approached, the *Prism* looked like nothing more than a rough cobbling of container modules and linkages, but he unfolded into a magnificent docking bay like an ancient paper puzzle. The *Capricious* settled onto one of the hull plates as directed by approach, and the *Prism* reformed, enveloping them.

Cordell tapped his intercom. "All crew, we have successfully docked with our hosts, so please be on your best behavior."

And after a moment's thought, he added, "That said, I expect everyone to be strapped at all times."

Chapter Sixteen

Revenant

The crew of the *Prism* were anything but welcoming as Boots and the others entered his halls. Staffers scurried like cockroaches away from Cordell's entourage, as though they, themselves, were the fugitives.

Though given what Boots knew of long-haul freighters, that couldn't have been too far from the truth.

The jump freight trade was full of people who'd skipped out on the bill life charged them—from parents who didn't feel like raising their kids, to outright murderers who found themselves more comfortable traveling through a half-dozen galactic jurisdictions. They weren't a particularly savory lot, only slightly better than the average eidolon miner. She'd rather not have dealt with them at all, but without a jump drive on board the *Capricious*, they needed a pickup.

Aisha made the mistake of staring too long at one of the cargo shipments, and a pair of *Prism* personnel showed up to glower and throw a tarp over it.

After a time, Cordell and the other crew members of the *Capricious* found their way to the vessel's central gathering area, which stank of dreamsmoke and old potions. There'd been more than a few debauched parties on board, and Boots wondered how they maintained a clearance to dock the damned thing.

Checo waited for them in the captain's seat, their eyes impassively counting the crew. "So, where would you like us to drop you?"

"The Masquerade, uh, Station," said Cordell, and for the first time, Boots saw a look of surprise on Checo's face. "Is it Masquerade Station, or just…"

"I'm sorry?" was Checo's response.

"Take us to the Masquerade," Cordell repeated.

Checo spread their arms. "I can get you anywhere you want to go, but I'd be remiss if I didn't warn my customers when they were making a big mistake. The Masquerade is the single biggest hub of underworld activity in the galaxy, disguised as a provider of… esoteric entertainments. It's the playground of the ultra-elite: the banking families, Gate Cartel officials, and most likely, some of the Gods of the *Harrow*."

"So you've heard of it," said Cordell.

"I have," said Checo, "but I'm not sure you fully comprehend your request."

"We're serious," said Boots.

"To get onto the Masquerade, you need two things: a ship with a docking key… and a mask for those going aboard," said Checo. "Neither of which can be bought. There are only five thousand of each, and their owners guard them fiercely. And before you suggest kicking in the door, their defense grid is perfect. You'd have an easier time flying into a black hole."

"I know," said Boots.

Checo cocked an eyebrow. "Do you?"

"When we were searching for the Chalice of Hana," Boots began, "a team of angel investors reached out to Stetson—offered to set up an office for us where major treaties and contracts could be negotiated without interference. We were offered two masks and a docking key if we found the chalice."

"So who were these guys?" asked Cordell. "If they've got two masks, they might have more."

"Never met them," said Boots. "Whenever I asked, Stetson would always say the details would come after we got the chalice."

"Maybe we could pretend to be Masquerade staff," said Aisha, "then sneak aboard and do what we need to do."

"That'll be remarkably easy," said Checo with a sarcastic groan. "All I need to do is plant neural spikes in your heads and sell you at auction. They do brain scans on all the help, you see. Either you're wearing a mask or you're brain-dead."

Cordell gave them a stunned look. "Oh, come on. You can't expect me to believe that everyone on that station—"

"Oh, yes," Checo said, pouring themself a drink before offering the bottle to the others.

"So you won't sell us entry into the station," Boots began.

" 'Won't' is such a crude word. I would if you could afford it. But unless you've got another *Harrow* to salvage in your back pocket, I don't think you'll have the scratch to spare for the rest of your little god hunt. I'd have to get you a key and masks, and as you might've guessed, I have neither."

Boots smiled. "But I bet you would sell us the name of a ripe target who visits the Masquerade on a regular basis. Someone really scummy, someone who absolutely deserves to be shaken down, or worse."

Checo craned their neck, appraising Boots's suggestion. "Rather bold of you, considering your target would almost certainly be a former client of mine."

"We didn't get this far being timid," said Boots.

"That's right," said Cordell. "I'm sure everyone would be willing to kick in a few argents to get a target dossier from you. Am I right?"

"You're a unique lot," said Checo, narrowing their eyes.

"No," said Nilah with a wry grin. "We're just bloody rich and angry as hell."

"Hear, hear," added Boots, taking the bottle from the table and pouring herself a glass. "I'm in for a deal."

"As are we," said Aisha, whose husband nodded his assent.

"And me," said Armin.

"There's always more money in the galaxy," said Orna.

Then all eyes fell upon the Ferriers, and Jeannie said, "Don't look at us. We didn't get rich off the first salvage."

"Yeah, I think I've got some pocket lint you can have, sir," said Alister.

Checo inclined their head. "I think we can work something out."

Cordell poured his own glass and clinked it to Boots's before taking a sip. "So that'll be one target, please. And how much extra for you to make me look like the poor sap you're selling us?"

"Oh, I doubt you'll be wanting that," said Checo with a poisonous smile. "You see, this fellow made his fortune in the Clarkesfall fighting pits."

Without thinking, Boots looked back at Orna. She cursed herself, knowing that every other member of the crew would do the same.

"Who is it?" asked Orna, her beastly voice straining against her marginally more civilized exterior.

"Only the leader of the whole racket," said Checo. "William Scarett."

Charger lowered its head. At long last, the quartermaster spoke. " 'Bill Scar.' "

"Captain, can we talk?" asked Boots, jogging up to Cordell in the spacious docking bay of the *Prism*.

Cordell had busied himself about the underbelly of the ship, making sure everything was perfect with the refueling lines. He was fretting, and it put Boots on edge.

"You know how much I love to talk," he said curtly, as he circled one of the landing pylons and checked the actuators.

She crossed her arms. "Was that supposed to be a joke?"

"Just say what's on your mind, Boots. We've got a lot of work to do before we come out of the Flow."

"I'm a little bit concerned for our dear friend Orna," said Boots. "You might've noticed she isn't herself."

He reached up and tested one of the cable couplings, making certain it would hold up to stress. "Why? Because we're about to hunt one of the many men who made her murder for sport and profit? Goodness me, I don't know how that could possibly be bothering her."

"Yeah, that's about the size of it."

"Okay, well...noted."

Boots rubbed the bridge of her nose. "I can't believe I'm asking this, but...I want to strongly recommend that you bench her."

Cordell stopped, his hand dropping to his side, and stared at Boots. "Excuse me?"

"Captain, come on," she pleaded. She'd been dreading this conversation, but as far as she could tell, no one else would have the guts to bring it up. "We all paid for that intel, and that means... you know...when she rips out Bill's spinal column before he gives us the authorization codes, we wasted all of our money."

He shook his head, jamming his hands into his pockets. "Well, now. That's some real insight. Have you ever considered becoming an officer, Bootsie?"

"Hell no, sir. I work for a living," she shot back, rehashing the old joke.

He sauntered closer to her, his eyes wrinkled with a lack of sleep. He hadn't been seeking Malik's help, and it showed. "Well, I'm going to let you in on a little secret: when you have a crew like mine, you're only marginally the captain. See, it's probably a bit like driving a race car, from what I've heard Miss Brio say."

"How do you figure?"

" 'Controlled explosions,' she once called it, like trying to guide a comet. You get to do some steering, but mostly, you're along for the ride. You make the right decisions in the blink of an eye, but there's no stopping it."

"Captain, if you bring Orna in there with us, you may be jeopardizing the lives of the entire crew. You know what happens when someone is a loose cannon."

He drew in a sharp breath. "If I don't, she will lose her goddamned mind, and who could blame her? And furthermore, who are you to talk about obeying orders? I seem to recall your insubordination when we rumbled with some of Mother's battlegroup. Or Nilah's when she refused to go on without Orna on the surface of the *Harrow*. Malik has made snap decisions against mine. So has Aisha, and god only knows what goes through the heads of those twins. As far as I can tell, the only person on this crew who listens to a word I say is my first mate. And you know why I tolerate it?"

He'd rekindled the old fires in his eyes, and Boots recoiled. During the Famine War, she'd once seen him shield smash an ensign across the cargo bay for refusing to shoot at the enemy. The poor kid took a pair of broken ribs and a fractured tibia, but the rest of his squad opened fire just fine, and they achieved their objective.

Starship captains weren't dashing heroes, they were calculating creatures of extraordinary violence and coercion—and sometimes Boots forgot that.

"Because every time y'all disobeyed my orders, you've been right." He jabbed a finger into her sternum. "But if you ever cross me and you're wrong..."

Boots's breath caught.

"You better hope your stupidity kills you." He fetched a cigarette out of his case and lit up before exhaling across her face. "Same goes for everyone, including Orna."

And just like that, his malice melted away. Sometimes, she lamented that Cordell's military had been disbanded, because he would've made a fine admiral one day. He certainly had the spine to win wars by any means necessary. His rigid stance went casual, and he stepped back a few paces to give her some space.

"Now you'd better stop this bullshit where you insult Orna behind her back, and treat her like the family she is, you feel me? We gave you more chances than you deserved."

Boots looked down at the scored deck plates of the *Prism* and sighed.

"Aye, Captain."

She made her way up the ramp and into the belly of the *Capricious*, her chest tight from the reprimand she'd been given. She hadn't meant to piss the captain off, but he'd needed to hear what she had to say.

Even if he wouldn't listen to her.

Even if he wouldn't act on it.

Once she was inside, Boots made straight for the mess hall. In light of their largess, the liquor cabinet was always fully stocked—something that had been sorely lacking during the closing days of the Famine War. They hadn't carried much booze during the *Harrow* conspiracy, either. It just hadn't been in the budget.

Boots dug through the cabinet until she found her Flemmlian Ten, then pushed it aside. She wasn't feeling particularly classy, just catty, and she wanted the kind of drink someone could make a mistake with. She found a decanter of heavy rum and unscrewed the top. It carried the bitter stink of yeast with the chemical chaser of a high proof—at least one fifty. She straightened up with the bottle halfway to her lips and noticed Jeannie sitting at one of the corner tables.

Boots froze.

"Mister Vandevere will kill you for drinking out of the bottle without a glass," said Jeannie.

"He ain't here," said Boots with a conspiratorial wink. "You going to stop me?"

The twin blinked her bleary eyes and shook her head.

"It looks like you could use a glass of your own," said Boots, fetching up two tumblers and taking her haul to the table. "Didn't know you went anywhere without that brother of yours."

"Yes, well…" She trailed off, as though that was supposed to satisfy Boots's curiosity. When Boots didn't let her off the hook or change the subject, Jeannie clarified, "He's asleep."

Pouring them both glasses, Boots said, "I see. And you're not asleep because…"

"This is the time when I get to do whatever I want." Jeannie raised the clear liquid to her nose and gave it a sniff, then a grimace.

Boots wrinkled her nose. "Such as drink things that totally disgust you?"

"I've been through worse," said Jeannie, and she tipped the tumbler's contents into her mouth, swallowing the fluid with unbroken eye contact to Boots.

"Seems exhausting."

"What?"

Boots refilled the other woman's glass. "Always guarding your brother. Can't be easy."

Jeannie's gaze drifted downward to the sloshing rum. "Maybe. But I owe it to him."

"To walk around at his heel all the time? I've seen you jump in to fix things every time he shoots his mouth off."

Her fingers wrapped around the cup, and she downed another

two ounces of booze in a single swallow. "I know he...seems normal."

Boots chuckled as she took her own first sip, then nearly choked on the gasoline taste of the drink. This Ferrier girl had a steel stomach.

"You all right?" asked Jeannie, reaching over to slap Boots's back.

"'Normal,'" Boots repeated, laughing, but stopped when she saw Jeannie's serious expression. "That's not the word I would've used."

"You've seen him get violent. Seen him cry. There's more. He gets confused easily. Forgets where he is. Sometimes he'll get so scared, and he needs a familiar face. You..." Jeannie froze mid-sentence. "You remember how you said I could come to you if I ever wanted to talk?"

Boots scooted around the table to sit by Jeannie's side. "Hey, of course, kid."

"What am I supposed to do if he'll never be happy?"

"You have to live your own life at some point."

"I'm just tired," she said, casting her eyes toward the ceiling. "I'm tired of finding him up wandering around in the middle of the night. Tired of the way he huddles in close every time he hears a footstep in the hallway, because he thinks someone is coming to beat him. I don't want to hear him cry anymore or see that look of confusion every time he forgets something he's supposed to know. He can tell there's something wrong with him."

Boots took another swig and rubbed Jeannie's back. "I've never seen him do that stuff."

Jeannie's eyes met hers, glazed and red. "That's because I'm always here to help him. It's a full-time job, and I'm...I'm not very good at it. And it's—it's so thankless because he doesn't understand how much I do for him. And...sometimes I hate him for it."

"Maybe you should ease off. Let him stumble a bit so he knows how much he needs you."

"I can't do that." Jeannie swallowed hard and refilled her glass again. Judging from her small frame, she'd be well on her way to intoxication. She opened her mouth to speak, but words failed her. She downed her rum and exhaled, then said, "It's my fault he's like this."

It was like the temperature around Boots dropped ten degrees. "What do you mean?"

Jeannie shoved her glass away, where it skidded precariously close to the far edge of the table. "Sometimes, I think fate asks us for too much. A moment comes when you need to shine, when you need to be better than you've ever been—but you're not shiny, you're dull. I just wanted to help him—help him forget. He asked me to help, showed me how, but... he's so much more powerful than me."

Boots pulled her close and squeezed her shoulder. "It's okay to tell me. What happened to Alister?"

"This is my fault," she whispered. "He's never going to be okay."

"Listen, kid—"

Jeannie shot upright, dabbing her eyes onto her sleeves, voice breaking. "Thanks for the talk."

Then she marched off in the direction of her quarters, leaving Boots alone with the half-empty bottle. Boots considered chasing after, trying to stick her nose in where it probably didn't belong. But maybe that's why Jeannie talked to her at all: because she didn't force the issue.

Thoughts roiling like storm clouds, Boots reached over and took Jeannie's tumbler. She filled both glasses, then proceeded to nurse them for the next hour.

She understood what it was like to have a duty to something with a grim future.

After a sizable transfer of argents to Checo DosSantos, the *Prism* was rerouted to the backwater world of Prothero, ostensibly to deliver a shipment of air purifiers to the wealthy inhabitants there.

The *Prism* came out of the Flow, reported engine trouble, settled down in a forested canyon below the scanners, and dropped off the marauder hidden in its cavernous interior.

Nilah stood on the bridge of the *Capricious* and watched the jump freighter rise away, bound for wherever the next smuggling job might take them. When the coast was clear, the comparatively tiny marauder rose into the air and took off. Twilight sun turned the forest below into orange spikes on a blanket of green. Here and there, idyllic cottages along a sunset river peeked out through the trees, their windows warm and inviting.

While it was no Taitu, Prothero had more than its fair share of civilization. According to Armin, the planet was 90 percent immigrant workers with only a tiny slice of native citizenry. Many of those citizens, however, commanded vast sums of argents that stunted Nilah's racing largess by a considerable margin.

The first mate manipulated the bridge projections to show the forbidden airspaces of the wealthy landowners below. Prothero's picturesque green hills turned red with scanner patterns. These people liked their privacy, that much was certain.

Nilah watched the threat analysis, noting the kinds of anti-air measures the Protherans possessed with some interest. Since hooking up with the *Capricious*, she'd gained a smattering of military knowledge, and she recognized a few of the autoturrets on the ground.

The wealthy of this world were equipped to repel a few goons in a light craft, not a marauder. She prayed Bill Scar would be no different.

"Distance to Scarett residence, forty klicks," said Armin. "We'll be in his airspace soon. Scanners indicate standard defenses."

"All right," said Cordell. "Looks like we won't be worrying about network attacks. Miss Brio, head to the cargo bay and get ready to drop."

Boots turned to her from the imaging station and nodded. "Hey, kid! Easier than jumping to the *Harrow*, right?"

Nilah smiled as she left, then rushed down the stairwell, leaping between floors in the combat gravity. When she reached the cargo bay, she found Orna prepping Charger's fusion blade. The bot's vents rumbled with pleasure as it tested the blinding sword before retracting it. The quartermaster, clad in a combat flight suit, spared Nilah a glance as she entered, then gestured to the nearby lockers where her own flight suit awaited her.

There hadn't been an opportunity on the voyage to explain to Orna just how she felt, to reassure her that she'd... what? That Nilah would always be around? That had never been the promise of their relationship; it'd just been a good time that turned into something more lasting.

Nilah tugged on the last straps of her suit as the cargo bay door howled open. She snapped on her helmet and pressed the test button on her descender. The all-good icon spun into focus—the ingredients were still ready to go. Striding over to Orna, she switched on her comm.

"Hunter Two here. Come in, Boss."

"Boss copies," said Cordell. "Hunter One, how we doing?"

"Ready to rock," said Orna.

The heads-up display in Nilah's helmet initialized, and she saw the world in shades of bright red. The words AWAITING AGGREGATOR FEED scrolled across the bottom of her vision.

"We're making a surveillance pass over the operational area now," said Cordell. "Going to see what sensors he's got the place equipped with. Once we're done with that, you two drop out the back and take down his networks. No alarms, you hear me? We're a day away from the closest jump gate if the local cops show up. Can't rebuild the jump dump again, either."

"Copy that, Boss," said Orna, slinging a bandolier of grenades across her torso and clipping it to her suit. "In and out like miner mice."

"Prince here," said Armin. "The only two priorities are getting station credentials and stealth for the duration of the mission."

"So any OPFOR casualties..." Orna began.

"Suboptimal, but acceptable," said Armin. "Just make sure they deserve it."

Nilah caught the glint of a smile through her girlfriend's helmet and her stomach lurched. Orna was always efficient and brutal, but Nilah saw something darker on her face. She was going to enjoy this.

Color returned to the world as the aggregator connection stabilized. Nilah tethered and walked to the wailing edge of the cargo bay to look down. Far below, she spied a sprawling manor house, dotted with bright red spheres.

"I've relayed the sensor pickup patterns to your visors," said Armin. "We're not seeing any personnel on the grounds proper, but that doesn't mean the coast is clear."

A small green *X* flashed in the center of one of the roofs, beside a large atrium window.

"This will be your optimal point of ingress," he continued. "There's a comm tower here, through which you can access the manor security. Depending on network topology, you may be able to access their power grid."

"Boss here. We're coming around for another pass. Stand by to execute."

Orna clipped in and stepped up next to Nilah. "Hunter One, acknowledged."

Charger crept up to the edge as well, its artificial balance able to easily compensate for any turbulence. It chirped its readiness.

The quartermaster's stance was sure and full of malice, as though she could reach down and tear the residence to pieces with her bare hands. She seemed so unlike the woman Nilah had fallen in love with in that moment: a wildcat that once loved to be stroked, now geared for murder.

Nilah reached out and touched her arm, and Orna jolted.

She didn't wait to see what Orna might say. "Hunter Two, acknowledged."

The ship made a slow bank, and the manor passed out of sight behind the ramp struts. When they completed their next loop, Nilah and Orna would get the orders to jump. She swallowed. It had to be easier than the *Harrow*, with its heavy cannons and surface-crawling defenses, but that didn't still Nilah's heart. A jump was a jump, and it could always end in a splat.

"You are go for jump," said Armin.

Leaping out of the back of a moving spaceship wasn't the sort of thing tackled lightly. Merely stepping off could cause a person to tumble uncontrollably, and so to survive, Nilah needed to commit. Following in Charger's wake, Nilah sprinted down the ramp and into the gathering twilight.

The air tore at her visor, seeking purchase on the seams of her flight suit as Nilah went spread-eagle to level off. Race car drivers were always thrill seekers, so this wasn't the first craft she'd jumped from—but she was accustomed to having a jetpack.

And there typically weren't security autoturrets at the bottom.

Charger's armor unfurled around it; its ordinarily sleek silhouette became feathered, each plate of regraded steel sweeping outward to create maximum drag. Orna soared through the air, landing on Charger's back and riding it like a skyboard.

The altitude counter on Nilah's heads-up display plummeted toward the inevitable, Armin's helpful addition to her data feed.

Then the words TRIGGER DESCENDER flashed in her face in bright white, and she nearly lost her balance recoiling from the shock. Nilah snapped the descender disc, and green phantoplasm enveloped her, bouncing her off the roof once before popping. She came to rest against a flat part of the building.

"Okay, Prince," she hissed. "I know you're trying to be helpful, but those warnings—"

"You're on the atrium glass! They can see you from below!" said Armin. "Get out of there!"

Nilah rolled to get her legs under her and looked around, seeing only a sea of red no-go zones. The bounce had disoriented her, and she cast about for Orna and Charger, finding them behind her. Orna waved frantically, and Nilah scrabbled off the thick panes of the atrium.

They held still for a moment, both listening for a siren, slinger fire, or even surprised shouts. When nothing came, Orna whispered, "Hunter One, package delivered."

"Copy that," said Cordell. "We'll be waiting up top."

Looking around, they spotted the comms antenna array—a series of a half-dozen dishes and metal pipes. The trio weaved through the plumes of red sensor detection, shimmying through canyons of falloff.

"How accurate are these projections, Prince?" Nilah grunted as she squeezed between two fields.

"Plus or minus one-point-two percent," he replied.

"Better not be plus," said the quartermaster.

Orna relaxed as she cleared the last detection zone, rushing to the comms array and drawing her glyph. She touched her glove to the antenna tower and her eyes rolled back in her head. Orna was in such a hurry that Nilah worried she'd botch the hack, but no alarms sounded and the quartermaster wasn't fried by any countermeasures.

Drawing her own glyph, Nilah pressed her palm to the junction box and psychically wound through the network. What she found was a path of severed circuits and burned-out relays rent asunder by a virtuoso. Not that Nilah liked to criticize, but Orna's typical attacks were brute force and a bit graceless. This was surgical.

Then her connection snapped closed as the system went dead.

"Nice work," Nilah breathed, eyeing her girlfriend for a response.

"I know." Orna took her hand from the antenna and clicked off the locking ring on her helmet. Testing the fit of her earpiece, she whispered, "This is Hunter One. Comms are down."

Nilah followed suit—no helmets meant better situational awareness. Charger flipped open its fusion blade, bathing them in a split second of startling light. It carved a perfect circle through the roof and snatched the core with its claws to stop it from falling. The blade went dark, leaving only orange glowing rings of molten metal as Charger gingerly placed the roof core to one side.

The pair of women peered into the darkness of the house for a moment before donning their echo imagers and drawing slingers. Orna would be able to see through Charger's eyes, too, which were much more powerful than Nilah's lenses.

The bot went through the hole first, landing absurdly silently for a creature made of regraded steel. Then Orna stepped off the roof, falling into Charger's arms and popping up to a ready stance, slinger barrel scanning for any sudden movements.

Fear gripped Nilah's heart. The distance between the roof and the ground was so much shorter than the jump from the back of the *Capricious*, and yet she didn't want to go inside; didn't want to follow Orna into the house. Though their slingers were full of overloader rounds to minimize casualties, Orna didn't need a weapon to kill someone.

The quartermaster looked back up at her, body gray in the echo imagers, and signaled the all-clear. Holding her breath, Nilah leapt into Charger's arms. It caught her and placed her to one side as easily as a doll.

The immaculate urmurex corridor before them shimmered with echo reflections like it was made of thousands of broken mirrors, disorienting her. Nilah just hoped Charger could spot any traps.

The bot sunk low, its head snapping to some unseen threat, and Nilah looked about for cover, settling behind a large buffet running along one side of the hall. She toggled her optics to visual and saw a long sliver of light just around the bend, a person's silhouette growing within its confines. The bot took off, and to Nilah's surprise, Orna followed in its wake. The quartermaster usually let the bot act as a shock troop, only diving in once the threat was subdued, but she was hot on its heels.

They rounded the corner, and a woman's gasp came echoing down the hall. Silently, Nilah sprinted down the hall to find the bot holding a guard by her neck, her eyes wide with fear.

"Where's Bill?" Orna whispered to her. "Two seconds to comply."

"I don't know—" came the woman's reply before Orna placed her slinger barrel against the guard's temple and pulled the trigger.

A brief flash of violet light erupted and snapped the woman's head backward, then purple smoke came snaking out of her nostrils and mouth. Charger tossed the stunned woman to one side like a piece of trash, and Orna leveled her slinger to continue advancing down the corridor. The stench of the stun spell almost gagged Nilah—she hadn't forgotten what it had been like for Boots to jam a sleeper into her gut. It'd been cruel to shoot that woman point-blank, but at least Orna hadn't killed her.

"This is Boss," said Cordell. "We've got some flashlights out on the grounds below. I think they know the comms are down. Some of the guards may be on alert."

"Copy," whispered Nilah.

"If Boots flies for me," said Aisha, "I can snipe those guards with a stun rifle. We're only two klicks out, and my scope can pinpoint targets."

"Copy that," said Cordell. "Be advised, Hunters, we're putting a thunderbolt in play. If you go outside, give us a warning."

Nilah swept the area on their phase, keeping her back to Orna and Charger. "Hunter Two, acknowledged."

The scent of clean water filled Nilah's nostrils. They emerged onto a landing overlooking the vast atrium. Overhead, stars twinkled through the panes of glass. She thought she could see the area where she'd landed almost directly above them. A gilded forest filled the floor below, jeweled leaves confusing her imager with their prismatic reflections. A light, resonant tinkling swelled in her ears as the metal branches chimed in meditative bliss. She switched into optical mode and saw winding brass trunks of corded wire, glimmering in the lights of floating lanterns. Through a clearing, past a murmuring fountain, stood a pair of double doors two meters high, lined on either side by statues of celestials in supplication. Directly before them, a spiral staircase to the lower level, open on all sides with no cover.

Orna motioned for Nilah to go down so Charger could provide cover. As she descended, Nilah tried to remember how it felt to ride inside the bot, and more importantly, whether Charger's imaging lenses would be defeated by the canopy of gemstones. They so fouled Nilah's optics that every shadow across the floor seemed impenetrable.

Once she reached the bottom, Charger leapt down after her with a quiet thwomp, followed lastly by Orna, her slinger focused on anything remotely threatening.

Reunited, the trio proceeded to the far wall, where they could at least make certain that there were no lurking dangers to one side. They wound through the synthetic forest, and Charger's head swiveled erratically to each leaf that dared chime out in the darkness.

Then everything went as bright as day as all the leaves became torches. A deafening, modulated screech filled the air, paralyzing in its intensity, nauseating Nilah and sending Orna to her knees. Charger's head shivered uncontrollably as it tried to isolate the sound, then a spell bolt slammed into it. Arcane energy crackled over Charger's exterior, and it collapsed into an inert sprawl. Orna was screaming for him, but Nilah couldn't hear what she said. They both ripped off their imagers, which had been fouled by the sonic and visual attacks.

The sound went dead, leaving only a ringing in Nilah's throbbing skull. Flashes filled the forest, red and white, disorienting her further. Only when they stopped could she see the half-dozen armed guards advancing on her, shouting for her to drop her weapon.

Chapter Seventeen

Overture

B worg!" was the guard's first word to her.

Nilah squinted, blinking at the guard with her hands up, finger hooked in the trigger guard of her slinger.

"Down!" the guard repeated, her words becoming clearer to injured ears.

Orna huffed on her knees, slinger clutched against the soft, synthetic grass floor.

"Hunters! Status!" called Armin, but Nilah's addled mind couldn't find the words to reply. "The atrium is all lit up. What's going on?"

Were there six guards? Numbers were so slippery after that attack. There was a word Nilah needed to escape the situation, but she couldn't quite muster it.

"Get down now!" the guard shouted, her fellows remaining steady where they were. "Toss your weapons aside!"

It started with a *th*. It made a flash and a rumble, and sparkly things. It could set fires in forests. This was a forest.

"Charger..." muttered Orna, her jaw working furiously.

"Th—thunderbolt," Nilah whispered.

"Copy that," came Armin's voice. "Zipper, pick a target and take them out on my mark."

"Focusing in on the leader," said Aisha. "Standing by for mark. In three…"

The guards closed in, still barking orders, but Nilah feigned being more stunned than she actually was. The hairs on the back of her neck stood up.

"Two…"

If she let go of her slinger, she'd be unarmed when the shooting started. She got down to her knees, making a show of compliance.

"One…"

The leader gestured to the side. "Now throw your weapon to—"

"Mark," said Armin, and a long, blue knock round shot through the roof glass, smashing into the leader, sending her sprawling across the ground.

Nilah spun her slinger to grasp the butt and planted an overloader into the next closest guard. The man's arms splayed wide and smoke roiled from his mouth before he crumpled. She took another shot, the spell bolt smacking another guard across the cheek and knocking her out.

Orna darted out from behind her tree and shot one of the guards in the hand. He sluggishly tried to bring his slinger to bear on her before she put another round into his chest. He stiffened and keeled over backward.

The last one hunkered down behind a tree, pinned by the two women. Nilah made sure he kept his head down while Orna advanced on his position with steely eyes. She reached him, and he tried to jump up and fire into her belly. She slapped his slinger aside and smashed the back of his head into the tree, ripping his weapon free of his stunned grasp. The rifle clattered to the roots of the tree, its chamber glowing the same blue as the bolt that had felled Charger.

Orna saw it, too. She pinned him by the neck and fired a bolt into the dead center of his chest. Purple smoke leaked from his lips. Then she fired again, intensifying the plume.

Then once more. She was trying to fry his brain.

"Orna, stop!" Nilah shouted, halting the woman's trigger finger.

Orna glared at Nilah, then released the convulsing man, who shook awhile longer before falling still. The quartermaster's shoulders rose and fell in long breaths, her lips twisted in an enraged scowl.

"Had to make sure he was down," she huffed.

Nilah nodded a little too quickly. "He's down."

Orna traced her glyph and rushed to Charger's side, tossing down her slinger. After slapping her palm to his chest plate, she let out a long breath.

"Is he?" asked Nilah.

"No. His eidolon crystals have been suppressed, but he's okay."

They'd been lucky the guards shot Charger first. Those goons could've put a flame round into one or both women if they'd wanted. Nilah expected Orna to remain behind with her pet, but the quartermaster picked up her weapon.

"Let's finish the mission," said Orna, gesturing to the pair of double doors. "Prince, do you have eyes on any other guards?"

"Zipper put down the ones outside," said Armin. "Looks like the coast is clear."

Orna checked her clip and rammed it back in. "Good."

They crept to the pair of double doors, flanking either side. Orna removed one of the grenades from her bandolier and twisted it, exposing a flat plate on one side. She fitted it to the entryway and cranked the primer.

"Breach."

They ducked aside as the doors imploded inward like they'd been kicked by a giant. The second the explosion cleared, the pair rushed inside, ready for anything—

Except the four screaming children in the master bedroom.

The next few moments came in such rapid succession that Nilah had trouble untangling them in her mind. There was a blond woman in her nightclothes, a double-barreled slinger, the light of scatterburst rounds, and Orna plowing into her space like a freighter coming out of jump.

And all the while the wailing of children rang out in the night. Nilah checked herself for hits, then her eyes swept over the kids for blood. Were they armed, too? Finding nothing, she bellowed, "Down! Get down!" in an authoritative voice she'd never had before.

Orna and the other woman scrabbled together across the ground, vicious blows thudding between them. Whoever she was, she held her ground against the quartermaster with surprising stamina—so when Nilah saw an opening, she rushed in and kicked the woman across the face.

Taking advantage of her stunned adversary, Orna clocked her twice in the jaw and knocked away her double-barreled slinger. It went skidding under the massive four-poster bed, and the quartermaster stood, pointing her weapon down at her bloody opponent.

Nilah, for all the shame it brought her, kept her slinger trained on the children.

Able to catch her breath, Nilah swept for targets. The bedroom was a parody of Expansion Era art, with sweeping golden lines folded into inlays of hundreds of different materials. Precious animated fabrics drifted overhead, sweeping through the rafters like phantoms. It was all expensive, but none of it worked together, like every part of the room was supposed to be the centerpiece. Between this and the metal forest, Bill Scar liked his wealth solidly on display in the most ostentatious fashion.

She transmitted the area-secure signal back to the ship. One of the kids started to cast, and Nilah slapped her hand, fizzling the spell.

"Don't help, baby!" the woman cried out at the kids. "It's okay. Mommy is fine."

"Ecaterina," Orna growled.

The woman propped herself up on her elbows and wiped the copious blood from her lips. "Orna," she croaked. "It had to be you."

Orna gritted her teeth. "Where's Bill?"

"Gone."

"Where?"

"You're older, but somehow, you're exactly like I remember," said Ecaterina.

"You know, I could've called the Clarkesfall Reconciliation Committee, told them I found out where Bill Scar was living, but I thought this needed a personal touch."

"Are you going to kill me?"

Her lips whitened, and Orna let out a hissing breath through her nose. "I should, shouldn't I? You stayed with him."

Even punch-pink, Nilah could discern a haunted look in Ecaterina's eyes, like guilt had died in her a long time ago.

"Of course I did," said the woman casting a glance to the quartet of children, who all favored her. "I deserved to survive. Deserved to be happy."

Dread welled inside Nilah. Her grip relaxed on her slinger, and she realized that she wasn't afraid of Ecaterina or the children, but of her girlfriend.

Orna pulled a long-bladed knife from her leg sheath and gestured to the kids, who gasped in unison. "Maybe I ought to take away some of that happiness."

Nilah straightened up and put herself between Orna and the kids. "No, you won't."

Those ice-blue eyes she'd always loved went wide, and the quartermaster began to tremble. Her jaw clenched.

"How old are you?" Orna gestured to the oldest child with a

knife. When no answer came, she screamed her question again, and everyone jumped.

"Twelve," mumbled the boy, head down, voice muffled by the rug.

Orna glared at Nilah, shaking her head like she was trying to shake a persistent thought loose. "That's two years older than I was the first time Bill Scar hauled me into a dusty arena and told me to murder a boy. We refused to kill each other, so he tossed a slinger into the pit with a single round inside. Bill liked to call it 'youth league.' This witch"—she gestured to Ecaterina—"was the nurse for the survivors. Patched up my wounds so I'd be ready for the next round."

The children wept. They didn't know. Half of them were too scared to listen.

"He stole so many kids," said Orna, her voice breaking. "The fast ones, the stringy ones who had what it took to survive in the wasteland without their parents. So it would only be fair if I took one in return."

Nilah kept her slinger pointed at the ground, but her grip was firm and ready. "They don't deserve to pay his debts." She looked to Ecaterina. "Listen, you want us to leave. We want the keys to the Masquerade. Protect your children and tell us what we need to know."

Ecaterina's red eyes cast over them, then to the youngsters face-down on the carpet. "The yacht. It's coded for entry and landing. Bill... likes to throw parties there. He keeps the masks on board."

"I remember his 'parties.'" Orna laughed bitterly. "Is that what he's doing, out where the law can't touch him?"

"I don't know. He never took me with him."

"Where's the yacht?" asked Nilah.

"We've got a hangar outside," she replied. "It's there." Then, to Orna, she whispered, "I'm not a monster. I thought about turning myself in... or killing myself."

The quartermaster's knife point twitched. "Really? It's not that hard. I could help you with both of those."

"I can't," Ecaterina sobbed. "I have to take care of the—"

"What, you don't want to leave the kids with Bill?" Orna spat. "I hear he's good with them."

The hostage affected a pleading face. "Stop. I thought about you for years—wondered what became of you and Heidi. Do you ever see her?"

The quartermaster's lip curled into a snarl. "No. And if Heidi knows what's good for her, it'll stay that way. You think bringing her up is going to change what happens to you?" Her head bobbed on her shoulders as she mocked the woman. " 'I thought about you for years.' Well, I thought about you, too—what it might feel like to clean out your ears with my slinger."

She sat up, her palms out like a beggar. "What else do you want from me?"

Orna thought on it for a moment, idly twirling her knife with a practiced hand. "Nothing. Lights out."

Then she shot Ecaterina point-blank in the forehead with an overloader. The woman collapsed backward, thunking her head against the ground and spasming before going still.

The children screamed even harder, and Nilah had to hush them, but they were terrified of her, too.

"What?" shouted Orna. "She'll wake up in six hours! Nil— Hunter Two, lock these brats in the bathroom so I don't have to hear their whining."

"Okay, darlings, let's go." Nilah urged them to their feet and took them to the restroom, which seemed palatial after being cooped up inside the *Capricious* for so long. White marble extended to a long window, through which Nilah could see the sprawling grounds illuminated in floodlight. Trees fluttered and swayed under the engine wash of the *Capricious* as it landed, bending the arbors to one side. A spotlight lit up on the ship's keel, brightening the bathroom and prompting another scream from the children.

She didn't want to stay in there too long—didn't want to leave Orna alone with Ecaterina.

"It's fine," Nilah said. "That's the ship that's going to take my friend and I out of here. You won't see us again. Now sit tight." She pointed to the oldest and said, "You're in charge."

Then she closed the door panel, traced her glyph, and coded a time lock into the circuit.

Back in the master bedroom, she found Orna standing over Ecaterina, regarding the older woman's features like she was studying a painting. Her knife remained in her hand. Nilah went to her and gave her a pleading look.

"Hey, we need to—"

"Yeah, I know," said Orna. "The yacht."

They rejoined the others in the front courtyard, and Malik checked the downed guards for injuries. He made a few concerned noises, but assured Nilah that they hadn't committed murder, only assault. Orna got the engine hoist from the ship and trussed up Charger's paralyzed frame, loading it into the cargo hold.

Once they'd secured the perimeter, Cordell ordered them to open the hangar.

Inside, they found an Exarch Systems Sunspray yacht, its archrome finish in brilliant rainbow hues under the hangar lights. Nilah had seen them at her races, even been on a few of them, but had never been able to afford her own. It wasn't a huge ship, with quarters for five crew, but every element of the interior would be bespoke, tailored to the interests of the customer.

And most importantly, it had an internal jump drive.

The captain whistled appreciatively. Boots gaped. The twins circled the ship, looking over every nook and cranny. And Orna let out a long sigh.

"Let's not forget how Bill Scar paid for this ship," she said. "Can we steal it already?"

The hack went better than expected. Without ever meaning to, Nilah had gotten to be something of an expert in ship security systems. Compared to slicing up the network on the *Harrow*, the Scarett family yacht was a simple matter. Nilah worked the sections that required finesse, like the ship's brain, while Orna messed with the power routings to stop the ship from discharging into Nilah's body. Armin ran simulations and aggregation, quickly identifying the next set of targets.

With a greeting of musical bells, the ship opened up before them, white leather interiors and cool blue lights beckoning them inside. Its ramp extended, coming to rest before Cordell's feet, and the captain shook his head with a smile.

"You looking for an upgrade, Captain?" Nilah asked.

He scoffed. "I know that's a joke, Miss Brio. There's no better ship in the universe than the *Capricious*."

"I'll captain him," volunteered Boots.

"You most certainly will not," countered Armin. "First mate, first pick."

Cordell crossed his arms and nodded his approval. "Too right." He picked up an empty plastic bottle from a nearby workbench and hurled it against the hull of the yacht, where it harmlessly bounced away. "I hereby recommission this ship the ADF *Scuzzbucket*. Captain Vandevere, the *Scuzzbucket* and all his riches are yours—for the duration of the mission. Any cash we make fencing this thing goes straight to the Clarkesfall Reconciliation Committee."

"After we're paid back for the DosSantos dossier," corrected Nilah.

"Fair enough," said Cordell. "Mister and Missus Jan, you're with me. You Ferriers are on the *Capricious*, too. The rest of you, take the *Scuzzbucket* and get him to our shipyard at Harvest. I want to stash our ship someplace safe while we hit the Masquerade."

"Yacht piloting?" Aisha nodded at Boots. "Looks like you're going to earn your commercial pips. When all this wraps up, you can do guided tours."

"Zip it, zipperjock," said Boots.

"No problem, Pips. When you get done with that bus, I'll have your fighter waiting for you."

"Enough chitchat," said Cordell. "The constabulary hasn't caught on to us yet, and I don't mean to give them cause. I want skids up in ten."

Nilah followed Orna and Charger aboard, the trio of them sweeping the interior in case someone hid inside during the assault. In the master quarters, they found their prizes: four animal masks hanging from the walls, gilded lines glimmering with rainbow energies. Even without her mechanist's mark, Nilah could sense the power of the spells encoded into them.

"The wolf is mine," said Orna.

With everything secured, they spun up the sleek engines and started charging the jump drive. Everything inside the Sunspray was perfectly calibrated, revving up with a performance whine usually reserved for exotic fliers. With a ship like this, they could run blockades, they could jump from world to world like royalty. They could do a lot of good with this marvel.

They made their way to the bridge, such as it could be called. Without a ton of tactical necessities, the *Scuzzbucket*'s bridge was little more than a windowed office with two chairs and some flight controls. They pressed in beside Armin, accidentally elbowing him as they passed. She doubted the bridge could comfortably hold any more crew.

Boots, noting their presence, turned to Armin. "Ready to launch, sir?"

The man had a strange, wistful gleam in his eye as he said, "Did you know that this is my first commission?"

"'Commission'?" Nilah repeated.

"Yes, Miss Brio," said Armin. "This is my first official captain's chair."

They scooted to one side to give him more room to appreciate the moment.

Boots, however, broke the mood by adding, "It's amazing how far a career can go with a little piracy."

Armin sighed and massaged the bridge of his nose. "Miss Elsworth, take us up. Confirm the *Capricious* is away, then initiate the jump to Harvest."

"Aye, Captain Vandevere," she replied with a grin. "You two might want to go strap in at one of the quarters. I'll let you know when it's safe to walk around."

The jump was smoother than any Nilah had experienced aboard the *Capricious*, and she'd almost forgotten what it felt like to fly in a luxury craft. When the all-clear came, she and Orna unstrapped from the crash couch to walk around and maybe raid the ship's stores.

Except instead, Orna went to the bed and collapsed face-first onto it.

Nilah prayed for her to make a joke about how tired she was, or to say anything at all, but she just lay there for long, quiet moments.

"Babe?" Nilah ventured.

No answer.

"I love you," Nilah added.

Orna's ears pricked at the words, and she turned so one cheek was resting on the mattress. She stared at the wall, some unpleasant phrase caught in her throat. Nilah's stomach churned with the fear that it would be the words, "I'm sorry, but I don't."

But Nilah waited all the same, refusing to leave until she knew. Orna's voice was hoarse when she finally spoke. "Why?"

"Because...you..." Nilah stammered as she tried to shift gears. "You're talented."

"You're drowning in talented friends. You could have someone sane. Lana seems sane."

"You've got a right fit body."

Orna blew out a breath. "Don't even get me started on your hordes of hot friends. You...you can't love me."

Her words chilled Nilah's skin, and she sat down beside Orna. "It's not about looks, love."

Those ice-blue eyes that Nilah treasured began to glaze with tears. "Then you really can't stay with me, because...because the deeper you go, the worse it gets. One of these days, you're finally going to understand me, and when you do, you're going to leave."

"What do you think I'm going to see?"

"That I'm a monster," she said, her voice cracking. "I wanted to kill Ecaterina so badly, right in front of her kids. I've killed so many people for less, and—oh, god, when I looked at your face..." Orna's gaze briefly met hers. "I saw how horrified you were with me."

She reached out to stroke Orna's hair, and the quartermaster flinched. Unlike in the cargo bay, Nilah didn't pull away.

"I was horrified, but not with you. I was furious that the galaxy would twist someone so precious to me." She laid down behind Orna, pushing her arms around the quartermaster and shushing into her ear. "You didn't kill her. That matters."

Her back shook as she replied, "I wanted to, so badly. And when you wanted to rescue Sharp, I just...thought we should cut and run...like a coward."

"You've been daring so many other times. People say we're two of a kind."

"You're, like, unflinching and I'm just, you know, selfish, because I can't stop surviving. I keep trying to live, but every damned day, something pushes me back to the sands. One of these missions, I'm going to do something truly terrible, and you're going to hate me forever."

Nilah tugged on Orna's shoulder, and she rolled onto her back, tears streaming down her face. She nuzzled into the crook of Orna's arm, resting her hand on the quartermaster's belly.

"What if I'd gone berserk? I wanted blood, Nilah. I might've... I might've settled for his wife and kids." She bit her lip and rubbed her reddened eyes. "I'm losing my mind."

"You're never going to go berserk."

"You don't know what I was thinking in—"

"Hush, babes." Nilah placed a finger to Orna's lips. "I do. That's why I stood up to you. And those thoughts... they aren't your fault, do you get that? You have every reason to be as angry as you are."

Orna rolled to face her, enveloping Nilah in those strong arms. "One of these days, you're not going to be there to stop me."

Nilah drank her in, the scent of sweat and slinger smoke, old rubber and her cheap mechanic's bodywash, and sighed into her bosom. No one sold perfume like that, but nothing in the galaxy smelled as good as Orna. She held her tightly for a few long seconds, eliminating every centimeter of distance between them.

"You're wrong," she slurred against Orna's collarbone, then pulled back to rest a hand on her girlfriend's cheek. "I will always be there."

Orna's breath caught and her lip quivered. "You'd be the first."

Nilah shook her head. "No again. The rest of the crew loves you. You're going to be okay, do you understand me? But if you need some reassurances...if you want me to prove I won't disappear..."

She swallowed, heart in her throat, Orna searching her face for some impending meaning.

"Maybe..."

In her career, she'd done dozens of press junkets. Stood on podiums across the galaxy. Headlined boatloads of events. Why was she having to muscle a lump out of the way of her words?

"...we ought..."

Deliberately jumped out of a moving starship. Helped kill a prime minister. Returned the single most powerful instrument of war to the right hands. Spent an evening drinking with Boots. Why was she so frightened?

"...to get married."

Orna gaped at her in shock. She'd made the wrong move. Every line on the quartermaster's face was about to spell out the word "no."

"You want..." Orna stammered, "to spend the rest of your days with a desert rat like me?"

Nilah, now crying, stupidly wiped away her girlfriend's tears instead of her own. "It'd be the greatest honor of my life, Orna Sokol."

"Deal."

And they sealed it with a kiss.

"Nice landing, Pips!" Aisha radioed to the *Scuzzbucket* as Boots docked him at Harvest.

They'd made multiple jumps in an effort to arrive at the same time, just in case someone was waiting on the other side. To Boots's delight, shoddy docking clamps and a stench like an open sewer were the only threats Harvest offered up. They'd even managed to get a private, sealed bay this time, which they could use as a home base.

Boots spent the next several hours on the comm with Aisha, learning how best to secure a larger spacecraft, as well as handle fuel-loading logistics, food, coolant, and all the things she'd never bothered with. There were seemingly endless forms to fill out. Now Boots understood why Aisha was always the last one out of the boat.

"If you're done with basic docking procedures," chuckled Aisha, "the captain wants to see you in his quarters."

"Armin's quarters are way nicer on the *Scuzzbucket*," Boots replied. "Along with my cushy pilot's chair, most of this place is pretty posh."

"He says just get over here," said Aisha.

When Boots arrived in Cordell's quarters, she found a delightful spread of breads, cheeses, and fruit laid out, alongside a bottle of Flemmlian Ten.

"You wanted to see me, sir?" she asked.

He came swaggering out from behind a closet door, having just donned his casual clothes. She could probably count the number of times she'd seen him out of his jacket on ten fingers. "Yes, I did, Bootsie. I figure we need to have a toast."

She frowned. He was spending too much personal time with the crew, and Boots most of all. What if he was losing his edge, going soft in his old age? She'd seen far too many of the Fallen give up on their decorum, and later, their lives.

"Why are you standing there like a fool?" he asked. "Get in there and pour yourself a glass. Pour me one, too."

She did as he bade her, and the scent of an uncorked Flemmlian was enough to set her mouth watering—smoky notes and a hint of cinnamon, with a vanilla finish. One for her, one for him, and she handed it off. As Cordell took it, a bit sloshed onto his hand.

"And...what are we toasting?"

"Dreams come true." He clinked his glass against hers, and she saw the empty bottle of wine peeking out from behind his cycler. He must've missed when he tried to throw it away—which meant he was already way ahead of her on drinks.

She crooked an eyebrow and snatched his glass, downing it and then hers right after.

"Hey! That's...that's insubordination!"

"To dreams coming true," she huffed, booze burning on her breath. "Now, you mean to tell me why I'm up here and you're piss drunk, raiding the ship's stores for all our carbs?"

"You can't talk to me like that."

She gestured to the closet. "You're not in uniform. How am I supposed to know what your rank is? Go put your crap on. I'll wait."

"You just love any excuse to be...a punk is what you do."

"That's right, sir," she said, easing him into a chair. "A punk is what I do. Very sensible."

"I just wanted to start a new tradition," he said, his head lolling back. "Starting by toasting you plugging that Stetson Giles."

"Yeah, except we haven't done that yet, so—"

His pointer finger shot up in objection. "That's the 'new tradition' part. You see, if you have the toast while everyone is still alive, they get to enjoy it."

She put her hands on her hips as the whiskey's warmth settled onto her bones. "With all the stupid crap we do, it's amazing we made it this far."

Cordell smiled and mocked a pathetic face. "Would you come to my wake, Boots?"

"Not on your life, reprobate." She pushed his chair hard to one side, then pulled up one of her own. "Shove over, dead weight. I've got a whiskey to murder."

He tapped his brow. "You've got to admit, previctory toasting is a solid idea. Would've been nice to have one last party with old Kinnard."

She splashed a bit too much into her tumbler, but it didn't matter since she had designs on the whole bottle. "Yeah. Maybe so. Look, you don't have a plan, do you?"

"What?"

"You're acting weird. Getting overly sentimental. You think someone is going to get killed, don't you?"

He scratched the back of his neck and sighed. "Any way you slice it, it's going to be dicey. If word gets around that we're there, Vraba will probably show up, or one of the other gods."

Boots took a thoughtful sip. "Why do you think they haven't thrown more gods at us? By my count, three of them are dead, but they've got a lot more."

Cordell laughed. "Ain't pissed them off enough yet. Destroying the universe is busy work—probably can't spare their most important folks to come after us."

"So that means if we keep going..."

"I'm not sure we want to be their top priority. We can barely handle one of them, much less two or three."

"Here's to being unimportant." She tipped her tumbler in mock toast. "So your problem is you can't figure out how to extradite Stetson Giles without getting your face melted by autoturrets."

"Hell, I haven't even figured out how we're going to identify the guy. He's going to be wearing a mask."

"What was it you always used to say? 'One problem at a time.'"

"Okay, so how do we get a positive ID?"

Boots leaned back in her chair, swirling her glass to peer through the long, amber legs that formed on the sides. "Stetson will probably be wearing the same mask every time. If we had some imaging, maybe Armin could do some pattern analysis."

"Could...like...install imagers in the masks' eye sockets. Let the crew fan out through the Masquerade for a few days. Just kind of walk around."

Boots blinked. Even drunk, Cordell was a decent strategist.

"That's good. Right then and there, we get a catalogued index of common routes for each mask."

Cordell's smile faltered. "Yeah, but that'll only tell us which masks go where on a regular basis. We still can't know which one is Stetson without...you know...a lot of data. Behavioral data. If we could get into his personal networks, that'd be one thing..."

Closing her eyes, Boots tried to think back to any way she might get ahold of Stetson's stuff, but she hadn't seen him in a decade. If he maintained a home outside of the Masquerade, she didn't know where it was.

"Like you said, we need behavioral data," said Cordell, drunkenly mistaking his idea for hers. "Can't train Armin's models without—"

"Except we have that," said Boots, smacking her forehead. "We probably have a hundred hours of genuine surveillance on Stetson."

"How?"

"The show. We make Armin watch *Finding Hana*."

Chapter Eighteen

Form Up

The next day, Cordell emerged from his room crisp and tight, his captain's jacket wrinkle-free. Boots, on the other hand, had to pay a visit to Malik for a hangover cure.

With all prep complete, they crammed into the *Scuzzbucket*, bound for a never-ending dinner party of power brokers and wanton indulgence. Boots couldn't believe she and Stetson had ever intended to work there; she couldn't stand regular dinner parties.

Also, Boots hadn't known about the spikes.

She'd never wanted to see Stetson Giles's face again, unless she was putting her fist through it. Despite her best efforts, it now filled the viewing gallery of the *Scuzzbucket*, projectors rendering his devious image in perfect contrast.

His face was a map of his checkered past. Stetson had a long, broad nose that terminated just above his extremely large, white upper teeth; both teeth and nose had been replaced after a bad scrap in a Gantry Station bar. Since his mouth could scarcely contain his ivory array, his lips were always pulled back in good-natured smirk; that smirk had charmed a dozen investors. His apple-red cheeks swelled with each smile, crinkling his eyes like a cowboy squinting into the sun; Gemma, the show's producer, used to love that look.

"I can't believe you ever trusted this guy," Armin muttered as Boots entered. They'd rigged up his datamancer's throne in there so he could better parse through footage of Stetson.

"Thank you, Admiral Hindsight," Boots said, crossing to the bar to pour herself a drink.

"Are you on duty?"

"Would I drink on duty?"

He sighed. "You might. Remember, I recruited you because I have trouble predicting you."

She toasted Armin and downed the fiery liquid. "But you can predict Stetson just fine."

"You know," said Armin, "I normally give myself a twenty-five percent tolerance for predictions. Every once in a while, I'm wrong. With you, it's like a thirty percent chance."

"Just five percent more?" Boots wiped her mouth with the back of her hand. "You made it sound like I was some unknown mathematical mystery!"

Armin shrugged and gestured to the playback. "But with Stetson here, I think I can give myself a seven percent margin of error. Watching him is like looking through a porthole. I swear it's like I can see the gears turning in his head."

Annoyance fluttered in her stomach like a match flame. "He's not that simple. It's not like we could've seen it coming."

The first mate glanced back at her and keyed up a few panes of transcripts. "This," he said, running a finger down the display, "is every instance of someone talking about finding the Chalice of Hana."

"So?"

He tapped one of the lines, and playback jumped to a much

younger Boots saying "chalice." Armin paused the feed, then pointed to Stetson's eyes.

"So what?" asked Boots. "He's looking at Gemma, the producer. She's pretty. A lot of people looked at her before he shot her."

"Again, then," said Armin, keying up the next instance of discussion.

This time, Stetson's eyes were firmly fixed in the center of Gemma's back.

"Okay, so you have two," said Boots. "That doesn't mean—"

"Let's look at another."

The playback jumped to Stetson speaking to Gemma about what they'd do the moment they held the artifact.

"You can't count it if he's talking directly to her—"

"Watch his index finger," said Armin.

And sure enough, it twitched. He keyed up another and another, and every time someone on the show brought up finding the chalice, Stetson would look at Gemma and stretch the fingers of his right hand—almost like holding a slinger.

"Okay," said Boots, plunking down her glass, "okay, I get it! We were dense and now she's dead. Thanks! You made your point!"

"That's not why I showed you that," said Armin.

"Okay, well I feel like crap now, so maybe you could tell me the upside?"

Armin sat up in his chair and gestured to the buffet service. "Pass me that bottle, would you? And a glass?"

Boots did as he asked her, and he poured himself a burbling serving of liquor.

"People crave absolution, Boots. A crew morale metastudy from 2987 showed that soldiers performed far better when—"

"You sound just like Kin sometimes," said Boots, "which is nice, but skip it."

"I liked that little cube," said Armin. "My point is this: there was never a question in Stetson's mind that he was going to double-cross you. He always intended to murder Gemma. His plans may have evolved over the course of the search, but it was always going to turn out the way it did."

She chewed her lower lip. "If I'd known, I would've shoved that slinger so far up his ass..."

"But you didn't, and what's done is done. Still, I almost envy you."

"Envy me? Yeah, we had a real blast right up until the murdering."

Shaking his head, he said, "No. I envy you because you have everything you need to achieve righteous justice. Our quarry's behavior reveals that he's subhuman. He always was, but he hid behind a mask of camaraderie strong enough to fool the two of you. And where we're going, he'll be hiding behind a mask once more. The difference is that this time..."

He paused to take a swig of his glass.

"...I have enough data on him to slice that mask to ribbons. No matter what else happens on this mission, Boots, we're going to get some damned justice for what happened to you."

"You sure know the way to a girl's heart," she said, toasting him, but she felt an unexpected warmth. Perhaps it was just the whiskey.

"All crew to the bridge," Cordell's voice interrupted over the intercom. He'd taken over command of the *Scuzzbucket* from Armin in an amicable, yet overly ceremonial, procedure.

"You sure about that, Captain?" Boots called back.

"What? Yes, I'm sure, it's—"

"Not a lot of room in there, sir. It's a yacht for five."

"We should listen to Pips," said Aisha, who'd become the main pilot after the two crews reunited. "She's flown this big boy before."

"And where would you suggest we cram nine people on this boat?" asked the captain, his voice tinged with annoyance.

391

Boots looked around the *Scuzzbucket*'s small yet luxurious theater. It was ideal for a tiny group of friends to get together and watch dramas, but it'd hold nine people. Armin saw her look and shook his head no—he'd taken over this room and wasn't keen to give it up.

She pretended not to notice. "Maybe the viewing gallery would work, sir?"

Nilah hadn't been so sweaty in a long time. They'd been in crew muster for ten minutes, and the *Scuzzbucket*'s climate control couldn't keep up. Tracks of perspiration ran from her armpits and under her bosom, and she crossed her arms over her chest to hide the stains.

"Whose idea was it to meet in this tiny box?" she grumbled.

"Oh, that would be Boots," said Armin, mopping his forehead. "Take a bow, Boots."

Cordell chortled, sauntering into the middle of the room with an unlit cigarette hanging from his mouth. "I told you lot that the *Capricious* is the best ship in the galaxy. Who agrees with me now?"

No hands went up.

"I mean," said Nilah, "if the rest of you guys weren't here, maybe it'd be nicer."

"Let's just get this done," said Cordell, and the twins dragged in a transit case from out in the hall.

They clicked it open, and the four masks from the ship's master bedroom arose on a lit tray, their features effervescing with woven illusions. There was a wolf, an eagle, a rabbit, and a bear. Viewed at different angles, their fur and feathers shifted from metallic to opalescent.

"Dibs on the wolf." Orna repeated her previous claim.

"That's what we're here to discuss," said Cordell. "You probably noticed that there are nine of us and four masks. We can get the ship into the Masquerade, but we need to talk options for board-ing parties."

He picked the eagle up and tried it on, and its cowl of feath-ers spread across his torso like a cloak, obscuring his body. In an otherworldly, genderless voice, he said, "Do I look as stupid as I think I do?"

"Less stupid than usual, sir," said Boots.

He turned on Boots with what Nilah assumed to be a glare, but she couldn't read his expression behind the raptor's eyes. "As you can see," said Cordell, "it changes my voice and height. It also"— he held up his arms, sheathed in luminous talons—"obscures any exposed skin."

"Wicked," said Orna, seeming for once like her old self again. "Do you mind?"

The eagle gestured to the lot of masks in their midst, and the quartermaster picked one up, turning it over to show Nilah a bril-liant pink stone set into a copper headband.

Nilah whistled appreciatively and said, "That's a very flawless eidolon crystal. Could probably power the ship's amps with one of these, and we've got four."

"Crystal crypto?" asked Orna.

"Almost certainly," said Nilah.

"Okay, but for the rest of us fools, what's crystal crypto?" asked Boots.

Nilah held up the mask and turned it around so the others could see the embedded gemstone. "Powerful stones like this cause minor anomalies all around them—beneficial, of course. Reduced aging, small flashes of light, minor gravitational dis-turbances, tiny arcane bursts. The purer the gems are, the more reliable the disturbances. A stone like this probably generates a thousand small events a day in repeating intervals. So, if you had a sensitive sensor array—"

"You could use the stones like a key," said Cordell, nodding. "Anyone without a stone is unauthorized, so zap go the autoturrets."

She nodded. "Exactly. This is why you need masks, and why they're so hard to get."

Malik picked up the bear, looking it over before donning it. The effect produced a clumsy-looking beast with an unreasonably upright posture. "If the crystals are the key, why make an animal-themed light show? They could've been bracelets."

"That's the marketplace," said Boots. "Anonymity is what attracts people to the Masquerade. All kinds of illegal trades go on inside that station. These masks are critical to doing business, because no one is going to show up if they think they'll get fingered."

"Our mission is to extradite Stetson Giles, get the index, shut down the Money Mill...and understand what the hell Henrick Witts is building out there in the darkness. If we can follow the cash, we ought to be able to do something about this Bastion we keep hearing about," said Cordell. "But here's the problem: who do we send in on reconnaissance?"

"I'll go," said Boots. "I know Stetson better than anyone."

Cordell shrugged. "That's kind of a given, but what about the other three?"

"I can subdue the man," said Malik, "get him sleep-drunk, and walk him back to the ship."

"I disagree," said Aisha. "You've gotten holes in you on the past two sorties."

"Which were over a year apart," countered Malik.

"You're presuming the dispersers don't pop your spell first," said Orna. "I think we can assume there'll be turrets, too."

"If you try to put the snooze on Stetson," said Boots, "you're definitely getting another hole."

"We could go," said Jeannie. "Alister and I might be able to read some minds—"

"Same risk, same fate," said Orna. "Besides, you two would probably stick out, masks or no. Remember how they ID'ed you on Pinnacle?"

"I should go," said Nilah. "I understand high society, and I'm quick on my feet."

"Then me, too," said Orna, wrapping an arm around her shoulder. "I'm not letting you out of my sight."

Nilah almost missed it, but Armin smirked at her.

"I'm inclined to agree. Miss Sokol is formidable even without a spell. So is Miss Brio," said Cordell, his eagle beak contorting to mimic his words. "That's three masks down. Who gets the last one?"

"You should take it," said Nilah. "If things go south, you've got a defensive spell."

"Which could get dispersed," he said.

"At least you can try to protect us with your shields," she replied. "You were brilliant on board the *Harrow*, or so Boots tells me. I was bleeding to death at the time."

"It's a solid bet," Boots added. "And if we run into any military types, you know what to say to them...better than we do, anyway."

"Is this what we want to do?" asked Cordell. "I know I'm the captain here, but this is a big decision. My stakeholders need to weigh in."

A chorus of ayes and yeahs went up.

The eagle adjusted its unlit cigarette, which hung unevenly from its beak. "All right, then. Miss Sokol, Miss Brio, I want these masks rigged for telemetry. I want to know exactly who sees what, and where they see it. You feel me?"

"Yes, sir," Nilah and Orna said in unison.

"Good. We make the Masquerade in twenty hours. The rest of you, get some rest. I want you ready for anything."

Gentle weeping issued from the darkness, and Boots's eyes creaked open. Dim shapes resolved in her view: a bedside table, a glass of water, a lamp. She had to shake away the feeling of being in two places at once. Was this her mansion on Hopper's Hope or ...

The sob came again, a man's voice. She remembered now—she was sharing a room with the Ferriers, and he wouldn't stop waking up like that. Jeannie had warned her that they were terrible bunkmates, but Boots had insisted that it'd be fine. There'd been plenty of late-night weeping during her soldiering days.

Rustling sheets interrupted the stillness, and Jeannie stood up from her pallet on the floor (thank god they'd let Boots have the bed) then padded around to Alister's place at the other side of the room. She laid down next to him, and he gave out a little sigh in his sleep. He whimpered, and she hummed a soft tune Boots had never heard before, which somehow reminded her of the mountains. Jeannie's voice soothed her, too, and her blinks lengthened until her eyes remained closed.

Bloodred light filled the cabin, and Alister sat up with a shriek.

"All crew ready stations," said Aisha. "We're on approach to the Masquerade in twenty."

Hell of an alarm clock.

Groaning, Boots leaned forward and massaged her neck. Had she slept five more minutes or five more hours? Smacking her lips, she called for water and chucked the cup into the cycler at the bedside.

The intercom chimed once again, this time Cordell. "Boots, can you report to the bridge?"

"I heard twenty minutes, sir," said Boots. "Permission to take a piss first?"

"Yeah, yeah. Hurry up, though."

"And brush my teeth?" she added.

"Boots, what do the ADF regs state about stank breath?"

It was too early for memory games. "I don't know, Captain."

"Nothing, so hurry your ass up here."

Jeannie helped a shaking Alister up. His stare remained fixed on some horizon known only to him.

Jeannie glanced at Boots and smiled. "He'll be right as rain soon enough. Go on."

The facilities were centrally located, and Boots found Nilah waiting outside. Orna opened the door, and Boots muscled past Nilah with a smirk.

"Hey!"

"Old lady. I get priority."

"Try not to break a hip, grandma," Orna said as the door closed.

Morning business under control, Boots rushed to the bridge, such as it could be called. Inside, she found Armin, Aisha, and Cordell—not a tight fit until she entered.

"Hi, Captain," Boots said, trying to stun Cordell with her bad breath.

He turned to face her, and she almost screamed when she came face-to-face with his eagle mask. Feathers fluttered and golden eyes bored into her skull. Good thing she'd gotten to the restroom.

"Why are you still wearing that, sir?"

"It's more comfortable than it looks," came his distorted reply. He handed her the bear. "Now put yours on. We need to call in an approach request, and I don't want our voices ID'ed."

Slipping it on, she grumbled, "Million-argent crystal in this thing, and he's using it for a cheap voice changer." Once the illusions had flowed down her arms like a fur cape, she said in a distorted voice, "Okay. Now I'm a bear."

"Good. Mister Vandevere, Missus Jan," said Cordell, "you're dismissed. I expect they'll want to see us wearing the masks, and I'd prefer you not to get spotted. Miss Elsworth, take the controls."

"Yes, sir," Boots acknowledged, scooting behind the pilot's console.

"Later, Pips," Aisha whispered as she moved aside.

Once they were out of the bridge, Cordell said, "Call it in."

Boots searched through the frequencies, shocked that the *Scuzzbucket*'s comm was inferior to the military-grade tech on her old fighter... the one in the shop back on Harvest, she remembered with a pang of longing. Approaching Masquerade without an escort wing left Boots frazzled, like there was something wrong with the ship. Not that it would matter, since the fighter complement on the station would be able to wipe them out in a matter of seconds if things went badly.

She pressed the transmit. "Approach, this is...uh..."

They had forgotten to agree on a name.

"Approach copies, unidentified Sunspray," came the tower response—a young voice, from the sound of it. "You're entering restricted space. Transmit docking codes or leave within thirty seconds."

Boots glanced back to Cordell, and the eagle gave an exaggerated shrug and mouthed some words. She couldn't make them out through his beak, but she guessed it was, "Make something up."

"Uh...yeah..." she said, but her mind went blank. "This is the recently recommissioned *Scuzzbucket*, ready to transmit docking codes."

"Copy, *Scuzzbucket*," said the tower with no hesitation whatsoever.

Consummately professional. The civvy spaceports could learn a thing or two from this guy.

"Receiving now," said the tower. "Codes check out. Give us a visual on the masks, please."

Boots tapped a button and the projectors spun a traffic controller's torso and head into being in the center of the room. She craned her neck to get a better look at the guy, but he turned to face Cordell. A neural spike glittered at the base of the controller's skull, and she felt a stab of guilt for admiring his professional demeanor. He turned to her, hollow eyes roving her mask, then disappeared.

"*Scuzzbucket*, you are cleared to dock. Bay five. The concierge will meet you there."

Boots pointed the ship toward the station and throttled up. The winking lights of a thousand windows spanned the sleek exterior of the Masquerade, and a large bay door opened along one side. Projectors spun out BAY FIVE in bright orange letters in front of the opening. She engaged the auto landing and the computer put the nose right through the holographic letters.

The bay had the standard atmos bubble shield, but everything else inside was beyond anything Boots had seen. Cushioned articulators reached out and grasped the archrome hull, gently lowering it into a suspension field. Attendants scurried to and fro, and Boots swallowed the sinking realization that they were all thralls. The ship bobbed once, then settled without the typical clank of a docking clamp. Boots had to check the readouts to be certain they were stable.

"Showtime," said Cordell. "Since your call sign is a bit famous, we'll have to call you something else."

"If it's Pips, sir, I will turn this ship around, so help me."

The eagle looked her over, appraisingly. "Let's just go with the animal names. You're Bear. Suits you."

"Thanks, Bird."

"I'm Eagle."

"My mistake."

Down by the docking airlock, they met up with Orna, now "Wolf," with a resplendent onyx fur cloak, and Nilah, now "Rabbit," sleek yet wild, with red eyes. A crimson ribbon flowed from her ears like a battlefield flag, dancing in a breeze that didn't exist.

"Okay, everyone," said Cordell. "First mission is just a recon. We go in, say as little as possible, and get a lay of the land. Even Boots—"

"Bear, sir," she corrected.

"—Bear," said Cordell, his golden eyes narrowing, "hasn't been inside the station before. For this mission, we remain together at all times. Fly casual, you hear me? Do not start anything."

They all turned to Orna, and the wolf snarled, "Why is everyone looking at me?"

Cordell punched the lock cycle, and the docking portal opened before them. A long, polyresin bridge grew from the nearest bay platform, its surface like polished alderwood under clear water. At the end of the bridge stood a tall attendant in a goldfish mask, dark black eyes set into a burnished, scaly face. Its long mouth curled at the ends, as though this fish knew a secret. Its ornate regalia, the color of firelight on solid gold, dazzled Boots.

"Never been impressed by a fish before," she whispered to Cordell.

The fish raised its hand in greeting and beckoned them over. Stepping out onto the bridge, Boots got a closer look at the docking bay crew scurrying about the underbelly of the ship—all in tailored suits of sumptuous, textured fabrics. She peered closer and found the neural spikes she feared.

They reached the fish, who smiled a disturbingly broad smile set with large, pearly teeth. Whoever designed that mask took anthropomorphism a step too far.

"Welcome to the Masquerade, revelers!" announced the fish in musical tones. The jovial voice indicated that—whoever was under that mask—they didn't have a spike in their head. "I'm the concierge, and I'm at your service for the duration of your visit. Years or days, I'll be here always. This ship has visited us before, but under a different name."

"It's a recent acquisition." Cordell extended his hand, which the fish shook. "Pleasure to meet you, mister...uh...miss..."

"Just concierge," said the fish. "Zie, zir, if you please. As your cultural attaché, I'd like to start you with a piece of advice: you'll find that identities are closely guarded secrets at our little party. Assume neutral pronouns here. In addition to taking offense at being misgendered, some of our celebrants may come to believe you've guessed their true identities and take action against you."

"Those are the rules?" asked Boots.

"No," zie replied with a good-natured chuckle. "Those are manners. We only have three real rules here in the Masquerade. One: if you're outside of the docking bay or your quarters, you must wear your mask. Without it, our automated defenses will deal with you."

Boots grimaced, easily guessing what that meant.

"Two," continued the concierge, "there is no fighting in the common areas of the Masquerade. Prize matches will be arranged from time to time, but those are strictly for entertainment, organized through station administration."

"Any fights coming up?" asked Orna.

"I'm afraid not," zie said, "though I feel certain we can arrange whatever amusements you desire. Three: a person's apartment is a sovereign territory. Security will not enter apartments unless there is a threat to the station. Those who follow others into their quarters may find themselves in dire situations. No government has jurisdiction over the Masquerade, and whatever fates befall you are yours alone."

They all exchanged glances, and the fish spread zir hands.

"Our revelers come for a variety of reasons and must be able to conduct their business without interruption. If you are good neighbors and mind your manners within the common areas, I'm sure we'll get along swimmingly."

"A little fish humor?" asked Nilah, and the concierge brightened.

The concierge rocked on zir heels. "I do find it shortens the days. Would you like to see your quarters?"

Cordell nodded. "Lead on, my friend."

They passed from the docking bay into a spectacular walkway of winding gardens and twisting streams of water that snaked through the air like blue dragons, all under a blanket of amplified starlight from the windows above. Chandeliers the size of starfighters hung from the roof struts, their crystal plates intermittently spinning out flashes of light. Jaunty live music filled their ears, the product of a ten-piece orchestra playing in a nearby amphitheater. Dozens of people filled the pedestrian streets, all clad in the ornate regalia of various animals.

The concierge spoke quietly as they walked. "I suggest that you don't gawk. The fact that you're new will only serve to help others unravel the puzzle of your identity."

"How many, er, revelers do you have?" asked Boots.

"Five thousand it has always been, never more, never less," said the concierge. "We do not make new masks, and those that exist are carefully guarded, which you likely learned when you acquired your own. This is the Central Promenade, where you may indulge in any of our fine dining and lavish performances."

"Probably not in the budget," said Cordell.

The fish laughed, zir mouth gaping to show those teeth again. "Oh heavens, no. We never do anything so vulgar as trade money in the common areas. Everything is already paid for by a trust, established by the purchasers of the original five thousand masks."

"No sweeter taste than free food," said Boots, eyeing a nearby open-air restaurant where a suited waiter carved bloody slices of meat from a muscular animal leg. But she wore no mask, and upon seeing the woman's vacant expression, Boots lost her appetite.

"Indeed!" said the concierge, stepping into a section of flooring marked with caution lights. Zie raised zir hand, and a spindly control deck sprouted from the hardwood. "Please join me inside the circle."

They did, and the concierge tapped a few numbers into the holographic keypad. Waist-high shields enclosed them, and the platform rose into the air, pulling away at an impressive clip. Sturdy oaks rushed underneath them as the stars streaked overhead, and Boots rested her hands on the translucent rails, savoring the breeze.

"How old is this station?" she asked. "This tech looks pretty new."

"One hundred and eighty-two years," said the concierge. "We keep it up to date with the proceeds of the trust, as well as charitable donations from some of our more dedicated patrons. This is a place where you can come for absolute privacy and serenity. Those who spend their days here come to understand its power and invest in our enterprise."

Wonder how serene it is when you've got a spike in your head.

The platform settled among gently swaying reeds beside a mirrored lake. The plants bowed out of the way, folding into a woven walkway so they could pass. Boots had seen a lot of interesting effects in her time, but the Masquerade was packed full of delightful surprises.

"This way, please," said the concierge, beckoning them down a slightly less gargantuan corridor.

A vertigo zigzag of silver lines painted the walls like a maze, with the occasional green stripe accent. Embedded in the green stripes were a series of brass plates, and at their approach, four plaques spun out stylized pictures of their animal heads. The silver lines twisted and turned, untangling into the shape of a door.

The concierge stopped. "This is branch twenty-eight. There are one hundred branches in total—fifty on each side of the station. Your masks entitle you to four flats with us, which have been configured into a single unit. Would you like to keep this configuration, or shall I divide them?"

"Keep it," said Cordell.

The fish clasped zir hands and stood clear of the door. "Excellent, my friends. This far I go, and no farther. If I'm needed for anything, please contact me with this." Zie handed each of them a card, and Boots touched it to her comm to embed the connection string.

Zie was keeping a fair distance, almost too precise, and Boots regarded zir sidelong. Beyond, the room breathed to life, glowing spheres rising from woven rugs to light the rafters.

"You can't show us the room?" she asked.

The concierge shook zir head. "I'm afraid not. Your apartments are your sovereign territory, and it's unwise for someone in my position to visit. If you need any assistance inside, I would recommend you bring a spike thrall to our administrative offices for inspection."

Boots grimaced. "We...uh...don't have any thralls currently, though, do we?"

"You have five," said the fish. "Good luck."

Nilah gulped as they stepped inside and sealed the door. The room beyond danced with shadows from the orbs circling overhead, and she squinted to discern any details.

The eagle raised his finger and whispered, "Fan out. I want those thralls dealt with."

Tendrils of her silver rabbit cloak receded as Nilah removed her mask, exposing her bare arms. She cycled her tattoos, ramping them up to a flash. Boots and Orna drew slingers, and Cordell cast his shield, cerulean and wavering, in the air.

The first of the thralls appeared in a doorway: a shirtless man, eyes wide and deep-set. Boots raised her slinger, and Cordell stopped her.

The thrall cocked his head. "State the passkey."

"Let's not make a mess unless we have to," Cordell said. "Miss Brio, could you please put this poor man down?"

Nilah traced her mechanist's glyph and held it in her hand, hesitating. As if reading her mind, Cordell added, "He's already dead, or he wishes he was."

She slowly approached the thrall, which became more agitated the closer she got. His lips were twitching, like he wanted to speak, which made the thought of ending his life even more nauseating. To her surprise, he did manage to speak, though his single word dismayed her.

"Intruder!" he bellowed, and other screams rang out from deeper inside the apartment.

Flashes of magic popped from the rooms beyond as the thralls in the darkness cast their marks. Nilah readied herself to leap out of the way, but instead of charging, he cast the breaker's mark, his muscles magically swelling to near bursting. With a howl, he ran at her, arms stretched wide, ready to rip her in half. Nilah ducked under his sweeping hands and kicked him in the kidney—but it was like kicking the face of a cliff. He wheeled on her and she blinded him with one arm, then rolled to one side to avoid a crushing punch.

The other thralls joined the fray, spells flying, and slinger fire rang out in the now-crowded room. She couldn't pay attention to them, though, or the breaker would get his hands on her. If he managed to secure a purchase, he could pull off one of her arms or legs as easily as destroying a doll. A lucky lunge brought him too close, and she juked, exposing his spine. She slammed her palm against the back of his neck, psychically connecting to his neural spike.

For a split second, she could see all his brain activity, how it was forcing him to fight, how it suppressed his sorrow. He wanted to die, and it wouldn't let him.

Nilah shorted the eidolon crystal into his brain, and he fell dead, tendrils of noxious smoke rising from his nostrils.

When she spun to face the other thralls, she found them bleeding out on the ground, slinger wounds in their heads and chests. Cordell stood in front of Orna and Boots, his shield still wavering where it'd been struck by some attack. She hunkered down and retreated behind him, as well. They cleared out each of the rooms without further resistance.

Returning to the foyer, Nilah couldn't help but stare at her handiwork. She wondered if her dead assailant had done anything to deserve the cards fate had dealt him. Had there been much left of the man in the end?

Cordell donned his mask and tapped his comm. "Concierge? Yes, I need to inquire about body disposal...Okay. Yes. What does that entail?" He held a brief conversation, then signed off. "Apartment interiors aren't covered by the trust. There's a service with a hefty fee," Cordell told the rest of the group, "or we can drag these poor bastards to our disposal chute. If we go with the service, it's eight thousand per head, and we've already bankrupted the ship's funds, so this would be a shared expense."

"Garbage chute it is. Boots, you want to get that one?" said Orna, grabbing a woman's corpse and dragging her toward the kitchen.

"We should do the service," Nilah blurted. "We're rich enough. These people deserve proper rites."

Cordell shook his head. "That's not what'll happen, though. They'll come pick up the bodies, scrub the place with a hotelier, and dump them in their own garbage chute. It's just a way to clean up. No matter what, these people aren't getting what they deserve."

"I know. I just feel worse because..." Nilah gulped, not wanting to say the words she knew should come out of her mouth. "We should harvest the spikes."

Orna looked at her in surprise. "What?"

"Look," she said, "those spikes are already coded to the station administration. That means they're tracked. We...I don't know...we might be able to reuse those codes somehow."

Cordell jammed his hands into his pockets and rocked on his heels. "So...a bigger mess."

Orna reached down to her boot and pulled out a long knife. "I'm game. They're not using them."

The quartermaster spent the next twenty minutes in the bathroom with each corpse doing her grisly work. Nilah couldn't bear to watch, but Orna handled it with all the casual professionalism of a butcher. She must've seen more than enough mutilated bodies in her time. When she emerged, she held five spikes, still wet with the blood of their former owners.

"Garbage now," she said.

Nilah helped the others drag the bodies, one by one, to the disposal. Every time she watched the soles of someone's feet disappear into the darkness, she said a little apology to the deceased. Boots joined in, then Cordell, and finally, to Nilah's surprise, Orna.

Their task complete, they remained in silence for a long while before Cordell spoke.

"I know what all of you are thinking, and I'd love to scuttle this place, too...but we have to focus on finding Giles and getting the index. The most important thing is finding out what resources we have at our disposal. Toss these rooms until you've got everything of value. In the meantime, I'll let the *Scuzzbucket* know we're safe."

They set to work tearing the place apart. The four units were more tasteful than Scarett's quarters on Prothero, which made the search more difficult. Each line of modern, minimalist design held yet another hidden cabinet, convenient recess, or access panel, and the handles, catches, and levers were so perfectly worked into their surroundings that they were hard to find.

And then there were the furnishings with blood on them, which everyone avoided until the end.

Slowly but surely, their resources began to pile up. A slinger here, a credit chit there, surveillance devices, emergency depressurization bubbles, two portable shields—not as good as Cordell's, but useful—and lastly, a plain metal case.

Nilah traced her mechanist's glyph and placed her hand atop the case, psychically feeling around for any hidden workings or traps. There had been a time in her life when a box was just a box, and she'd have opened it immediately. Many devious ploys later, she trusted nothing on its face.

A powerful energy resonance met her mind, and she nearly broke contact in surprise. Carefully flipping open the top, she found a palm-sized eidolon crystal so pure she felt as though she could fall into its facets. Her breath caught.

"Uh..." But words failed.

Most crystals had a milky surface, a vaguely pinkish hue that spoke to their impurities. They had to be used in series to get the desired throughput, reducing efficiency. The *Capricious*'s main power plant was a set of eight cloudy, head-sized stones.

She cleared her throat again, but the magical rush of the crystal swooned her. "Hey..."

"What is it?" Cordell called from the next room. "Everything okay?"

She suppressed her spell, and her intoxication dissipated, though her tattoos still radiated pink pleasure. "Yeah. We've just...got a new piece on the board is all."

"What's up, babe—" Orna rounded the corner and drew up short when she saw the crystal sitting in its protective case. "Whoa. Is that—"

Nilah shook her head.

Orna's cheeks flushed. "We could..."

"I know."

"Wow."

"Right?"

Boots and Cordell followed shortly after, but they only saw future argents when they looked at the stone.

"Just how powerful are we talking here?" asked Boots.

"Capital ship jump drive," said Nilah. "Or main amp. This could power a small city."

"Or obliterate it," Orna added.

Cordell folded his hands behind his back and sauntered to the large porthole window that dominated the bedroom. "Now isn't that something? Looks like ol' Bill Scar just gave the *Capricious* his freedom, because we are definitely turning that into a jump drive."

Nilah blinked. "You want to put this in our ship? That's overkill."

Cordell shook his head. "No more Gate Cartel. No traceability. Just jump on and off whenever we want. Hell yes, I want to put that on our ship. And in the meantime, I want to put it in Charger so that we've got the most badass beast in the galaxy."

Orna let out an annoyed sigh. "Not how it works, Cap. Overcranking his subsystems would probably wreck them."

He grimaced. "Okay, fine then. All I'm saying is that we use this thing to blast some deserving punks."

The window adjusted its tint as the light of a large jump spilled across it. Nilah blinked, trying to make out the shape of the ship that had just entered their sliver of space, but only saw blackness and stars. Except some of the stars had aligned into long rows of grid lines. Only then did she understand what she was looking at:

The black hull of Izak Vraba's warship.

Chapter Nineteen

Duet

Nilah had last seen it in the skies of Hammerhead, sleek and sinister, and had prayed they'd never have to deal with it directly. Twin streaks of engines filled the porthole view as the Masquerade scrambled its fighters.

Cordell nodded approvingly. "Two dozen fighters versus a ship like that? It'll be a knock-down, drag-out if they go at it."

Boots spoke up. "You think they're posturing maybe? Telling him not to try anything?"

The captain smirked. "I wish that asshole would. Those fighters would cut him down, and that's not counting station defenses."

Nilah shook her head. "You're not counting his godlike magic, Captain."

"True that." He tapped his comm. "Eagle to Prince."

"This is Prince," Armin replied over the comm.

Cordell cleared his throat. "Be advised: Vraba is here, and we're not sure why yet. Keep all systems online in case we need to beat a hasty retreat. Jump coordinates Murphy Belt. If the shooting starts, give us five minutes and get the hell out of here."

"Copy that, Eagle," said Armin. "Be careful out there."

They watched the vanguard of fighters crisscross around the warship like a pack of sharks, but no glowing shots joined the starscape.

"I think he could easily destroy this place if he wanted," said Boots. "Just snap it in half. He cracked into the Pinnacle like a candy shell. I'd hate to see godlike glyphs through military amps."

"He's not here for us," said Nilah, "or we'd already be in pieces. He's here for the Money Mill index."

"You can't know that," said Orna.

Nilah took a few steps closer to the window to watch the action. "He knows we caught Maslin Durand. He knows we looted the bloke's vault box on Mercandatta. If he hasn't been able to find the contract anywhere else, he can assume we have it. That means we're after the index, and he intends to get to it first."

Boots smiled. "I almost wish he knew we *were* here, since he can't blow the station or he might destroy the index."

"Making his contract and the Money Mill inoperative," said Nilah. "But... that also means that if we destroy the index while we're on board, he might just kill everyone in retaliation. There'd be nothing stopping him."

"The way I see it," said Cordell, "we've got three obstacles: we don't know where Giles is, we can't just grab him in the Promenade, and even if we could, getting him back to the ship would be nightmare."

"He doesn't have to make it off the station," Boots added with a dark expression. "Only the index does."

In the distance, one of the launch bays slid open on the warship, and a marauder exited, flanked by enemy fighters. The Masquerade's vanguard fell in behind the formation, escorting them toward the station.

Cordell donned his mask, eagle feathers spilling down his shoulders. "Let's get to the docking bay. I want to see this bastard in the flesh."

They rushed back into the gardens of the Promenade, and as they walked, Nilah noticed other masked figures joining them. Before long, the palatial Promenade filled with flying platforms, all headed toward the docking bay. They gathered at the head of the station, eagerly watching as Vraba's marauder entered its final docking stages.

"Why is everyone turning out?" Nilah whispered to Boots in her strange, masked voice.

"Probably just want to see the important guy with the unregistered warship."

They arrived at the docking bay, taking their place along the mezzanine railing, where they'd have a good view. Several dozen revelers had gathered in the bay, and thralls set up an impromptu cordon to keep them back. The *Scuzzbucket* lay peacefully nestled among the other ships, its archrome finish scarcely the most exotic thing there. The concierge waited alone on the platform at the end of the line as the blast door slid open.

Vraba's marauder glided through the atmos bubble, its polished hull like the iridescent carapace of a midori beetle. Anchor servos reached out and gently guided it onto the clamps, and a bridge grew from the concierge's feet to the ship.

The hatch opened, and Nilah squinted to get a better look, cursing herself for not installing zoom optics on her mask. A figure emerged—an elephant with bulging shoulders and wide gray ears swept backward. A crust of gems sparkled along his trunk, which curled at the end like a question mark. Then came a badger, a weasel, and a marpo; Nilah enjoyed more than a little schadenfreude at that person's expense.

"How are we going to know which one is Vraba?" asked Orna.

Boots glanced at them. "Maybe we could—"

Then a stately crow emerged from the ship, every feather of its jet-black coat tipped with a golden arrowhead. Gilded chains

413

encircled its head, resting across its reflective beak. It swept down the bridge, and the others fell in behind.

Boots the bear nodded. "Well, that makes it easy."

"I have to say," said Nilah, "I'm a little disappointed. It's a bit on the nose, don't you think?"

"Cut the chatter," said Cordell.

"All crew, come in," said Armin. "This is Prince."

Cordell tapped his comm, which was a little disturbing, since he had to reach inside the illusory eagle's head to make that happen. "Go ahead, Prince."

"You need to spread out, now," said Armin. "We don't want him to see you following, or he'll be leery of your masks. If you can get visual coverage of the Central Promenade, you may be able to see where he goes."

"Copy, Prince," said Cordell, turning to the rest of them. "We've got twenty-five corridors on each side of the Promenade. Bear, head to the intersection of six and forty-four. Rabbit, take twelve. Wolf, take eighteen. Go now."

Nilah raced down the mezzanine in search of one of the mobile platforms, but so many of them had been taken by gawkers eager to see Vraba's arrival. It must've been a rare occasion for a warship to appear outside of the Masquerade. She hopped on one of the circles and raised her palms, guiding the control panel to her hand. She dialed in twelve, and it set off.

She glanced behind herself. Aside from her own, the only platforms headed away from the docking area were the ones with Boots and Orna. The wolf quickly overtook her, racing toward the far end of the Central Promenade.

Upon landing, Nilah took quick stock of her surroundings: a few benches, a drug dispensary, a nightclub that either hadn't opened yet or was winding down after a lengthy evening cycle. She hadn't been on the station long enough to get a feel for the local time. She scurried toward the dispensary, trying to blend in among the other revelers selecting their highs for the day.

A fox in a tuxedo came to her and smiled a toothy grin—another one of the free-willed staffers. How zie could live with zirself among the thralls was beyond Nilah. "Good morning! Perhaps I could be of some assistance in selecting a—"

"Something obscure and wicked. Artisanal. Handcrafted," she said, cutting zir off. "I expect you to take your time and really impress me."

"O . . . okay. Of course. How do your tastes run?"

She turned to face the window, to the Promenade, folding her hands behind her back. "Give me something to regret. Blow my mind so hard it'll take days to put the pieces back together."

Zie brightened at that prospect. "I see. Would you like it delivered to your—"

"Do I not sound like I'm dying for it? Stop asking daft questions and brew me something."

"Right away," said the fox, bustling toward a doorway deeper into the dispensary.

On the way, a reveler caught the apothecary and added, "I'll have what zie's having."

Nilah stood on the front stoop to watch the skies for Vraba's platform, and before long, she was rewarded with the sight of his retinue approaching. Their transport descended in front of the corridor opposite her shop, along with the effusively helpful concierge. The fish babbled away at zir party, but none of Vraba's guards paid any attention.

"This is Rabbit," Nilah whispered into her comm. "I have eyes on the crow. Corridor thirty-seven."

"Copy that," said Armin. "Eagle, Bear, Wolf, back her up."

"Please, you mean," corrected Cordell, huffing. He must've been running. "The captain doesn't take orders. He does favors."

"Please," hissed Nilah in Armin's stead.

Vraba set off down the path, and Nilah followed along at a decent distance, strolling as though she had every right to be there. It was strangely liberating, wearing the mask. Even when Vraba's guards glanced back at her, she merely nodded at them like a friendly local.

They came to a reindeer with silver vines hanging from obsidian antlers, and zie lazily waved at the crow in greeting. The concierge fish took zir leave, and the party traveled onward, deeper into one of the side gardens.

It was trickier to follow there. The paths curved more sharply, and sturdy elm trees blocked much of Nilah's sight. When they reached a set of benches around a roaring waterfall, they stopped. Vraba's guards fanned out, facing away from the crow and reindeer.

If she stopped to watch, she'd be suspicious, so Nilah kept walking. She tapped her comm. "I think I might've seen Stetson. A reindeer with lovely black antlers. Near corridor...um, fourteen."

"I'm almost there," said Boots. "Stay with them."

"Can't stop," she replied. "They'll see me. Going to the mezzanine."

She hopped a platform, which boosted her up to the second level. "I can't get close enough to hear what they're saying."

"Just keep them in your sight so the imagers can capture," said Armin. "We can run speech analysis back at the ship."

She walked to the railing and peered over, trying to get a better look through the trees. The shifting leaves provided her targets ample cover, and she searched back and forth with mounting frustration. She finally found a spot with ample coverage and watched the conversation unfold.

"This is Wolf," said Orna. "I'm in position."

"Bear. In position."

"Eagle still inbound," said Cordell. "These jerks took all the platforms."

"We've got three angles," said Armin. "Perhaps you'd better hang back, sir."

"Oh, good," he sighed. "Not getting as much cardio as I used to."

Nilah glanced around. The only people nearby were a couple of revelers, laughing and joking on their way elsewhere. She returned her eyes to the targets.

The crow's feathers bristled. The reindeer had said something to offend him, and the guards turned their attention to their master. The reindeer laughed, and Nilah's gut tensed. But miraculously, instead of killing him or turning the place into a shadowy nightmare, the crow spun and walked away with his entourage. Whatever defenses the Masquerade had in place, even the Gods of the *Harrow* wouldn't dare step out of line.

"That's interesting," said Nilah. "Whatever he did got Vraba pretty hacked off."

"Good," said Armin. "Get back to the ship so we can strategize."

"Copy," Nilah said straightening up to leave. "I—"

"Hello," came a voice beside her.

She turned to find a bull with horns like flowing fire, and she was so surprised she almost took a swing. "Oh, god, you startled me. Sorry, but I'm—"

"And which one are you?" asked the bull, zir distorted voice growing low and rumbly.

"I'm afraid I don't know what you're talking about."

"You're wearing my favorite mistress's favorite mask," said the bull, savoring the repetition. "Let's have it back, eh?"

Her stomach turned as she said, "Bill Scar."

He grinned as he clapped a hand to her shoulder. "Did you think I wouldn't have friends on the station who could lend me a few masks? A way to get back?"

She brushed his hand away, looked him in the eyes, and said,

"This place has more defenses than most military bases. Try something and get roasted."

The bull regarded her for a moment, rubbing his bare skin where she'd touched him. "Oh, I will, bunny rabbit. Watch your back."

Then he walked away to join his friends. She tapped her comm. "Bill Scar is on the station."

Orna hadn't spoken a word since they arrived, and Nilah worried about what was going on in her head.

They crowded into the cramped viewing gallery of the *Scuzzbucket* as Armin cued up the video of Vraba's conversation. He quickly located the sync point, and all three videos began playing at the same time.

"I hate these masks," grumbled the first mate. "Impossible to read their damned lips."

Nilah sighed. "So it was a bust?"

"Of course not," Armin said. "I just need to train the model."

He riffled through the Link, bringing up a dozen white papers on surveillance and analysis of distorted imagery, his eyes flickering over them. Since the masks all used the same vocal puppet pinning algorithm, he could get data from recording the crew talking. He lined everyone up in their masks and had them make weird faces and say nonsense lines until he was satisfied.

"Okay," he said, interrupting their third chorus of *The azure zebra fights fragrant granite*. "Let's see what we can see."

They turned their attention to the projection, where the three angles interwove to create a rough, three-dimensional space. It had a couple of holes in it, but they could make out most of the action.

"I know why you came here, Mister Vraba," the reindeer said in a computerized voice, its intonation flat. Apparently, Armin's model couldn't suss out tone, only content. "I already heard about what happened to Durand."

"Good. Then you have the index ready for me?" asked the crow.

"You do understand how I make my living, right?" replied the reindeer.

Boots pointed to the reindeer. "That's got to be Stetson, then. Who else is going to be talking about an index?"

Armin sighed and paused playback. "I thought that much was obvious. Can we please get back to it?"

"Sorry, sir," said Boots, and Armin gestured for the playback to continue.

"You drink from a cup and wave your hands around," countered Izak Vraba. "Show me to your room and turn over the index."

The reindeer shook his head. "Not happening. It's safe with me."

"You've misspoken."

"Have I?" asked the reindeer. "See, friend, only a small portion of my cash comes from the signing commission. Most of it is licensing fees, which you pay to me for keeping your precious index. You might be one of the most powerful men in the galaxy, but you can't touch me here, which means that those losers from the *Capricious* can't, either. Hell, I've even got a curse on one of them."

"Guess again, punk," muttered Boots.

"I won't ask another time," said the crow.

The reindeer shrugged. "So don't. Grab yourself some drinks and pills and have a nice vacation. But if you think I'm handing you the most lucrative index in my collection, you can go suck a comet."

Cordell snorted.

The crow cocked his head, the edges of his beak pulling into a cartoonish frown. "In time, you'll come to regret your mistake."

"Will I?" asked the reindeer. "You hire independent contractors, you get independent thinkers. Sorry I'm not more like your stooges over there. You're not going to blow the station. You're not going to attack me. That, goodly Mister Vraba, is what we call 'game over.' Have a nice day, will you?"

"Our organization will brook no insubordination from the likes of you."

The reindeer mocked the crow's delivery of a threat, then said, "Go back to your ship, and make sure the money keeps coming in, or I'll burn the index and release all of your people from the contract."

"If you did that, I'd swat the Masquerade from the sky like so much stardust."

"Stop posturing," the reindeer said. "I've got other things to do, so get out of my face."

The crow shook with anger, then smoothed down his feathers. "We'll buy the index from you for the remainder of your contract."

The reindeer nodded. "There's a win-win if ever I heard one. There was no reason to get all dark and threatening. Besides, I've got dozens of other contracts going through you—all of which would end if you tried something. Why ruin a beautiful friendship?"

The crow folded its arms, and the illusory wings clipped through one another. "You should count yourself lucky."

"Smart. Never lucky. You bring me the closeout fee, here in the Promenade, in two cycles...and I'll give you the index."

The parties took off and the conversation ended. Mercifully, Armin cut the feed before Bill appeared. Nilah didn't want to imagine the effect it'd have on Orna.

Cordell sucked his teeth. "Nice to know we're not the only ones in the galaxy who can talk back to those cats."

"Please don't compare us to that traitor piece of crap, sir," sighed Boots. "It's bad enough having to hear him again."

"Duly noted," he said. "This mission is getting way too complicated with Giles, Vraba, and Scarett all on the station."

"What's complicated, sir?" asked Orna. "Kill two, capture one. They're making it easy when they show up like this."

Cordell crooked an eyebrow. "Miss Sokol, I appreciate your enthusiasm, but you know that every mission dimension adds risk. This is bordering on unacceptable."

"You've told me about plenty of unacceptable sorties, Cap," she countered. "You took those odds and made them work."

Cordell's eyes were the calm before a supernova. "Because I was ordered to, Sokol. When I'm in charge, I pick the odds. Got any other tips on how to captain a ship?"

Orna pursed her lips but said nothing in return. Nilah swallowed and raised her hand, and Cordell turned his cool gaze on her. That marked the first time he ever looked at her like that, and it gave Nilah a few extra kinks in her guts. In fact, no one had ever given her such sternness—not her father, not Claire, not the prime minister.

"Captain..." Nilah began, "I know you may think I'm taking her side because, um, we're together, but I really do think she's right."

The look on Orna's face soothed Nilah's quivering heart, and she took another breath.

"In racing, we have rules, but the teams do anything they can for an advantage. And they have this strategy group, and my old boss was on it so she could lobby for rules changes. That's done by a quorum of—"

Armin gave her a polite fast forward motion. "Skip to the point, Miss Brio."

She caught herself before she could wring her hands, forcing her posture upright. "Um, yes, well, when you change the rules, many teams are too slow to respond, and it costs them the title."

Cordell leaned forward in his chair, resting his elbows on his knees. "I'm not sure I take your point."

"The laws of the Masquerade are strict," said Nilah, "and they're probably well-enforced. But if we could change them, even for a few minutes, we'd be the only ones with the new rules set. We could kill another god, grab the index—"

"And the Chalice of Hana," Boots added.

"Right. That, too. Why not?" Nilah looked to Cordell, wondering how he'd take her plan. It wasn't direct insubordination to side with her fiancée, but it didn't look great.

"Okay," he said. "How do we change the rules?"

"Orna and I hit their data center and hack it apart," Nilah said. "That'll take down the dispersers and autoturrets. It'll be their most-guarded area, though."

"And we can only field four combatants," Cordell pointed out.

"Five, sir," said Orna, tapping her circlet.

The captain gave her a skeptical look. "They're not going to let Charger in there."

The quartermaster nodded to the door. "About that..."

A two-meter-tall bipedal black wolf came ducking through the door, and the assembled crew shot to their feet in surprise. Its animal eyes glowed with the expressive green light of Charger's lenses. The sight of the robot in resplendent costume stole Nilah's breath away.

"The mask fits anyone with a head and a body, sir," said Orna. "It doesn't care if you're alive or not. So we could take the data center with the right mix of two others."

"I'm obviously one of the two," said Nilah.

"And I'm the other," said Aisha. "You need a good slinger."

Cordell popped open his case and put an unlit cigarette in his mouth. "Going in there hot, eh? That'll inflict significant casualties."

Boots shrugged. "Who cares, sir? These people are thieves. They steal lives and turn them into spike thralls. How is that any different than Witts?"

Only the gentle white noise of the lagging climate system filled the hush that followed. Nilah shifted uncomfortably in her seat, taking stock of the others. Jeannie and Alister totally agreed. The Jans seemed fine with the assault. Boots was obviously in favor, and Orna was nothing if not eager. The executive staff, on the other hand, weren't so keen.

Cordell cleared his throat. "Do we really want to treat everyone on the Masquerade payroll as an enemy combatant?"

"That puts us at war with them," said Armin.

"And I'm completely fine with that," said Boots, and the rest of the crew nodded their assent. "Some of these people need shooting."

The captain nodded. "So your suggestion is: shut down the data center, then whack Vraba and kidnap Giles...except one person would be on the hook to do the assassinate-kidnap part. If Miss Brio, Miss Sokol, and Missus Jan have a mask, that leaves one for the rest of us. I don't know about you, but I don't think anyone on this crew is up to that task."

Nilah gestured to the table running along one edge of the room, where they'd put the five neural spikes they took out of Bill's thralls. "I've been thinking about that, too. The easiest way to get everyone else into the station is as thralls."

Murmurs went up and she held up her hands to silence everyone. "The scanners on board the Masquerade are looking for two things: the spike codes and higher-function brain activity. We've got the codes right here. Captain Lamarr could wear the mask, and Boots, Malik, and the twins could be armed backup. Mister Vandevere would stay on the *Scuzzbucket* and keep him hot for a jump."

"And the brain scanners? If you've got a way to stop someone from thinking, I'd love to hear it," said Cordell.

Malik smiled at Nilah, recognition in his eyes. "She does."

"There's a sodding good trick that Mister Jan taught me back on Carré," Nilah said. "We flatten out."

"We can be at that index deal, Captain," Boots urged. "All of us."

Around the room, each of the crew members endorsed the plan until it came to Armin.

"I'll have to run simulations on all known brain-wave scanners against 'flattening out.' If we're wrong, the Masquerade will automatically gun you down at the docking bay exit."

Cordell licked his lips. "Then you've got under two cycles, Mister Vandevere. Let's ice these chumps."

Nilah and Orna spent the next cycle inside their quarters, prepping the neural spikes. It was a tricky task, since they needed the transponders the most, and those were housed inside the part that penetrated the brain. If they decrypted the data shards, they could write the codes onto new hardware, but they didn't have time to redesign a chipset. Worse, the *Scuzzbucket* wasn't exactly an engineer's dream workbench.

Before long, they'd littered the floor with bits of wire housing, shards of shaved data crystal, and globs of solder. The Backstrom Ellis designer tables where they worked quickly transformed from priceless antiques to scratched-up junk, pockmarked with scorches. It was, as Armin would put it, a suboptimal situation.

Still, every time Orna finished a section and handed it to Nilah for assembly, Nilah could sense her fiancée's art in the design. The quartermaster had a primal simplicity to her work that bordered on elegant. Most mechanists couldn't stand to work together, constantly stepping on one another's toes, but she fit together with Orna like a nut to a bolt.

Orna handed Nilah the fourth spike look-alike, and Nilah admired her handiwork. It looked like the silver hexagonal head of a neural spike, but they'd crammed the transponder inside so they could glue it to the surface of someone's neck. When Nilah took it, Orna's fingers closed around hers, and the quartermaster looked her in the eye.

424

"I never say it first," said Orna, "and I'm sorry."

Nilah smiled gently, trying to wash away the strange frown on Orna's face. "Say what?"

"I love you. I really, really do. I don't deserve you."

"Of course you do, darling. You're a sodding hero, and everyone knows it. What's wrong?"

Orna looked away. "You didn't have to back my plan to the captain last night. I know I said you always run off on your own, but...I didn't mean that you had to, like, endorse everything I do."

Nilah laughed, and her exhaustion amplified it a bit louder than she intended. "I backed you up because you were right, love."

"You promise?"

Nilah scooted her chair down the table to be right next to Orna and snaked her arm around her waist. Then she leaned in and kissed Orna's bare shoulder, just below the strap of her tank top. Then, she worked her way up Orna's neck, and the skin around her white scars went pink.

"I'm sorry you have to deal with my...with my past," said Orna. "I don't know why you want to marry someone like me."

Nilah lightly bit the skin just above her collarbone. "Have you *seen* you? You know you have a following on the Link, right?"

"Stop. I'm being serious."

"So am I. You're so brave, and I admire everything about you."

The quartermaster smirked and shook her head. "I think soldering gets you riled up."

"Not really. It's engine timing calibration that makes me want to tear off your clothes," she whispered into Orna's ear, then leaned back and stared into her eyes. "I just want you to know how much I want you all the time."

Orna chuckled. "You'll just have to wait until we're done."

"I don't mean like that," Nilah said. "I mean today. Tomorrow. In a hundred years. If I'm breathing, I want you."

Orna reached over her and wrapped her arm around Nilah's shoulders, and her heart stilled. Nilah rested her head against Orna's chest, pressing her ear to her skin and listening for her pulse.

"I have so many good memories of you," said Nilah. "When I saw you the first time."

Orna snorted. "You mean when I choked you?"

Nilah cleared her throat. "There was a certain fun in, uh... well... it might be something to try again later, love. But not just that. Every moment of this year is full of you. We cried together. We fought together—"

"I'm from a dead world, but..." Orna nodded. "You've become my home."

"You know," said Nilah, kissing her once more, her fingers traveling over Orna's arms. "We haven't promised these to the captain for another two hours. We've been working so hard. Perhaps we could take a little nap."

The quartermaster laughed and glanced back to the bed. "After all, we might die tomorrow."

Nilah, Orna, and Aisha gathered at the docking portal with Cordell and Armin. The quartermaster had already climbed into Charger, and Nilah couldn't help but do a double take every time she saw the giant wolf. Aisha pulled on the bear mask, which fit her poorly compared to Boots. Slight and skinny did the costume little justice.

"Zero hour," said the captain, clapping Nilah on the shoulder. "If this plan isn't going to work, now is your last chance to back out."

"Uncharacteristically noncommittal of you, Captain," Nilah replied.

"You're supposed to give us an inspirational speech, sir," Aisha added.

"This isn't the *Harrow*," said Cordell. "We're on offense now, and we can leave if we choose. I just want to hear you say you've got this."

Nilah smirked. "You know what? Next week, when we hand over the names of every corporation funding Bastion's construction, I want you to turn to me and say, 'Good plan, Miss Brio.'"

"That's the spirit," Cordell said as she donned her rabbit mask.

"You're to begin your assault on our cue," said Armin. "We want the meeting to be ongoing when you fight, since you'll almost certainly sound some alarms. Will you be able to cut the power to the defense grid?"

Aisha shrugged. "Not my department, but I'll shoot some people."

"Mister Vandevere," Nilah said, "it'll probably be more delicate than that. Simply cutting the power will likely trigger a defensive response."

Armin narrowed his eyes. "So you're going to slice apart one of the most sophisticated security systems in the galaxy faster than you did the *Harrow*?"

"We don't have to hack the main computer," said Orna. "We just have to get control of one of the stupid security thralls. Slavery is their biggest security hole, and we're going to breach the hell out of it."

"Yes. Perhaps leave the hacking to us, sir?" Nilah added.

Armin nodded in defeat. "As you wish. God speed you."

"Keep the ship hot for us," said Aisha. "I'll be glad to get off this hulk."

They said their goodbyes, cycled the airlock, and stepped into the docking bay. Nilah's eyes traveled to Vraba's marauder, flanked on all sides by his soldiers. They caught a couple of confused looks at Charger's lupine form, but no alarms went up.

They stepped on a platform and swept down the Central

Promenade, trees passing soundlessly below. Within seconds, they'd be in position.

"Are you ready?" whispered Orna as the platform slowed its descent toward the guard station.

Nilah looked through the ample windows at the armed spike thralls patrolling the interior. "Is anyone ever ready to do something so foolish?"

"I am," said Aisha. "Let's kill another god."

Chapter Twenty

Standoff

The spike-alike was cold against Boots's neck, and the skin glue they used stank like a cross between denatured alcohol and burnt rubber. It was supposed to be used for sealing cuts, but Malik swore it would hold the small device.

They were working in Boots's shared quarters, and they'd already managed to drip chemicals and makeup all over the nice rugs.

"Hold still. I have to set it," said the doctor as he spritzed a frosty liquid onto her neck that ran down the back of her shirt.

She ducked away, slapping at the middle of her back. "Cripes! Come on, Doc!"

"You'll live."

"Oh, is that your medical opinion?"

Cordell rounded the corner with the twins in tow. "Are you complaining again, Boots?"

"In my defense, sir, it was like having a corpse run its finger down my spine." She dodged away as Malik went to spray her again.

"I'll run my boot up your ass if you don't let the doc do his job."

"If it makes you feel better," said Malik, "I'll let you attach mine."

"Ten minutes to mission start," Armin's voice came over the

intercom. "I'm getting remote feeds from three of the four masks. Captain, can you check in?"

"Copy," said Cordell, pulling on the eagle mask. Feathers flowed down his shoulders into a cape, and he cracked his neck. "Are you seeing what I'm seeing?"

"I'm seeing Boots," said Armin.

"Yeah," said Cordell. "I'll try to look at something prettier. Maybe I could find a mirror."

"Har har," said Boots, wincing as the last of the cold-set fluid managed to trickle down her back, past her shirt, straight into her pants.

Once Malik attached the spike-alikes to the twins, he was true to his word, letting Boots spritz him to her heart's content. Unfortunately, the doctor's stoicism carried the day, and he wasn't nearly as fun to torture. When they were all suited up and ready, Cordell inspected his troops.

"Today, we're going to get up close and personal with a god," he said. "When we get the signal, I want you to fill Vraba up with so much slinger fire that his own mother wouldn't recognize him. The index takes priority next. Then we're going to grab Giles, head to his quarters, and get the Chalice of Hana. Understood?"

"There's no chance this flattening is going to get dispersed, right?" asked Boots.

"It's a passive spell," answered Malik. "Just like your curse was. Can't disperse something inside you."

"Enough gabbling," said Cordell. "Y'all ready to be legends again?"

"Yes, sir!" came the unified chorus.

The eagle gave them an approving nod. "Sweet. Mister Jan, do your thing."

Malik gestured for Boots and the twins to gather around him. "Stare into the glyph, if you please."

His veins bulging with strain, Malik carved out a one-meter purple glyph, which began to turn like a vortex. Boots watched as each smoky ligature stretched and twisted, forming layers of laminar flow. She found herself transfixed by the interplay of skeins of magic, sparkling and shifting before her eyes. The tension in her gut dissipated, and she let out a long breath.

It would be okay. Everything was going according to plan.

All her concerns faded away, and the knots in her brain began to untangle. The room swelled before her, gently swaying in her vision. The spell filtered through her nervous system like soothing medicine, relaxing every aggravated muscle. The load upon her shoulders lightened; she could almost drift away on the breeze if she wished.

The room's lights smeared and wavered as she shook her head to and fro. She giggled a little, making them dance before her.

"Are they under?" asked Cordell.

She was walking. The eagle said to follow him.

You're my only wing, so you'd better stay on this bird.

The first time he'd said that to her, explosions pumped the air like a bass beat. Spells slammed their tiny outpost, and the *Capricious* took off in pursuit of the attackers. She'd hated him then.

Hated. Then loved. Then hated. Then loved again.

A long forest stretched before Boots. The eagle took her soaring through the trees. They passed a lake. Did the eagle want fish? This place had a fish, and his name was the concierge. He was annoying. Maybe they could eat him. Bears and eagles both ate fish, and she was a bear.

Or was she a wing? Wasn't someone else the bear now?

Somewhere, on another world, she lay dormant and broken, her canopy shattered, her eyes glazed over. Was it Clarkesfall? No. She'd been shattered there, but her body rested in the docks of Harvest. The mechanics were putting her back together, and while they did, her spirit traveled the galaxy to this horrid place.

So many other animals filled this forest: squirrels, sparrows, beavers, ducks, and even the goldfish.

"Eat the fish, eagle," Boots said, pointing to the goldfish from her perch.

The eagle pressed his wing tips to her lips and whispered, "Please shut the hell up," because he was a wise bird. And then they were landing, steadily descending toward a much larger prey. With the flesh of the reindeer, they would feast for many cycles. All they had to do was kill a crow. It was a simple task for an eagle, but what did she know? She was only a wing.

They'd reached a clearing where other animals stood vigil in totemic silence. Many of the animals turned to them, but the crow and the reindeer continued talking.

The eagle opened his beak to speak once more, his voice soft and full of wisdom.

He said, so quietly as to be profound, "The eagle has landed. We're in position."

"Copy," said god. Or was he a prince? They were all royalty in the heavens.

"Excuse me!" called the eagle in his vast knowledge. His voice was so sonorous, so musical that all the other animals in the clearing perked up at the sound. "Before you make that trade, I have something you might want."

"And what might that be?" called the crow.

And Boots nearly shouted, "You, Crow! We want your meat!" But she didn't, because she was only a wing, and wings had no mouths.

When the eagle spoke again, it didn't sound quite right. "I've got the people who've been making trouble for you all along, Lord Vraba. These are crew members from the *Capricious*."

"Team Wolf," Armin said in their comms, "Eagle is in play. Execute mission."

"I'll take the lobby disperser. Bear, get the autoturret when I do," said Orna, and Nilah jumped onto her back, scrabbling for handholds under the illusory wolf cloak.

"Let's go!" Nilah shouted, and Charger launched on all fours underneath her.

The lobby doors came up on them fast, and Nilah ducked close to Charger's back plates to avoid crashing safety glass. They smashed into the clean, white foyer of the guard station, and Nilah tossed down a portable shield around them, absorbing the initial volley of autoturret fire.

The walls went bloodred with alarm lights as spells splashed against her shield. The energy of the disperser began to eat into the defense, sending hairline cracks across its luminescent blue surface. Thralls leapt from their stations, drawing slingers and firing upon them with merciless impassiveness.

"Get the disperser!" Nilah shouted over the cacophony, and Charger leapt into the air, latching onto the antimagic device like a tiger.

Charger ripped the housing off the wall and hurled it into the distant autoturret, crushing both into molten slag. When the bot hit the ground, it took a glancing shot from one of the thralls. Before the thrall could fire again, however, a lancer round from outside hollowed out his head.

"The turret was supposed to be mine," called Aisha.

The pilot strode into the room, slinger barrel hot, taking out thrall after thrall, even before Nilah could close ranks with them. Aisha rarely had occasion to cast a glyph in front of Nilah, but she could snap them out almost in the blink of an eye; they didn't have to be large to aim a pistol.

Nilah leapt the front desk into a pair of thralls who'd taken cover to reload. She landed a savage kick across the first's face before hooking the other in her elbow. With a spin, Nilah hurled the woman's head into the corner of the desk. The thrall convulsed, sliding to the floor with a smear of blood.

Only one thrall remained upright after their grim work, and he staggered forward with his jaw hanging at an awkward angle. Nilah traced her glyph and readied to hack his spike with a quick combo of punches and—

Aisha shot him, too.

"What did you do?" Nilah shouted.

The bear's eyebrow twitched, Aisha's annoyance showing through. "There are two left, Rabbit."

Nilah spun to see Charger soaked in blood as it dropped two bodies.

"Did you hack the guy behind the desk?" asked Orna.

Nilah jerked a thumb at Aisha. "Bear shot him."

Their comms chimed as Armin said, "Focus, Team Wolf. If the thralls are down, cut your way in."

Charger snapped out the fusion blade, blinding Nilah in the stark white room.

Her eyes adjusted as Charger closed the gap to the interior door and took a slash. The sword bounced harmlessly off the wall, leaving no damage save for a few smoky streaks.

Oh, no.

Orna took another swipe as the lockdown alarms blared. The lobby blast shutters slammed down behind them, and the room began to flood with gas. Nilah took as deep a breath as she could and held it, gesturing for Aisha to do the same.

"Hold on," said Orna. "Never liked this sword, anyway."

Charger pulled out the eidolon crystal they'd found in Bill Scar's quarters, now in its hyperbattery induction housing. When Orna attached it to the sword, heat washed from the blade like a blinding star. Nilah would've screamed if it weren't for the copious amounts of neurotoxin filling the lobby.

Charger made a trio of white-hot slices through the lobby door and kicked it into the corridor beyond, metal edges dripping syrupy orange. The fusion blade turned to ash, and Orna ejected the hyperbattery cable from the spent sword handle, where it spooled away.

Slinger bolts lanced out from the opening as thralls fired from cover. Team Wolf couldn't charge inside without taking too much fire.

Charger threw down the second expendable shield, and Orna bellowed, "Bear! Let's go!"

Aisha forced the opposition heads down with her pinpoint shots, but she couldn't hit everyone at once. With clean air, she was able to shout, "Rabbit! Get them out of cover!"

Nilah sprinted down the hallway toward the nearest collapsible barricade. When their assault had stuttered, it gave the guards inside time to erect defenses. Nilah leapt the first barricade to find a furious thrall completing a poison glyph. Not giving him a chance to lay his hands on her, Nilah pounded his gut with her boot, sending him stumbling into the open.

Aisha's shot took the top of his head off, and his spell popped. Nilah raised her hand before peeking over the cover to find Aisha advancing on her position.

"Next!" called the pilot.

Zigzagging down the hallway, Nilah made her way toward the next target. Her heart raced with each step in the open. She'd almost reached the second mobile barricade when a metallic chittering filled her ears—something she hadn't heard in over a year—springflies.

The mechanical beasts rounded the corner and leapt for Nilah's face, their scything arms stretched wide in all directions. There was no time to cast her mechanist's mark. There was scarcely time to blink.

Aisha's slinger bolt whizzed by Nilah's head, and the closest springfly exploded in a comet of shrapnel, bits of metal digging into Nilah's skin. It knocked the others off course, and she had just enough time to slide to avoid having her head lopped off.

Charger pounded into the melee, its AI-calibrated manipulators snatching the bots out of midair in graceful sweeps. It smashed the bots against walls and into each other, their thin blades tinking harmlessly off regraded steel plates. Aisha blasted the ones that managed to crawl onto Charger's back to take a swipe at sensitive electronics.

At the far end of the corridor, the thralls took advantage of the distraction to mount a heavy slinger on a tripod. Nilah would never reach the emplacement in time and grabbed her slinger to take a few shots. A blue shield descended over the tripod, and her bolts bounced harmlessly off.

"Get out of the way, Rabbit," grumbled Orna, scraping off the last springfly like a barnacle. She jammed the hyperbattery cable into Charger's legs, and the bot made a noise like a race car in top gear. Its lenses went white, and it sunk into a crouch.

Nilah flattened against the deck as Charger launched shoulder-first, slamming through the series of barricades. Thralls, guns, and duraplast were scattered through the hall, but Orna smashed against the emplacement shield without penetrating it in the slightest. She reared back and gave it a supercharged kick, and this time it tore like gelatin. With the shield down, the bot made short work of the tripod crew.

Crawling over to the nearest downed thrall, Nilah checked his pulse—still alive. She shoved him onto his stomach and traced her mechanist's glyph, psychically linking with the neural spike. Security was heavier on this one than Bill's, but she could power through it with little difficulty.

When the thrall's eyes flickered open, he smiled at her, turning

Nilah's stomach. He'd gone from murderous to servile, and she knew he probably wanted neither.

"Good day, mistress. How can I be of ser—"

"Give me the codes to shut down the dispersers and autoturrets," she ordered.

"Uh, folks," called Orna, peering through the door at the end of the hallway. She ejected the hyperbattery cable from Charger's legs, which had begun to seize up from overloading.

"I'm afraid that's not possible," said the thrall, cocking his head. "Those must run in perpetuity."

Nilah shook him by the collar. "I know the sodding directive! How do I shut them down?"

"The Masquerade data grid is a human-in-the-loop system," said the thrall. "So there's only one way to shut it down."

She released him, stepping back. He climbed to his feet, limping. When she looked down, she saw his ankle turned at a strange angle, though the smile never faded from his face.

"What's going on?" Aisha said as she approached, checking her clip. "We've got to keep going!"

"Damn it, Rabbit and Bear, get the hell over here!" said Orna, stepping down out of Charger's exoskeleton.

The bot made a few sad noises and pointed to its legs.

"I know, I know," Orna sighed, unholstering her slinger. "Look, I'm sorry, but we needed the speed. Just walk on your hands, and I'll fix you later."

Nilah and Aisha jogged to the end of the hall, stepping over thralls and shattered barricades. When they reached the opening to the data center, they stopped dead. The overwhelming stink of body odor and disinfectant washed over them.

"Team Wolf," said Armin, "your signal is degrading. I can't make out what you're seeing."

Row upon row of thralls sat wired into consoles, tapping away at projections. Goggles covered their eyes, and bedsores covered much of the rest of them. Nilah tried to make a quick count, but there had to be over a thousand of them locked inside the arched structure.

"It's a . . ." Nilah breathed. "It's horrible, sir."

Nilah's thrall came limping up to her, his ankle making a chilling crackle noise. Sweat coated his brow, and his skin was ashen. "Welcome to the Hive. This is our distributed, human-in-the-loop logistics, navigation, and defense center. A single servant is enough to run the entire defense grid, so even if one dies—"

"The others can take their place," Orna finished.

"We're running out of time," said Armin. "The dialogue isn't going well, and Eagle Team won't stay flat forever. Shut it down."

All those innocent people sitting helpless before Nilah. Even if she wanted to put her slinger to each of their faces, she'd be slaughtering them for hours.

"Sir, it's not a normal data center," said Aisha, her knuckles going white around the butt of her slinger. "They're thralls. Hundreds of thralls."

Static came over the line as Armin's next message broke up. Of course the Hive would be comm-shielded.

"They're already dead," said Orna, quietly. "They were killed when the spikes went in. I know I've been a monster in the past, but—"

"It's okay," said Nilah. "We have to do this."

"If you attack any of them," said Nilah's thrall, "they'll all wake up and fight back with any spells they have."

Even if they didn't cast, the team's meager slingers wouldn't be enough to fight off a barrage of bodies. Nilah cursed and snatched the hyperbattery from Charger's utility belt. Orna took one look at her and knew exactly what her plan was.

Orna pulled out a snapwire kit and handed it to Nilah. "Oh, man, the captain is going to be pissed when he finds out what you did with the power source for his future jump drive."

"Give me a C-PROM, too," said Nilah, pulling a single round out of her slinger mag. "I need to set a timer." She peeled the snapwire contacts and placed them against the glowing head of the bullet, then connected the tiny controller chip.

"Why? What's going on?" asked Aisha.

Within seconds, Nilah had rigged up the slinger round in series to the pure crystal of the hyperbattery. The device began to heat up in her hands as the feedback loop caused a runaway reaction. She traced her mechanist's mark and psychically connected the C-PROM, writing a few lines of primitive code—just enough to make a detonator.

"Remember that super-expensive eidolon crystal we found in Bill Scar's quarters?" Nilah gave Aisha a pained look. "We're going to use it as a bomb."

Boots dreamed of a reindeer, standing before her and inspecting her like a piece of butchered meat. He gently reached toward her face, though his hands were human.

"Damn, girl," he said, in the cadence of her most-hated enemy, Stetson Giles. His murderous grin flashed through Boots's mind: the moment he gunned down Gemma. "That bad attitude finally caught up with you, didn't it?"

A musical voice echoed in her empty head, and everyone looked to the heavens; another god was speaking. *Code black. All security personnel, code black.*

"Their minds still contain all of the information you require," said the eagle, inclining his head to look down his beak at the crow. "I'll sell them for a million argents apiece."

"How very convenient that you should bring them to me," said the crow, "when they've been a thorn in my side. Do you think I'm stupid, Captain Lamarr?"

Stetson straightened up and took a short step backward. "I don't know how you got here, Boots," he whispered, "but you can't touch me. And even if you could—"

A low rumble filled the station. Was it the thunderous anger mounting in her flattened mind?

As if in answer, the Central Promenade went bloodred and klaxons rang out. A gentle voice said, *"Emergency: All celebrants report to your quarters. Repeat—"*

Then the eagle took a long slide and slapped the hell out of Boots. Her dulled senses returned and the world shifted into perfect focus. She wasn't dreaming; Stetson Giles stood before her, the grin fading from his face.

"Guess again, bastard," she growled, snapping out the hidden blade in her metal arm. She leapt toward him and jammed it into his gut as far as it would go. The air rushed from his lungs and she shoved him backward into the deck.

Slinger fire lit the Promenade as Cordell opened up on the crow, putting five shots into its head and chest. The corvid went down in a spray of blood, and when the last shot hit the center of its mask, the gem inside exploded into glittering pink mist, taking most of its face.

Boots slapped Jeannie, instantly awakening Alister, who was linked to her mind. He, in turn, smacked Malik, and all of them focused fire on the downed crow, not taking any chances. A strange calm followed as the enemy guards took in what had just happened.

Then a huge black glyph erupted from the weasel in the back, smashing into the air like a hammer strike. A horrible wail, a symphony of fury, filled the Promenade. Boots had heard that song before in the Special Branch Archives.

The crow was a decoy.

Cordell jumped out in front as the shadows rose around them, hammering his shield with bladed tendrils. Blackness encapsulated them, reaching out, slicing at their bodies, and it took everything Boots had to jump out of the way. To flee outside his shield was to die in the many-bladed night.

Against Mother, they'd had a trick up their sleeve—grenades filled with indolence gas. Against the old prime minister, they'd had a sound containment strategy, and the greatest sharpshooter they could've acquired. Their strategies had hinged on rock-solid planning around keystone moments—just like with Izak Vraba. However, the keystone of this plan had just crumbled, and hungry magic swirled through the Promenade, rising like a tide to devour them all. Slinger bolts impotently pinged across the slick black surface of Vraba's spell, and Boots could just barely make out the weasel's smile before he disappeared in a swirl of shadows. Without intervention against the unopposed magic of a God of the *Harrow*, they'd be skewered in seconds.

Good thing Boots had brought a backup plan.

She pulled the bolt on her arm and locked the firing pin for her ship-to-ship slinger round.

"Suck on this," she breathed, taking aim at Vraba.

The flash blinded her. The boom deafened her. But through it all came the sharp pain of her arm turning to hot shrapnel. Bits of metal sliced her face and chest.

The shock wave tossed all of them from their feet, and she went sprawling across her back, then her shoulder, then her neck. Each individual cobblestone of the Promenade's walkway tore at her body. When she finally skidded to a halt, the world swam in her periphery, and blood leaked from her brow into her eyes.

"Captain!" she cried out, but she couldn't hear her own voice over the ringing. Through the blur, she tried to make sense of the raging inferno she'd caused. It was all heat and light, hungry flames coming for her in the dusky red light.

All except an inky spot, a black sphere with a ragged edge.

The orb unfolded, revealing Vraba, his illusory weasel mask half blown away. When her eyes adjusted, she could make out the rivulets of blood running from his furious face, his flowing black hair, and a gaping wound where his shoulder should've been.

She'd missed.

The god let out a primal scream of anguish, and the shadows leapt to stanch the bleeding, working their way into his shoulder like snakes. He centered up for another attack as howling wind replaced her deafness. The air whipped at them, and she realized in horror that she'd caused a hull breach.

Stetson lay on the ground, clutching his gut, a data crystal at his side. He reached out with shaking fingers and pulled it under himself, blood spilling out around the stag-head disguise's mouth. Hull sealing spells rolled from their emergency emplacements, popping out of hidden recesses in the walls to seal the breach. The roar became a high-pitched whine, then went silent.

Cordell rolled onto his back and ripped off the eagle mask, cramming it into his pocket with a groan. The twins were already helping Malik to his feet, and he clutched his side, trying to hold his guts in. Vraba's guards had been blown to pieces in the exchange.

The thousand wails of the shadow song harmonized into the words, "You die today." Night spread around Vraba into the form of a colossal spider, each foot tipped with a hammer. The god screamed, suspended at the center of the creature like a foul heart consumed with rage. He made no illusions of his hatred—he wanted to look them in the eyes as he crushed the life from them.

Apparently, losing his arm had pissed him off pretty good, so at least he and Boots understood each other.

The spider raised its forelegs above itself, preparing to smash Cordell with a pair of mallets. Boots clambered to her feet as Cordell staggered to his. He was so dazed, she doubted he'd see the end coming. And so she did something she never would've imagined two years ago—she barreled straight for him on unsteady legs.

Boots tackled Cordell out of the way as the hammers came down, shattering the floor of the Promenade. Stone slabs came loose like puzzle pieces, battering the pair as they rolled clear of the blow. Hundreds of spikes lanced out for her, and Cordell traced his glyph, blocking them out with a weak shield.

Other blades of darkness circled around the back of them, cutting off their escape routes, and bright cracks formed in their blue energy field. Her panicked eyes met his, and through Cordell's concentration, she could almost read his thoughts.

This is it, Bootsie. We tried.

She dropped her slinger and took his hand as the first tendril wound through the shield and held it tight. The shadow sprouted a scalpel and reared back to strike at Cordell's neck. When the shield went down, they'd both be skewered.

A bright bolt sailed through the air, striking Vraba in the stomach, and the shadows recoiled, giving them some air. Boots traced its path back to Jeannie, teeth bared and screaming as she fired again and again.

A wall of night spilled over Vraba's exposed form, blocking the rest of her shots. The slinger spells splashed against it, tiny pops of lethal fire rendered harmless.

"Get back to the ship!" Jeannie roared to her brother, who bore Malik over his shoulder. "Go now!"

A lash of darkness swept toward Jeannie, and she barely dodged out of the way, but she didn't retreat. She stood her ground, emptying her clip into black space around Vraba.

The shadow spider lumbered toward her, snapping down trees

and crushing park benches. It made no attempts to dodge her fire, barreling through the barrage toward Jeannie's tiny body.

But she stood her ground and reloaded once more.

Boots snatched up her slinger from the ground and sprinted for the beast's backside, trying to get a good angle, hurdling over ruined furnishings and downed revelers.

Then she spied the chink in Vraba's armor—he'd only covered the front of his body. She took careful aim with her shaking arm at the back of his head and gritted her teeth. One half of her body was on fire from the recoil of her slinger round, the other half was a wobbly mess.

But she had to fire.

The spell lanced out and splashed against the inside of Vraba's bubble, striking just shy of his head. A spray of flame blinded him, and he wheeled on her, smashing the mezzanine walkways with a shower of sparks. One of the god's eyes was closed, his face burned, but he still carried on.

She scarcely noticed his good eye dart toward something behind her, and when his hammers came rushing in her direction, they were shattered by disperser bolts. Boots turned to see an approaching set of platforms, armed to the teeth with angry thralls, portable dispersers, and autoslingers. So the Masquerade had more defenses after all.

"Eagle team, status!" called Armin.

"Vraba is tearing up the Central Promenade!" Boots shouted into her comm. "He's turned into some kind of huge spider thing!"

"Damn it! Just hold on!"

"What the hell does—" But she had to duck out of the way of a falling strut.

Vraba wrapped himself in a cocoon of thick, liquid darkness as the dispersers zapped impotently at the core of his spell. More security forces swarmed from the other side, and a hail of fire illuminated both sides of him.

Boots tapped her comm with her slinger hand. "We've got wounded, but Vraba is dead to rights. Only a matter of time before—"

The black bubble swelled to twice its size, sucking in nearby atmosphere with a loud hiss. A pair of sledgehammers rocketed out of the top and bottom of it, wedging against the floor and ceiling of the Promenade. The Masquerade reverberated with a horrible groan as its load-bearing struts began to bend, and Boots was rocked from her feet.

"I'll sift the wreckage for my index," wailed the polyphonic voices, and muscular darkness reinforced the hammers, pressing harder.

Boots tapped her comm again, staggering to her feet. "Prince, he's going to rip apart the station!"

"Copy that. Prince inbound."

And what good would a datamancer be? There could be no running from this. Boots and the others would be swept into hard vacuum, and Vraba could await rescue by his marauder in his perfect cocoon. Boots watched the thralls reload their slingers and redouble their fire, but it would be no use. Again and again came the bass thump of heavy dispersers, targeting Vraba's thick appendages to no avail. The creak of the load-bearing supports became a bone-grating screech, and any second, the vacuum of space would rip them all from this life.

Cordell called to his comrades, his voice breaking with the force of his shout. "Everyone get to the—"

A new noise joined the creaking of the Masquerade's hull—the whine of a high-performance luxury yacht, barreling down the Central Promenade. The sleek archrome form of the *Scuzzbucket* rammed through trees, crosswalks, and security thrall platforms as it blasted toward Vraba's cocoon.

A pair of pincers erupted from the shadows and caught the hardened nose of the ship, stopping it dead in its tracks with a screech. Giant knives spiked into the bridge, shattering the windows and perforating the *Scuzzbucket*'s frame. Still, the blue flames of the yacht's engines roared; its maneuvering thrusters popped with gas to keep it upright.

"Armin!" came Cordell's voice over the comm. "Armin, damn it, what the hell are you doing?"

"I'm bringing the engines to full, Captain," grunted Armin, and the *Scuzzbucket*'s tail flared even brighter.

The thousand voices cried out as the pincers began to give, centimeter by centimeter, shaking as their strength failed them. Then, like a knife slipping between a pair of ribs, the *Scuzzbucket* ripped through Vraba's cocoon, splattering the god across its nose.

The shining yacht lost control, crashing against the wall of the Promenade, grinding Vraba's corpse into nothing more than blood and bad memories.

With the shadows gone, Boots finally got a good look at her comrades on the other side. Cordell was scarcely upright, and the twins fared little better with Malik. She ran to them, even though every bone in her body urged her to lie down and die.

"Armin!" screamed Cordell. "Armin, answer me!"

More klaxons rang out, and the gentle voice of the station said, "*Attention all celebrants, there has been an incident. Primary reactors breached. Containment at thirty-two percent. Please report to your rooms immediately for station escape protocols.*"

Out of the corner of her eye, Boots saw Stetson climb to his feet and drag the mask off his face. Blood ran down his brow into one eye, but he glared at her with the other. She raised her slinger to shoot him, but he turned to hobble away.

If she shot, she'd never find his room, never get the chalice, and if he went to ground, she might not find him again.

"Damn it!" she cried. "Captain, I've got to go after him."

Cordell snatched her wrist as she made to run. "Containment failure! Do understand that? This station is going down, Boots!"

Stetson's betrayal had cast a shadow over every day of her life after the war. He had ruined her, cast her out of her future, and she would take what she was owed. She bored into Cordell with her gaze, a display of insolence she'd never dared in all her days aboard his ship.

"Don't stop me." In the space between explosions, she said, "I need this."

He released her and took a step back. "Good luck to you, Boots. If you can, get back to the apartments for evac. I'm going to get my first mate."

She gave him an Arcan salute, and he returned it. Then she looked to Malik, who was being loaded onto a platform by the twins. "I'm sorry."

The doc said nothing, his breathing too ragged to speak.

Boots turned and ran, following Stetson's trail of blood deeper into the station.

Nilah had expected the small army of thralls greeting her when she emerged from the lobby door. The surprise had come when a grenade landed in the middle of the enemy forces, scattering them to the wind. Automatic slinger fire sawed through the little group from the mezzanine level, cutting down each soldier with bright lances.

Team Wolf had only just managed to get out of the way when the data center blew behind them, sending a gout of flame pouring into the Central Promenade like a volcano eruption. When Nilah got her bearings, she located the source of the automatic fire: a pair of tripod-mounted slingers on the mezzanine, operated by a snake and a goldfinch.

"Orna Sokol!" bellowed a voice from up top, the flame-horned bull emerging into view. "Drop your weapons and raise your hands! Unless you're planning on walking back into that burning guard station, that is."

Another explosion lit the distant Promenade, rumbling through the deck. Nilah craned her neck to see if she could somehow spot Boots and the others through the trees, but there was no way.

The tripod-mounted slingers sprayed the area around them with gunfire, as if to prove a point.

"Hey, Bill," Orna called back, face twisted with hatred.

"You grew up, kiddo," said the bull. "If you weren't so cut up, you'd be a pretty woman."

"That bull mask is a big improvement for you, too," Orna replied.

"If you don't throw away your heaters in three seconds," said Bill, "I'm going to turn that famous girlfriend of yours into a fine red mist. One..."

Nilah tossed her weapon aside, and Orna did the same.

"Two—"

Aisha snapped up her slinger and put a shot right between Bill's eyes—or so Nilah thought. With a bright arc, the flame round bounced off and went straight back the way it came, thunking into Aisha's shoulder. It passed through her with a trail of sparks before splattering against the deck. She fell with a shriek, clutching her smoking wound.

"I told you to drop your weapons! It appears some of you didn't hear me," cackled Bill. "That's called a reflector, and it's one of the perks of being richer than god." To his minions, he added, "Light her up so they know we mean business."

Charger bolted out of the shadows, clanging along on its hands before skidding in front of Aisha. When the volleys came, they riddled its torso, shattering steel plates and spilling lubricants.

"No!" Orna screamed, fetching her weapon, but her finger froze on the trigger. She couldn't shoot Bill without getting shot in return.

Nilah cast her mechanist's mark, looking for something, anything to use, but she came up empty. She darted for her slinger, but a line of automatic fire tattooed the deck in front of her, shattering her pistol.

Orna threw the slinger to one side and raised her hands. "Stop, Bill! You got me!"

The bull gestured for his soldiers to stand down and the fire stopped. Aisha shook uncontrollably, balled up underneath the collapsing robot, and Nilah couldn't make out if she'd been hit again. Charger's servos whined pitifully as it tried to support its weight with a failing power plant.

"I didn't like what you did to my wife," said Bill. "Coming into my house, scaring my kids, stealing my ship."

"Sorry," said Orna with a shrug. "At least she was accommodating to us."

"Not anymore. I don't brook betrayal, not even from my own woman," he said darkly, giving it a moment to sink in. "Is that Ranger? God, how I missed that little rescue armor. Needed to pay him back for what he did."

When he removed the bull mask, Nilah understood exactly why they called him Bill Scar. His face looked like it'd been snatched off and no one had bothered to put him back together. Mottled flesh gave way to soft features and sunken eyes.

"That was a mean trick for a little girl," said Bill. "Throwing eidolon powder in my injury like that. When I saw you on the news, I hoped to god I'd get a chance to peel your face off like you did mine."

"Here we are, Bill," said Orna. "Come on down and do it."

When the next explosion rocked the station, a voice told them the reactor was breached. A hideous shuddering traveled up the Central Promenade, and Nilah could swear she saw it swaying like a bamboo reed in the breeze.

Bill shook with laughter, nodding his head. "Okay, Orna. Okay, yeah. But I'm not going to take your face. I'm going to slide this knife into your belly until I feel better about what happened. Then I'll take Miss Brio and leave you here to bleed out. She'd be worth a lot of money to the right people. How does that sound?"

"Sounds like you need killing, Bill," said Orna.

Nilah inched toward the safety stripe around a nearby platform and shouted up to Bill, "Or you could walk away. We'll even let you live."

Bill cocked an eyebrow, such as it could be called.

Nilah dropped to her knees, placing her palm to the ground and psychically wending her way into the platform circuits. The platform shot upward underneath her, and she adjusted the angle to send it flying toward the nearest turret. A hail of spells sizzled through the air, but she kept to a low crouch, using her vehicle as a shield. When she was over the mezzanine, she leapt, fanning her arms and overcharging the strobes in her tattoos.

She rolled her landing and came up in front of one of the autoslingers, sinking a boot into the snake gunner's groin. When zie doubled over, she rammed her fist into zir throat and hip-checked zir as hard as she could. The gunner went over the railing, unable to scream through the impending fall.

Nilah spun the gun on Bill, but remembered the reflector before she pulled the trigger. With all her strength, she picked up the tripod and charged him with the legs. With a shout, Nilah shoved him into the other gunner, toppling that tripod, too.

Slinger bolts tore into the goldfinch goon from the ground below, and Nilah glanced down to see Orna, slinger in hand and fury in her eyes. The gunner collapsed dead, leaving Nilah alone with the slaver who had ruined her fiancée's childhood. He made to shoot her, but she easily dodged away, closing the distance with distracting flashes from her arms. In the blink of an eye, she'd seized his arm and twisted his slinger free, hooking his trigger guard and breaking his index finger in the process.

"You want to hurt Orna?" growled Nilah. "Go give it a try."

She ripped the slinger away and clubbed him with it across the temple. Blinding him with a spray of light, Nilah smashed his knee sideways and took hold of his arm. She twisted his wrist up over her head and brought it down, snapping his elbow and hip-tossing him over the edge.

Bill screamed all the way to the bottom.

When Nilah peered over the edge, she saw a broken man, blood streaming from his nose and mouth, shivering and struggling for breath. And like a spreading forest fire came Orna, tossing the slinger to one side to free up both of her bare hands.

Nilah didn't need to watch, didn't wonder what her fiancée might do to the monster of her nightmares. It wasn't her revenge to take.

Even though every muscle in her body ached, Nilah rushed to a mezzanine platform and took it down to Aisha and Charger. The bot was critically damaged, and her heart thumped in her chest at the thought of losing another one. When she pulled Charger aside to find Aisha, the pilot was intact, though shaking and sweating, pouring blood.

"Okay," she whispered, turning Aisha over. "I've got you."

"I know," whispered Aisha. "I wasn't worried."

Nilah dug in Charger's utility belt, but his first-aid pack had been ruptured, styptifoam pouring out the side in a hardening white lather. She scooped up some of the fresh, sticky suds and slathered them across Aisha's wound. Though Nilah tried to shake away the excess, the foam hardened her fingers into claws, and she had to smash them against the deck to get free.

"It's fine," grunted Aisha, trying to stand up. "Flame rounds mostly cauterize and—"

She slumped into Nilah's arms, barely hanging on to consciousness.

"Orna!" Nilah shouted, turning to face the quartermaster. She found her straddled across Bill, thumbs pressed into his eyes, and turned away.

"Orna," Nilah repeated more calmly and waited.

After a moment, Orna joined Nilah at her side, hands slick with Bill's blood. "Thanks."

Nilah nodded at Charger, whose power banks had failed. No longer did its rib cage carry the hot flame of a heart; only cold shadow. "I'm sorry."

"He's fine, the big baby," said Orna, walking over to the bot and taking hold of its skull. She wrenched one of the plates free and pulled loose a data crystal, holding it up. "Just a little smaller now. After Ranger, I...I was more careful. Let's go."

They gingerly loaded Aisha onto a nearby platform and took to the skies. The forest, which had been so verdant and lovely, was now ablaze. No sprinklers triggered to fight the fire, since all station defenses were down. Sparks flitted through the starry atrium like fireflies. The world below raged out of control.

Orna followed Nilah's gaze to the inferno and said, "Good. Burn it all."

"Yeah."

Then the *Scuzzbucket* came into view, its frame damaged and hull breached in so many places. There was no way it would be spaceworthy again.

Nilah's heart sank as she set the platform down before Cordell. "Oh, my god."

"Armin!" Orna cried out, leaping the last meter to the ground.

Cordell greeted them, nodding to the twins and Aisha. "It's bad. I can't raise him, and we can't get in."

"Leave it to me," said Orna, rushing toward the downed yacht.

"Vraba?" asked Nilah.

"Just a stain on the front of the *Scuzzbucket*," said Cordell. "Boots?"

The captain grimaced, as though swallowing a bitter pill. "On her own."

Gravity shivered as the central drive began to fail, and Nilah's stomach lurched.

The station voice came again. *"Attention all celebrants: an enemy warship is targeting the Masquerade. All point defenses failing. Please report to your rooms for immediate—"*

"Okay, so it's worse," he said. "They're not going to risk letting us get off the station with Vraba dead."

Chapter Twenty-One

Last Dance

Nilah hoisted Aisha over her shoulder, carefully moving the downed woman toward her husband. The twins had found a medpack in one of the emergency sconces, and they were pushing gouts of bloodstained styptifoam into Malik's gut.

"Malik...baby..." Aisha moaned at seeing her husband's sorry state.

Then a lone figure stepped out into the Promenade before them. Nilah recognized the scales of the goldfish glinting in the firelight. A pair of tube launchers glinted in either hand, their barrels aglow with the light of the grenadier's mark. If he fired, he'd vaporize them and probably melt a sizable hole in the station, too.

"You!" bellowed the concierge. "This was my life's work!"

Aisha let go of Nilah and gently slipped the slinger from her holster at her back. The pilot was scarcely able to stand, much less cast—but Nilah heard the whisper of a glyph forming behind her. She only hoped the concierge wouldn't notice.

"Don't bother with the marksman's glyph," cried the fish, "unless you want another hole. Half the people on this station have reflectors."

Nilah sneered. "I take it they were on sale, darling? Get lost."

"We were the elites!" zie screeched. "We were the chosen! The true power brokers of the galaxy! We were the star around which the rest of you trash orbited! And at the center of it all, I was the fusing spark that—"

"Cool," Aisha interrupted, firing.

Except she wasn't aiming for the concierge. The spell bolt struck the mooring anchor of a chandelier high in the atrium, and the assembly came down on zir like an ice floe breaking from a glacier.

Aisha watched bitterly as a mountain of glass crushed the fish, then she fell unconscious once more.

"She's lost too much blood," said Nilah, scooping her up, surprised at how light the pilot was. She set Aisha down before the twins. "Take care of her. I'm going to help Orna open the ship."

"Get him out of there as fast as possible," said Cordell, catching her arm. "I want us in those rooms in the next three minutes."

Through the atrium's magnified starfield, Nilah spied other rooms, detached from the Masquerade, launching into the great beyond, Vraba's black warship looming over all of them with every cannon ablaze. Swarms of fighters tangled overhead, and antiship rounds flitted through the skies like fireflies. Then one of the escape apartments went up in a fiery explosion. Then another.

The enemy fighters were targeting the fleeing revelers.

"Captain," said Nilah, her voice almost a whisper, "even if we get to the room...without air support..."

He nodded at her. "One problem at a time, Miss Brio. I've still got my mask, so we've still got an escape pod."

Nilah rushed through the shattered scene to Orna's side. The quartermaster had already traced her glyph and had her palm pressed to the *Scuzzbucket*'s dented airlock.

Despite her own onrushing demise, the only thing Nilah grieved was Orna. Her mind kept turning the problem over and over, trying to imagine a way to save her fiancée from all of this. Orna didn't deserve to die on the Masquerade, surrounded by the lavish wealth she hated—not after the burden of her childhood. The quartermaster had suffered enough for ten lifetimes, and a measure of happiness should've been her reward—not being swatted from the skies like a pesky wasp.

"The damned door is jammed!" Orna shouted. "And the power is still online. If there's been a breach, the engines could go up at any second."

Nilah traced her glyph as well and slapped her hands to the hull. She wound her way through security, past the critical systems, to the control surfaces...and found someone giving them inputs.

Without warning, the *Scuzzbucket* lurched backward, screeching against the demolished wall. Nilah and Orna leapt back as its maneuvering thrusters fired once more, lighting up the deck with gouts of hot gas.

The pair rushed back to a safe distance and Orna tapped her comm. "What the hell, Armin?"

The maneuvering systems brought the yacht to an unsteady level, where it listed to and fro like a drunkard. With a whine, the *Scuzzbucket*'s main engines kicked on, twisting the Promenade smoke into cyclones, and it swiveled to face the far docking bay from whence it came. A long strand of twisted metal moored it to the wall, and it pulled the wreckage out like ripping a seam. Lights flickered inside the ship, spilling out through its numerous wounds. The bridge lit up, and Nilah spotted Armin's tiny silhouette inside.

"Get him out of there now!" shouted Cordell, but the ship hovered five meters out of anyone's reach.

"Don't bother, Captain Lamarr," said Armin. "I'm busy."

Cordell's face lit up. "Armin. Oh, thank god! Come down so we can get to—"

"I don't think so, Captain," Armin cut him off, his voice

ragged. His silhouette disappeared from the window as he headed for a different console. "It's time we deal with that warship."

The hairs on the back of Nilah's neck stood up, and she cast her glyph. Even without touching the ship, she could feel the power of what was happening inside. She put a hand on Cordell's shoulder, and he wheeled on her in confusion.

"Not right now," he growled. "Armin, do as I say, damn it!"

"He's spinning up the jump drive!" she cried.

The captain's face contorted in surprise. "What? No!"

Orna took a few hesitant steps toward the unsteady ship's hull, staring up at it like a child left behind. "Listen, Armin. Listen to me. You and the captain rescued me, so now I'm going to rescue you. Do not do this. You're family, all right? Just—"

"I know, Orna," he said, quiet and calm. "That warship. Those fighters. They're going to kill all of you. I can take them down. Break their ranks."

Orna ran her fingers through her hair in frustration. "But their defenses... They've got serious firepower, and your ship—"

Armin cut her off. "Those won't stop a jump. I'm not going around their defenses—I'm shooting through them. I can hit their reactor."

"You're not a pilot!" Cordell bellowed. "You can't possibly do this alone!"

A long pause followed, and the jump drive's whine grew loud enough to be heard by the naked ear. Arcs of pink energy crawled across the hull as the ship's reserves filled with power.

"Armin!" called Cordell, fury in his eyes.

"I am a datamancer," said Armin. "I know the odds. And furthermore, I am the commanding officer of this fine vessel, and I demand your respect, Captain Lamarr."

"If you jump in the atmosphere, we're all dead," Orna begged.

"I'll get outside the shields—even with the holes in my ship. I won't have to hold my breath for long," said Armin.

"It wasn't supposed to go down like this," said Cordell.

"What we want doesn't matter," Armin replied. "They have us walled off. This is the only winning play in our game."

Cordell nodded bitterly. "And what are the odds, Mister Vandevere?"

"Sixty-eight percent. Two out of three."

The Sunspray yacht pulled free of the tangle of debris, shearing off even more bits of its fragile hull. It wasn't spaceworthy—it wouldn't even hold pressure—but it didn't have to if it was only jumping a hundred klicks. It lazily roved away down the Central Promenade, barely scraping past all the damage it had done on the way in.

"I've followed you most of my career, but today, we are equals," Armin said. "So give me this, okay?"

Cordell's hands clenched and unclenched as he watched the vessel depart. Nilah took Orna's hand, and the quartermaster squeezed hard before dragging Nilah into her arms and holding her tightly.

"Orna," Armin said, his voice quiet.

"Yeah?" the quartermaster mumbled into Nilah's hair.

"I'm so glad Cordell and I answered your distress signal...all those years ago."

"You saved me," she said, voice quivering, "but you're not going to let me return the favor?"

"I'm sorry for yelling at you so much when you were a teenager," Armin chuckled. "And I'm so proud that I got to see you become a real sailor."

"And you got to be a captain," she sobbed. "It's just like we always talked about, right?"

"Right," he replied. "And duty calls."

"I'll miss you, Captain Vandevere," Orna whispered into her comm. "Thanks for always being there."

"Godspeed, Captain Vandevere," Cordell added, tapping his heart with an Arcan salute.

The *Scuzzbucket* picked up speed and faded from view, disappearing behind the veil of smoke obscuring the docking bay.

"For Arca," whispered Armin, his voice disappearing with a rush as his ship passed out of the bubble, venting into nothingness.

Then a blinding pink flash penetrated the black clouds of smoke, painting their edges fiery gold like a sunrise.

They waited for long seconds, watching the atrium overhead, and the dark warship that should've spelled their doom. Nilah kept blinking, trying to knock the jump strobe from her eyes so she could see into the great starscape beyond the bubble.

Then came a distant, pale spark the color of a cherry blossom.

Inside of Vraba's warship, a star was born, leaving no survivors save for Armin Vandevere's glory. Its brilliance expended, the star collapsed into nothingness.

The station hallways coruscated with alert lights as blast shutters fell in front of rooms. The various animals of the Masquerade sprinted in panic for safe havens, completely ignoring the bleeding deer and the woman following in his wake with murderous eyes.

"Attention all revelers: debris cloud detected," said the station's pleasant voice over the intercom. *"A catastrophic event has generated a significant threat to the Masquerade. You have five minutes to reach minimum safe distance. Seek shelter in your quarters immediately."*

Boots limped after Stetson, shouldering her way through panicked celebrants, slinger in hand. If he reached his apartment, he might be gone forever, and she'd be damned if she let him walk out of here.

It wasn't hard to find him if she ever lost sight. She just followed the trail of blood, fixating on his lumbering form, a wounded animal to be chased to a clearing for slaughter.

He spun and popped off a shot, missing Boots, but not an unfortunate calico cat, who went down like a sack of bricks. He fired again, piercing a turtle through the chest. Boots shoved a reveler out of the way and shot back, and through some miracle, she actually managed to hit him in the arm, ruining flesh and splintering bone. Stetson cried out, and his slinger went spinning off into the chaos.

Despite his new injury, the man continued attempting to flee. As they turned down another side passage, the crowds began to thin.

"How does it feel, Stetson?" she called to him. "Losing an arm sucks, doesn't it?"

Her own shoulder tortured her; her prosthetic mounting screw was twisted at an odd angle, and frayed muscles burned underneath. She'd probably fractured her stump. She might find herself fighting off blood poisoning if she didn't get significant medical help in a couple of days.

"Attention all revelers, reactor containment at four percent. Seek shelter in your quarters and engage escape protocol."

Stetson stumbled to the ground, crying out in agony, and she waited patiently for him to stand back up. She couldn't have him giving up and dying here.

"That's right, buddy," she urged him. "Keep on going back to your safe, comfy room. You can make it through this."

"Go to hell, you dull-fingered—"

She blasted the wall beside his head without thinking. Relief settled over her when she realized she hadn't hit him by accident. Her track record with a slinger was less than stellar, and she didn't need to press her luck.

"What'd you say?" she taunted him.

"Crazy!" he cried, hobbling for his room. "You hear me?"

Boots considered the insult, not feeling like he was wrong. "You know what's crazy, Stetson? Watching one of your friends murder another one of your friends. You remember doing that, you goddamned thief? You remember standing over me with your slinger cursing me with your first contract?"

"Boots," came Cordell's voice, "this is Boss. We're leaving if you care to join us. We're in Bear's quarters on branch twenty-eight."

"Get clear, sir," said Boots. "I can find my own ride."

"Copy that." His voice was hoarse. "Prince...said to tell you goodbye."

"Goodbye? What do you—" But she knew what he meant. "I'm sorry."

"See that you make it back to us, okay?"

"I'll finish things, and you'll see me on the other side."

The brass plate nearest Stetson lit up with a stylized representation of a deer, and the lines untwisted to create a doorway. Stetson turned and flung the index down the hall, where it bounced into a burning pile of wreckage, leaving Boots with a choice: sift through the fire for the index and expose more of the conspirators, or take her revenge.

There were ten paces between the pair, and Boots was drop-dead tired, but she charged him.

When she slammed into Stetson's body, they toppled through the portal into his room. He rolled onto his back, and she straddled him, bringing the butt of her slinger down on the bridge of his nose.

She pressed the warm barrel into his forehead and said, "Hold still if you don't want to die right now."

And he did, because he was a broken man. He'd lost so much blood, and his eyes lolled in his head, so she slapped him back to the present moment. Then, she pulled off his mask to see the hated face underneath.

He hadn't changed much. Wealth did that to people—kept them young and healthy. Though now, his rosy cheeks had gone ghostly pale, and one of his front teeth had been chipped away.

"*Welcome,*" came an automated voice from the quarters as a hologram spun up in the far corner of the room. "*Escape protocol is in effect. If your party is all present, and you would like to depart now, please select 'acknowledge' on the projection above.*"

Boots gestured to the opulent quarters, filled with trophies of adventures she'd never seen. "Is this what you bought with Gemma's blood?"

His lips parted so he could speak, but a splutter of crimson came out instead. After several aborted attempts, he finally managed, "How did you b-break the curse?"

Boots stood, keeping her slinger on him. "Sheer spite, buddy. Where's the cup?"

She didn't have to look hard. It occupied a place of honor among Stetson's many lavish possessions: the centerpiece of a shelf full of relics. After the war, she and Stetson had bonded over their mutual love of history—that was why they'd been on the Link together. Once he'd murdered Gemma, Boots had been on Gantry Station scraping together enough argents to buy pieces of paper, and he'd been scooping up original paintings and sculptures. She limped to the bookshelf where the Chalice of Hana lay ensconced.

Many of the priceless titles dated back to Origin, and she ran her fingers along the spines before returning her gaze to her enemy. He hadn't moved a muscle and lay on the ground taking labored breaths.

With only one hand remaining, Boots had to set her slinger down to take the chalice from the shelf; she'd forgotten how light the cup was. It made a resonant sound when she bumped it on the edge of the shelf—a tonal hum that refused to stop, even when she clutched it close. For the second time in her life, she held the instrument of empires and the genesis of the alliance that created Clarkesfall hundreds of years ago. She ran her thumb along its features; doves rose from a golden base in a long stem, encircling a pristine bowl.

"She was twenty years old, Stetson. We were already grizzled veterans in our thirties," she said, admiring the cup's figuration.

"Do you hate me because I killed her, or because I robbed you?" he rasped.

"A whole lot of both."

She took the cup over to his bar, where she filled it with a generous pour of Humphrey '62 whiskey. It wasn't her favorite, but it'd have to do in a pinch. She swirled the whiskey around and around, watching as motes of light traveled through the amber liquid, bubbling up to the surface in glowing chains.

She'd wanted this for so long. She could have magic if she desired it, powerful and real, far beyond that of any of her contemporaries.

"But you know," she sighed into the cup, "after a decade of thinking, I'm starting to realize something: this stupid thing shouldn't exist. It's the kind of garbage that makes a person turn on their friends, that gives rise to evil empires, that can be used to enslave a free people."

His hoarse laughter filled the apartment, and he descended into a coughing fit. "What did you think was the point, you sparkless fool?"

"To enforce trust."

"If you have to enforce trust, it don't exist, Boots."

"We were supposed to build something together."

Blood tinged his derisive snort. "I built better without you slowing me down. So, what, you're going to destroy the cup?"

She held it aloft so she could look one more time at the sheen traveling along the sweeping line of stylized doves. In the era of the Landers, this chalice had secured their homeworld.

Now it had been a tool of those who devoured Clarkesfall.

"Yeah," she said. "I am. But I've got something to do, first. You're going to swear to me that you'll never cast a spell for the rest of your life, nor will you ever willingly allow a spell to be cast upon you."

She drained the scintillating liquid from the bowl in a single shot, and it burned all the way down her gullet. She'd seen how it worked when Stetson cursed her aboard the *Saint of Flowers*. It'd been like his very soul exuded golden fire through his hands, and he'd cast a huge, masterful glyph. Boots set down the cup and stared at her calloused fingertips, waiting for the glimmering magic to work its way through her veins.

But her flesh remained flesh.

Her magic remained dead.

To everyone else in the galaxy, the Chalice of Hana was a life-changing artifact, the beginning of a new era. To her, it was a fancy cup, wet with a whiskey she didn't even like. As she stared into the bottom of the basin, one of her tears joined the droplets, infusing with magic.

Even her teardrops were too good for her, able to absorb the power of the chalice that she could not.

Stetson's vile, wracked laughter echoed in her ears, drowning out her own shaking breath.

"Once a sparkless dull-finger, always a sparkless dull-finger…"

He coughed once more, and the air caught in his throat. His fingers began to shake, then he fell dead still, eyes wide in surprise and fear.

"Attention all revelers—"

Boots tossed the cup aside and grabbed the bottle of Humphrey. "Yeah, yeah, you nag."

Then she slumped out from behind the bar and over to the projection, where she placed her hand against the "acknowledge" button. The blast shutter slammed shut, and the countdown began.

Sitting down cross-legged on the floor, she took a generous swig, then lay down and waited for whatever hand fate decided to deal her.

With the *Scuzzbucket* destroyed, their only way off the station was inside Bill Scar's former apartment. In the event of catastrophic damage, all the apartment modules were designed to separate and seal, protecting the wealthy clientele and ejecting them from the station. They buckled in and launched, Nilah's heart in her throat as the room hurtled away from the doomed structure.

When the Masquerade's reactor went up, it filled the stars like a supernova. Whatever remained on board was instantly turned to carbon or fused into a ball of molten metal and gas. One or two small pieces of debris struck the escape pod, but they'd been lucky for the most part. The apartment next to them had been crushed by an errant server cluster.

Much like a Fixer contract, every apartment pod had an insurance policy, entitling them to individual extraction to the destination of their choice. Jeannie and Alister were able to keep the Jans stable while Nilah and Orna checked the apartment pod's internal systems. For a house, it had a considerable amount of guidance and navigation intelligence. The party had enough food and supplies for three weeks, though their ride was due to arrive within the day.

While the marooned residents of the Masquerade waited for pickup, their apartment pods drifted in formation in relative peace and stability. Of the five thousand pods on board the Masquerade, Nilah estimated some three hundred had successfully jettisoned. Perhaps the other residents had died in the explosions. Perhaps they simply hadn't been on the station at all during the fire.

Either way, Nilah couldn't say she felt any real sorrow for those who'd perished. They were little more than slavers, rubbing elbows with some of the most horrid people in the galaxy.

Cordell called Boots to check in and confirm the news about Armin's death; Boots told them she was fine and simply wanted to be alone to grieve. Since they were several hundred kilometers apart, that was easily arranged.

Nilah couldn't say for certain how the galaxy would take the news of what they'd done. Certainly, there were gangsters and garbage humans on board the Masquerade, but some of them were bound to be notable diplomats, heads of major corporations, and other tossers the civilized universe considered "important." Some of them must've died in the explosion...or become bystander casualties of the firefights.

Would the truth about their deaths come out? Would they be reported missing? As the adrenaline faded from Nilah's mind, only questions remained. Beyond caring, she laid her smoke-stained, blood-spattered body down on Bill's pristine sheets.

Within seconds, she was asleep.

The shudder and clank of a docking clamp roused Nilah from her slumber, and she found Orna snoozing beside her. Nilah was cold—Orna had stolen the blankets.

What if they weren't being rescued, but kidnapped? She fetched her slinger from the nightstand and checked the clip: knock rounds. In truth, she didn't have much fight left in her if the docked ship was hostile.

The nearby projectors registered an incoming call, and Cordell pulled on his mask, gesturing for Nilah and Orna to join them in a private area—out of the view of imager lenses. An attractive man and woman spun into existence before them.

"Hello, revelers!" said the man. "I'm Captain Kenichi and this is Navigator Koyuki of the *Yamada*, and we're—"

"Harvest. Ceresport Docks. Slip eighteen F," interrupted Cordell.

"Of...of course!" said Kenichi. "Right away! While you're waiting—"

Cordell repeated himself, and his voice sounded beaten even through the eagle's distortion field.

Koyuki gave them a worried look. "After such a difficult time, we hope you'll consider joining us on the ship for some of our luxury offerings. We have a wide range of spells and salubrious company to soothe your—"

"How many more times do I have to say it?" Cordell bellowed, jamming his finger at the projection. "Is no one going to follow my goddamned orders today?"

Kenichi looked to Koyuki, his face swelling with embarrassment. "I assure you, sir, we take your orders very seriously."

Cordell took a step toward the projection, seething. "Then *Harvest. Ceresport Docks. Slip eighteen F. Right. Now.*" Then he added. "We don't want your drugs or your food or any of that other crap. Just leave us alone and take us where we want to go."

He terminated the call without another word.

"Captain," said Nilah, placing a hand on his arm as he skulked away toward the couch where he'd camped out.

He stopped and pulled off his eagle mask, head hanging. "Please don't ask me to be in charge right now."

She gave him a pained smile. "I'd say you've earned a vacation."

He pulled out his cigarette case and seated a smoke in his mouth before offering her one. She took it, rolling the delicate paper between her fingertips. It smelled a little like raisins, with the faint acidity of eidolon dust.

"I've never smoked before," she said.

"Don't tell Boots," Cordell replied. "She'll call me a reprobate."

Nilah's laugh was louder than she intended. "Oh, I've had more than my fair share of mind-altering substances. Some of the parties at my flat on Morrison Station would've probably killed poor Boots."

"It just calms you down a little," he said. "Makes you breathe evenly."

"In that case..." She handed it back. "Any calmer and I'll be unconscious. But you go ahead."

He lit his cigarette and shook the lighter closed. After drawing a deep breath, he said, "Armin used to sneak a smoke with me on the bridge whenever we were alone."

She thought of them alone with the stars, passing a cigarette back and forth, and her mental image of Armin twisted a little bit. He'd always been so professional whenever others were around. The idea of the man cutting loose was antithetical to all of Nilah's experience.

"He was saving up for a ship of his own one day," Cordell said. "Was planning on having a commission and running legit cargo."

"Did he get close?"

Cordell nodded. "Oh yeah. He hit that five years ago, playing eidolon futures and mineral subsidies. I've never met a poor datamancer... Then when he got the *Harrow* salvage, he doubled his fortune."

"So why didn't he..."

Cordell set the rooms to privacy mode, and they walked to the panoramic window so they could gaze out into the stars. The pristine underbelly of the *Yamada* filled the top of their view, and endless space stretched below.

"Always said he wanted a bigger ship," said Cordell. "It was like his go-to line every time I asked. The dude didn't have any family, so the cash just kept snowballing in his bank account."

"So he was lying?"

"He was scared, maybe... or lonely. Didn't want to strike out on his own."

Nilah thought back to the moment they first hit the bridge of the ADF *Scuzzbucket*, and the look on Armin's face as he settled into the captain's chair. It was nothing like the *Capricious*; the yacht was only large enough for someone to command a tiny ship full of rich weirdos, but Armin's expression had been one of pure amazement.

For the first time, the galaxy had rested at his fingertips, and that hadn't been lost on him.

"Before the end," said Nilah, "he liked being captain, I think—getting his own commission for a few days."

Cordell chewed on his lip and ashed his cigarette into the apartment carpet. "That's the gateway. Don't ever command a ship, because once it gets in your blood, there's no stopping it." He sucked in a breath and wiped a tear from one eye with his thumb. "God, you know? He'd felt that call...gotten to taste it. I know he would've left us after taking his seat on that yacht. And—"

He couldn't keep going. He pressed the heel of his palm into his brow and sobbed quietly. Nilah placed a hand on his back and left it there; petting her captain was like stroking a lion's mane. There had only ever been mutual respect between the pair, and a loving, supportive friendship fit them poorly.

"He would've been so great," Cordell said, voice breaking. "Not like me. Never taking my stupid risks."

To embrace him would've been too much, so she took the cigarette from his hand and said, "I'll share one with you, sir. You could lead me into the dark heart of a black hole, and you know I'd follow."

"As it happens, Miss Brio, that doesn't work out for everyone."

She took a drag, then promptly sputtered out hacking puffs of smoke. The bitter blend tore at her lungs and throat, and a vague nausea descended upon her as her tattoos went bright green. He slapped her on the back, chuckling.

"Boots was right," Nilah gasped as he took it from her. "That's a bad habit."

"We all do stupid crap on this crew, basically a hundred percent of the time," he muttered around the stick.

She straightened and caught her breath, eyes locked on the stars as the *Yamada* initiated its jump. Four of the gods were dead, and they'd personally killed three. Henrick Witts's financial engine would unravel underneath him. They'd destroyed the filthy center of pan-galactic politics in the process.

"That's what makes us legends, sir."

Chapter Twenty-Two

Rendezvous

The *Ardor* touched down in the staging area of Boots's farm on Hopper's Hope, and she winced as it blew another set of barrels down·the hill. It released the docking clamps and blasted away, leaving Stetson Giles's apartment in the middle of her farm. At this rate, she'd have to build a little spaceport if she wanted people to stop wrecking her barrels.

Her transport had, thankfully, taken Stetson's body off her hands to dispose of it. Her apartment's insurance policy apparently included "inconveniences," such as incriminating corpses. Unless she leaked it, no one would ever know what became of the traitor.

Better to consign his fate to obscurity than allow him to be a part of her story.

Boots fetched up the Chalice of Hana and stepped out the door into the dusky evening, taking in the earthy scent of barley. As much as she loved ship life, there was no substitute for the smell of a healthy field.

She took a few shaky steps to her warehouse, adjusting to her planetary weight after being cooped up in a small house with weak gravity for three days. Reaching the door, she set down the cup and dug in her pocket with her good hand for her paragon crystal. The door unlocked just fine.

If she didn't do this now, she'd lose her nerve.

The scent of steamy sour mash and live yeast wafted from the open portal, and she crept inside. It was after hours, and her employees should've been at home resting. Hell, since she wasn't here to watch them, they'd probably been at home the entire time she was gone—the lazy bastards.

Mash tuns burbled in the hazy light, and Boots wound between them, bound for the press. They used the press to smash leftover barley and corn waste into bricks, which could then be sold off-world for a variety of garbage artisanal breads, soaps, and anything else rich jackasses liked. With her windfall from the *Harrow*, she'd bought a far more powerful press than she needed. It'd be more than enough to turn the Chalice of Hana into a golden disc.

Boots placed the cup into the press cradle with the sickening feeling that she'd be buying new equipment after crushing something so powerful. She shuttered the gate, yanked down the safety shield, and stepped back to grab the dangling control console. She flipped the arming switch and the piston thrummed to life, priming the pressure chamber.

It'd only take a half kilo of force to press the go button—only a moment of clarity or insanity to remove one of the greatest treasures from the galaxy.

"No one needs this, right, Gemma?" Boots asked the empty mash house.

Even if she kept it, even if she could've used it only for good, she couldn't hold on to it forever. One day, she'd die. Hell, she'd already lived a lot longer than the average person with arcana dystocia. Someone would take it. Someone would gain enough leverage to enslave those around them.

Given the clashes they'd had, that someone would most likely be Henrick Witts.

She pressed the button, and the piston let out a loud buzz as it lowered into place above the cup. When it met the rim of the finely sculpted bowl, its buzz grew deafening. The machine began to shake, and Boots took a few more paces away as golden fissures formed in the surface of the cup like magma under hardened rock. She detected a rising whine, and she decided that maybe staying indoors with the press wasn't the smartest decision, so she rushed outside.

The sound that cracked through the picturesque valley was like the cannons of old. Boots winced as the windows of her warehouse popped with a lightning flash. Barley-fattened grackles took to the skies in their gibbering flocks.

She crept back inside, and the steady sound of running fluid greeted her ear. To her dismay, she found one of her thousand-liter mash tuns pissing away its product though a small gash in the side. When she reached up to see how bad it was, she pried loose a single golden dove, which had been wedged into the surface. She'd been right to worry about her hydraulic press—the piston had been launched out of the roof like a rocket.

But in the press cradle, she found a half-collapsed chalice bleeding fiery magic, the spray of power sputtering and dying. As the seconds ticked by, it dimmed before finally growing inert.

She pocketed the dove and fetched the patch kit, fixing the leak before she lost more than a few gallons. She half wondered what being struck by a blazing artifact shard would do to a batch of mash. There were plenty of products out there "infused with magic," but not so many outright attacked by it.

Though she had sworn she wouldn't partake of her own supply again after Cordell and the others got so wasted, she dipped into her white dog with a tin cup.

Then, she walked over to the crushed Chalice of Hana, the ruined embodiment of her dreams, and proceeded to get too hammered to walk back to her house.

"Hello, Boots!" came Ai's voice the second she finally stumbled through the door.

"Painkillers," said Boots.

Her kitchen dispensary lit up with a cherry-scented mixture in a silica cup, and she downed it in one. Pleasure radiated throughout her body as it slid down her throat, a sign of the dispensary's superior quality. At least one of the mansion upgrades had been worth it.

"You have thirty-two thousand, eight hundred seventy-four new alerts," said Ai.

"You're about as useful as marpo perfume," grunted Boots. "Did you do anything while I was gone?"

"I answered your distillery messages every day."

"So these... aren't about Kinnard's Way? How old are they?"

"The oldest alert is from the day before yesterday," said Ai. "They're news items."

Boots inhaled sharply. The cops would probably be kicking in her door any minute to charge her with some trumped-up crime or another.

Or maybe they'd just go with murder. The Masquerade existed outside of jurisdiction, but surely she'd just made some powerful enemies.

She could add them to her rapidly growing collection.

"Play the newest item, Ai."

A newscaster spun into being before her, hands folded at his waist in the classic corporate stance.

"Pan-galactic markets soared today with the revelation that Captain Cordell Lamarr and the crew of the Capricious *dismantled an*

illegal contract servicing Henrick Witts. Witts rose to prominence last year with the revelation of the Harrow *conspiracy, and authorities have been tracking his movements ever since. Members of the* Capricious *executed a daring raid on an illegal—"*

She swiped him away, and a woman's torso replaced him.

"Forensic datamancers have taken the so-called Giles Accord and traced market ripples for effect, though experts believe they will only be able to isolate one percent of the companies who participated in the contract. At this point, Taitutian authorities report that they've already made two hundred and twenty-eight arrests, with more pending. The Special Branch was able to link the contract to the cult group Children of the Singularity, *a Link-based organization that denies the* Harrow *conspiracy. In the wake of these cases, GATO planets have declared the* Children *a terror group."*

She swiped again, this time landing on a fresh-faced young man in casual clothes. His hands rested in his pockets, and she could tell from his spiked hair that she'd probably hate the guy.

"So much for freedom of expression! You know, when these people can just roll around the galaxy as they please, blowing up whoever gets in their way, they're the real tyrants. I, for one, am glad to hear that Vandevere died in the assault. He doesn't deserve a state funeral. He deserves—"

The glass left her hand before she had a chance to stop it, shattering into silica powder on the far wall. Ai, sensing her agitation, shut down the recording.

"Admiral Benjamin Woods of the Landers," Ai began, "once said that courting controversy is the surest sign of righteousness."

Tiny robots skittered out of the wall, brushing away the powder and mopping away droplets of sticky medicine.

"Ai, deactivate whatever subroutine caused you to tell me worthless platitudes," said Boots. "I don't need your help."

A chime. "Acknowledged."

She shook her head in disgust and made her way to the bedroom, peeling out of her smoky clothes. A nice bath would sort her out. It might at least help her feel like a human being again. She winced as she touched her shoulder stump, which had grown swollen and feverish.

"And call my prosthetic therapist," she said.

Once the bath was filled with inviting suds and scented water, Boots dipped into her tub, letting the accumulated grime of several days soak from her weary bones. She folded a towel and rested her head at one end, closing her eyes to take in the steam. In the past, she'd always brought a glass of whiskey with her, but with her recent escapade, the thought was less than appealing.

"I have a call for you," Ai said, projecting the phone interface for her.

"Take a message."

"It's Taitutian Special Branch Agent Cedric Weathers. He says it's important."

"Watch me not care," said Boots, hitting the ignore button.

She slid deeper into the tub, looking across the white bubbles like a field of snow. She stared into them, seeing the frosty peaks of Hammerhead, and she could almost feel the chill on her exposed cheeks.

"I have a call for you," Ai repeated, projecting the phone interface. "It's Taitutian Special Branch—"

Boots slapped the answer button, sending bits of foam across her floor. "What the hell do you want?"

Cedric Weathers's face appeared before her, somewhat softened since the last time she saw him. "Good day, Miss Elsworth."

"I think we have different definitions of 'good,' Agent Weathers," she said, wiping the bubbles from the side of her face. "As you can see, I'm busy saving the galaxy from body odor."

He smiled. She'd have to mark her calendar.

"I wanted to convey thanks on behalf of the Taitutian government for your actions at the Masquerade."

You mean the part where I gunned down Stetson, or the part where I lost my first mate?

"And who told you about my 'actions,' Agent?"

"Captain Lamarr has given us a full debrief," Cedric replied. "He's the one who passed us a copy of the Giles Accord."

"Cool," she spat, reaching for the termination button.

"Please wait," he interrupted. "I'd like to extend an invitation to Taitu for you to receive the Medal of Valor."

"Box it up and send it over."

"The ceremony will immediately follow the state funeral of Captain Vandevere."

"Armin wasn't a captain," she said, but her fingers kept their distance from the termination button.

Cedric gave her a pained smile. "It appears there is a lot you don't know. We'd like to get your side of things."

"That's a first."

"Please, Miss Elsworth. Captain Lamarr has told us he'd value your presence. We can send our fastest ship to fetch you."

Once again, she found herself with her hand hovering over a button. She could tell them to go away and never bother her again, but she'd probably just be waiting to die at the hands of one of the gods.

Or she could face the fact that the job wasn't done.

"Send it," she sighed. "I'll pack my bags."

When Nilah arrived on Taitu in the *Capricious*, her father greeted her at the spaceport. They'd had to cordon it off from journalists and gawkers as a matter of galactic security, though she spotted them at the perimeter fences, hungry for a glimpse of her crew.

Darnell Brio threw his arms around her and picked her up as though she were still a little girl, kissing her forehead and laughing.

When he finally let her feet touch the ground, she said, "I've got some news for you."

He gave her a worried smile and asked, "What news isn't about you these days?"

"It's good, Papa, I promise," she replied as Orna came up beside her.

"We're getting hitched," said the quartermaster, chucking him on the shoulder. With a mischievous grin, she added, "Say you don't mind. I'm not asking."

Darnell looked from Nilah to Orna, elation swelling up in his breast, then pulled them both in for a bear hug. For the second time, Nilah introduced him to Cordell, Malik, and Aisha, then brought Jeannie and Alister over to see him.

"These are our recent acquisitions," said Nilah.

"It's an honor," said Darnell. "Shall we get back to the estate? I've had dinner prepared, and your stepmother would like to meet your friends."

Nilah grimaced but relented. She wasn't overly fond of the recently minted Theodora Brio, but her father seemed happy, and that was what mattered. They traveled in a protected escort to the Brio estate, where government security held the perimeter against any and all intrusions.

Upon arrival, they found a courier waiting in the foyer, a sealed case in his hand. Nilah's father turned to them and said, "I think it's best if I wait for you in the dining hall."

The courier strode to Cordell and held out a pad. "Captain Cordell Lamarr? I need you to sign for this."

Cordell traced his glyph across the pad, which lit green with acceptance. The courier then passed over the case and excused himself.

"What is it?" asked Nilah.

"Damned if I know," he said, checking for latches.

The others gathered around as he placed it on a table and clicked it open. Inside, they found eight chits, each inscribed with one of their names, as well as a letter. Cordell took the piece of paper and read it aloud to the others.

I, Armin Vandevere, being of sound body and mind, hereby order the law firm of Harris & Lincoln to execute my last will and testament. Over the years, many crew members of the Capricious *have come and gone, but Cordell Lamarr and I remained. In troubling days, we learned that we were the last stalwarts against oncoming terror, and we fused like a family. It is my final wish that my cash assets be evenly divided among the crew, the closest thing I have to living relatives.*

I've never been good at spending money. Enclosed, you'll find my share of the Harrow *salvage, along with much of the rest of my fortune. A portion of my estate has gone to found the Clarkesfall Heritage Museum on Taitu, which should be completed within two years of my demise.*

If you're reading this, I want to apologize. I know how I must've seemed to some of you—rude and cruel—and I want to assure everyone that I bore them no ill will.

At least, not after I got to know you better.

I hope that you have all survived me, and this letter isn't falling upon your families' heads, further complicating their times of grief.

You're the most wonderful assortment of people I've ever had the pleasure of meeting, and I love you all very much.

Even Boots.

Your friend,
Armin

"Punk," said Cordell, smiling. "Should've bought a ship instead."

"This wasn't how we were hoping to get a share," Jeannie said, taking her chit from the velvet lining, "but we appreciate it."

"Armin never treated us any differently," said Alister, wiping his nose. "Never looked at us like we were freaks. He...he always saw the potential in people."

Nilah picked up the silver drive, turning it over in the light to see her name inscribed on its ornate surface. It was so frustratingly like him to always be prepared. But she didn't want money, she wanted her friend back.

She tucked the drive into her pocket, then ushered her friends into her ancestral home. That night, they would drink themselves stupid, shout and sing, and most importantly, tell stories of the friends they'd lost.

The Capitol Weather Agency arranged for sunny skies on the day of Armin's funeral, and brilliant rays filtered down through fluffy white clouds onto the steps of the Green Palace. It was a crime to bury him on Taitu, considering that two years ago, they wouldn't have given him the time of day.

Boots ascended the steps as crowds thronged behind her, the formal suit itchy on her skin. A blustery wind swept in from the west, and she was thankful for the warm protection of her RVC jacket. A veritable who's who of Clarkesfall personalities was there, from Jack Rook to the members of the Reconciliation Committee. The government hadn't done any of this for Didier—his grave lay unadorned on a little grassy hill on a Carrétan terrace. She'd always meant to visit; Boots heard his family was good about bringing flowers.

She hadn't seen Cordell since they'd parted ways in the Central Promenade. They hadn't spoken by voice, only by messages delivered between their assistants, and she had no idea how he'd react to her the next time they met.

In the foyer, Boots found her crew, and despite her best efforts, she rushed to their side to embrace them one by one. She pulled Nilah in so close that she thought she might squeeze the life from the poor woman.

As they parted, Nilah whispered, "Orna and I are getting married soon. Want to come?"

Boots nodded her head, unable to speak.

"You're not even going to say hi to me?" came the captain's voice behind her. "That's cold, Bootsie."

She hadn't wanted to keep flying with them. There had been so much pain, but the moment she saw Cordell in the flesh, all of it melted away. She threw her arms around her captain and crushed him to her with all her might.

"I'm sorry," she whispered. "I'm sorry I wasn't there."

His hand fell across her back. "We've all got things we have to do sometimes. Are you satisfied?"

"Yeah," she said, blinking back tears.

"Then forget about it. You're with us again, and that's the end of it." He stepped back and gestured to the Jade Parlor, where a casket bearing Armin's stand-in statue awaited the mourners.

An Arcan-born singer rendered a dirge from her homeland, and in turn, each of the crew members got to speak. First came Cordell, then Malik, Aisha, and Nilah. Orna gave a stirring speech about the meaning of mentorship. Jeannie and Alister skipped their turns, having pled to remain out of the limelight. Then Boots ascended the dais. She looked over the crowd of mourners, finding a menagerie of power players from across the various planetary governments. She spied socialites and captains of industry.

"Armin Vandevere was too good for all of you," she began, and a quiet gasp arose from those gathered. "When we discovered the treason arising in your ranks, where were you? When we bled and fought to save your galaxy from the rot festering inside, where were you? Callous. Careless. Foolish."

Her eyes drilled into the members of the Special Branch, then Prime Minister Bianchi, who gave her a defiant look.

"But he was too good for me, too. When we first met, he threatened to throw me out the airlock. He was probably the saltiest, meanest officer under which I have ever served, but he was fair. Bluntly, I probably should've been thrown out an airlock."

Cautious laughter tittered in the crowd.

"He gave me more shots than I ever deserved, and while I was on Hopper's Hope, playing at being a distiller, he was out in the stars trying to protect you lot from yourselves."

They'd butcher her for this in the media. The prime minister wouldn't take this embarrassment lying down. Boots couldn't help but feel like a betrayer, but she couldn't stop the words coming out of her mouth, either.

"I never met an admiral who had half the bravery and sound judgment of Armin Vandevere. I never met a politician who had his backbone and clarity of morality. And because we weren't taken seriously, his life was squandered. There should've been an armada at that station, blasting those murderers and slavers into space dust. Instead, you had a lone man in a damaged starship doing what needed to be done."

She gripped the podium on both sides and glanced back at his effigy. It was a poor approximation, lacking his sour frown and furrowed brow. He looked entirely too peaceful for a man with such fire. When she returned her gaze to the audience, she found them conflicted—some of them wouldn't meet her eyes.

In her debrief, she'd been warned not to discuss sensitive

information with the general public. The funeral was live simulcast across the galaxy.

"The thieves who took him from us are still out there. They're building something bigger than ever, waiting for their chance to strike. They would've stolen the life of every last person in the galaxy, and you all jump on the Link to wonder loudly if we've 'gone too far.'"

Fire burning in her heart, she said, "Until every one of you is willing to stand up, we haven't gone far enough. So keep on betting your futures on a single, tiny starship crew. Take a load off and leave the rest to us. I wouldn't trade your entire police force for one Armin Vandevere, so keep your damned medals."

Stunned silence followed her from the podium, until Cordell shouted, "Hear, hear!"

As one, the crew of the *Capricious* rose and filed out of the Jade Parlor, leaving only murmurs in their wake.

A tremendous feast spread before them, but Nilah wasn't hungry. None of them touched a single thing on the table as they waited for Armin's service to end, save for Cordell, who wet his lips with a glass of wine. Nilah nuzzled into the crook of Orna's arm, holding her close for comfort.

"I hate this dress," Orna whispered. "Why did you convince me to wear this?"

"It looks good on you," Nilah replied, then added wryly, "though everything looks better off you."

Cordell choked on his drink and Jeannie laughed.

"Y'all need to get a room," he said, wiping his lips with a napkin.

"We've got one on the ship," Nilah replied.

"I thought you wanted a fancy Taitu wedding, Miss Brio," said Alister, reaching out and plucking a kinsberry jam cracker from the spread.

Nilah looked up into Orna's eyes and kissed her. "I'd rather do something small at my father's house. Maybe Kristof could come."

"Hate that guy," grumbled the quartermaster.

The doors to the banquet hall spread wide, and Agent Cedric Weathers came storming in, face red. "Do you think that was entirely wise, Miss Elsworth? Talking down to the Assembly Government like that?"

"Your cowardly police force is what's unwise," countered Boots. "You keep letting powerful people off the hook, we're going to keep killing them."

The agent straightened his cuffs. "On that, we'll have to agree to disagree."

"Funny," said Cordell. "Agreeing to disagree seems to be what got us into this pickle. The Children of the Singularity never would've picked up steam if your people had the stones to put them down."

Nilah cleared her throat. "Do you have a reason for disturbing us, agent? As you can see, we're busy mourning."

"Before Miss Elsworth's public outburst, I had been authorized to make a deal with the lot of you, though I'm not sure anyone cares to see you again after today," said the agent.

"Caring about public opinion isn't our forte," said Malik, and Aisha added, "Or your opinion in general."

Cedric pursed his lips and shook his head in disappointment, then snapped his fingers. An attendant entered, holding a data cube transit case, and he placed it on the long banquet table. The special agent flipped open the latches and extracted a scuffed-up cube, placing it into the contacts along the wall closest to him.

"Perhaps you'd like my opinion, then?" asked Kinnard, his voice rendered in perfect clarity over the dining hall.

That got their attention. Nilah looked around at her friends, and though Jeannie and Alister didn't get it, the others couldn't hide their elation.

"Kin!" cried Boots. "Is that really you?"

"Authorized user Elizabeth Elsworth identified," said Kin. "Ratifying voice print." Then came a short beep. "Indeed it is! I'm so glad to hear from you again."

"They unlocked you," said Nilah, sounding a little sadder than she intended.

"Of course we did," said Cedric. "We had to, in the interest of global security. Now I'd like to offer you a special opportunity, provided Prime Minister Bianchi doesn't withdraw the recommendation."

"And what's that?" asked Cordell, looking down his nose at the man.

Cedric clasped his hands behind his back. "You've been remarkably effective at dealing with Henrick Witts's coconspirators, and Miss Elsworth, you were right about the level of governmental support you've received. We didn't believe you, and we should have."

"I'm sorry, can you speak up?" Aisha asked. "It sounded like—"

Cedric glared and said, "The Galactic Alliance Treaty Organization worlds have an extrajudicial task force, dedicated to the pursuit of high-value targets, code-named Compass. We'd like you to join us, and in return, you'd get top-level access to sensitive archives, weaponry, and transport, and most importantly, we would outfit your ship with a jump drive."

Nilah narrowed her eyes. "So you want us to be cops?"

"No," the agent replied. "You'd make regular reports to the minister of defense and the prime minister herself, and your actions would be classified at top levels. GATO police and military would be bound by treaty to intervene on your behalf. We'd also return your AI. Provided, of course, Miss Elsworth's stunt didn't ruin your chances."

Nilah found her friends a rightly skeptical group of people. Each one had proven themselves a hero, and in return seen obstruction at best. And yet, she couldn't shake the feeling that this was a chance for vindication, and perhaps when it came to Henrick Witts, retribution.

Cautiously, she ventured, "Perhaps, Special Agent Weathers, if the prime minister lets a few reasonable criticisms impair her judgment, we'd prefer not to be beholden to her."

"Fair enough," Cedric replied. "And if all goes according to plan, I'm offering you the chance to take this fight a step further on your own terms."

Cordell uncrossed his arms and pushed off the wall where he'd been leaning. "Well, we'd have to think about it."

The agent nodded. "Of course. Take your time."

"Better guns and gear?" said Boots. "I'm in."

"Alister and I would like recognized citizenship," said Jeannie.

"And maybe some backup from time to time," said Alister.

"No trackers. No funny business," said Aisha. "I don't want you people keeping tabs on our ship."

Cedric spread his hands. "You only get the assistance you request as a member of Compass."

"And I expect you to update the med bay," said Malik. "We cannibalized our last bot and needed a new one, anyway."

"Of course," replied the agent.

"Give me crap to rebuild my battle armor. Oh, and one for Nilah," said Orna, "and maybe I'll sign on."

Cedric looked to his associate and smirked, but then nodded his approval.

"What about you, Miss Brio?" asked Cordell, turning to Nilah. "I don't know about you, but I'd like to stick it to Witts sooner rather than later. What do you say?"

Her beloved friends were sure in their purpose, tall with pride. With the help of Compass, they might be able to score a real win. They might be able to avenge Clarkesfall once and for all and rid the galaxy of the greatest thief it'd ever known.

She nodded, looking dead into the eyes of her captain.

"I'm in, too."

The story continues in ...

THE WORST OF ALL POSSIBLE WORLDS

Book 3 of the Salvagers

Keep reading for a sneak peek!

Acknowledgments

I can't start thanking people without professing my undying love for my editors, Brit Hvide and Nivia Evans. Your clear and competent guidance turned my story into a book, and I'm always grateful for that.

Thank you to JesReadsBooks for my first ever video review. Watching you take the journey through my story was such a thrill, and the closest thing I've ever had to real-time feedback.

Thanks to Stephen Granade for letting me ask him all sorts of ridiculous physics questions, and to Christopher Rapin and Scott Hutchton for answering my obtuse military queries. It's always a privilege to have access to so many experts.

And where would I be without the Orbit publicity team: Ellen Wright, Laura Fitzgerald, Paola Crespo, and Alex Lencicki! People can't buy a book unless they know about it, and you made sure the word went far and wide. I look forward to working with you again.

As always, a deep and abiding thank you to my spouse, Renée White. Without your love and support, I'd never have the strength to do this.

extras

orbit

meet the author

Photo credit: Rebecca Winks

ALEX WHITE was born and raised in the American South. They take photos, write music, and spend hours on YouTube watching other people blacksmith. They value challenging and subversive writing, but they'll settle for a good time.

In the shadow of rockets in Huntsville, Alabama, Alex lives and works as an experience designer with their spouse, son, two dogs, and a cat named Grim. Favored pastimes include Legos and race cars. They take their whiskey neat and their espresso black.

if you enjoyed
A BAD DEAL FOR THE WHOLE GALAXY

look out for the next book in the Salvagers series

THE WORST OF ALL POSSIBLE WORLDS

by

Alex White

The crew of the legendary Capricious *may have gone legitimate, but they're still on the run.*

With devastatingly powerful enemies in pursuit and family and friends under attack planetside, Nilah and Boots struggle to piece together rumors of an ancient technology that could lead to victory.

CHAPTER ONE

Spectrum

Nilah Brio was so tired of having the dress conversation. They'd settled it once before in the Green Palace of Aior. They'd talked it out in the quiet hours of a *Capricious* night cycle. They'd negotiated the topic in the ruins of Gelding Colony.

And now, beside the rush of Mizuhara's spectacular Thousand Falls, Nilah's comm chimed so Orna Sokol could once again say, "I'm just going to be honest, I really don't like dresses."

Winding up a set of serpentine steps, Nilah emerged onto the landing of a small infinity pool. It was empty, save for a few bathers, but none of them interested her. The view over the Delta Valley, with its intertwined golden rivers like circuit boards, should've arrested her heart. She should've been taking in the salubrious mist of an entire mountainside of hot-spring waterfalls, shot through with dozens of rainbows. Instead, she had to strain to keep her annoyance in check.

"You do understand that a wedding is a ceremony," Nilah quietly replied, trying to keep her conversation disguised. People came to Mizuhara for peace and relaxation, not to see each other gabble on their comms. "And my family has *ceremonial dresses.*"

498

"Arnie Camden offered to design me a suit," said Orna. "Not Camden Cross. Arnie himself."

"You're not marrying Arnie Camden."

A short huff entered Orna's voice. She must've been climbing stairs, too. "If he keeps sending me custom suits, I might. I don't like looking girlie."

Nilah did a one-eighty and marched back into the bathhouse caverns, restraining herself from taking the next set of stairs two at a time. It wouldn't do to be seen in a hurry. "We're wearing sodding bikinis, darling. That's about as girlie as one can look."

There came a scoff on the other end of the line. "As a disguise, babe. Not for my wedding. Speaking of which, are the mods holding up okay?"

Nilah glanced at her arms: no visible dermaluxes, no dark skin, no sleek combat suit or hidden slinger holsters—just bare flesh, glistening with droplets of condensation. Typical illusion spells weren't great at concealing an entire human body, but the headbands from the Masquerade were a million argents' worth of bespoke tech and top-quality components. The masks had been designed to make people look like animals, but Nilah and Orna had cracked them open and changed out a few parts to make them general purpose.

"All good," Nilah replied. "I look like a tourist. A 'girlie' tourist, as you put it, and I'm fine with that."

"There's a difference between what you wear and projecting a spell," said Orna. "If you'd have told me to come in here in a real bikini, I'd have told you to shove it up your ass."

Nilah moved to one side of the pathway as a large party of drunken bathers came streaking past, giggling. She couldn't have them bumping into her, finding a rough body sleeve instead of skin. "I'm surprised you didn't want to go swimming as a giant onyx wolf."

"Oh, I kept wolf mode. Going to bust it out when I want to put the fear of god into someone."

"Ladies, you are *killing me*," Captain Cordell Lamarr's rich voice cut into their comms chatter. "Do you have the target or don't you?"

"Hunter One, negative," said Orna.

"Hunter Two, negative," said Nilah.

"Then can you both please find her?" asked Cordell.

Nilah wound past a set of cordons designating the upper levels as "diamond suites," and the security computer beeped an acknowledgment, automatically billing their ship's account. That, in turn, would be funneled through a set of staged, unsigned accounts, and finally come out of the GATO Compass Special Operations budget.

They'd been a part of the elite secret unit for almost six months, and Nilah quite enjoyed the perks: exotic flier rentals, fine dining, and an all-you-can-shoot buffet of weapons for Orna.

"Boss," Nilah began, "if I paid you a thousand argents, would you order Hunter One to wear a dress at the wedding?"

"You are approaching thin ice, Hunter Two," he grumbled. "And to answer your question, you didn't factor in my danger pay."

Climbing higher through the caverns, Nilah passed by a server bot with a tray of sparkling wine. She snatched one, taking a sip as she stepped onto one of the many lifts.

"Need I remind you," came Kinnard's voice on her comm, "that you're on duty?"

She was already regretting giving the AI access to her mask telemetry for imaging analytics, but in the absence of Armin Vandevere's datamancy, Kinnard was the next best thing. They'd gotten Boots's old Arcan military AI back from the Taitutians when they'd joined Compass. His return after a year stuck in a dark corner of the Special Branch Archives had been a balm on everyone's souls after the tragic loss of their first mate.

He died a hero, but he died all the same.

"It's part of the disguise, Kin," she whispered. "Not all of us look like interchangeable data cubes."

"I assure you that I am unique and beautiful on the inside," said Kin. "Also, you just passed your target. On your ninety."

Nilah turned right to find the green-haired Rebecca Grimsby sauntering past in a swimsuit, an array of strapping lads in tow. Grimsby was an attractive woman, but the number of men with her was simply ridiculous—there had to be at least five, all intent on her. This part of Thousand Falls twisted serpentine through the rock, hot mist billowing through the caverns to obscure Nilah's vision. Splashes echoed from the walls as Rebecca and her party dipped into the hot springs of the chambered mountain.

"Hunter Two," Nilah breathed. "Target acquired. I'm, uh…"

Kin cut in, "I've relayed Hunter Two's coordinates to your heads-up displays. Hunter One can reach her in the next minute and a half."

"Yes, what he said," Nilah agreed, sliding off the path into the pools. "I'm in pursuit."

" 'What he said.' A strange turn of phrase," Kin repeated and laughed, and Nilah shook her head in annoyance. Ever since coming back, he kept laughing at even her blandest jokes, and it came off as clingy.

"Hunter One here. Can you *please* hang back this time?" asked Orna. "Grimsby threw a dude out of an eighty-story window on Taitu."

Nilah's eyes sifted through the mist, but she couldn't make out anyone else in the cloud. "So? She probably caught him off guard."

extras

"This place is literally a bunch of waterfalls and infinity pools," Orna grunted, her breath coming in quick bursts. She must've been sprinting. "It's just stuff to throw people off of."

"Or bathe in," corrected Nilah, feeling her way along one of the slick walls. "Why can't you get your mind off murder for two seconds?"

A gentle horn sounded out from the depths, hearkening back to an ancient time when lighthouses protected the mariners of Origin. Though in the case of Thousand Falls, it meant the mountain was about to bellow out a cloud of magical gases to delight and pacify the bathers.

"Here comes the euphoria," said Kinnard. "Clip in, Hunters."

Nilah fetched a rebreather from under her illusory swimwear and fitted it to her nose and mouth, snapping it to her face with a little clip on her septum. A thin film of metabolizing gel coated the inside of her mouth and the back of her throat so she could speak. The Spectrum Ops rebreathers were so much more comfortable than the old sweaty ones from the *Capricious*. It was regrettable that she couldn't relax in the baths and enjoy herself. She probably hadn't had a decent soak since the Prokarthic pools in the late Duke Vayle Thiollier's palace.

"Got mine," she whispered.

"Clip thecured," lisped Orna, who hadn't yet figured out the trick to the masks, and insisted they weren't well-fitted for her.

Nilah watched in awe as prismatic energies filtered through the mist, spilling random hues through the caverns. Clouds coalesced into iridescent raindrops, settling on the surfaces of the pools like oil slick, and then, with a great bellowing, the mountain exhaled.

It was like being pelted by a warm typhoon, as channels of healing wind replaced the mists around Nilah. Even with her rebreather on, her muscles began to relax and her mind yearned for her to sink into the springs for a long soak. Those who

502

breathed in the arcane air would be out of their minds with pleasure for a few minutes, which worked well for Nilah's plan. This was an extradition mission, after all.

Except when she turned to survey the caverns without their heady fog, she found Rebecca Grimsby's entourage of pretty boys with their own rebreathers. With a sad sigh, Nilah realized that these sculpted men weren't a retinue of admirers, but a complement of guards. Rebecca, for her part, sank into the water with a stupid laugh and swam away, high as a kite.

They were staring at her mouth. They had to be looking at the rebreather.

"Oh, my god," said the nearest one. "I think she's choking!"

Nilah caught her reflection in the stilled water and saw that her illusory mouth had wrapped over the rebreather, and the computer—not knowing what to project—was smearing it every which way, like she'd swallowed a whole apple. She turned away from them as one man stepped forward with genuine concern in his eyes.

"Miss! Are you all right?" he asked, advancing on her.

If she spoke, her muffled voice might give away the mask, so she attempted to wave him away while trying to unclip her rebreather. If she could just get it off without them seeing, she might salvage this.

"She *is* choking!" he cried. "She's swatting at her mouth! Give me a hand!"

To her genuine surprise, they rushed her, hoisting her from behind and giving her abdominal compressions—which caused her to lose her grip on the rebreather and rupture the metabolizing film.

Which caused her to start choking.

"Hunter Two is in trouble," said Kin. "Hunter One, you'll reach her in—"

"I've got it, Kin!" barked Orna.

On the racetrack, when Nilah played chicken through a hairpin, she had a cold iron backbone. When she faced down an enemy mech in the Pinnacle with nothing but her bare hands, she kept it together. But when that bag of metabolizing film ruptured, sending shards of gel down her airway, she couldn't help but panic. This was further exacerbated by being surrounded by a bevy of shouting, ultra-fit male specimens, one of whom currently had her wrapped up from behind. He could definitely feel the rough shell of her advanced combat suit, which tensed in time with his blows to stop her from dislodging the obstruction.

"Something is off!" he called to his compatriots.

"She's got something caught in her mouth! Sweep the airway!" replied another, and the hunk in front of Nilah hooked a finger behind the mask and pulled.

To everyone's horror, the palm-sized rebreather unit emerged from her mouth, trailing a glistening, wet glob of destroyed film. To them, it must've appeared as though her mouth split wide, disgorging the large device. The man behind her released his hold in shock, staggering back. With a violent cough, Nilah hacked up the broken piece of film and spit it into the pool in a slimy glob. The guards were already backing away, some of them falling into fighting stances.

Sucking in a chestful of sweet, glorious air, Nilah gasped, "Thanks, mate." Then she delivered a heavy side kick directly into her rescuer's solar plexus.

She took in her arena: a winding shallow path along a wide hot-spring pool. A curtain of water roared over the far wall— the cliff face on the outside of the mountain. Beyond the waterfall would be a sheer drop. The quintet of model-quality bodyguards spread out between Nilah and Rebecca, forming a sloshing line through the shallow pool. Her target lounged beside the roaring falls, pointing and giggling.

The closest man withdrew something shiny from a pocket in his swimsuit and tossed it onto the walkway not far from them. Nilah braced, expecting an attack, but light spilled from the device, coalescing into the projected form of a man, square jawed and presentable for mass media.

"Attention," said the projection. *"You are interfering with a Willingham McCabe client. If you surrender to the authorities now, your only worries are lawsuits. If you attempt to attack us or flee, we will have no further recourse but to end your life and the lives of your conspirators. Our firm has kept this promise for over fifty years, and you will not be the first exception."*

This was what passed for intimidation? Nilah was embarrassed for them.

"Surrender!" shouted the nearest one, making a face like a toddler in mid-complaint. "You're unarmed, and you have no chance against—"

Nilah deactivated her mask, revealing the black mesh of her combat suit, along with holsters bristling with trip sticks, sleepers, and a slinger pistol. Dermaluxes pulsed to an unheard beat, magnified through glassy inlays in her suit sleeves. Her favorite piece of kit was the set of shock knuckles she'd borrowed from Orna, which rounded out the affair with fashionable malice. She flexed her fingers, lightning arcing over the contacts.

"No," she replied, "you surrender."

The guards began to cast glyphs in unison, and Nilah struggled to identify the marks. Without a clear picture of who to target first, she launched herself off the nearby wall and onto the wide, antislip pathway. Then she dipped her shock knuckles into the pool and discharged the battery.

The shock wasn't enough to fry everyone in the water; they

weren't trying to kill Rebecca Grimsby, after all. Nilah did, however, experience the distinct pleasure of seeing five spells pop in their owners' faces in perfect unison. She sized the men up: all too jittery to cast a glyph, but not remotely out of commission.

Then Orna came sprinting past, diving into the pack of guards like a wrestling ring.

The brawl that followed was as vicious as any barroom scrap, Nilah and Orna taking their opponents to task with brutal efficiency. They were supposed to use the trip sticks, then hit the downed enemies with sleepers, but in the battle-fueled rage of the quartermaster, all plans evaporated like the cavern mist.

"What's your girl's ETA?" Orna grunted, shoving one of the guards against another before delivering a savage backhand to his jaw.

Nilah concentrated, feeling the connection through her mask to a robot trapped at the base of the falls. It desperately recalculated its climbing path over and over again, its processors working overtime. She came back to her senses just in time to dodge a meaty fist.

"She's stuck," Nilah replied, spinning her flashing arms to blind her assailant. She deployed the Taitutian art of Flicker—the near-unbeatable fighting style of those with dermalux tattoos.

Orna drew out her sleeper stick, and instead of using the pointy end to deliver a spell, she bashed a fellow's nose with the blunt side. "I told you to copy Charger's pathing code!"

A goon caught hold of her hair, shoving Nilah under the water. She twisted free with a rising rocket, possibly snapping one or two of his ribs, breaking through the surface like a dolphin mid-leap. "And I said I wanted to figure it out on my own!"

"That's all fine and good until we're stuck mopping up these clowns while your bot walks into walls. You're a good tuner, but"—Orna popped a guy across the jaw with a right cross and he went down—"you suck at AI. I'm calling Charger."

An alert sounded inside Nilah's head, followed by the image of leaping up the embankments of waterfalls. It scrabbled over rocks, launching from boulders to sink its claws into any purchase it could find.

Nilah caught a glancing blow across her temple, dazing her. "It's fine!" she slurred before regaining her balance. "She's coming. Stop nagging me."

Hefting her sleeper, Orna clicked the discharge button and pegged her poor foe in the forehead. Purple smoke poured from his nose and mouth as he went flying backward into the water—

Water which suddenly sunk a lot lower than it should've.

Nilah spun to find Rebecca, completely awake, standing atop a swell of clear liquid. A fresh mariner's glyph faded from her fingertips, drawing the water into any shape Rebecca could desire. Nilah and Orna already knew about the target's control of fluids, so they'd prepared emergency oxygen in their combat suits. Most mariners tried to drown their adversaries.

But Rebecca's animated wave carried her out over the terrace, through the curtain of water and off a cliff.

Nilah ducked past her opponent and laid into his kidneys, buckling his knees. "How is she awake enough to flee?"

"I don't know," Orna growled, putting down the last guard with an elbow to the chin. "Maybe someone delivered her a mild electric shock?"

Nilah felt out her connection to her robot. It wasn't half as strong as Orna's link to Charger, but she was still new to bot construction. To her delight, she found it halfway up the falls, less than a hundred meters from her. She grinned at Orna.

Nilah paced the distance to the pool's edge, now only ankle-deep. "I know the fastest way after her."

"You're not." Orna's hands fell to her hips.

"Oh, but I am, darling."

She jogged back and dashed for the edge, pumping her legs for all their might. Then she planted her foot on the lip and leapt out through the falls into the clear, tropical skies of Mizuhara.

Boots had parked their cargo cart just down the street from the valet stand, and she watched in utter boredom as staff rushed to and fro, charging a hundred argents to park a lousy sports car one block away. At least the Thousand Falls facade was pretty, a summit of mossy waterfalls extending up into the heavens with a perpetual column of mist.

"We should've brought the Midnight Runner for this," she sighed, taking another bite of her bean paste bun. She would've done just about anything to be back in her ship—there hadn't been a decent sortie in months.

"Seems a bit exorbitant, though, doesn't it?" asked Malik. "Using a starfighter when a glorified van would do?"

"Heads up," said Cordell over their comms. "Hunter team is encountering some static on the top level. Be ready for anything."

Boots and Malik exchanged glances.

"According to my analytics," Kin began, "it's well under the Hunters' control and . . . spoke too soon. Look up!"

A long slug of water poured from the topmost waterfall, like the mountain had popped a cyst. It slithered down the side at breakneck speed, and Boots squinted to identify the nucleus of it: Rebecca Grimsby floating, green hair splayed at all angles. It changed its trajectory, splashing into the valet parking, enveloping the sports cars and sweeping their owners and resort staff out onto the sidewalk.

Quick as a wink, Rebecca hurled one of the drivers from an

idling car with a tentacle of water, then leapt into the controller's seat. She peeled out of the lot in a spray of droplets.

Boots slammed the cargo cart into drive, chucked her bun out the window, and floored it. The truck roared mightily for such pathetic acceleration, but came up to speed. Malik leaned out the passenger-side door, traced his glyph, and hurled a bolt of purple energy at the sports car, missing by a sad margin.

"I'm regretting not bringing your wife along!" Boots barked.

"Someone has to fly the *Capricious*," Malik replied, hurling another spell at the swerving vehicle. The bolt slammed into a nearby condo, knocking a cat off the fence with sudden sleep paralysis.

"She's not flying it right this second!" Boots said, taking a turn so hard the chassis bucked up on two wheels before firing emergency stabilizers. "You're casting too much, old man. Save your juice and use this."

She passed him a slinger and he checked the mag.

"Discus rounds?" he scoffed. "We're in a resort colony, not a war zone. You're going to hit someone's kid!"

Boots dodged down a side street to avoid a delivery bot trundling through the middle of the road. "If you've got time to gripe, you've got time to reload. Spare rounds in the console."

"Where did everyone go?" Nilah demanded over the comms. "Anyone have eyes on Grimsby?"

"Boots and Sleepy here," called Boots. "In pursuit. It's an archrome car. Fancy spoiler on the back with pulsing lines running the sides. Goofy roof spike-fin-thing."

"Sounds like a Preston Exa," Nilah mused. "You'll never stop her in your truck."

Rebecca's car slalomed through a set of road barriers like a fish through a reef. Boots simply bashed through with her six tons of mass. A rare swear word burst from Malik's lips as he dropped a box of spell cartridges into the floorwell.

"That depends," said Boots. "If I don't have to dodge stuff or turn, we'll make up ground!"

"Hunter Two," said Cordell, "find a way to catch up."

Flashes filled the cart's rear imagers, and Boots's heart sank. If she had to pull over and explain to the local authorities what she was doing, the mission would be over. Her Compass clearance would get her off the hook, but Rebecca Grimsby would escape.

"Oh, I have, sir," Nilah cooed, and the high-pitched whine of a performance engine filled Boots's ears.

The jumper craft came down hard in front of the truck, its undercarriage spitting sparks over their windscreen. It was a sleek number, with roaming magenta stripes streaking along its lime-green surface, culminating in a dazzling gold "Tobiuo" logo. What held Boots's attention, however, was the startling white-and-gold bot perched atop its roof.

She'd seen the bot before in the makeshift lab of the cargo bay, but locked onto the roof of a beach jumper was another story entirely. The humanoid armor leaned gracefully from side to side, surfing the vehicle between oncoming traffic. Glorious and majestic, it stood with all of the poise of a dancer. Its arms flashed with caution lights as it steered through a busy intersection.

"Oh, yes!" Nilah whooped. "Teacup's hacking interface works like a charm!"

"Please tell me you're not still calling it that," Orna groaned over the comm.

"Of course I am, love," said Nilah, and the jump jets put her astride the fleeing Rebecca Grimsby. "What did I tell you, Boots? Preston Exa."

"Enough with the car crap!" shouted Boots. "Knock her off the road!"

Nilah's Tobiuo drifted across into the Exa, shoving it a bit, but Rebecca was on tires, and Nilah was on hoverlifts. With no traction, the Tobiuo bounced right off. Worse still, Boots could make out the silhouette of a frantic passenger inside Nilah's beach jumper, beating on the glass.

"Bloody—" Nilah began and knocked Rebecca again with the same result, sending the passenger sprawling in the cabin.

"Hunter Two, you've got someone in your car!" Boots said, laying into the horn to warn people as best she could.

Malik snapped in his clip and leaned out the window to put a few shots into Rebecca's rear bumper. They glowed with the orange light of eidolon suppressors, and each shot took a few ticks off the Exa's speed.

"Now we're talking," growled Boots, slamming into the Exa's backside with the full force of the cargo truck.

The Exa spun with the hit, coming to rest at the driver's side of the truck. It peeled out, leaving a cloud of black polymer smoke as it raced away in the exact opposite direction. Nilah and the Tobiuo whipped around, easily swapping ends on performance hoverlifts before coming to a halt. The jumper's gull-wing doors popped open.

"Out," Teacup boomed over its speakers, and its terrified passenger scurried from the cabin. At least they wouldn't have any civvies tagging along for the chase.

The jumper launched in the direction of the Exa, and over the comms Nilah chuckled. "Leave the driving to me, loves. I'll bring her back in one piece."

Struggling to get the cart into gear, Boots grumbled, "Cheeky little punk."

The cart roared left through the intersection and up a long

straightaway. Finally starting to get the hang of it, Boots whipped past a gaggle of joggers and around a shocked fellow on a sports bike.

"Where are you going?" Malik demanded, loading another clip.

"Going to cut ol' Becky off," said Boots. "I'm not letting Nilah get her after showing us up!"

A high-caliber slinger melted the tarmac just in front of the cart. Checking the imagers, Boots spotted a pair of fliers closing in on her.

"*This is the firm of Willingham McCabe,*" came their loudspeakers. "*You are in pursuit of a client under our protection. Surrender or be destroyed.*"

Boots squinted at the imager feed, trying to make sense of the threat. Any halfway decent outfit would've just opened fire. "What the hell?"

Another round struck the light pole ahead of her, sparks gushing from its base. Pedestrians scattered, and her heart jumped into her throat at the thought of one of them getting crushed.

Boots narrowly swerved to avoid the collapsing pole, then gunned it—as much as the cart would allow. "What was that about not needing the Runner?"

Malik fired up at them, his shots flying so wide as to be laughable. "Just keep us in one piece, Boots!"

"Boss, come in," she shouted into her comm. "We're taking fire from private security and need air support!"

"I'll handle it," said Orna. "I'm almost to you."

Boots flinched as another round struck a little too close. "You can't just shoot security guards out of the sky over a town! Have Zipper come knock out one of their engines with her marksman's mark."

"*Capricious* en route," said Cordell. "Hold tight."

"We just turned up Fifth Avenue!" said Nilah.

Boots checked her guidance display—two blocks up. They were never going to make it to a cutoff point. She spun the large steering wheel to the right, skidding around a corner insofar as the lumbering machine could skid. Another shot pounded the pavement ahead of them, spraying the front grill with molten glass shards.

"I have an idea, Lizzie," said Kin, and she couldn't help but smirk at his use of her name.

"All ears, Kin!" she said.

"I'll call their management and explain the situation. They'll have to listen."

Boots jerked the wheel to avoid another flaming round. "Yeah, you do that, buddy."

The cart sagged with a brutal hit as something landed on the roof. Had one of the shots struck home? Boots checked the camera feed to find Charger perched atop them, a huge piece of spinning tech in its hands. The bot's bloodred armor gleamed in the sun, and its dorsal vents sizzled with pleasure.

It'd almost knocked Boots off the road, and she fumed. "What the hell are you doing, Hunter One?"

Orna scoffed. "You were the only ones slow enough to catch on foot, grandma."

Charger traced out an amplified mechanist's glyph and jammed its fingers into the piece of gear in its hands; arcane energy crackled over the surface as the device spun up. A jagged mounting bracket hung from one side where it'd been ripped free from something.

One of the fliers fired a shot, and the device came to life, shattering the spell on approach.

Boots gaped. "Where did you get a full-sized disperser?"

"Stole it. They didn't need it," said Orna, and a bump in the road shook her hold on the gyroscoping spinning head. "It's like wrestling a damned bear, though." She scarcely brought the system up for the next incoming shot and laughed. "Whoops! Almost got us. Not really, sucker. Try harder."

Malik grimaced. "Please don't taunt the people with cannons."

"I've connected to the Willingham McCabe answering service," said Kin.

"Hello?" came a smooth voice.

"Hi!" said Kin. "You're currently conducting security operations in the Mizuhara Colony, which put your men in danger of violating GATO Commissioning Treaty Article Fifty-Seven Dash A, Subsection Eighty-One. If you persist along this path, your soldiers may be killed, and your organization may become enemies of the Taitutian State."

"Who is this?" demanded the voice.

"I'm afraid I'm not authorized to say," Kin chuckled, "but I can assure you"—a pause, then—"they terminated the call."

Broken spell threads spattered the cargo compartment, hissing all around them as another round detonated in midair.

"Boss," said Orna, "give me weapons free so I can blast these assholes."

The truck ramped a hill, nearly shaking Charger loose, and the bot dug a huge row of furrows down the side panels. They wouldn't be getting the rental deposit back, that much was certain.

"Boss here. Denied. *Do not* shoot those assholes."

The truck screeched as Charger curled its toes in frustration. "But they're assholes, sir!"

"Not a capital crime," said Cordell. "Air support inbound in twenty seconds."

They swung around a long curve, and the town opened up a little. Along the distant shoreline road, Boots spotted Teacup, perched atop its Tobiuo beach jumper as it raced after Rebecca's

Exa. The jumper leapt past magical walls of water summoned into its path by the fleeing woman; Rebecca's magic was fierce and strong.

The roads intersected ahead, just as Boots had hoped. She kept the accelerator to the floor, praying that she'd be able to T-bone the Exa and end the chase.

She made it to the intersection one second too late.

Rebecca blasted by, but Teacup and the Tobiuo came crashing into the rear bed of the truck, demolishing it and knocking Charger free. Gravity went all funny as the car's emergency drives kicked on to spare them a horrific death, and they went rolling into the embankment. When they came to a stop, Boots found Teacup and Charger lying in the middle of the road, scuffed all to hell and floundering in each other's arms.

Boots struggled upright in the driver's seat, checking to find Malik glaring at her.

Rebecca's Exa made it a hundred meters before the *Capricious* raged over a nearby mountainside and plastered the hood with a shot from the keel slinger. The Exa flipped end over end a few times before skidding to a halt on its roof.

Then, the *Capricious* lanced the two pursuit fliers with a shot each across their engines, forcing an emergency landing from both.

"I'm afraid that's how it's done, people," said Aisha, her aim perfect as always.

"Yeah, I'll try to remember to bring my starship to the next car chase," grumbled Boots, creaking open her door.

"Don't blame your failings on my wife," said Malik, jumping out beside her.

"I said we should've brought the Runner!" Boots shot back. "Hunters! Are you done playing grabass over there? We've got a target to catch."

Teacup disentangled itself from Charger as Boots advanced on the downed Exa, slinger at the ready.

"Boots!" called Malik, tossing her a clip, which she fumbled. "Take these overloaders. Suppressors don't hurt organics."

She picked it up off the ground, finding a few rounds inside. "Thanks." Then she turned to the car. "Grimsby! Come out with your hands up and fingers interlocked! I will shoot the piss out of you, you hear me?"

No response came from the flipped supercar, just the gentle spin of the tires and ticking of cooling metal. Teacup unfolded, and Nilah stepped down out of its interior in her dark combat suit. She wore her Compass gear like a natural, and if Boots hadn't known better, she would've assumed the ex-racer was a cold-blooded killer.

"You should've seen the truck coming!" Nilah screamed at Teacup, and the bot recoiled. "Now come with me." As she strolled past, she muttered, "Back in a tick, Boots. Just let me handle this."

As requested, Boots hung back while Charger, Teacup, and Nilah closed on the vehicle.

"Now, I'll show you something she can do that Charger can't," said Nilah, and Orna gave a bitter laugh.

They surrounded the vehicle, peering inside. Boots kept her distance, since she was neither a martial artist nor made of regraded steel.

"Door off, please," said Nilah, and Teacup shredded the metal from its frame. "Thank you, gorgeous. Now please apprehend the woman inside."

Like a snow leopard fishing from a mountain stream, Teacup ducked in and removed Rebecca Grimsby from the vehicle. It popped open its front armor plating and jammed the screaming woman inside, its restraints locking to her limbs. Then, her cries were instantly silenced as the armor snapped closed.

Nilah clapped the dust from her hands and turned to her compatriots. "She can't cast. She can't see. She can't hear. She can't move."

"And all you had to do was let scum into your battle armor," Orna mused from the safety of Charger's cockpit. "I'd rather cut off her hands. That'd stop her from casting, too."

The *Capricious* touched down in the middle of the nearest intersection, much to the chagrin of a waiting delivery driver.

Boots tapped her comm. "Well, Boss, we got her."

"Finally?" he asked.

"Yep. Claire Asby's daughter is all ours."

if you enjoyed
A BAD DEAL FOR THE WHOLE GALAXY

look out for

ONE WAY

by

S. J. Morden

Andy Weir's The Martian *meets Agatha Christie's*
And Then There Were None *in this edge-of-your-seat
science fiction thriller about one man's fight for
survival on a planet where everyone's a killer.*

1

[Internal memo: Gerardo Avila, Panopticon, to Data Resources, Panopticon, 10/2/2046]

We are seeking inmates who fit the following profile:

- serving either an indeterminate life sentence(s) or a fixed-term sentence(s) that extend beyond the inmate's natural life-span.
- has had a prolonged period (5 years +) of no contact with anyone on the outside: this includes, but is not exclusive to, family, friends, previous employers and/or employees, lawyers, journalists and authors, advocacy groups, external law enforcement, FBI, CIA, other federal organizations including immigration services.
- has professional qualifications, previous employment, or transferable skills in one of the following areas: transportation, construction (all trades), computer science/information technology, applied science, medicine, horticulture.
- is not suffering from a degenerative or chronic physical or mental condition that would cause death or debilitation in the immediate (5 years +) future.
- is currently in reasonable physical and mental health, between the ages of 21 and 60.

Please compile a list of potential candidates and send them to me by Friday.

Gerardo Avila,
Special Projects Coordinator, Panopticon

"Put your hands on the table."

Frank's hands were already cuffed together, joined by three steel links. His feet were also shackled. The seat he sat on was bolted to the ground, and the table in front of him was the same. The room was all wipe-clean surfaces. The smell of bleach was an alkaline sting in the back of his throat and on the lids of his eyes. It wasn't as if he could go anywhere or do anything, but he still complied with the order. Slowly, he raised his hands from his lap, feeling the drag of the metal biting into his skin, and lowered them onto the black vinyl covering of the table. There was a large hole drilled in it. Another length of chain was run through the circle made by his cuffed arms and into the hole. His guard put a padlock on it, and went to stand by the door they'd both entered through.

Frank pulled up to see how much slack he'd been given. The chain rattled and tightened. Ten, maybe eleven inches. Not enough to reach across the table. The chair didn't move. The table didn't move. He was stuck where he was for however long they wanted.

It was a change, though. Something different. To his left was a frosted window, bars on the outside, a grille on the inside. He looked up: a light, a length of fluorescent tube, humming slightly and pulsing in its wire cage. He could see the guard out of the corner of his right eye.

He waited, listening to the nearby hum and the more distant echoing sounds of doors slamming, buzzers rasping, voices shouting. These were the sounds that were most familiar to him. His own breathing. The soft scratch of his blue shirt. The creak of stress as he shifted his weight from leaning forward to sitting back.

He waited because that was all he could do, all he was allowed to do. Time passed. He became uncomfortable. He could only rest his hands on the table, and he couldn't get up and walk around. Eventually he grunted. "So why am I here?"

The guard didn't move, didn't smile. Frank didn't know him, and wasn't sure if he was one of the regular staff anyway. The uniform was the same, but the face was unfamiliar. Frank eased forward, twisted his arms so he could put his elbows on the table, and put his weight on them. His head drooped forward. He was perpetually tired, from lights on to lights out. It wasn't an earned tiredness, a good tiredness. Having so little to do was exhausting.

Then there was the scrabble of a key at a lock, and the other door, the one facing him, that led to the free world, opened. A man in a suit came through, and without acknowledging Frank or the guard, put his briefcase on the table and pushed at the catches. The lid sprang open, and he lifted it to its fullest extent so that it formed a screen between Frank and the contents of the case.

The briefcase smelled of leather, earthy, rich in aromatic oils. The clasps and the corners were bright golden brass, polished and unscratched. They shone in the artificial light. The man pulled out a cardboard folder with Frank's name on it, shut the briefcase and transferred it to the floor. He sat down—his chair could move—and sorted through his papers. "You can go now. Thank you."

Frank wasn't going anywhere, and the guard was the only other person in the room. The guard left, locking the door behind him. It was just the two of them now. Frank leaned back again—the other man was close, too close—and tried to guess what all this was about. He hadn't had a visitor in years, hadn't wanted one, and certainly hadn't asked for this one, this man in a suit, with his tie and undone top button, his smooth, tanned skin and well-shaved cheeks, his cologne, his short, gel-spiked hair. This free man.

"Mr Franklin Kittridge?" He still hadn't looked up, hadn't looked Frank in the eye yet. He leafed through the file with Frank's name on the cover and *California Department of Corrections and Rehabilitation* stamped on it, turning the translucently thin pages covered with typeface. Paper and board. Everybody else would have used a tablet, but not the cash-starved CDCR.

"Well, if I'm not, both of us have had a wasted journey."

It wasn't much of a joke, but it seemed to break the ice, just a little, just enough for the man to raise his chin and steal a glance at Frank before looking down at the contents of the folder again.

Of course, no one had called him "Mr" Kittridge for years. Frank felt a long-dormant curiosity stir deep inside, where he'd shut it away in case it sent him mad.

"Can I get you anything?" the man asked. "Something to eat, drink?"

Frank cocked his head over his shoulder at the locked door behind him. Definitely no guard. He turned back. "You could start by telling me your name."

The man considered the request. "You can call me Mark," he said. His tell—a slight blink of his left eye—told Frank that he wasn't really a Mark.

"If we're on first-name terms, Mark, why don't you call me Frank?"

"OK, Frank." The man not called Mark closed the folder, opened it again, turned some pages. "So what are you in for, Frank?"

"I'm assuming you're not carrying that file in front of you because you're short of reading matter. I know you know what's in it. You know that I know. So while this is a pleasant change of scenery, I'm still going to ask you why you're here."

Mark finally looked up, perhaps surprised by the directness aimed at him. "You know you're going to die in here, right?" he said.

"I'm eligible for parole in eighty-five years. What do you think, Mark?" Frank twitched the corner of his mouth. That was his smile these days. "Do you reckon I'll make old bones?"

"You'd be—" Pause. "—one hundred and thirty-six. So, no. I don't think so."

"Well, dang. I was so looking forward to getting out."

"You killed a man."

"I know what I did. I know why I did it. But if you're looking for contrition, maybe you should have asked for someone else."

Mark put both his hands on the file. His fingers were long, with buffed, tapered nails. They glowed as brightly as the brass furnishings on his briefcase. "I want to know what you think about the prospect of dying in jail, Frank."

After a moment's reflection, Frank concluded: "I'm not a fan. But I factored the possibility in when I pulled the trigger, and now? I don't see I have much of a choice."

Mark took one of his elegant fingers and circled it around the seven-pointed star on the cardboard file's cover. "I might be able to help you," he said. "I might be able to give you a choice."

"And how would you do that?" Frank raised his hands, and eased them down again, slowly enough for every link of the chain that bound him to the table to catch against the edge of the hole, then fall. "*Why* would you do that?"

"A private company owns this prison, and runs it on behalf of the state."

"There's a logo on everything I'm wearing. Few years back, the logo changed, but it was the same old prison walls. You're telling me a lot of things I already know, Mark. I'm still waiting for you to tell me things I don't."

"You don't want to hear me out?" said Mark. "That's OK. That's your right. But what if it's something you might be interested in?" He sat back in his chair, and examined his pampered hands.

Frank put on his compliant face again. Inside, he was mildly irritated, but no more than that. "You asked for me, remember? Not the other way around. So, this company, this Panopticon? You work for them?"

"Technically, no. But I've been authorized by their parent company to see if you'd be interested in an offer. And before I tell you what it is, I want to tell you what it isn't." He left a gap to see if Frank said anything, but that wasn't Frank's style. "This isn't a pardon. You'll remain guilty of second-degree murder. This isn't commuting your sentence. You'll serve the rest of your hundred and twenty years. This isn't parole. You'll be at all times under a prison regime. Neither will you get time off for good behavior."

Frank considered what he'd heard so far. "Go on," he said. "You're really selling it to me."

"We can't give you any of those things because we're not allowed to. The State of California—the law—wouldn't permit us to cut such a deal with you. What we can offer you is a transfer."

"Panopticon have another jail somewhere else?"

Mark pursed his lips. It was the first emotional response he'd really shown. Frank thought him, despite the expensive suit, the leather briefcase, and the manicured hands, or perhaps because of them, a cold fish. A dead fish, even. "In a manner of speaking."

"So why don't you just transfer me? You don't need my permission to do that."

"No, that's true enough. We need your cooperation, though."

"Do you? I'm not really getting this whole thing, and you seem a straight-up kind of guy, so why not just lay it out?"

Mark doodled with his finger on the cover of Frank's file again. "Given everything I've said, are you still in?"

"In for what? All you've told me is that I'm still going to die in jail. Does it really matter where the jail is?"

"You weren't just chosen at random, Frank. You have skills. A lot more than many—most—of the inmates incarcerated here. Skills that are going to waste. Would you like to use them again?"

"You want me to build you the prison that I'm going to die in?"

"In a manner of speaking," Mark said again.

Frank tried to sit more comfortably in his chair, but his chained hands wouldn't let him. He frowned at the pristine Mark opposite him. "And this is to save you money?"

"To save the parent company money," Mark corrected him. "Yes, that'll happen."

"Mark, I have to say I'm struggling to understand what's in this for me."

"The benefits will be: better food, better accommodation, a small team to work with, a challenging, stimulating environment, an utterly unique project, and considerable personal autonomy. It won't feel like jail. It certainly won't feel like the regime you're under now, that I can guarantee you."

"But I still wouldn't be able to leave, would I?"

"No. This would be a transaction where you'd have to remain on the site in order to help maintain it," said Mark. "That doesn't mean there wouldn't be free time for you to, how do I put it, enjoy the surrounding countryside. You'd always have to return, though. It's in a somewhat isolated position, and there's literally nowhere else to go."

"Where is this, then? The desert?"

"Initially, yes. You'll need to undergo some specialist training at a privately owned facility. Medical tests, too. If you refuse to co-operate in or fail to complete any of the tasks the company set, you'll be bounced straight back here. No appeal. No hesitation, either. Likewise, if you fail on medical grounds." Mark put his hands back flat on the folder. "Are you still interested?"

"Without committing myself, yes, sure. I'm still waiting for the sucker punch, though. Tell me there's a sucker punch."

"If you accept the conditions I've already stipulated, then I'll outline the project more explicitly."

"You're starting to sound like a lawyer."

Mark gave his tell again, and said nothing other than: "Do you accept the conditions?"

"OK."

"Yes?" He was playing games with the language, and it seemed Frank had to play along too. This was legal boilerplate, and it had suddenly become obvious that this whole conversation was being recorded.

"Yes. I accept the conditions," he intoned.

Mark took a deeper breath, and Frank felt like he'd crossed some sort of threshold, an invisible line in his life. A faint wash of sweat broke out across his face, and his hands grew slick.

"Your training will take almost a year. There's a specific deadline we can't go beyond, and either you're ready, or you're not. The training facility is, yes, in the desert. There's some very specialized equipment you'll need to be totally familiar with, and your background in construction and project management will hopefully mean you won't have a problem with that. You'll be introduced to the rest of your team, and you'll learn to work together, learn to trust each other, learn to rely on each other."

"How many?"

"Eight altogether."

"And are they in the same position I am?"

"Seven of them, yes. One company employee will be on site to oversee the project."

"Will the others be ex-prisoners too?"

"Serving prisoners."

"And they have to stick around after we've finished this building work, too?"

"Yes."

Frank looked over to the bright window, then back. "I'd better like them, then."

"That's not the company's concern. Merely whether you can work with them."

"So where is this place, that you want to send seven cons to, to build you a prison and then stay there for the rest of their lives?"

"Mars."

Frank turned to the window again, and stared at the blurred parallel lines of the bars that divided the outside from the inside. There were seven of them, maybe six inches apart. They'd be iron, swollen with rust, peeling and flaking paint pushing off their surfaces like sloughing skin. "You did say Mars, right? As in the planet?"

"Yes. The planet Mars."

Frank thought about it a little longer. "You have got to be fucking kidding me."

"I assure you the offer is most genuine."

"You want a bunch of cons to go to Mars? And build a prison? And then stay there?"

Mark wiped his hands on his suit trousers, a luxury that Frank didn't have. "It's not designated as a prison, but as a federal scientific facility. Let me explain, in order. A convict crew will be sent to Mars. Once there, they will construct a base from prefabricated parts and make it habitable. When the facility is finished, the crew will continue to live on Mars and serve out the rest of their sentences, helping to maintain the facility, expanding it as and when required, and assisting visiting civilian scientists in their work. That the facility will also be your prison is, I suppose, a somewhat technical detail. But as I've already explained, there'll be nowhere to escape to."

Frank nodded slowly to himself as he digested the information.

"You haven't rejected the idea out of hand," said Mark.

"Just give me a minute. I'm thinking."

Once the insanity had been stripped away, it was actually a straightforward offer: die in prison or live on Mars. He was never getting out of this penitentiary alive: he'd been sentenced to a hundred and twenty years for shooting a man in the face, in broad daylight, in front of a crowd of witnesses. Only the fact that he could prove that the dead man was his son's dealer saved him from going down for murder in the first, and onto death row.

He hadn't contested the charges. He hadn't spoken in his own defense. He'd taken what was coming, and he was still taking it. By mutual consent, his wife and his son had disappeared after the trial, and they'd both moved a very long way away. Bad people, like the associates of the man he'd killed, had long memories, and longer reaches. No one had ever contacted him subsequently, and he'd never tried to contact anyone either. No, tell a lie: he'd had one message, maybe a year into his sentence. Divorce papers, served out of a New Hampshire attorney's office. He'd signed them without hesitation and handed them back to the notary.

There was literally nothing for him here on Earth but to die, unremembered and unremarked on.

But Mars?

He'd heard the news about the plans for a permanent Mars base, back when he was a free man, but he couldn't honestly say he'd paid much attention to it: he'd been in the middle of hell by then, trying to do the best thing for his family, and failing. And afterwards? Well, it hadn't really mattered, had it? Someone was putting a base on Mars. Good for them.

He hadn't thought for the smallest fraction of a moment of a second that it might include him.

Now, that would be a legacy worth leaving. Somewhere, his son was grown up, hopefully living his life, hopefully doing whatever he was doing well. He'd been given a second chance by Frank, who had loved him more than life itself, even if he'd had a strange way of showing it.

Did the boy think about his father? At all? What would it be like for him to suddenly discover that his old man was an astronaut, and not a jailbird? "This is the big Mars base, right?" Frank asked. "The one they announced a few years back?"

"Mars Base One. Yes."

"That's . . . interesting. But why would you pick cons? Why wouldn't you pick the brightest and the best and let them be the goddamn heroes? Or did you already throw this open to the outside world, and there weren't enough young, fit, intelligent people with college educations and no rap sheet beating down your doors for an opportunity like this. Is that it? You're desperate?"

Mark stroked his top lip. "It's because, while the company wants to minimize the risks involved, it can't completely eliminate them. And when a young, fit, intelligent person with a college degree dies, the publicity is terrible. Which is why they've offered you this opportunity instead. There's also the need to prove that this isn't just for the very brightest. Antarctic bases need plumbers and electricians and cooks. Mars bases will too.

The company wants to show the world that, with the right training, anyone can go."

Frank hunched forward. "But couldn't you just hire the right people?"

"Frank, I'm going to level with you. Arranging a big space-ship, that costs a lot of money and time to build, which will take people out there, and will also bring them home? That isn't a priority right now. As it stands, the company get something out of this, and you get something out of this. They get their base built, quickly and yes, cheaply. You get to spend the rest of your life doing something worthwhile that'll benefit the whole human race, rather than rotting to death in here. Quid pro quo. A fair exchange."

Frank nodded again. It made some sort of sense. "OK, I get that you don't want the pretty people dying up there, but just how dangerous is this going to be?"

"Space is a dangerous place," said Mark. "People have died in the past. People will die in the future. Accidents happen. Space can, so I'm told, kill you in a very great number of different ways. We don't know what your life expectancy on Mars will be. We've no data. It may well be attenuated by a combination of environmental factors, which you'll learn about in your training. But you'll be able to minimize the risks and increase your chances of survival greatly by following some fairly straightforward rules. Whereas the average life expectancy behind bars is fifty-eight. You're currently fifty-one. You can do the math."

"Mars."

"Yes, Mars."

Frank poised the tip of his tongue between his teeth, and bit lightly. He could feel himself on the threshold of pain, and that was the closest he ever got these days to feeling anything.

But to feel pride again? Achievement? To think that his son would be able to look up into the night sky and say, "There he is. That's where my father is."

Were those good enough reasons? He wouldn't be coming back: then again, he wasn't really here either. It'd be a second chance for him, too.

"Where do I sign?"

orbit

Follow us:

f **/orbitbooksUS**

𝕏 **/orbitbooks**

▶ **/orbitbooks**

Join our mailing list
to receive alerts on our
latest releases and deals.

orbitbooks.net

Enter our monthly
giveaway for the chance
to win some epic prizes.

orbitloot.com